THE TOWN TIME FORGOT SERIES BOOK THREE
TERMINUS
NOT EVERYTHING DIES

LISA COLODNY

Copyright

Terminus is a work of fiction. All names, characters, locations, and incidents are the products of the author's imagination or are used fictitiously. Any resemblance to actual events, locales, or persons, living or dead, is entirely coincidental.

TERMINUS: A NOVEL
Copyright © 2019 by Lisa Colodny
All rights reserved.

Editing by KP Editing
Cover Design by KP Designs
Published by Kingston Publishing Company

The uploading, scanning, and distribution of this book in any form or by any means—including but not limited to electronic, mechanical, photocopying, recording, or otherwise—without the permission of the copyright holder is illegal and punishable by law. Please purchase only authorized editions of this work, and do not participate in or encourage electronic piracy of copyrighted materials. Your support of the author's rights is appreciated.

Dedication

To Madeline,

Thank you for standing by me all these years. What a ride we've had; I can hardly wait to see what's next!

Always your friend,

Lisa

Table of Contents

Copyright 3
Dedication 5
Table of Contents 7
Chapter One 9
Chapter Two 21
Chapter Three 28
Chapter Four 44
Chapter Five 57
Chapter Six 62
Chapter Seven 72
Chapter Eight 80
Chapter Nine 93
Chapter Ten 103
Chapter Eleven 114
Chapter Twelve 126
Chapter Thirteen 136
Chapter Fourteen 150
Chapter Fifteen 161
Chapter Sixteen 173
Chapter Seventeen 186
Chapter Eighteen 196
Chapter Nineteen 207
Chapter Twenty 216
Chapter Twenty-One 228
Chapter Twenty-Two 240
Chapter Twenty-Three 249

Chapter Twenty-Four 260
Chapter Twenty-Five 271
Chapter Twenty-Six 283
Chapter Twenty-Seven 295
Chapter Twenty-Eight 307
Chapter Twenty-Nine 317
About the Author 332
About the Publisher 333
Extras 334

Chapter One

The breeze from the sitting room into the kitchen was cooler than the old farmer thought it should be. Had Benjamin, his son, forgot to drop a few more logs on the fire in the fireplace, before he'd run to the barn to tend to the animals?

Gabriel Ennis pushed his tired body away from the table, not concerned with the sound the chair's legs made as it scraped across the floor, leaving a scar across the floor where the grains of the wood came together. It was only a few steps from the kitchen table into the hallway that led to the other room, he knew before reaching his destination that the fire was out. He could smell the last of the embers and see the fine trail of smoke from the ash, as the fire took its last breath and died out.

Without thinking, he grabbed the small hand shovel and scooped as much of the ashes as he could out of the hearth, before dropping them into an old metal bucket nearby. His knees cracked as he knelt to select a few smaller pieces of kindling from the wood bin and tossed them where the warm ashes had been.

Benjamin was no more absent-minded than anyone else in the Ennis household these last few weeks, since their "guests" had been married. Gabriel considered thinking how two nights ago, they ate dinner without any bread.

Edith, his wife, had buried her face in her hands laughing. "I'm so sorry, Gabriel. My mind is just not in my head tonight." She'd pointed to the icebox and laughed, wiping tears from her eyes. "I kneaded it, set it to rise, and forgot to bake it in the oven."

That night, the three of them had taken their places at the supper table, looking only a few times at the two empty chairs between them.

Gabriel used his hands to right himself to his feet, waiting for the kindling to lite before adding several more slabs of thick, dry wood to the blaze. Only a minute or two, he thought to himself, as he looked around the rustic contents of the room.

The immediate years after the war between the states had been hard ones. There were hundreds of Confederate soldiers looking for work, and even more former slaves who'd left their homes on the plantation looking for a place to build a new life. Many of them had drifted to Hamilton, Nebraska. They all had the same hungry look in their eyes upon arriving. He saw the same drive in Christopher's every time their eyes met.

"Did Benjamin forget the fire?" Edith asked from the doorway, adjusting the loose strands of hair around her ears and tucking what she could into the tight bun.

"Yeah." Gabriel moved closer to her, opening his arms to embrace her once she was close enough. He was so much bigger than she was, it was easy for him to rest his chin on top of her head. "Do you think we should check on them?" he asked, his words muffled.

"No." She pulled away and moved closer to the front door, so she could look outside without stepping onto the porch to the small house a few hundred yards away. "They've been through a lot."

He came up behind her and slipped his arms around her waist. "I'm still kind of confused. They weren't really married all the time they've been here. They were just pretending?" Gabriel stepped away from her and moved closer to the threshold of the door. "And what about this time burp that brought them here?"

Edith nodded. "I don't understand it either, but I think it has something to do with those lights in the night sky."

"The ones Heimdail keeps talking about being a bridge between this life and the next one?" He paused. "That old Indian is crazy, Edith. You know that, right?"

"I don't know that, Gabriel and neither do you." She pulled him back, more fully into the sitting room. "He's probably in the barn, do you want him to hear you?"

"Makes no difference to me," Gabriel argued. "Christopher told me that he and Devon were transporting a prisoner from one jurisdiction to another, when they were hijacked and left for dead in the woods. He didn't mention anything about lights in the sky."

"Devon mentioned it to me," Edith answered, wringing her hands out in front, "one of the days when she was upstairs recovering from the deputy's attack in the jail." She turned to face him. "Have you spoken to Ray or Tom?" She paused. "Is Devon in any danger?"

"Not since the wedding, but Ray didn't mention anything to me that leads me to believe Devon might be compromised. And Ray would know, he is after all, the sheriff?"

"What about Thomas, Jr?" she added quickly.

"Tom sent his son to Colorado to manage the Hayden mine right after Devon was hurt. Thomas Jr is many things, but he's not a dumb man. He has to know, he'll be arrested if he returns to Hamilton." Gabriel paused. "It won't matter that he used to be the deputy, or that his father, Thomas Sr, is the richest man in town."

"Devon hasn't pressed any charges, Gabriel," Edith said. "She's not going to."

"Thomas Jr doesn't know that, Edith. There's nothing for him here anymore, he has to know that." He walked back to the door to get a good look at the guest house. "She's recovering from the attack and Christopher's shoulder is all but healed from the bullet wound." He smiled. "And they exchanged marital vows for real during Abby and James wedding last week. It's going to be okay." He looked back to where she was waiting. "We're all going to be okay."

****

Mrs. Ennis moved quickly, setting the platter of meat and bowl of scrambled eggs in the table's center. She turned back to the stove and grabbed a smaller pot of fried potatoes she'd already sliced and oiled. The handle of the pot was warmer than she expected, and she let the pot drop loudly against the table to alleviate the heat radiating her hand.

"Ma," Benjamin exclaimed. "Let me get the rest." He pushed his chair away from the table and took several large steps to the stove. Without ceremony, he dropped a small pot of oatmeal on the table and retrieved a baking tray of bread from the oven.

"I wish you'd tapped on the door, Mrs. Ennis and let me help you get breakfast ready." Devon advised, before placing several big, heavy plates on the table close to where Gabriel and Gates were sitting and to the empty places for Benjamin, Mrs. Ennis, and herself.

"There will be plenty of time for you to help, dear." Mrs. Ennis placed her hand on Devon's shoulder. "It's important that you and Christopher have this time together, alone." She looked fondly to Gabriel. "The time goes so fast; you blink and thirty years have passed."

She moved to the other side of the room and popped the seal on a glass jar of tomatoes. "These are from the ones you and I canned," she said to Devon.

"I can't wait to try them," Devon smiled, taking her seat next to Gates and waiting for Mrs. Ennis to take her place at the table.

Once everyone was at the table, prayers were said and the food was passed around, talk was minimal as the plates and mouths were filled with food.

"Devon," Benjamin asked. "Can I get another piece of bread?"

Devon grabbed the bread plate and passed it across the table to Benjamin, noticing how intently he was studying her wedding ring. "I wanted to thank you, Ben, for your gift."

She held her hand out in front to better admire her ring and pulled Gates hand into hers to inspect the matching set of wedding bands. "Once we're able, we'll buy our own and you can get these back."

Benjamin shook his head, scooping several spoonfuls of scrambled eggs from the bowl and onto his plate. "I don't want them back; I wanted you to have them."

"Wouldn't you rather give them to your own wife, someday?"

"The rings were never supposed to belong to me. I got them by default after my sister died. Wearing them would be a reminder every day that my sister's life was cut short. That's not how I want to start my life out as a married man."

Gabriel pointed toward the stove where the coffee pot was warming and held his coffee cup up for Mrs. Ennis to fill with coffee.

He slurped from the cup and asked Gates. "You feel like riding out to the blonde field sometime this week?"

"What's a blonde field?" Gates asked. "Why do we need to go there?"

"It got its name because of the pale, yellow trees that make up the tree line. I picked out the place several years ago to build a home for Mary and Thomas Jr when they were betrothed." Gabriel paused. "It will still be a good place to build a house, start a family."

"I'll leave that to you, Gabriel. No one knows the land better than you. If you say that's the place, then I'm sure it will be perfect." Gates looked quickly at Devon, hoping she felt the same way.

"You don't want to ride out and take a look?"

"Not today, I've got to ride into town and meet with the Sheriff."

****

Deputy Gates walked past the door to the sheriff's office again, stopped at the end of the alley, took a deep breath, and returned to the office door. He'd made the trip twice already, but couldn't bring himself to open the door and go inside the office; couldn't stand to see the jail cell where the former deputy Hayden and his friends had raped Devon.

He took a final breath and pushed his way through the door and into the office, stopping as Sheriff Ray Callahan emerged from the cell corridor twirling a large metal ring of old keys in his hand.

Callahan stopped short, noticing Gates standing near the front door. "Thought for sure you'd still be honeymooning with your wife?" He hung the key ring on the wall behind a large desk, its top was covered with papers and dirty plates, some with remnants of food still on the face of the plate. "Wasn't actually expecting you in till next week."

Gates nodded, but didn't respond. Instead, his eyes were fixated on the door that led out of the office to the corridor that bordered the cells where the prisoners were held. Like lightning across the sky, Gates remembered being dragged by his feet, down the corridor and into a cell. He'd been barely conscious; blood stained the front of his shirt.

In the cell next door, Devon struggled with several men trying to hold her down on the cot. Gates remembered how helpless he felt, as his hands were tied to the bed and he heard Devon being raped in the cell next door.

Callahan approached him quietly from behind and placed his hand on Gates' shoulder. "Maybe you should take some time before crossing this bridge, son?"

Gates nodded and approached the door to the cells, preparing to walk through and into the corridor to the cells. "It isn't something I'll forget no matter how much time passes, Sheriff." Gates paused and exhaled another big breath. "But I am hoping to get to a place where I can process and accept what happened to us and we move on with our lives."

Callahan watched as Gates disappeared through the door out of the office.

****

Gates stood quietly, solemnly, looking back and forth from one cell to another. He hadn't been able to see what was happening in her cell; he could only hear the sound of the struggle and her plea as she begged them to stop. His mind could only imagine the rest of the events as they unfolded. He saw Devon on the cot with hands tied above her head to the metal rail of the headboard. Her naked legs were visible on either side of a partially clothed cowboy, most of the rest of her body was covered by the cowboy.

Sheriff Callahan appeared behind Gates and pushed a shot glass of liquor into his hand. Gates gulped the drink in a single swallow and handed the empty glass back to Callahan.

"Put it behind you, boy," the Sheriff advised. "She's certainly trying to." He indicated back toward the office area and waited as Gates made his way out of the cells and back to the office area.

Callahan pointed to a smaller desk on the other side of the room, before falling into a chair behind the larger desk, his desk. "That's your area over there. Course you'll be using this one most of the time. Normally, we wouldn't both be here at the same time unless there's a problem."

Gates couldn't help but think of the former deputy when the sheriff mentioned the problem. "Do you think Hayden, Jr is really going to stay away from Hamilton?" Gates shook his head. "I can't see him walking away from his father or his family's money."

"I've known Thomas Hayden, Sr. all my life. He's a good man, just has a blind side where Thomas Jr. is concerned. I think Tom will do what he can to keep Thomas Jr away from Hamilton and your wife."

"I hope so. I promised Devon she'd be safe. Now that he's not your deputy, there's nothing preventing me from killing him."

"You're a lawman now, son. Remember that."

****

Even with the snow on the ground, the small guest house had never been warmer. The heat was only partially generated by the fire burning in the fireplace. Mostly, it was a result of the coed bath currently taking place in the washtub, a tub both Gates and Devon were very grateful for.

They were spooned together in the old antique bathtub. Gates had climbed in first, his back pressed tight against the back of the tub. Devon stepped inside his legs, her back tight against his chest.

"It's so nice to have you home, not rushing off to town or a field with Mr. Ennis." She dipped a small washcloth in the water and wrung it out over his knee.

She leaned in and kissed his knee. "Remind me to thank the Sheriff for giving us the day to spend together." She leaned back as close against him as she could. "It feels longer than a few weeks since you became deputy."

"Having second thoughts about me taking the job?" He folded his arms around her, clasping his hands at her waist.

"Not at all. I just miss having you around."

"I won't ever be very far from you, Devon." He kissed her shoulder and slid his hands under her arms for better access to her breasts. His kisses dropped to her neck and jaw as his hands worked her breasts, teasing them till they were hard as nails and red as blood.

"Remind me to thank Ben for dragging this old tub from the barn. I think Mary would approve that we've put it to good use," his words distorted by his lips on her neck and shoulders.

"I don't think this is the purpose Mr. Ennis intended when he got it for her." Her demeanor changed, her words were sadder and more thoughtful. "I can't imagine how hard it must be to lose a child."

"Doesn't it seem odd to you how little they speak of her? I mean, the tub was buried in

the barn until Ben drug it out and upstairs for you." Gates dropped his head back against the rim of the tub.

"I think it's easier for Mr. Ennis not to have her things around. Benjamin was explaining to me how his father couldn't mourn for her. He just blocks it out and tries to deal with it in his own way. Per Ben, his father doesn't deal well with emotions his or anyone else's." Devon thought about her own father, missing him was an endless exercise. As much as she loved Gates and the Ennis', she'd never get used to being without her family, not seeing them ever again.

"But he's a very caring man and I think he feels things very deeply. He just doesn't know how to express it," Gates laughed. "Which is the complete opposite of Mrs. Ennis."

"I know, it's sad really. How hard she works to keep her mind off Mary. When we first came, her proximity to me, especially when I was dressing or bathing was concerning. I realized after Ben brought the tub to the washroom, that I was kind of a substitute. The intimacy made her feel closer to Mary."

Both jumped as a result of the tap at the front door. Gabriel's voice was strong at the door. "Christopher, I'm heading to the blonde pasture if you want to ride over with me. Girl, can you see to the animals?"

Gates rose from the tub, pulling her to her feet and over the rim with him. "Just a second, Gabriel." Quickly, they dried off and pulled on their clothes, before Gates opened the door and ran to catch up with Gabriel.

****

Gabriel's horse was antsy, pacing from hoof to hoof, as if it were getting ready for a race and was anticipating the blast of the start gun. Gabriel pulled the reins, removing any slack and guiding it closer to where Gates horse was waiting. Gates stepped from the porch, mounted the horse as Devon watched from the doorway.

"The sow is probably going to give birth sometime soon," Gabriel explained to Devon. "And Marston's mare needs some salve on that wound. Can you check on the sow and put some medicine on the mare?"

"Of course," Devon nodded. "We'll see you for supper." She disappeared through the big, open barn doors, watching as Gates and Gabriel rode away toward the blonde field.

It shouldn't take long, she considered to check in on the sow and mix up some more salve for Mr. Marston's horse.

Devon finished applying medicine to the hoof of Marston's big, white mare before climbing to the top rafter of the stall occupied by a huge sow. She balanced herself comfortably to sit across the plank and observed as the big sow moved unsteadily on its feet, before finding a comfortable position in the stall and dropping on its belly.

The engorged sow turned on its side, ready to deliver piglets as Mrs. Ennis' entered the barn and called up to her. "Be careful up there, Devon."

"I will, want to join me?" Devon called down to her.

"No, tending to the animals is man's work. I don't understand why you enjoy it. Have you ever seen a birthing, it's messy?" Mrs. Ennis pushed both her hands into the front pockets of her apron.

"Actually, I've seen several births, delivered a few babies before we came here."

"You were a sheriff, back in your own time?"

"Yes, of sorts. Gates was a Detective; I worked with the Marshall's service."

"Must be hard; adjusting to a slower, steadier life?"

"Sometimes, yes. But I think if we ever get home, I'll miss this life, too." She smiled. "My grandfather was a vet, he doctored all kinds of animals. My brothers and I spent every summer and holiday with him in his clinic. Sometimes when Mr. Ennis and I are in here working, I feel very close to my grandfather."

Devon climbed down from the stall, dropping herself next to Edith.

"I know what you mean." Mrs. Ennis explained. "I feel close to Mary when I spend time with you." She hugged Devon. "I know you miss your family and all, but I'm glad you are here with us, dear."

"Me too, Mrs. Ennis."

****

Gates was glad Emma, his horse, knew the way home. He couldn't be positive, but he was almost certain, he'd dozed off twice during his ride home. He slid off the horse once she came to a stop just outside the stall and made quick work of removing the bridle and reins.

He tossed two scoops of oats into the bin and refilled the water bucket inside the horse's stall, before turning the lantern down and closing the barn doors behind him.

The main house was lit like a Christmas tree with lanterns burning in every window, as if the Ennis' were marking the path home with breadcrumbs. Conversely, the tiny guest house with a single lantern burning in the window was overshadowed, lost among the lights as if to deceive and confuse.

Gates stepped up the steps slowly, each step taking more effort than the next. He'd already unbuttoned his jacket as he entered through the door, tossing the thick coat against the nearby chair.

"What happened?" Devon asked, folding the last of the laundry and practically running to him to address his stained trousers, and the shirt collar that was barely hanging from his shirt.

"Bar fight, Turner twins." He toed off his boots and hung his gun belt over the back of a kitchen chair that they didn't usually use at the kitchen table. He eyed the linen-covered plate of food sitting on the kitchen table in the place he usually sat.

"I thought you went to the blonde field with Mr. Ennis. I didn't realize you went into town today." She poured him a glass of milk and sat it close to his plate of food.

"I did," he took a big drink from the glass. "Didn't take that long. On the way home, Gabriel went to check the damage on the bridge while I went into town."

"Brought your dinner over, it's probably cold. If we had a microwave, I could warm it." She yanked the linen cover off the plate, as if she were a magician performing an act.

"I'll get you one in another, ninety years? For now, this is fine."

He moved delicately in the chair and pulled the plate closer to him, as she took a seat at the table to join him.

"I could heat it in Mrs. Ennis' oven?"

Gates forked up big pieces of meat and stuffed them into his mouth and shook his head. "It's fine. I'm so tired, it doesn't matter. Being deputy here is harder than being an NYPD Detective. I'm going to finish eating and rinse off at the pump behind the house. Then I'm going to sleep. I'm beat."

Devon pushed herself between his chair and the table, before sitting easily in his lap, facing him and leaning closer. "Planning on going right to sleep?"

She kissed his chest and neck, before finding his lips. Her hands toyed with the hair on the back of his neck, near the ragged collar.

Gates swallowed slowly, returned her kisses, his hands pushing her as close against him as he could. "You have something else in mind?"

She pulled away, just enough to unbutton her shirt and slide it off her shoulders, before unclasping her bra and dropping it to the floor. "If you're too tired…"

Gates stood with her still in his lap, lips connected and carried her to the bed. He fell into bed with her wrapped around his waist. Their laughter echoed throughout the room.

He whispered into her ear. "I might have an hour or two still left in me."

Chapter Two

Devon wasn't awake when the sun began its ascent up into the clouds, but she wasn't exactly asleep either. Even with the chill that circulated in the air of the small guest house, and the fact that she was naked under the covers in the small bed she shared with him, she was warm. Throughout the night, they'd moved around in the bed, but neither had moved far from the other.

She was never out of his reach, enveloped within his embrace and warmed by the flames burning low in the fireplace and by the heat from their last session of lovemaking. Although it had already been a few weeks since their wedding, they found themselves making love several times a night and into the early hours of the morning.

Gates shifted his weight from one side of the bed to the other, trying to free his arm from underneath her body. He heard her groan as soon as he moved his arm free. Initially, he thought the sounds were simply the result of Devon being in a half-asleep, half-awake state.

But he felt her body tense and jerk as if she was in pain. Before he could ascertain what the problem was, he recognized her sounds as those of distress. When he propped himself up to determine what was causing the distress, he realized she was still asleep.

He knew she was having a nightmare. Her hands were clenched close to her chest, and her knees were pulled as close to her torso as she could get them into a fetal position.

"Get off of me," she demanded.

Gates barely missed the force of her fist as it passed by his face. He caught her wrist and soothed her. "Devon, it's okay. Wake up."

She kicked at him, still pleading and fighting with him. "Please, stop," she whined.

"Devon!" His voice grew louder and more frantic. "Devon, wake up."

She lurched upward in a single motion, her eyes wide, her arms thrust in front of her in a defensive position. She pulled the blanket up and over her chest and held it in place with one hand; her other hand was still out in front as if to ward off any unwanted advances.

It took a few minutes for her to realize where she was and that she was safe. She leaned back against the headboard panting deep breaths in and out, taking the blanket with her. "Oh God, Gates, I thought I was over it," she said, in a shaky voice.

He slid back into bed next to her as close as he thought he should and turned to face her. "Devon, it was just a nightmare." He opened his arms out to her and was only partially surprised when she leaned into his embrace.

Rubbing her back tenderly, he asked, "What can I do?"

She shook her head. "Just hold me."

Before he could reply, there was a tap at the door, and it opened quickly without the occupants inside consenting. Gates's feet were already on the floor, his hands reaching for his gun before he made out Gabriel's form standing just outside the doorway, rifle in hand. He was only wearing trousers, and he hadn't bothered to fasten them. They were hanging loose around his waist. "Everything okay? We heard crying?"

Devon backed up to the headboard as far as it would allow and pulled her knees close against her chest. She tucked the blanket tight around her chest and nodded, wiping the tears from her face, but she did not respond.

Gabriel took a few steps into the room and drew nearer to the bed. "Is everything okay?"

"Yes, it was just a bad dream. I'm sorry I disturbed you," she said, her voice shaky.

"No need to apologize; just wanted to make sure you're okay." Gabriel shifted his weight uncomfortably from side to side then added, "Can I come in?"

Gates stood up and took one of the blankets with him, which he draped around his waist and gathered his clothes before stepping behind the curtain to dress. "Of course, Gabriel; excuse me a minute."

Gabriel took a seat close to Devon. "I thought you were better." He patted her knee in a fatherly, non-threatening way and added, "Actually enjoying a wife's duties?"

She shifted in the bed to see if there was any chance that Gates was coming out soon and could address the issues in a more appropriate manner. "Mr. Ennis," she advised, "I don't mean any disrespect, but I don't think it's solely my duty to please him. We have a duty to each other ... and it's making me uncomfortable to have you asking about our private moments together."

"What happened to make you start thinking about what Thomas Junior did?" he asked, genuinely curious.

"I don't know." She pulled the blanket tighter around her. "The wedding ... spending the night at the Hayden ranch." She finished talking, but thought to herself as she added mentally, *making love repeatedly*.

Gabriel handed the rifle to Gates as he appeared from behind the curtain, fully dressed for the day. "You should keep this over here. I got several over at the house."

Gates took the rifle and poised it by the front door. "Something you're concerned about?"

Gabriel stood up and nodded, heading toward the door as he answered. "Just want to be sure everyone's safe. I got a rifle in every room, including Benjamin's." He pointed to the rifle as he exited. "Just make sure it's loaded and everyone knows how to use it."

She smiled. "I know how to use a gun, Mr. Ennis, but thank you."

He looked anxiously between Gates and Devon. "Finish getting dressed. Breakfast will be ready soon." As he got to the door, he asked Devon, "Can you take Marston some medicine this afternoon for his mare?"

"Of course," she answered.

Before he walked out the door, Gabriel added, "Christopher, you should go with her. There's not much to be done today in the hayfield."

Gates nodded, secured the door behind him, and paused to listen as Gabriel headed back toward the main house. Gates then turned to find Devon still wrapped in her blanket looking through the bureau of clothes for the white button-up shirt Mrs. Ennis had just laundered for her. She grabbed her skirt, underpants, and bra, and disappeared behind the curtain. She looked longingly at the metal tub that Gabriel and Benjamin had moved from the washroom of the main house into the back area of the guesthouse.

Gabriel had stumbled over his words as they lugged the heavy basin down the stairs as to how the idea had been Edith's. But Devon was certain the idea had been his all along. For whatever reason, it was easier for Gabriel to divert gratitude elsewhere than to acknowledge that he'd had a role. It was difficult for him to simply say the words, "you're welcome."

****

Mrs. Ennis had just set the eggs on the table, when Gates and Devon came hurrying into the kitchen. As Gates slid himself into the chair next to Gabriel, he motioned toward the empty seat where Benjamin usually sat. "He's not going to school?"

Gabriel sliced several large pieces of ham and forked one onto Gates's plate. "He left early to meet Hannah Travis before school." After sipping cautiously at the hot coffee, he forked another slice of ham onto Devon's plate next to where she'd already scooped a small portion of eggs. He shoveled a spoonful of eggs into his mouth and spoke around the food in his mouth. "Can you mix up some salve and get it over to Marston before it gets too late?"

Devon nodded and glanced toward Mrs. Ennis. "I won't be gone too long, then we can clear the patch behind the house you've been eyeing for spring planting."

"That will be fine, if you're sure you feel up to it. Not too tired?" she replied, looking over the cup she was drinking from, as if she was trying to evoke a response.

Devon finished eating and pushed away from the table. "I won't be long."

Gates caught her by the hand and pulled her back to the table. "Give me a minute to finish and I'll get the team hitched."

"Hitched?" she repeated. "You're going to Marston's with me?"

Before Gates could respond, Gabriel answered, "Yeah, Christopher's taking some feed over for me. Marston's running a little short."

"I'm surprised we've any to spare with the fire in the barn and all." She nodded and left through the kitchen door. When she got to the barn, she didn't bother to close the door behind her.

"She brings up a good point. Do we have any to spare?" Gates peered out after her and then looked questioningly at Gabriel, who was finishing his breakfast.

"Just toss a few bags of feed in the wagon," Gabriel said, reading his thoughts. "She won't know the difference. And I'll go by one day next week and bring it back home."

"Everything ok?" Gates asked, looking behind to see where Devon was.

"I had a dream last night," Gabriel nodded, his eyes downcast. "It was Mary."

"Mary?" Mrs. Ennis questioned. "You had a dream about Mary?"

"She was sitting here at this table, there was a big vase of yellow flowers," he paused. "I felt like she was warning me."

"What did she say?" Mrs. Ennis swallowed down her tears.

"She looked me right in the eye and said he's coming."

Gates bit his lip, his fingers twitching as if they were itchy. "Let's keep this between us, if you don't mind?"

Gabriel nodded. "I'll be over at the field across the river. The bridge needs more work, especially before the weather turns colder."

Gates nodded. "Soon as I get back from town, I'll meet you and help finish whatever's left to do."

Gabriel pulled his warm coat on and added, "Stop by the school and pick up Benjamin when it's out. He can help with the bridge."

****

As the wagon lurched to a stop in front of the Marston ranch, the familiar lanky form of Simon Marston's body was detectable in the field behind the house. He turned curiously toward them when he heard the wagon's brake being set. He walked briskly toward them, tucking his gloveless hands into his front pockets to keep them warm.

Gates and Devon met him just in front of the house. Gates quickly unloaded the bags of corn, while Devon explained to Marston how often to apply the salve on the mare's front leg. Simon smiled his toothless grin, nodding his head up and down as Devon spoke. She smiled and made her way quickly back to where Gates was standing near the wagon, hands tucked inside the front pockets of his jeans.

He looked up at the sky to assess the time of day, making note of the pink and yellow lights that were clearly visible in the morning sky. At that time of the day, the lights looked more like a rainbow after a summer rain, but they were still noteworthy, and Devon and Gates just stood and gazed at the colorful reflections.

After a few minutes, Gates climbed up into the wagon and waited for Devon to pull herself up and take the place next to him. "Come into town with me," he said. "We're already halfway there. We'll get Benjamin at the school before we head back."

She nodded and slid her arm through his and nearly into his pocket. She didn't realize she had fallen asleep against his shoulder, until the wagon came to a gentle stop and her body fell forward just enough to dislodge her chin from his forearm. He smiled apologetically to her. "I won't be long. Why don't you browse in the mercantile for a few minutes and see if there's anything you need?"

She jumped down to the ground and noticed how loud her boots were on the frigid soil. "Anything specific?" she asked, as she was walking away from the wagon and toward the mercantile at the end of the street.

He disappeared through the door of the sheriff's office, and then reappeared and said, "I don't know, something black, lacy, and tiny?"

"Yeah, right," she called out with a laugh. "I'll see if they have anything black in the flannel nightgown department."

He grinned as she turned her head and made her way to the store. Several minutes later, she exited the mercantile carrying a small linen pouch under her arm and chewing on a piece of chocolate.

She saw Gates waiting for her near the wagon, and waited for him to cross the street and join her, playfully pulling at the bag in her hand. She held him off with one arm and protected the pouch with the other making sure to keep it just out of reach. Finally, she handed him the pouch and said, "Calm down, cowboy, it's chocolate. I got some for Benjamin, too. It's his favorite."

She looked around for Benjamin as they neared the wagon. She was surprised to see that he was not already sitting in it ready for the trip home. She tossed the bag of chocolates to Gates. "Don't eat it all, save some for him. Where is he anyway?"

"I asked the teacher while you were still in the mercantile," Gates replied. "She said he left right after school. She didn't see him leave, but said he didn't stay and play after school. I suppose he's on his way home. We'll pick him up along the way."

Chapter Three

"Where is everyone?" Gates asked, as he pulled the bridles from the horses and led them into their stalls. He dropped several scoops of oats in the bins and sat a bucket of water nearby each horse.

"Gabriel's probably working on the bridge, maybe Benjamin went straight there after school," Devon mentioned, before peering around the barn's door to look behind the main house. "I figured Mrs. Ennis would be hoeing the weeds from the field behind the house."

"I don't think Gabriel's left yet. His horse is still in the stall." Gates pointed behind them where a chestnut-colored mare with a mane as black as coal, stood patiently in the stall.

"Maybe they're having an early lunch?" Devon asked, taking Gates' arm as he walked toward the house.

"Or a really late breakfast," Gates added, laughing and taking the steps two at a time, until he was on the porch and waiting by the door for her. He held the door open and allowed Devon to step into the mudroom first.

To determine if Benjamin was in the house, he called out, "Hey Benny, did you run all the way home from school?" There was no definitive response, but they heard moving about from the sitting room and opted to venture farther into the house.

Gates latched the kitchen door and took Devon's arm as they moved from the kitchen into the sitting room. He noticed three of the kitchen chairs were missing as they passed by the kitchen table, just about the same time as he heard a familiar voice.

"It's about time. We've been waiting for you."

Gates and Devon stood speechless at the door facing the former deputy. Thomas Hayden Jr. hovered over Gabriel and Edith Ennis bound tightly to two heavy wooden chairs. Gates pushed Devon safely behind him, she moved as if frozen in place.

It was obvious that Edith had been crying; her eyes were swollen and red. Her hands were tied behind her back to the chair with a thick rope. Each foot was bound to a chair leg with the same type of rough, thick rope. Other than the strand of hair that was hanging just to the left of her ear, nothing else was out of place.

Gabriel, however, looked as though he'd put up a good fight. His shirt was torn down the middle, and there were bloodstains on the front of his shirt just under his chin. There was a small trail of dried blood from his left nostril trailing across his lip and down his chin.

Thomas Jr. waved his gun to motion for them to come further into the door. "Come on in and join us, Deputy Gates, Mrs. Gates." He stressed the word 'deputy' as if it were a new word for him, as if he hadn't spent the last four years as Hamilton county's only deputy.

Once Gates and Devon were more fully into the room, they were able to make out the recognizable form of Thomas Sr. bound and gagged and lying on the floor along the wall beside where the Ennis' were secured.

Hayden Sr's feet were tied together from his knees all the way to his ankles. Like Gabriel, he looked as if he'd put up a good fight. His bottom lip was swollen and bleeding, his left eye was so swollen that it was nearly closed shut.

"Hayden," Gates said. "I know you're upset about losing your job, but your father, Devon, and the Ennis' had nothing to do with it. This is between you and me."

"Shut up!" Thomas Jr. yelled. "I don't care about that stupid job." He smacked the empty chair next to Gabriel and replied to Gates. "Get over here and have a seat. I saved this one for you."

To emphasize his point, he pushed the gun up against Mrs. Ennis's temple so that her skin became red and wrinkled from the pressure of the muzzle. If he was hurting her, she didn't let on. Instead, she sat solemnly, eyes glazed, loose strands of hair clinging desperately to the bun atop her head.

Gates held up his hands making his way closer to the chair where Hayden had indicated. "No one has to get hurt, Hayden. We can work this out."

Before Gates finished the sentence, he was assessing the situation. As a trained police officer, he knew he could easily overpower Thomas

Jr., but he couldn't guarantee the safety of the hostages. Reluctantly, his negotiating skills took over and he moved slowly toward the chair where Thomas Jr. had indicated.

Thomas Jr. looped two pieces of rope around Gates's ankles and pulled it around the leg of the chair, pulling it so tight that Gates could barely feel the blood rushing through his veins. Then, he doubled a second strand of rope and pulled Gates's wrists through the chair's rungs, until his hands poked through and he were tied against the thick pieces of the chair.

Thomas Jr. pointed his gun toward Devon who was making her way cautiously toward Mrs. Ennis. "Not you; you're over here with me."

She exhaled a breath she didn't realize she was holding. "Hayden?" she implored but complied and walked in the direction he indicated.

Once she was close enough, he lurched forward and caught her around the shoulders before pulling her by the back of the hair toward his chest.

"Don't put your hands on me!" She elbowed him in the groin, causing Hayden to drop to his knees, one hand clutching his groin, the other hand still holding the gun against her.

"No, you don't," he warned, motioning with the gun back toward the sofa and pulling himself painfully to his feet.

"You'll have to kill me this time, Hayden," she warned him, her voice strong with conviction as if to calm the fear that burned like a brushfire all the way to her throat.

Hayden Jr. anticipated her stand and moved closer to where Gates was bound to the chair. Hayden Jr. placed his hand on Gates' shoulder as if they were friends, buddies even.

He pointed his gun at Gates and said to Devon. "How about him? What if I kill him instead?" He jerked Gates's head backward by his hair and cocked the hammer on the gun, making a show of pushing the gun barrel roughly into Gates' testicles. "What if I shoot him in the balls and just let him lay here and bleed to death?"

She hesitated, pondering his question, but Gates chimed in. "Don't listen to him, Devon; take this perp down."

Hayden Jr. smiled an arrogant smile, then slammed the handle of the gun across Gates' face so that the right side of his lip practically burst open and poured blood onto the floor. Hayden announced as if he were speaking to a very large group of people, "You should know that if I don't walk out of here unharmed, Benjamin dies."

Devon stood motionless against the wall, her mind only partially absorbing the implications. The sound of Mrs. Ennis whimpering brought her mind back into focus. "Where is he? You bastard!" Devon yelled.

Hayden Jr. made his way back to her, the way a hungry animal might pounce on a weaker animal. He grabbed her around the throat and pushed her roughly against the wall, so that two of the framed photos on the mantel slammed to the floor. "He's safe for now. But if I don't get back to him within the next few hours, he will die."

As if to taunt her even more, he laid his gun down on the table close to where she was standing, so that it was well within her reach. "Go on," he said calmly. "You don't believe me? Take the gun and shoot me. Save yourself from what you know is coming, again." He walked closer to her. "But if you do, the boy dies."

Devon heard the arrogant voice of her former prisoner, Esteban, in her head. She pondered the implications of the two choices he'd given her the night she and Gates had secured the prisoner in the motel room during their trip from New York to Washington. "You'd be surprised what desperation can make you do," he had said.

She eyed the gun that Hayden placed on the table near her. It was within her reach. It would take little effort on her part to grab the gun and shoot him. A quick shot to the chest, and all her problems would be solved.

Thomas Hayden Jr. would never hurt her again. Then she thought of Benjamin's smile and his warm heart, and the joy that he brought to everyone who knew him. She knew in her heart that there was no other choice for her to make. She ignored the gun and braced herself for what she feared was to come.

Devon could hear the sobs of Mrs. Ennis growing louder from her place in the chair. "It's okay, Mrs. Ennis," she comforted. "I won't let anything happen to him. I promise." She pushed Hayden's arm away from her neck in one drastic downward swing of her hand and ignored the gun. "What's this about, Hayden? What do you want?" she asked, keeping the couch between them.

Hayden placed the handgun on the table next to the sofa. "I want him to know that you belong to me."

After that, he pushed himself away from her and made his way purposefully to his father, who was still lying semi-conscious against the wall. He pulled at the older man's arms, until Thomas Sr. was on his feet and leaning against the wall.

Hayden Jr. pulled his father roughly to his feet and slung him over his shoulder and into the sitting room, where he dropped him into the overstuffed chair that sat parallel to the far wall, facing the sofa where Devon was standing. "Place of honor for my father," Thomas Jr. said through clenched teeth, spewing spittle in his father's face, "to show my gratitude for all his support."

As soon as he dropped his father into the chair, he took big steps back to Devon and pushed himself close against her, so that she was pushed tight against the wall, knocking the remaining framed pictures to the floor.

He kissed roughly at her neck, pulling at the buttons of her shirt, so that he could kiss the swell of her right breast. They continued to struggle along the wall surrounded by ceramic vases and trinkets that plummeted to the ground as a result of their struggle.

Gates fought frantically against the ropes. "Hayden, you son of a bitch, I am going to kill you this time." If Hayden heard him, it wasn't evident by his actions. He continued to battle with Devon along the wall, so that their actions looked more like a wrestling match than anything else.

She moved from left to right to push him away, but he pushed at her throat with his right forearm, making it hard for her to breathe. Both her hands clawed at his hands around her throat, but his grip was too tight.

She pulled her right knee up toward his groin again, but he was prepared this time, and he pushed her knee away as a defense. He ripped through the shirt with his left hand, so that it tore open in front and was hanging open at each side. His eyes lit up when he saw the lace of the black bra tightly securing her breasts in place. "Very nice," he purred, poking at it with his right hand."

He cupped both breasts with both of his big hands, pulling at the lace cups until her breasts peeked out over the top. She moved her hands to her chest to afford some cover, but he caught her by the wrist and pulled her toward his groin.

"Touch me like I was him," he ordered.

She pulled her hand away and looked instinctively to Gates, but Hayden grabbed her chin and forced her gaze back to his face. "Don't look at him; look at me." He looked over his shoulder to his father who was trying to get to his feet. "Enjoying the show, Pa? She's beautiful, huh?"

Gabriel broke in. "Thomas, don't do this here. Take her upstairs and afford her the respect of some privacy."

Hayden pushed his right hand hard between her legs, rubbing her ineffectively through the material of her skirt. She cried out and pushed him backward so hard, that he was knocked off balance and stumbled toward the sofa.

He regained his balance and advanced toward her again, knocking her backward into the piano so that the sound of them hitting the keys resonated through the house loud and angry.

He thrust the piano bench out of his way, splintering it into several pieces against the wooden floor of the living room. Jerking her by the hair, he pulled her toward the sofa and threw her down like a rag doll against it. He hovered above her and motioned to her skirt and shirt, yelling his commands. "Get undressed, now!"

"What?" she asked, even though she'd heard him very clearly the first time. She pulled herself up to a sitting position, pulling her shirt together in front, but remaining on the couch.

She looked anxiously toward Gates and the Ennis'. "You can't be serious?"

Devon realized the high back of the sofa would afford some cover, but not all that much.

He pulled her shirt open again to emphasize his point. "I'm very serious. Take your clothes off! I had to tear them off the first time. I don't want to do it that way this time."

He rubbed her chin almost gently. "You're going to give it to me this time. I don't want to just take it."

She could feel Gates' frustration as he fought effortlessly with the ropes that bound him. She looked behind the sofa where Mrs. Ennis, Gabriel, and Gates were still tied to the wooden chairs, and she realized that at least for the time being, she was on her own. Once again, there was no backup coming.

"Let's go upstairs," she said barely above a whisper; her eyes looking downward to the floor, her head bowed in defeat. She thought maybe she could gain the advantage by leading him into a false sense of security upstairs. In any event, she didn't want to undress here in the middle of the sitting room with everyone watching.

He took a knee to the sofa, almost straddling her where she sat. He grasped her chin with his thumb and pointer finger and pushed her back against the arm of the sofa until her back was nearly bent across the arm. "They have to know you're mine. He has to see you touch me, kiss me, make love to me."

Hayden Jr. leaned in and kissed her as he finished his sentence. He pulled his mouth from hers but remained close against her. "Don't make your lips so tight."

He manipulated her mouth, touching her lips almost gently. "Make them soft." He kissed her again and then pulled his face away slightly. "Softer," he said. Finally satisfied, he fell onto her again, kissing her lips and pushing his tongue full into her mouth, until she thought she'd choke.

He ran his hands over her exposed chest again pulling at her bra so forcefully, that the band dug and tore painfully across her back. Hurriedly, he unfastened it at the front, so that her breasts fell free against his chest.

He pushed at her shirt still hanging over her shoulders. "Take it off and the black thing."

She raised her torso into a sitting position and slid the shirt and bra off her shoulders. He fell against her again like a thirsty animal in need of water, pushing his hands around her back, pushing her fully against him so that her breasts were fully in his face and mouth.

He traced the outline of each breast with his tongue, his thumbs pulling at her nipples until it hurt. She bit her lip and tried to ignore the pain.

He mumbled into her neck. "Undo my trousers."

She turned her head to her right to assess how the audience was handling the exhibition. She wasn't surprised to see that the Ennis' and Hayden, Sr. had affixed their gazes elsewhere except on her, and Hayden Jr. Gates, however, was looking directly at them. His eyes were cold and unblinking, and his jaw was clenched so tight, that he didn't look like himself.

Thomas Jr. squeezed her right breast hard. "Look at me," he warned. He pushed himself to his knees and sat back on his heels, pulling at the waistband of her skirt. "Take this off."

"Thomas, please don't do this here, take me upstairs," she begged again.

He adjusted himself, so that his groin was just above her waist. "Undo my trousers and push them down."

Reluctantly, she obeyed him and pushed the dirty brown trousers down his waist and around his ankles. He waited patiently. "Touch me, like you do him."

She shook her head again. "No, just do whatever you're going to do and get this over with."

"One more chance, Devon; touch me, just like you did him the other night," his voice was eerily calm.

She shook her head and refused, looking to Thomas Sr. for assistance, but the older Hayden was of no help to her. Instead, he sat still in the chair, his eyes watery and fixed on the wall behind them as if he were in a trance.

Hayden Jr. stood on his feet and stepped out of the trousers. Almost at the same time, he slid his shirt off and let it fall to the floor.

Hayden Jr.'s movement from the couch had made all three of the hostages look up to see where he was going. Gates was surprised at how young Hayden looked standing there naked before them. He'd always assumed he was much older, but it was obvious how young he really was.

Hayden didn't say a word. Instead, he walked over to where the shotgun was propped against the back wall and collected it; then he returned to where Gates, Gabriel, and Edith were bound. Without a word, he slammed the handle of the shotgun into Gates' groin.

It was like a thousand fireworks exploded inside his head, as Gate slumped forward with a scream so loud, the noise of everything else in the room was silent.

When Gates was able to sit up in the chair again, Hayden walked back to the couch to where Devon was sitting, clutching her hands over her breasts for cover.

"Now," Hayden continued. "Take off your skirt and touch me, like I asked you to."

Devon reached out and cupped him in her hands, before running her hands up and down the sides of his shaft. She felt him responding, grinding himself into her hands.

He pushed his fingers into the waistband of her skirt and pulled her up to a standing position next to him. Devon's attention was drawn to the necklace he was wearing, her necklace, the one he'd yanked from her neck as he left her broken and bleeding in the dark jail cell that night.

Thomas Jr. pushed his erection against her buttocks stretching against the material of the skirt. "You like my necklace? Every time I look at its reflection in the mirror, I get hard just thinking about how good you were."

Hayden Jr. ran his hand up under her skirt and between her legs, moving his thumb almost tenderly atop the dark, wiry curls he encountered there. He bit at the back of her neck, pushing her as close against him as he could.

He raised his head from her neck and looked straight at the hostages tied to the chair. "You have to watch her give herself to me." Devon couldn't be sure he was directing the statement to Gates or Gabriel, but it was obvious it was intended for one of them.

She let out a cry she couldn't contain anymore, as he buried his hand deeper in the dark triangular patch of hair and stroked her folds almost tenderly. "Reach behind and touch me," he ordered.

"For God's sake, Thomas," Gabriel pleaded, making sure to keep his gaze on Thomas's face. "Let her go upstairs."

Tears were streaming down her face freely now, but she never made a sound. She reached behind and stroked him as he'd requested. She could feel him pressing against her buttocks. "Harder," he advised, pumping against her hand.

He pulled them toward the sofa, falling into it first, then pulling her atop of him. He slid himself between her legs, pushing as close against her as he could. His pleasure was obvious. "God," he moaned, pushing himself closer to her. "I'd forgotten how good you felt."

She let out a small cry as his fingers dug deeper into her. "I want to feel what he felt. I want to feel when it pleases you."

He began to grind her body against his fingers, grabbing her breast with his free hand as he did so. After a minute or two, his pace was frantic, but she felt nothing. "Harder," he yelled. She continued to thrust against him until she was hurting. "Harder," he yelled, louder this time.

It was obvious to her that he couldn't maintain the erection. She felt him push up against her even harder, squeezing her left breast as he did so. "I know you like it this way. I watched you with him the other night against the barn."

As if to better make his case, he pulled himself up into a sitting position, so that they were nearly chest-to-chest. His mouth found her breasts again and he took advantage of how close they were. He suckled them from left to right then back several times, finally grabbing her right one and pulling her back into his mouth. "You're hurting me!" she called out, pushing his mouth away from her.

"Not as much as last time though, huh?" he replied, pushing himself up so that he could see over the back of the sofa to where Gates and the Ennis' were looking away from them. "Last time, mmmm, you were so tight. I must admit it took me a bit for surprise."

She slapped him across the face, but it hardly had any effect on him or his intentions. In fact, it hardly fazed him at all. "You're a pig, Hayden."

"Shut up, Hayden!" Gates warned from his chair.

Gabriel spit a mouthful of blood toward the floor between his chair and the one Edith was tied to. "I don't understand; what's he talkin' about, boy?"

Hayden pushed his whole body upward, taking her with him and flipping them both toward the arm of the sofa, so that her back was almost draped across it. He looked up toward Gabriel, his light brown bangs falling into his eyes, almost obstructing his view. He continued thrusting into her. "Let's just say, Mr. Ennis, I've had two virgins in my life, and both of them came from this house."

Gabriel's anger and frustration seemed to implode at that moment against the ropes binding him to the chair. He struggled vehemently to acquire enough slack to free his arms, his breath coming in great gasps, as he grunted and moaned in an effort to move the chair back and forth.

Devon raised her hand to hit Thomas again, but he caught her wrist in midair and held it snuggly against her side. Then taunted her. "Still feels good though, right?"

She didn't answer. Instead, she squirmed from left to right, right to left, almost bucking him off her. Hayden let her hands go, but grabbed her by the back of the head and forced her still. He bent his body close enough, so that her necklace was resting against her breast. Almost gently, he took the charm between his fingers and stroked her nipple with it until it grew erect and hard against his fingertips. "You like that?" he asked, as if he was concerned about her satisfaction. When she didn't answer, he pulled it from the chain and placed it almost between her legs, just above her core, careful to stroke just above the nerve center.

"So, tell me what you need me to do then. I want to hear you moan like you did with him," he spoke almost sincerely. He scratched at her clitoris with the charm, taking time to hold it in place against her. "Come on, Devon, scream my name. You can pretend it's his tongue or finger, whatever you need."

He opened his mouth to her breast again and stroked her roughly with the charm still between his fingers. "Come on, Devon, just move against my hand; just like it was him. Soon as you come, I'll let you go. I promise." He was pumping his fingers harder in and out of her, rubbing her in perfect rhythm. "Come on," he chanted. "Just tell me what you need to finish. You want me to do what Ferris did down there? You liked that."

She leaned in closer to him. "Nothing that happened that night was pleasurable, Hayden. Nothing!"

He tightened his hold on her hair and yanked her head, so that it snapped back again.

"Thomas!" Mrs. Ennis screamed. "That's enough."

"No!" he yelled back, losing his composure. "I wanted it to be different this time." He pulled his hand from between her legs and smacked her square across the jaw, so that she was propelled sideways off him and landed almost beside him. In a single motion, he pulled himself to his feet and pushed her onto her stomach. He forced himself between her legs, fighting with the skirt and using brute force to hold her face down into the cushions of the sofa, as he attempted to penetrate her from behind.

Gabriel cried out, "Thomas, you're going to kill her. Let her up; she can't breathe."

"All I wanted," Hayden was saying," was to touch you like he did; pleasure you like he did."

He pulled her up again by her hair and kissed her neck. "Why couldn't you just let me?'

She cried out with such conviction, it was if she'd gotten a second wind. "Because I don't love you!"

He pushed her against the cushions.

"I love Gates!" It was almost as if the confession surprised her more than anyone else.

Hayden pushed her face against the sofa. No one really noticed when the front door opened quietly, and Benjamin walked into the room, carrying the rifle his father usually kept hidden in the barn.

"Thomas?" he called, as he closed the door. He was dressed in the clothes he had worn to school, but they were saturated with mud, especially the trousers.

Thomas stood up from the sofa and dragged Devon toward the door with him. "Benny, I didn't expect you to break out of the old springhouse. Very impressive," he said, in a manner that reminded Gates of the tone his older brother sometimes used with him.

Benjamin motioned the rifle toward Thomas Jr. "Let her go, Thomas, and step away from her."

Hayden pushed her down against the sofa but didn't step away. "Benny, I've been like a brother to you. You really gonna kill me?"

Benjamin cocked the rifle but kept the barrel on Hayden. "I'm not gonna kill you, Tommy." He lowered the rifle's aim from Hayden's chest to his groin. "You'll just wish you were dead."

Hayden hesitated for a minute, and then he smiled as if he'd told a dirty joke. "Benny, come on, it's me. We grew up together. You'd really throw our history away for her? You barely know her!"

Desperately, he grabbed her by the wrist and pulled her to stand next to him. Devon seemed to be stunned by Benjamin's entrance; she hadn't moved since he'd come into the room, except to cover her breasts as best she could.

Hayden pushed her toward Benjamin but didn't let go of her wrist. "You like what you see, Benny? I'll hold her for you so you can have a turn."

Benjamin flinched at the implication but didn't lower the rifle. "Don't think so, Tommy." Benjamin motioned to Devon. "Devon, walk to me," His words were soft and comforting.

She grabbed the afghan off the back of the couch, as she pulled away from Hayden, and wrapped it around herself before leaning closer to Benjamin. "There's a knife in my Pa's ankle sheath," he informed her. "Take it and cut them loose. Sheriff Callahan isn't far behind me."

Devon went to untie them. She pulled the leg of Gabriel's trousers up and slid the knife out of the sheaf, slicing the rope binding his ankles and then freeing his wrists.

Once he was untied, he took the knife from her and began cutting Edith and Gates's ropes. As soon as Gates's feet touched the floor, he made a grab for Thomas Jr.

Gabriel caught him by his arms and pulled him back toward the wall, and almost into the kitchen. "Back off, Deputy," he said. Then he took the rifle from Benjamin and handed him the knife instead. "Cut Thomas Sr. free." Gabriel held Thomas Jr.'s arms behind his back while Benjamin freed Thomas Sr.

Thomas Sr. handed Thomas Jr.'s clothes to Gabriel, who told him to get dressed and not to make any sudden moves. By the time Junior had put on his trousers, Gates had made his way back into the living room. Thomas Sr. pulled the handgun from his holster and held Gates at arm's length. "Son, I know you're upset, and you have every right to be, but the law will be here in any minute. Just stand down until Ray gets here."

"I am the law," Gates reminded him. "Step aside, Mr. Hayden."

By now, Devon had reemerged from upstairs dressed in a white, fuzzy, worn robe, escorted by Mrs. Ennis whose arm was wrapped protectively around her shoulders. "Thomas!" Mrs. Ennis called out. "You have your weapon drawn in my home, and it is pointed at someone I love like a son."

"Edith," he whispered, tears in his eyes. "He's my son."

Mrs. Ennis made her way between the two of them and positioned herself between Gates and Thomas Sr.'s gun. "Put it down, Thomas. I know Christopher will do the right thing."

Hesitantly, Thomas Sr. let his gun drop to his side just as Sheriff Callahan stepped through the front door and into the living room where Gates was handcuffing Thomas Jr.

"What's going on?" he asked. "That old Indian friend of yours came into town a while ago and said you needed help out here."

Gabriel pointed toward Thomas Jr. "He took us hostage. Had us sit here and watch while he forced himself on her again." He pushed angrily at Thomas Jr.'s chest, so that Hayden lost his balance and stumbled backward. "Ought to take him out back and shoot him like the rabid dog he is."

Gabriel fought back tears as he turned to Thomas Sr. "I'm sorry, Tom, the little bastard doesn't deserve to live." He pushed past Gates and exited through the front door. "Get him out of my house."

Ray pulled at Thomas Jr.'s shackles and drug him outside. "Come on, Thomas, let's get you back to town and processed." He looked at Gates. "I'll take the statements sometime tomorrow. I'll need everyone to come down to the office to be interviewed." He took off his hat and held it out in front of him, and then he leaned toward Gates and whispered, "You'll need to take her over to the doc, so he can make a statement on her injuries."

Gates looked over his shoulder as Mrs. Ennis poured some whiskey into a glass for Devon. He pretended not to notice how badly Devon's hands were shaking; her face was still flushed, and eyes were only partially dried. "I'll have to see how she feels about that. She didn't report anything last time."

The sheriff nodded and pulled Thomas Jr. out the door and onto his horse. After tying the horse's bridle to his own horse's reins, he mounted his horse and headed back to town.

The sun was just setting on the horizon, its yellow rays dancing off pink and blue clouds cascading from the gray sky. Ray Callahan pulled his jacket tighter around his chest, regretting he hadn't worn thermals underneath his clothes. The evening was colder than any fall night they'd had so far. His breath formed little clouds with each exhale.

He was sure the Ennis' would press charges of kidnapping, assault, and the attempted murder of Benjamin. Thomas Hayden Jr. was sure to hang whether the girl testified or not. He thought of his old friend, Thomas Sr., and how his life was about to change. What a tough road the older Hayden was about to take. He doubted Thomas Sr. would ever recover. Thomas Sr. never had much objectivity when it came to his son. If Senior hadn't been there tonight to witness what Junior was capable of, Ray doubted that Thomas Sr. would have believed it.

Chapter Four

Mrs. Ennis embraced Benjamin. "Honey, we were so worried he'd hurt you. What happened? How'd you get away?"

Benjamin wiped at his trousers. "Thomas jumped me as I left the schoolhouse. I woke up gagged and tied down at the old springhouse. It was cold, and I was wet. I was shivering so badly that I could hear my teeth chattering." He pulled his trousers off, assessing the dampness of his long johns before deciding they were dry enough. He slid into another pair of trousers that were lying in the wicker basket by the stairs. "I thought I was going to die. Then Heimdail showed up and untied me; said a brown-haired spirit bird told him where I was, and that I needed help."

He sipped from a shot glass filled with an amber-colored liquid that his mother handed to him. He swallowed slowly to ease the burn he felt all the way at the back of his throat and into his stomach. "I had a feeling he was here, so I stopped at the barn and got Pa's rifle. I stood out on the porch until I was sure, and that there was trouble."

Devon pushed past them, making her way toward the door. "I'm going over to the house, Gates. I'll see you there."

Mrs. Ennis tried to brush back the hair that had escaped from her bun. "Devon, I'll bring some tea over for you to drink in a minute."

Devon shook her head awkwardly and answered in a hushed voice. "There's no need for the tea, Mrs. Ennis. He didn't actually ... you know."

"Just to be sure, honey, you should drink the tea."

She smiled. "No thanks. I'm just going to wash up next door."

Mrs. Ennis looked to Gates for assistance, holding her hands up in surrender. "Christopher, can you think of any reason she doesn't need the tea?"

Gates collected his gun belt from the floor. "I don't know, Mrs. Ennis; she should know what he did or didn't do." He slid his hat back on his head and made for the back door, holding it open, but not going through it. "I have to trust her judgment, especially now when she's probably doubting herself."

He kissed Mrs. Ennis on the cheek and went out the door, disappearing into the darkness. Mrs. Ennis heard his shoes echo faintly on the steps of the guesthouse and heard the front door open and close. She stood there a minute looking into the darkness and to the small window where the illumination glowing from the fire burning inside the house was visible.

She looked back at Benjamin who was sitting at the kitchen table, picking at a plate of food she'd put out for him.

"I'm sorry, Ma," Benjamin stated, his eyes looking at the floor. "I promised Devon he wouldn't hurt her ever again." He looked past his mother to the kitchen door, where the light of the lantern was visible against the blackness of the night. "Did Thomas Jr. hurt her again?"

"Yes," Mrs. Ennis wiped her eyes. "But not like before. Thank goodness you came when you did."

"I should have shot him at the river when I had the chance. This is all my fault."

"I hope I haven't raised the kind of young man who would shoot another man whose hands are in the air in surrender?"

They heard the wagon roll to a stop behind the house, its big wheels grinding against the frigid ground. She heard footsteps going back and forth to the water pump behind the main house.

Benjamin got up and stood next to his mother. "Who is it?"

She slid her arm around him. "Your pa, most likely."

He leaned closer out of the door, peering into the darkness. "Is he filling up the buckets?"

She wiped her hands on the apron. "Yes, I think so."

"What for?" he asked.

"I think he's getting water for the tub for her," she answered so matter-of-factly, that he couldn't come up with a reply.

Benjamin smiled and stepped out through the door to help his father.

****

Gates hadn't bothered to knock before he went in; he doubted it would make much difference anyway. At first, he thought the room was empty; perhaps she'd gone to the outhouse. But that didn't seem likely, because he knew how much she hated going out there, especially at night.

Then he saw her, sitting toward the back of the cabin near the corner, tucked into a ball.

He tossed his hat at the rack, not noticing when it fell to the floor. After undoing his gun belt and hanging it over the back of the chair, he approached her, taking care to keep a comfortable distance from her as if she were a wounded animal.

As he got closer, he could see she was still wearing the robe she had put on earlier. Gates knelt, rubbing his chin while pondering what he should do for her. After going over a few mental scenarios, he sat cross-legged on the floor next to her.

"Devon," he whispered. "You want to change into your own clothes?"

She nodded. "In a minute ... I like sitting here, the smell of the fire, winter chill in the air."

"Do you need anything? Anything I can do?" he asked.

She shook her head. "I can't tell you what these last weeks have meant to me." She held out her hand to admire her wedding ring. "I can't find the words to tell you how complete you make me feel ... how good it felt this morning to wake up naked in your arms, my skin touching yours."

He looked at her with soulful eyes, hoping to come up with his own words to match what she was sharing with him. Instead, he sat quietly and let her finish her thoughts.

"I love you, and I am so afraid," she admitted.

"Devon, Ray has him in custody. He can't hurt you anymore." He moved closer to her.

"No, I'm afraid I won't be able to feel like that ever again," she answered, tears welling in her eyes.

"You will," he said, edging closer to her, so that they were facing each other nearly knee to knee. He reached out and placed his hand on her knee. "I'm here with you no matter what it takes."

She wiped her eyes and opened her mouth to reply, but was interrupted by a tap on the door. Gates spun around and called out, "Come in, it's open."

Benjamin came through the door, weighted down with a large bucket in each hand, which he carried to the fireplace. Gabriel followed close behind him also carrying a large bucket in each hand.

"I'm so sorry, Devon." Benjamin's eyes were teary as he approached her but kept his distance. "I know I promised you that---"

"I'm so grateful, Benjamin, that you came when you did. You've nothing to apologize for."

Gabriel dumped the buckets into the tub and motioned for Benjamin to return to the wagon and collect some additional buckets to pour into the tub.

Benjamin had filled the tub only about halfway, when he announced the buckets were all emptied. Gabriel pointed to the back of the main house where the handle of the pump was visible. "Take the wagon back and get another load," he told Benjamin.

Obediently, Benjamin collected the two buckets from his father's arms and exited the guesthouse, tossing the empty buckets into the back as he climbed into the wagon.

Gabriel cautiously approached Devon. "I know it's hard and all, dealing with everything that's happened. You've got to put this behind you and pick up where you were."

Devon just sat quietly and listened, wiping her eyes as the tears spilled out.

He smiled at her. "You've both been so happy the last week or so. I'd hate to see you regress back to the way it was. Nothing Thomas Junior has done has to matter unless you let it."

It was the first time she'd spoken since he and Benjamin had entered, and it took her a few minutes to find her voice. "I know," she whispered. "I'm trying."

Benjamin returned, lugging two more buckets and sloshing water furiously from side to side, until it drizzled into large puddles onto the floor. He made about four more trips in and out of the cabin, pouring the buckets into the tub. "Devon," Benjamin asked, "You want me to pour the hot buckets in?"

Gates shook his head and answered for her. "No, I'll pour them after she gets in. It'll stay warmer longer than if we dump the water in now."

Gabriel patted Benjamin's shoulder. "Let's say goodnight, son."

Benjamin waved to them as he made his way out of the door. Seconds later, Gates and Devon heard the wagon pull away from the house and head in the direction of the barn. Gabriel followed him, pulling the door closed as he went out.

When they were alone again, Gates helped Devon up. "Get in the tub and I'll pour the hot water in. You can rest for a while in the tub."

Reluctantly, she untied the belt around her waist, slid the robe off her shoulders, and stepped into the tub. Almost as soon as she lay back and eased into the water, Gates poured the hot water into the tub.

He poured some scented powder into the tub and sat a full glass of wine atop the table near the tub just within her reach. He stood and looked anxiously around the room as if he'd lost something. His eyes lit up when he spotted Gabriel's guitar propped against the wall opposite the couch. He snatched it up with one hand and took a seat on the bed, sliding the base of the guitar onto his lap. As he played, a soothing melody resonated throughout the cabin. It was the same melody he'd played the first week they'd arrived at the Ennis'. He hummed along with the music, and to her surprise, he began to sing along with the music.

She reclined her head against the tub, intoxicated by the warm water against her body and the performance by Gates and his guitar. Devon was surprised, not only by how good he sang, but also by how meaningful the lyrics were, especially because he'd penned them himself.

The song was about a broken road and true love. The song told how all his loves before had led him to this place and time, so that he could be with her. It had a contemporary, country rhythm and a meaning that was painfully genuine and raw.

He didn't realize that she'd fallen asleep, until the knock at the door caused him to turn to see how she was doing. He opened the door, not surprised to find Mrs. Ennis holding a basket of fruit and nuts and some sandwiches.

"I thought you might be hungry," she said, stepping into the room as Gates stepped aside to allow her to enter. She placed the basket on the table and motioned to the tub where Devon was slumped on her side, snoring gently. "How is she?" she asked.

"I truly don't know. She's so calm, it's scary," Gates answered, looking back to where Devon was asleep in the tub.

"It's the shock of seeing him again; hurting her again. Should I expect to make a trip tomorrow to see James?" Mrs. Ennis tucked the loose strands of hair back into her bun.

"She says nothing happened that requires an examination. I have to trust her to make the right decision."

Mrs. Ennis opened her mouth to speak, but Gates interrupted. "And no tea."

Edith almost laughed aloud. She probably would have if the time and topic had been different. She walked toward the tub and dipped her fingers in the water. "It's getting cool. You should get her out."

Gates nodded and pulled the blankets on the bed down to expose the white sheet. He laid a heavy floral blanket from the couch on top of the sheet. Gently, he lifted her from the tub and carried her toward the bed, mindful of the trail of water he was leaving with each step.

She stirred slightly, turning immediately to her right side with her back facing them. Gates looked at the wineglass, not surprised to see it was nearly empty. Good, he thought to himself, she needed the sleep.

He dried her off with the floral blanket and pulled it out gently from under her.

Mrs. Ennis handed him a nightgown for Devon, but he shook his head. "I don't want to wake her up." He pulled the blanket from the foot of the bed and covered her sleeping form, careful to tuck it softly around her chest.

Mrs. Ennis noticed that the fire had died down to embers that rose like smoke into the air, only to fall back, ash as black as coal. "Better put some more wood on the fire; don't want her to get cold."

Gates tossed several large quarter logs into the fire bay, stacking the logs close to each other with a long, skinny, metal rod. "We'll be fine, but thank you."

She kissed him on the cheek and walked to the door without looking back. As soon as he heard the door close, he undressed and slid into the bed next to his wife, then he blew out the flame in the lamp, so that the room fell into a soft blanket of darkness; only a small ray of moonlight radiated through the window and cast a shadow on the bed.

****

He awoke with a jerk at the sound of the rooster bellowing from a rooftop nearby. He rose up on one elbow just enough to determine if she was still asleep. The relief was evident on his face to find her expression calm, content, and at ease. Sleep had found her easily last night and had held on tight.

He felt her inhale deeply next to him, raising her arms fractionally overhead and stretching, so that her back arched against his chest. Gates could tell she was awake just by her breathing. Without saying anything, she turned toward him so that she was enveloped tight against his chest embraced by his arms on either side of hers.

She took a moment to take in her surroundings; her last conscious thought had been relaxing in the tub. Devon was not surprised to find she was warm, naked, and in their bed with her husband watching over her. He pushed himself away from her as if to get up from the bed, but she held on to his forearms, effectively holding him in place.

She exhaled, never breaking eye contact with him. "I love you, Chris."

He kissed her on the forehead. "I know."

She leaned in to kiss his lips, but he pulled away. "Devon, I don't think we should …"

Silencing him with her lips, she made contact, urging him to react to her and engage her physically.

She locked her arms around his neck, pulling herself closer to him, intensifying the kiss so that their lips and tongues were battling for control.

It was an odd feeling for her, awakening naked with him to find that he was not erect. Under normal circumstances, he was rigid and waiting before the sun was up. She moved her knee back and forth between his legs, rubbing gently against his shaft and testicles. It was not difficult to feel him tensing as she contacted his sensitive member.

He felt her hand moving down his abdomen and just above his groin, before he felt her wrap her hand around him pushing and pulling until she felt him respond. She'd never considered that his erection might be painful until she saw him cringing. "You okay?"

He laid his hand on top of hers and stilled her ministrations. "I'm a little sore, but I'm fine." Gates leaned in closer to look directly into her eyes. "I'm more concerned about you."

Devon contemplated her response before saying anything. It wasn't that she didn't trust him with her thoughts; she trusted him with her very life. But she couldn't find the words to tell him that she needed it all to just go away, every moment of yesterday from the time they returned from Marston's ranch, to the time they were finally safe in the guesthouse.

For her own preservation, she desperately needed him to hold her so tightly, that none of the recollections could break through. It was her sole desire to bury herself deeply within his embrace, until she could find her voice again.

She pushed herself into a sitting position, wrapping her arms around her knees and leaning back against the headboard. "I don't want to talk about it," Devon whispered so low, he almost didn't hear her.

She traced his forearm with the tips of her fingers. "I can't think about it anymore."

He knew she was filtering her thoughts and carefully planning exactly what she was willing to share with him. "I want to focus on how good you make me feel," she swallowed slowly, realizing for the first time how dry her throat was. "I want all of that back, Chris." She licked her lips and before looking up to face him, she added. "Before it's too late."

He moved his hand off hers and ran his fingertips from her rib cage to her breast, rubbing the nipple with his thumb until it piqued and hardened. "I can't just erase what happened, Devon. We can't pretend it didn't happen."

"I know that," she added, scooting closer against his side and pushing herself into his hand. "I just want you to remind me why it doesn't matter."

"It matters," he reminded her, "because everything that has happened has brought us here to this place and time." He moved his hand from her breast and gently caressed her cheek with the back of his hand. "You can't separate them in time, Devon."

She held his hand within her own and took a deep breath. "You know, Gates, before I met you, my life was full." The fact that she'd reverted to his last name was not lost on him, but he didn't acknowledge it in any way.

He reclaimed his spot next to her and pulled the blanket over her chest, tucking it carefully around her breasts. Devon continued. "I had a career that I was proud of and good at. I had great friends and family; I dated when I wanted to."

Leaning her head against his, she added, "Then you came along and toppled my balance. I didn't realize what was missing in my life until I found you here."

Her eyes were tearing as she finished. "I don't think I can go back to the way it was before; I can't live without you and the way you make me feel."

He leaned close against her and covered her body with his own, pulling awkwardly at the blanket to expose her chest, and dropping feather-light kisses along her neck and shoulder. "You sure you want to do this now?" he asked, as he wrapped his mouth around her right breast.

"Yes," she moaned. "Make love to me now."

He rolled them so that she was on her back, almost flat against the mattress, and he kissed a trail of wet, warm kisses between her breasts and down to her abdomen. He raised his hands over his head and each found a breast, palming the mound and pulling at the nipple in one fluid motion. His kisses made a path between her legs burning every inch he touched. He moved his hands between her thighs, pushing her legs apart as his mouth found her center. It was as if he hadn't eaten in months; his mouth, lips, and tongue were everywhere all at once, inside and outside, tip to end. He pushed her folds apart, teasing her with his finger first, then with his tongue.

He felt the long muscle of her outer thigh tense and her arms clench alongside her hip. He pulled his mouth away and looked at her. "You okay?"

She nodded and smiled. "Yes, I'm fine."

"You want me to stop?" He was unsure of what he wanted the answer to be. As much as he loved being buried between her legs, he knew she was struggling to finish what she'd started. He pulled himself back to face her. "Devon, I can't do this—not like this."

She pushed him closer against her, so that his groin was nearly flush against hers. "Chris, please. You've always implied my needs take precedence over yours." She pushed her hand between their bodies and found his penis again, stroking him almost frantically up against her opening. "I've never asked you for anything; please. Make love to me, now."

There was something in her eyes that he'd never seen before. He wasn't sure if it was desperation, fear, or surrender. He found himself kissing his way back down her body until his mouth was resting between her legs. Sliding his hands up and under her buttocks, he pushed her as close to him as he could, almost lifting her up to him. She could feel his hot breath on her center, as she ground herself harder against him.

He could tell by her frenzied pace that she was close to her climax. He pulled his mouth away long enough to push at the engorged bundle of nerves quick with his finger, so hard and fast, she cried out and pushed at his hand.

God, he thought, she is beautiful. Her face flushed red and hot, her breath arriving in deep inhalations, so that it almost sounded like a hiccup. He held on and continued stimulating her with his finger, until she squeezed her legs together so tight, he had to withdraw his hand.

He kissed her again and pushed himself between her legs, probing gently for penetration. He pushed into her, careful to watch for any signs of distress. Thankfully, there were none. She moved rhythmically to meet his thrusts, opening her legs wider to accommodate the bulk of his body. He dropped his weight back against her so that her breasts were in his hands again, then in his mouth, and finally back in his hands. She slid her hands up and down his back coming to rest on his buttocks. Pushing him almost desperately down into her, she whispered, "Just a little harder."

His movements against her were almost snakelike, the lower part of his body undulating dance-like into and out of her. As she requested, he increased his motion so that he was almost slapping against her.

It was taking all his concentration to hold back his release. Licking his lips, he tasted the remnants of her on his face. It was more than he could take, and he pumped with such intensity, he exploded into her before he intended, calling out her name into her shoulder as he finished. Gates flipped over onto his back, pulling her with him. "I love you, Devon. Don't ever doubt that."

She smiled to herself, laying her head against his chest and rubbing the puckered skin around his nipples. "I don't doubt you, Chris." She sat up against the headboard taking the bulk of the sheet with her. "Are you going into town today?" Although, she already knew the answer, she felt compelled to ask anyway.

Reluctantly, he made his way to his feet, grabbing his clothes from the back of the chair and dressing quickly. "There are some things that have to be decided over the next day or two: what Hayden will actually be charged with, where he'll be processed, and so on."

After grabbing his coat from the couch, his hat from the rack, and his gun belt from the back of the chair, he hesitated before going out the front door. "You sure you're declining to make a statement?"

She nodded. "Yes, I'm declining."

He adjusted his hat so that it sat straight on his head. "Your decision. I'm going to grab some breakfast and head into town. You coming over to eat?"

Devon shook her head and ran her hand through her hair, pulling it back behind her ears. "No, I'm not hungry."

Before leaving, he returned to the bed and sat close to her. "Rest for today. I'm sure you'll get your appetite back tomorrow."

She kissed him on the cheek, her fingers trailing the spot she'd just kissed. Tangling her finger in the dark hair at his neck, she ran her fingers through it, enjoying the feel of it. She liked his hair this length, longer and curlier at the ends where it bent upward and onto itself. He usually wore it much shorter; she smiled, delighted at how much younger it made him look; how reckless he appeared.

"You should stop by the barber and get a cut. Sheriff Callahan won't like the shaggy look," she advised.

He kissed her knuckles, stepping to his feet almost at the same time. "You sure you'll be okay?" His reluctance to leave was evident in his voice.

She nodded, stepping into the robe as she made her way out of the bed. "Yes, I've some animals to tend to today, and other odd chores, nothing noteworthy." She hooked her arm through his and led him toward the door. "I'll be fine. Go eat, and I'll see you for dinner."

He made his way out of the door, glancing back at her one last time, before closing the door and heading to the main house.

Chapter Five

Mrs. Ennis dried the frying pan furiously with the thick cloth, checking several times to make sure there weren't any damp places before putting it away. She hated trying to undo the damage to the iron pots and pans once the rusting process had started. Sometimes, it was easier to just throw the pan away instead of trying to clear the rust away with oil.

Gates stepped quietly into the kitchen, hat in hand. "Morning," he kissed Mrs. Ennis on the cheek. "I could smell the bacon all the way from the outhouse."

He accepted the cup of coffee from Mrs. Ennis' hand, and turned to Benjamin who was standing near the breakfast table binding his school books together, with what looked to Gates to resemble an antique bungee cord.

Benjamin's empty breakfast plate was still on the table as was Gabriel's.

"Where's your Pa?" Gates asked, sitting at the table behind one of the two linen-covered plates of food.

"Went back upstairs for something." Benjamin didn't look up from his work.

Gates pointed to the other the one intended for Devon. "I don't think she's coming over for breakfast." He pushed the plate closer to Benjamin. "No need to let it go to waste."

Mrs. Ennis stepped between them and collected Devon's plate. "I'll walk it over to her later."

Mrs. Ennis returned and took the empty chair on the other side of Gates.

"It's been three days, Christopher. We've hardly seen her."

"Just give her some time, Mrs. Ennis," Gates said, stuffing eggs and bacon into his mouth and listening for Gabriel's boots on the stair steps. "She's a little better every day."

"Does she know you're going to be away for a few nights?" Mrs. Ennis asked, looking anxiously behind her as if she could see through the kitchen wall and into the guest house.

"I haven't been able to tell her, every time I try to talk to her about anything serious, she distracts me." Gates pushed his empty plate away and swallowed the last drop of coffee from his cup.

"Distracts you? How?" Mrs. Ennis refilled his coffee cup and set the pot to warm on the stove.

Gates looked awkwardly to Benjamin. "Let's just say her appetite has returned and she's hungry a lot."

Benjamin looked up from his task. "You don't have to use code. I know you're talking about sex."

"Yes, I'm talking about sex." Gates stood up and leaned against the kitchen counter, turning back to face them and running his hand through his hair. "I've tried for the last three days to tell her I'm transporting Hayden to Kansas City to stand trial. Ray doesn't think he can get a fair trial here. Every time she's near me, she initiates sex and I can't think clearly."

"Can I go with you to Kansas City?" Benjamin moved across the room closer to Gates, and leaned against the counter in a similar fashion.

"No, you're needed here. Keep an eye on her," Gates answered, feeling guilty about taking the deputy job again and leaving all the work to Gabriel.

"You know I'm going to be your deputy when I'm old enough," Benjamin paused. "And there ain't nothing here to hurt her now that Hayden is in custody."

"I don't think it would be a good idea for you to come along." Gates pushed off the counter and walked to the door, peering out the back door.

"Why not? I'm old enough, I could be of some assistance," Benjamin's words were tinged with frustration.

"That's not what I mean. I'm afraid you'll retaliate against Hayden."

"I could have shot him, twice already. You don't give me enough credit." His words were precise, loud as he made his way back to the kitchen table and swept up his school books in a single, swift motion. "You should tell her the truth and stop using sex as an excuse." He left the room, letting the kitchen door slam behind him.

****

Mrs. Ennis watched Benjamin stomp across the snow-covered yard between the main and guest houses. She could tell by his pace that he was angry, probably mentally continuing to argue with Christopher in his head.

She turned back to Gates. "I'm sorry. I don't know what's gotten into him; making him so protective of her. Lord knows, she doesn't need protection from you."

"I'll try and speak to him tonight. I've got to go and talk to Devon about my trip."

"Christopher, she's not coming to breakfast?" Gabriel asked, entering the room from the hallway and taking the seat he'd previously occupied at the kitchen table.

Gates sat down at the table where Gabriel indicated, removing his hat again and laying it on the table next to the plate of leftovers in the middle of the table. "She's fine, Mr. Ennis. Just give her a little breathing room."

Hurriedly, almost desperately, Gabriel scooped the left-over eggs and ham onto a clean plate so quickly, that the food was mashed together in a big pile in its middle. Gates laid his hand on Gabriel's shoulder gently to stop him from spooning the food. "I know you're worried about her, but we have to trust her to tell us what she needs when she's ready."

Gates took the plate from him and set it down next to the one Mrs. Ennis had set aside for Devon. He continued talking, but his discussion was not directed solely to Mrs. Ennis, but to Gabriel as well. "When she's ready, I know she'll let us in." He forked a thick, juicy piece of ham into his mouth and continued. "Until then, we just have to wait."

Gabriel nodded his agreement. "You sure she'll be okay here today? You want Benjamin to stay home from school?"

Mrs. Ennis did not answer but looked curiously to Gates who sipped hot coffee from the cup before answering. "No, Hayden is in custody. There's no threat to her now. She'll be fine."

Mrs. Ennis smiled and kissed Gabriel on the cheek. "He left about an hour ago anyway."

Gabriel looked at Edith with a quizzical expression. "Travis's girl again?"

She nodded and looked anxiously out the kitchen door, as if she could see his retreating figure running down the winding path to the driveway. She caught movement from the guest house, where she could just barely make out Devon's figure at the window.

Mrs. Ennis' first inclination was to wave at her, but when she saw the look of anguish on Devon's face, she decided against it. For now, she'd do as Christopher had requested and give her this time to regroup and gather herself.

She nodded to Gabriel as he stood up from the table and went out the back door toward the barn, probably to ready the team. Now that Christopher was working in town with Ray, Gabriel was hard-pressed to get the daily chores completed before nightfall, especially now when the days were shorter and the nights were longer.

Seconds later, she heard the horses pulling the wagon out of the barn and onto the path. She knew Gabriel would guide the team in the opposite direction Benjamin had taken, heading instead for the northeast field where the last of the hay was stacked and waiting to be loaded into the wagon and transported back to the barn.

When Gabriel and the team were just a tiny speck in the distance, Edith looked at where Gates was still sitting at the kitchen table pretending to drink from the coffee cup, she'd just refilled for him. "Something on your mind, Christopher?"

"I think Ray is going to recommend that Thomas Junior hang for his crimes. I know that Mr. Hayden will be devastated. And I know how close he is to your family."

He paused and made his way to where she was still standing by the door. "I need for you to understand how hard this will be for her and for me-- for everyone. As long as he's alive, I believe he will be a threat to her."

She rubbed at his hand that he'd placed on her arm. "I know Ray will do what he thinks is right and fair. And I believe you'll support him whatever that decision happens to be."

Gates pretended not to see how she looked at the framed photograph of Mary that hung on the wall in the foyer, near the stairs to the second floor. "I learned a long time ago how to mourn the dead and breathe with the living, I'll do no less for Thomas Junior."

Mrs. Ennis handed him his hat and a saddlebag that she had filled with his lunch for the day. "That man who held us hostage the other day, is not the young man I helped to raise. The boy I remember was kind and gentle, and he had an infectious laugh."

She rubbed at his back urging him through the back door. "I didn't see any resemblance to that boy in the eyes of the man who did those horrible things."

As Gates stepped through the door, she added, "He wasn't always like that; something happened, and he changed."

Gates nodded. "I'd like to think that's what happened, Mrs. Ennis."

He kissed her on the forehead and made his way to the barn to saddle Emma. Seconds later, he came out leading the horse from the barn. He mounted the horse effortlessly and nudged her toward town.

Chapter Six

He opened his eyes before his brain registered that dawn was breaking just off the horizon. Gates seldom slept on his back; usually, he was more comfortable on his side. He slid his hands behind his head and watched out the window as the darkness slipped away and the daybreak hung just above the horizon, then climbed slowly into the sky until the sun was above the clouds. Despite the peacefulness of the morning, he felt as if something was off-- as if he was waiting for something.

Only seconds later, he heard the rooster announcing the coming of a new day. Devon stirred next to him, burying her face deeper into his chest and almost gathering him in her arms.

He smiled to himself, comforted by the feel of her against his chest, the smell of her on his skin. He embraced her just at the waist and clasped his hands around her. "You awake?" he whispered.

She didn't open her eyes, but nodded that she was, and then she adjusted her head on his chest so that she could see the daybreak.

"Devon," he began, swallowing as if his throat was dry. "You want to get out some today, go into town for dinner, maybe?"

She shook her head. "No, not really. I have to tend to the animals …"

He cut her off. "The animals will be fine for a day. It's been several days and all you've done is tend to the animals in the barn and work out."

She rose up and placed her chin in the middle of his chest. "I've been trying to clear my head. You know running helps me do that." She smiled as if she were a child asking for a second cookie. "I'm feeling better now."

He traced her lips and moved his head toward hers for a kiss. She accepted his kiss and moved closer to him, so that they were nearly chest to chest. He slid his hands down to her buttocks and pushed the white nightshirt up to her waist, toying with the waistband of her underwear.

She stilled his hand and replied into his neck. "We can't."

He pushed at her hand more urgently, while his lips pressed hers in a long kiss. "Why not?"

She replied almost mournfully. "It's not that I don't want to, I do," kissing his neck and shoulders.

He flipped them so that he was on top, pushing between her legs gently, grinding his erect penis against her nightgown. "Then what's the problem?" His hands found her breasts through the gown and caressed her so roughly he heard her cry out.

"What's wrong?" he asked, his voice registering his concern.

She held on to his hand. "I'm having my period, that's all."

"Should I get one of my shirts?" he asked, almost laughing, remembering a time that seemed significantly long ago.

"No, I use the cloth rolls Mrs. Ennis keeps from old clothes and blankets." She playfully punched his arm.

He resumed grinding his erection into her groin. "I don't mind," he announced, his kisses gently circling her breast, making the fabric covering it wet and sticky.

She reached down between them and took him in her hand, pulling his shaft toward her, up and down, delighted at his reaction to her touch. "I do," she answered.

Gates clutched her hand and stilled it. "Then we'll wait, what, a day or two?"

She nodded. "Most likely."

"Good," he said, and he pulled himself up and swung his legs over the edge of the bed to put his feet on the floor. "I've got to make a run to Kansas City, so when I get back tomorrow night, we can celebrate."

She tossed the blankets away and got to her feet. "What's in Kansas City?" she asked, standing in front of him as though demanding an answer.

"I've got to transport a prisoner," he answered matter-of-factly. She knew who the prisoner was without even asking.

"Why Kansas City?" Devon asked, toying with the belt on the white robe, as she threw it on and fastened it around her waist.

"A marshal will meet me and take custody of him. Ray doesn't believe Hayden can get a fair trial here, and I agree with him. This is best for everyone."

"Why you?" she asked. Her voice was so strained, he thought she might cry.

"I think it's a test," Gates admitted. "If I get him there in one piece, Ray will know I'm a man of honor. I think he's trying to reassure himself that he made the right choice."

"And if he doesn't get there in one piece?" she asked, only half-joking. Gates stepped into his underwear and then his trousers. "Then he'll know I'm just a man."

"I'm coming with you," she argued, hands folded across her chest. "You'll need back-up."

"I don't think that's a good idea. Hayden is still Hayden. I'll be fine."

"Tomorrow night?" she confirmed.

He nodded, biting his lip, surprised at how well she'd accepted the news. "I'll kick Emma into overdrive. If not late tomorrow night, early the next morning for sure."

"You're leaving today?"

"Probably from town, once I collect Hayden from the jail. We're on our way."

"I'm missing you already." She kissed him innocently, liked she'd done before they'd slept together. "Be careful," she paused. "I love you."

"Love you more." He handed her a skirt and shirt. "Get dressed and have some breakfast with me. You've hardly eaten anything all week. I miss the company."

She wasn't sure if it was the pout or the devious look in his eyes, but she found herself dressing quickly and accompanying him to the main house for breakfast.

They nearly collided with Benjamin as he bolted out the kitchen door and jumped from the back step in a single giant leap. His jacket was hanging loose at one shoulder, as he made his way down the long dirt driveway, and toward the main road that ran parallel to the house.

Gates turned to watch him run past, calling to him as the distance between them grew. "What's the rush?"

Benjamin turned back to them. "Heimdail's leaving today, heading back north into the mountains."

"Give him our best," Gates called out, and then he waved him off and turned back toward the house, pulling Devon's arm into his.

****

The morning went by quickly. Devon busied herself with the animals. First, she washed them, and then she fed them, and then she mended half of them. If she had to admit it, she did the work more out of habit, more than need.

The thought of Gates being away from her tonight and most of tomorrow, was weighing heavily on her mind. It wasn't that she was scared; she really wasn't, at least not scared for herself. But the thought of him being on his own in the middle of nowhere without backup, without her, was more than she could bear.

If the prisoner he was transporting hadn't been Hayden, she'd have most likely tagged along to make sure she had Gates back. But she knew she couldn't handle seeing Hayden again so soon after the attack. The wounds were still too raw and too deep.

She smiled to herself, finding comfort in the memory of being in Gates arms, breathing in his scent, the sounds he made as she writhed against him, satisfied and satiated. Her cycle was all but finished, and now she wished she'd let him make love to her this morning after all. She bit her lip, missing him already and longing for the day to end and bring him home to her.

Devon didn't hear the barn door open, or the approaching figure until she felt his breath against her neck. Initially, her posture was defensive, but as his arms gathered her lovingly against his chest, she relaxed and was lost in his embrace.

"I was just thinking about you," she said to him, as his lips found hers and she dissolved slowly into him. He took her face in his hands and held her to him, pulling her so close, that she could hardly get her breath.

He suckled at her neck, nibbling at her collarbone just above her throat, all the way to her shoulder and then back again. "I hate being away from you tonight."

Unbuttoning her shirt so that it hung open at her arms, he unlaced the thin corset and pulled it away from her chest, dropping it to the ground so that he could nuzzle her breasts against his face.

The prickly sensation of stubble on his chin against the tender and sensitive skin of her breasts, was overwhelming and she shook in response. She found herself pulling his shirttail out of his trousers and unbuttoning the tiny buttons of his shirt so forcibly, she was surprised that none of the buttons were torn off. As soon as she tossed the shirt away, she was undoing his pants and pushing them down to his knees.

He pushed her backward, guiding her toward the back of the barn to a warm pile of hay stacked almost waist high. As soon as her back hit the hay bed, he was already positioned between her legs, pushing her skirt and petticoat off her waist and down to her knees.

His mouth clamped down hungrily on her left breast, paying careful attention to the nipple, already swollen and engorged. His tongue pulled it in and out, guiding it into his mouth, suckling almost childlike, and then pushing it out again.

Devon felt his fingers probing her center before she realized her pantaloons were off, lying near his trousers on the barn floor. He slid his fingers in and out of her several times, trailing his thumb in soft tiny circles around her core.

Eagerly, she opened her legs wider to accommodate him as he pushed himself closer against her until he'd penetrated her fully, moving quickly to redistribute his body weight onto his arms.

He set a pace that was slow and steady at first, pushing so deeply into her that she couldn't manage to respond. Instead, she slid her arms around his waist until her hands met on either side of his buttocks. She pushed him harder into her, biting at his chest as his thrusts brought her mouth close enough to have easy access.

He sat up with her still connected to him and spun her around so that she was nearly sitting atop him, her breasts hanging easily within reach of his mouth again. Gates placed a hand on either side of her hip and lifted her just enough to raise her off his shaft fractionally. Then he let her fall against him, repeating the act several times, until she picked up the pace herself.

Between the sensations of his mouth pulling at her nipple and the feeling of him pushing so far inside of her that it was almost painful, she knew she was close to climax. As soon as his fingers pinched at her folds, she felt the pressure between her legs building with such intensity, she knew she would not be able to muffle the scream against her arm.

She fell against his chest instead, almost crying into his neck as she came. Gates held out as long as he was able to; as soon as he felt her pulsating against his penis like a hundred tiny pins, he flipped them over so that she was on her back again and pumped himself dry into her. He had pushed himself so high up on his arms, that tiny beads of sweat dripped from his chin onto her chest and trailed like rain down her abdomen, disappearing somewhere below.

He asked her between deep breaths, "I couldn't wait the two days. I'm sorry."

She pulled him as close against her as she could, pushing the hair out of his eyes. "I'm glad you came back. Where's Hayden?"

Gates pushed to his feet and bent down to collect their clothes. He handed her the skirt and pantaloons first, then tossed her shirt and bra into her lap. He watched her button the shirt just above her breasts, and then slid to her feet, stepping into her shoes. "Ray's bringing him to me."

Gates held up his hands in response to the look of panic on Devon's face, thinking Hayden was coming back to the ranch. "I'm meeting Ray back at the mercantile. I've got to pick up some supplies before we head out."

"I don't like you transporting a prisoner without backup," she mentioned, almost casually, looking up to gauge his reaction.

He zipped his pants in a single action, looking at her nervously as he answered. "I'll be fine." Stepping into his boots, he snatched his shirt off the bed of hay and picked some loose strands of hay from the collar before putting it on.

Gates put the shirt on and let it hang open. "I'm meeting a federal marshal about fifty miles out of Hamilton." He pulled her to within arm's length of him. "As soon as I hand Hayden over, I'll head back in double time." Gates kissed her on the forehead, letting his lips linger against her skin longer than was necessary. "I'll be back in time to make love to you again before the sun sets tomorrow night."

She kissed him again, gently on the lips this time, smiling at him as she buttoned his shirt against his chest. "I love you; come home safe."

He reluctantly pulled himself away and disappeared through the doorway to the barn. Seconds later, she heard his horse trotting away, the mare's hoofs echoing fainter and fainter as the horse galloped away.

****

Devon watched him against the horizon, until he was little more than a dark speck. Then she turned her attention back to the animals and busied herself with their needs to help pass the time. She had been working for about an hour, when she heard the distant sound of a rider approaching.

She looked awkwardly around the barn for something to wipe her hands on. By the time she found a worn, ragged bag, the rider had made his way to the house.

Devon peeked through the slits of the wood-plank walls of the barn and saw Ray bringing his mare to a quick stop before he slid off the horse and his boots hit the ground with a loud scuffling noise.

"Edith? Gabriel?" he yelled, looking around anxiously.

He hitched the horse to the post and made his way toward the barn. He'd only gotten a few steps, when Mrs. Ennis came hurrying out the front door, wiping her hands on a large kitchen towel. Devon knew by Mrs. Ennis' pace and body language, she knew something was wrong before Ray had said a word.

Devon had felt it all morning, just like the storm that was brewing in the distance. The red and yellow flashes of light barely visible in the late afternoon sky were like a painted canvas. Although it had been a cool day, a warm wind out of the west was blowing the limbs of the trees back and forth as if they were waving.

"Ray, what's wrong?" Mrs. Ennis asked, biting her lip and tugging the hair that had fallen loose back into place.

Ray pulled a crumbled piece of paper from his jacket pocket and pushed it toward her, his hand trembling slightly as he spoke. "This was in Thomas's cell."

Mrs. Ennis took it from his outstretched hand and inspected it cautiously. It was nonsense, a series of random numbers and letters. "I don't understand, Ray. What's this about?"

He took it from her and ran his hand over it, as if smoothing it out would make it easier for her to read. "At first, I thought it was just trash, but look here at these initials on the bottom: NF."

Mrs. Ennis' lips moved as she read silently to herself, but she still looked confused. "NF?"

Ray nodded. "Nick Ferris," he answered, matter-of-factly. He looked around and asked, "Where's Gabriel?"

She pointed behind the house. "At the lavender field," she said, named for the fragrant scent it gave off in the spring.

"That's a half day's ride there and back," he murmured, his eyes moving frantically back and forth as he considered what to do.

"Ray?" she asked, the concern in her voice making her sound almost angry. "What's wrong? What is it about this cryptic message that concerns you?"

He pointed to the last line of numbers. "Abby was over this afternoon, helping me clean up once Deputy Gates took custody of Thomas. She recognized this code from when they were kids."

"What does it mean?" she repeated. "I don't understand."

Ray pointed to a series of numbers near the end of the second sentence. "She couldn't remember it all. But she swears this last line reads Intercept Idresil Nov 24."

She pushed the note back toward him and echoed, "Idresil?"

"Abby says it is the name of the huge ash tree about twenty miles from your ranch. The kids used to call it the family tree. "Today is November twenty-fourth, Edith."

"That's right, it is. I just realized that, too. You think Christopher is in danger?" she asked, wiping anxiously at her brow and pushing her hair into place.

"I think this telegraph is from the Ferris brothers. I think they're planning to ambush Deputy Gates at that huge ash tree and free Thomas Junior."

He tugged at his mustache, as though pondering the ramifications of such an ambush before looking past the house. "I'll ride as hard as I can and get Gabriel. We'll head to the ash tree as fast as we can and try to help."

Before either could say anything else, they heard the gallop of a horse from inside the barn. Devon came blazing out of the barn, leading the horse frantically away from the barn in the direction of the large ash tree. She looked like a character in an old Western movie with her coat opened at the front, its tails flailing like a flag behind her.

As she rushed past them, she was pushing the heavy barrel of the rifle, into the rifle sheath mounted on the saddle. She kicked her feet into the sides of the horse, urging him to move faster. As she made the last turn out of the fence and toward the long dirt road, all she could think of was that she had to get to him in time.

Ray looked curiously to Edith, uncertain of what to do. Should he follow the girl? No doubt she had heard everything from the barn and was on her way to Gates. Would it make more sense to bring Gabriel as a backup?

In his musings, he'd been looking toward where Devon had taken off, and he didn't realize that Edith had gone into the barn and saddled another horse from a stable near the entrance. Ray recognized it as

Benjamin's horse. He looked quickly back to the house, just in case he'd missed the boy.

Edith mounted the horse like an expert and guided the animal toward the front gate of their property. She hesitated, stilling the horse with the reins. "You go after Devon. I'll get Gabriel."

Ray made his way quickly to his horse, almost jogging as he grew nearer to the animal. He pulled his body into the saddle in a single fluid movement and kicked his horse into action before he was even fully in the saddle. As his horse neared Edith's, he called out, "You sure you can get to the lavender field alone?"

She nodded and pushed the horse forward, until she passed Ray at the front gate, and then she headed in the opposite direction. She kicked at the horse's ribs to propel him forward. Ray waited until she was almost out of his sight, before he urged his horse through the front gate in pursuit of Mrs. Gates.

She had about ten minutes on him already; adjusting for their weight difference and the endurance of the horses, she would probably get to Gates a good twenty minutes or more before he could. Ray was keenly aware of what could happen in that span of time. In fact, a gunshot could take a life, and a woman's honor could be taken in far less time. Callahan pushed his horse harder in the direction she'd taken. The last time these five people had converged together, it had been catastrophic. Ray was hoping he could prevent yet another tragedy. He looked overhead at the dark clouds lingering above him, illuminations of yellow and pink lights peeking out from behind them. In all the excitement, he hadn't bothered to pack any rain gear. All he had was whatever was stashed in his saddlebags or stored in his bedroll. He didn't have a warm coat or even a canvas he could use as a tent.

All he could do was pray that the storm was mild, and that he reached the deputy and the girl in time. He pushed the horse as hard as he dared, looking anxiously as far ahead as he could see.

Chapter Seven

Deputy Gates tugged in frustration at the rope that secured Thomas Jr.'s horse to his own. They were so off schedule; he'd be lucky if they were anywhere near the drop off location by nightfall. So far, he'd had to stop three times as a result of Hayden's moaning and bellyaching over one thing or another.

Once Hayden had said he was sick and needed to vomit. Despite fifteen, twenty minutes of dry heaving onto the fresh, crisp snow, Gates hadn't seen anything to indicate Hayden was physically ill.

Twice, Hayden had asked to stop to take a piss. Gates was certain, Hayden had urinated only one of those times, the other time he was just killing time, making it almost impossible to get back home quickly to be with Devon. Gates knew Hayden was doing it purposefully.

Gates looked up to the sky where the sun was making its descent through the clouds and behind the horizon. It was nearly sunset and they hadn't even made it to the big ash tree yet.

"Guess our little honey will be lonely tonight?" Hayden Jr. baited, laughter evident in his words. "Huh, nothing rooting between those luscious legs to keep her warm."

"Shut up, Hayden, don't make me put a gag on you." Gates fists clenched in response.

"What do you think satisfies her more? Getting it from behind or up close and personal in the front?" Hayden paused. "You know what I enjoyed the most, the way she tasted. God, it was sweet."

Gates abruptly brought the horses to a stop, sliding down and yanking Hayden off the horse in one swift motion. Gates delivered several punches in the center of Hayden's gut, not flinching when Hayden dropped to one knee, breathing heavily, and guarding his stomach.

"I promised Devon I wouldn't kill you. Don't make me break another promise to her." He stepped back, his fists opening and closing as if the act of stopping the assault on Hayden had utilized all his restraint.

He pulled Hayden up by the collar of his jacket and heaved him in the direction of the horse. "Get back on the horse and shut your mouth."

"What promise have you already broken?" Hayden asked, between heavy breaths, his lip bleeding where he'd bit it during Gates beating.

"That you wouldn't get close enough to hurt her again."

Hayden nodded, his arms tucked close into his stomach, torso folded into himself so that he looked more like a child than a full-grown man.

Gates mounted his horse and pulled the rope as tight as the horses would allow and continued the path to Idresil.

****

Devon kicked the horse again, urging him onward to where she hoped to find Gates. What was he thinking, transporting that lunatic alone? She'd known better than to let him go alone. Since she'd awakened that morning, it had been a heavy weight on her mind.

She gripped the saddle horn so tightly, that her hand was nearly blue. Of course, that could have been from the coolness of the evening as well. She could tell by the way the wind had turned cold and the breeze it had brought with it; it was going to rain again.

All she could do was hope the storm was mild, or that she intercepted him sooner rather than later and could turn him back toward the ranch. They could transfer Hayden some other time with more support and better resources.

She pulled the hair from her face, untangling it with one hand and hanging on to the saddle horn with the other. Devon thrust her shoulders forward in a fruitless effort to ward off some of the rain that was just beginning to fall.

Although it was a steady rain, it was not a hard rain. Neither she nor the horse was saturated. She swallowed long and slow, almost holding her breath. God, she prayed, please let him be safe.

She finally had to acknowledge to herself something he'd already admitted months before. She couldn't live in a world that didn't include him. Closing her eyes briefly, she vowed that if he were hurt in any way, she'd kill them all, officer of the court or not.

The sun had disappeared behind the horizon an hour or so ago, its rays reflected off the clouds and bounced off the frozen ground as if it were a mirror. Devon shielded her eyes from the glare, searching in the distance for any sign that she was close to him, that he was near.

A flash of lightning caused her to turn in its direction, and she tried not to be distracted by the sound of the rolling thunder as the winter storm approached. Once the sky was darker, she was able to see the outline of the pink, yellow, and red lights barely visible high in the evening sky.

"Oh God," she said to herself. "Those dam crazy lights again."

Devon saw movement far off in the distance. At first, she thought her eyes were playing tricks on her, but as she squinted ahead, it was obvious there was someone not too far ahead of her. She urged the horse to work just a bit harder to get her close enough to identify who it was. Within minutes, she could see that there were two figures on horseback, and one rider was several paces ahead of the other.

It was ironic how the rain began to fall harder, as soon as she assured herself it was him. She could easily make out his form on Mary's horse. As she got closer, she could see the rope that ran between the two horses. Gates had given Hayden's horse a fair amount of slack on the rope, but she could see that Hayden's hands were bound in front of him near the saddle horn.

The rain was falling harder now, so hard that he'd never hear her calling him over the sound of it slapping the barren ground. She kicked the horse harder, calling Gates's name above the roar of the wind and rain. Holding herself steady, she pulled her gun from her holster and grabbed the reins again to reestablish her body position.

She called to him again, as loud as she could, praying that he'd stop and turn around.

As her horse drew closer, she felt rather than saw his body turn in her direction. She wasn't close enough to see his reaction, but she could feel that he was confused. He had brought his horse to a full stop by now and forced Hayden's horse to stall as well.

She knew they were close to the old ash tree, because she could make out its massive form just ahead of Gates and Hayden.

"Chris!" she screamed, several times through the howling wind.

Not far in the distance, Gates huddled as small in the saddle as he could, seeking protection from the storm. Above the howling wind, he heard his name, stopped and turned to see a rider approaching.

He knew it was Devon. He pulled the slack from the line between the horses, turned the horses around, and traveled back toward her.

"What is it? What's wrong?" he yelled.

The storm raged all around them, the wind whipped at their faces and the exposed skin of the neck and hands. The temperature dropped dramatically since the storm started, Gates could see her expelled breath, thick in the air as she made her way closer.

By now, he could easily make them out, riders on horseback just ahead of him as they made their way anxiously toward them. He knew who it was even before they were close enough for him to identify them. It was the Ferris brothers; guns drawn, coats trailing open behind them, as they pushed their horses to such an extreme pace that it was cruel and obscene.

"Intercept!" Devon screamed through the rain, just as a gunshot echoed behind her.

Gates heard the bullet whiz by his head and searched the area quickly to identify its origin.

Several minutes passed, before he realized the riders were firing at them. He kicked the horse harder, urging her to go faster, pulling Hayden's horse with him. When the second bullet whizzed by, he watched in horror as Devon was propelled off her horse backward and landed with a thud on her back in the soggy terrain.

Devon kneed her way to her feet, staggering as a result of the impact she'd made with the ground. It was almost as if she was lost, unsure of which direction to run, where to go for refuge.

"Devon! No!" Gates kicked the horse to move faster through the storm, when he was about a hundred feet from her, he could make out her form, rising unsteadily to her feet. As he neared her, another round of gunshots rang out. Gates slowed the horse just enough to hold out his arm and snatch her from the ground. He ceremoniously placed her in front of him, snug against the saddle horn.

"What's going on?" he yelled through the storm, holding onto her tightly as he zigged and zagged the horses through the wind and rain, trying to put some distance between their horse and the other riders.

"They're here for Hayden," she groaned, closing her eyes against the stinging rain.

He realized when he first collected her from the ground that she was hurt. But he thought it was most likely the result of the hard contact with the ground. Once she recovered from the wind being knocked out of her, she'd be fine. But as he propelled the horse out of the clearing and toward the heavy growth of forest, he realized she'd been shot. He could tell by her stance and positioning that she was trying to contain the bleeding.

Gates pulled Emma's reins tight bringing the horse to an abrupt stop. At the same time, he wrapped his arms around Devon's waist to prohibit her from being propelled off the horse when he brought it to a stop.

He surveyed the proximity of the Ferris brothers and weighed his options. Gates wasted only a second before he drew his gun and fired several rounds into the head of Hayden's horse, cut the reins, and kicked his horse as hard as he could to put some distance between them. As the horse fell to the ground, he fired again and wounded Hayden in the upper thigh. As both Hayden and the horse lay on the ground, moaning sounds coming from the both, Gates kicked his horse into action, hoping to put as much distance as he could between the intruders.

The rain fell heavily, synchronized with intermittent bouts of thunder and lightning. Gates swiped his gloved hand across his face to wipe the rain out of his eyes. He pushed the horse harder and searched for a place to make a stand.

The Ferris brothers slowed their horses, Nick stopped to collect Hayden who slid up on the rear of the horse. Even though the horse's pace was slower than Franks' horse, it was faster than Mary's old horse, especially now that she was carrying two riders.

Even in the darkness, thru the cold raging wind and burning rain, Gates knew Hayden was closing the distance behind them. Gates could feel him, like an ache just under his skin.

"They have Hayden, why are they still chasing us?" Gates screamed, turning in the saddle to see how much distance was between them.

"He's here for me," she whispered.

"Devon?" he called above the storm. "Can you shoot?"

She nodded that she could and pulled the rifle out of the sheath; she managed to get off a few shots before Emma lunged to her left, taking a path that Gates probably wouldn't have even seen.

It was uncanny how Emma seemed to know where she was going. Gates loosened his hold on the reins, partly to allow Emma some control, but mostly to hold on to Devon as she bounced up and down on the horse's back, she seemed to defy the laws of gravity.

She called to him just as a flash of lightning lit up the sky, leaving behind waves of red and pink lights. "It's those weird lights again!"

Gates shook his head and yelled back to her. "I see them."

She looked behind them to assess how close Hayden and the Ferris brothers were. "Chris, they're gaining."

Devon held her hands up over her eyes to shield them from the rain, but the storm was relentless; she couldn't see more than fifteen feet in front of the horse in any direction.

Emma made another series of turns, left and then right, passing so close under some of the trees that both Devon and Gates had to bend over to avoid being tossed off the horse. "We've got to find some shelter," he called to her. "Make a stand."

She nodded and scanned the landscape to look for something they could use as cover against their pursuers. Gates pointed toward three huge trees with massive trunks. The branches were thick and bent almost at ninety-degree angles, so that they were nearly horizontal with the ground.

Just as Emma passed by the trees, her forward motion coupled with that of the riders was no match for the angle of the descending terrain. Emma stumbled, trying frantically to regain her footing and her balance. But the landscape had transitioned from flat to almost mountainous in a second. Both riders and horse found themselves tossed through the air, until they tumbled head over feet several times, before crashing into the massive body of cold, black water whose waves crashed and rolled over them like a train.

****

When Gates first hit the water, he thought, this is odd. Where did all the water come from? It wasn't until they were submerged under the water and stroking wildly for the surface, that his mind registered that they were in the river.

Emma and Devon appeared at the surface at almost the same time, inhaling large breaths of air and fighting to stay above the water. Emma had gotten about to the middle of the river when she hesitated, allowing Devon to grab hold of the saddle horn.

The raging current pushed them along the river, tossing and turning them above and below the water. Gates grabbed a stirrup as Emma and Devon passed by, using the power of the big horse to stabilize his movement to some extent. If he noticed that they were gaining momentum along with the river's current, he didn't let on. He was aware that at some point, they would encounter a waterfall and most likely would cascade into an even larger, deeper basin of water. Gates pushed himself high up on the horse's back where he could make out the outline of the waterfall just ahead. He yelled to her, "Devon, we're coming up to where it empties. Get ready for a drop."

She nodded that she heard him and listened as he yelled to her again. "Hold on tight to Emma, and when I tell you, take a big breath and hold it. Okay?"

She nodded and slid her fingers up and under the horse's bridle. He raised himself up again, noticing they were about ten feet from the drop. He called to her again. "You ready?" She nodded once again and called out over the roar of the falling water. "I love you, Chris."

He smiled at her and screamed, "Big breath," just as the three of them tumbled over the waterfall and were dumped into an even larger river. Like the smaller one, its current was wild and raging. Emma hit the water first with Gates and Devon still attached to her. It seemed like they fell forever, drifting deeper and deeper into the water. Beneath the surface, it was calm and peaceful, but as they sank deeper, everything around them grew dimmer, colder, and darker.

The last thing Gates remembered was admiring the view, and then everything faded to a black circle no larger than a pinpoint. Then there was nothing; no light, no sound, nothing at all, just darkness.

Chapter Eight

His first thought was that he was hungry. Gates hoped Devon had remembered to pack some food. He was not up to another meal of nature's bounty; meaning squirrel and berries. He moved his left arm first, to announce to her that he was awake. Then, there was that persistent annoying bird chirping and calling somewhere nearby. Chirp, chirp, it called rhythmically. Chirp, chirp, chirp, its persistent cadence rang through the open window.

As he became more aware, he realized that the bed was softer than the one in their tiny guest house. He wondered if Mrs. Ennis had purchased a new bed after he'd left for Kansas City. He slid his right arm up and down in the space next to him, searching for her.

Gates had a moment of panic when he realized it was empty. She wasn't beside him. He stirred restlessly, pushing himself up against the headboard. "Devon?" he called out, his voice dry and strained. If he hadn't felt his lips moving, he'd not have believed he was the one speaking. Chirp, chirp, sang the bird again, only louder and angrier.

The window next to the bed had no curtain or shade, and the sunlight streaming into it was so blindingly bright, he held an unsteady hand in front of his eyes to block it as much as possible.

He couldn't make out the silhouetted figure sitting next to him. Initially, he thought it was Devon, but as his vision cleared, he knew it wasn't his wife. He was sure it was a woman, though, because he could make out the curve of her breast against the sunlight. "Where's Devon?" he murmured, impatiently.

The figure next to him stirred upright, and Gates realized that whoever she was, she had been sleeping. "Chris," the voice said, her voice pained with concern. She placed her hand against his chest as if to restrain him from getting out of the bed. "Relax, you're safe."

He continued to push his upper body up. "Where's Devon?"

"She's fine; she's just in the next room," the voice answered.

He smiled when he recognized the voice. "Abby," he whispered weakly, and then, his voice growing stronger, he asked, "How'd we get home? Where's Hayden?"

"Chris, it's me. You're safe, Devon's safe," she advised him again. "You're hurt, you both are, but you'll be okay. Just be still and rest."

"I want to see Devon," he insisted, pulling the blankets off and pushing himself to his feet.

Small, delicate hands pushed him back more forcefully than before. "Chris, it's me, Kaitlin, your sister. Who is Abby?"

Once Gates maneuvered his face out of the sunlight, he could see her clearly; he exhaled a breath he didn't even know he'd been holding. His sister was the spitting image of Abby, only a little shorter and with darker hair. Her voice, her smile, everything was Abby Callahan.

Why hadn't he seen it before?

He looked around the room in confusion, before he realized he was in a hospital bed. At the same time, he knew that the "chirping" of the bird was the beep of the IV pump to the left of the bed. His breathing became deeper, harder, more erratic, and his hands plucked at the blankets and tubes as if to clear a path to exit the bed.

The woman took both his hands in hers and pushed him back against the bed. "Chris, please, just calm down." She glanced anxiously to the monitors he was attached to, taking in the fact that all his vital signs were rising at an alarming pace.

The blood pressure and heart rate monitors whined and beeped, and his breathing grew more intense and strained. She yelled behind her back hoping the nurses at the station nearby would hear her. "I need some help in here!"

He swallowed; the room was spinning faster and faster until his eyes rolled up into his head and he fell back against the pillows. The darkness enveloped him again, and everything went black.

****

The media room was bustling with activity; people and cameras were stuffed in every corner and in every spot that could hold a figure or equipment. Although the room was large, today it didn't look very big at all. Just in front of the room to the right of a large picture window that overlooked the parking lot, and just beyond the street, was a podium with a dozen or so microphones pointed at odd angles in almost every direction to where the podium stood.

Some were unmarked, but many contained TV station call numbers and logos. To the left of the podium stood several people; some were obviously physicians and nurses dressed in scrubs and lab coats, and others were more formally dressed in suits. To either side of the group, several men and women stood, including several hospital security officers were dressed in uniforms, but they were not armed.

A woman in her fifties stood closest to the podium, looking anxiously at her watch and then around the room, as if she was looking for someone. The light-colored suit she was wearing stood out in great contrast against the dark brown paneling that covered the length of the wall. She was a pretty woman, with blonde hair cut just to her shoulders, and she had intense blue eyes. It would have been easy to imagine her thirty years earlier playing volleyball on a beach in Southern California.

After checking her watch one last time, she tapped anxiously at a single microphone mounted to a stand on the podium, and its logo read Memorial Hospital. "Excuse me," she announced, waiting for the crowd to give her its attention.

Gradually, the room grew quieter until it was silent; everyone's gaze was on the blonde woman at the podium. "Good morning, my name is Susan Miller. I am the chief operating officer here at the hospital." She made a waving motion toward the people standing with her. "I want to thank you all for coming out. We have been inundated with telephone calls since Agent McKenzie and Detective Gates were brought into our Emergency Department earlier this week. If you'll be patient, we'll try to answer as many of your questions as we can."

She leaned into the microphone and said, "Before we take your questions, let me introduce some of the people up here with me." She pointed toward the man closest to her. "This is Dr. Mark Lawson, the medical director for the Emergency Department."

Before anyone could ask any further questions, she added, "He is also the doctor who treated Agent McKenzie when she was brought in."

She pointed just beyond Dr. Lawson. "This is Colleen Adams, one of the nurses working in the Emergency Department, and next to her is Dr. Jeff Williams, the physician who worked on Detective Gates."

Mrs. Miller leaned into the microphone and said, "We will answer your questions as best as we can." She pointed to one of the reporters standing close to the podium.

The man called out above the roar of the crowd, "Has either of them regained consciousness?"

The physicians glanced at each other before answering. Dr. Lawson pulled the microphone closer to his mouth and answered, "Agent McKenzie has not, and I do not believe Detective Gates has, either. Has he Jeff?"

The other physician shook his head that Gates was not yet conscious.

Another reporter called out, "Any idea where they've been for almost three months?"

Mrs. Miller motioned toward a man dressed in a police uniform. "Captain Whyte?"

Captain Whyte was a huge, African American man with a chiseled chest and arms. He looked more like a mountain in a police uniform than an officer of the court. His uniform was pulled so tight across his chest, that it seemed as if the buttons would fly off at any minute. "We can't really speak to that at this time. Two days ago, just after dawn, an employee of the electric company who was walking the line to identify a malfunction due to the recent storm, and discovered the officers unresponsive near the Missouri River at the Nebraska state line."

He read from a paper he held out in front of him. "After the police were notified, the area was secured, and the officers were airlifted out of the area and brought here to the hospital."

"How'd you know who they were?"

Dr. Lawson motioned for one of the nurses to come to the microphone. "Colleen is the one who recognized them," he said. "I'll let her answer that question."

He pulled the microphone closer to her. "Nurse Adams?"

Colleen Adams was younger than she looked, but after completing her fifth twelve-hour shift in a row, she was drained physically and emotionally, and it showed. She ran a nervous hand through her auburn hair and licked her thin lips. "I actually recognized Agent McKenzie first."

She looked awkwardly around the room. "I was up for the next call that morning. As usual, I went outside to wait for the ambulance. As they were unloading the patients, I helped take the first stretcher off the truck, and it just happened to be her. Once I got her inside the trauma bay and started prepping her, I remembered seeing her photo on the news a few months ago."

She looked at the physician standing next to her. "I remembered thinking that she was too pretty to be a U.S. marshal." Her attention went back to Mrs. Miller. "When they rolled him past me, I knew it was them. I remembered thinking he was a good-looking guy, too, and that they were probably holed up in a motel somewhere."

She stepped back into line with the others and smiled as the laughter of the crowd died down. Someone else called out, "What can you tell us about their injuries?"

Dr. Williams stepped up to the microphone. "We can't comment about the specifics of their injuries at this time."

Before he could reclaim his place, another reporter asked, "Can you comment on their status?"

He glanced at the other medical personnel to get a consensus from the group. "Both are listed as critical at this time."

The same reporter posed a follow-up question. "How come Detective Gates was moved to the ICU while Agent McKenzie was held in the emergency room for several hours longer?"

Dr. Williams indicated for the other physician to answer the question. Dr. Lawson anxiously stepped up and adjusted the microphone. "As you know, their disappearance is an ongoing investigation. The Emergency Department has certain protocols and policies that we must follow. We hadn't completed Agent McKenzie's initial consultations. Once she was stable, and we'd completed everything we had to do, she was also transferred to the ICU."

From the back of the room, someone yelled, "Are you referring to trace evidence?"

Dr. Lawson shook his head. "No comment."

After a few more questions, Mrs. Miller said, "We want to thank you for your interest today. We will update you as soon as we can regarding the status of the officers. Please respect the wishes of the families. Although they are very appreciative of your concern and interest, they ask that you honor their request for privacy. At this time, I'd like to invite the families to make their way to the family conference room located on the second floor, just across from the ICU. We've reserved the room for the families. We will try and answer your specific questions as best as we can."

She exited through a small door behind the podium, with the physicians and the nurse following close behind her. Captain Whyte waited until he heard the click of the security lock, before he made his way back to the occupants of the media room and ushered them out the door.

****

Kaitlin Gates leaned as far back as the chair would allow her to, taking great pride in tucking her feet up underneath her so that she was completely engulfed in the big, green chair that she had pulled close to the hospital bed where her little brother was sleeping.

She sipped nervously at the coffee in the white Styrofoam cup and pushed an errant strand of long brown hair behind her ear. After pushing her head as far back along the edge of the chair as her neck would allow, she arched her back almost as a counterweight.

She'd hardly moved in almost two days; she squeezed the arm of the chair almost intimately as if it were an old friend.

Kaitlin looked at her watch to check the time; her parents would most likely return soon. She had practically forced her father to return to the hotel with her mother to get some rest. They were all dead tired; no one had dared to leave since they'd gotten the call that Christopher was alive.

She placed the cup on the metal table and looked tenderly at her brother. He was covered from the neck down by a thin white hospital gown except for his right arm, which was bent at the elbow, his hand near his head. She smiled to herself, noting how peaceful and childlike he looked. If it weren't for the dark mass of hair peeking out from the sleeve of his gown under his arm, he would've looked like he was seven years old and resting at naptime.

The rhythmic hum of the monitors was relaxing to her, and she realized she was fighting to stay awake. She thought back to two days ago, just after ten in the morning when she received the telephone call from the police that her brother and the other officer were being treated in the emergency room.

She had barely managed to gather her things and throw them into a travel bag before she was out the door. She had called her parents en route to the airport. Within three hours, they were all in the emergency room, waiting patiently in the waiting area for someone to come out and update them on his condition.

While they were waiting, a couple about her parents' age were hurried into the waiting room by hospital staff. Even if she hadn't recognized them from the newspapers and television newscasts pleading for information of their daughter, she'd have known who they were by the look on their faces.

Kaitlin knew these were Devon McKenzie's parents; they had the same forlorn look of relief and curiosity she'd seen in the eyes of her own parents. Within the hour, the brothers had appeared in the waiting room taking their places close to their parents. By the time her own brothers had joined the party, the waiting room was practically bursting at the seams.

Several times, the nurses caring for Devon and Chris had come from behind the metal doors and in hushed tones, updated the families on their condition. By the time they were all moved to a private media room, an assortment of official-looking people in various police uniforms crowded in, until there was literally standing room only.

Kaitlin had watched with curiosity as Devon's brothers, Kevin and Brett McKenzie, took in the news of their little sister's condition. Since both were police officers, they were very familiar with the term trace evidence, and knew exactly what it inferred.

She watched their expressions change from pain to anger in a matter of seconds. Kevin was only a bit taller than Brett, but Brett was the bulkier of the two. Kaitlin wasn't sure what their ranks were, but as Kevin stood there in his dark suit and tie that he'd loosened at the neck, she could tell he was used to giving commands.

Brett, dressed in worn blue jeans and black sweater and black boots, was no doubt a more relaxed person than his older brother was. Ironically, it wasn't until Jason emerged through the doors, pushing them so wide as he entered, that he nearly collided with Mr. and Mrs. McKenzie, that she noticed how much Devon and Jason shared their mother's dark hair and features, while the older brothers were blonde and of a fair complexion, like their father.

If Kaitlin remembered that Devon was a twin, she'd forgotten until she saw Jason McKenzie and his wife, Melissa, rushing into the media room to join Devon's family. Jason was still wearing his firefighter's pants and boots, but had changed into a civilian knit shirt and jacket. Kaitlin could hear him growing louder and angrier, as he talked to his brothers. "What do you mean they're collecting trace evidence?" he demanded.

Kevin McKenzie pushed his hands into the front pockets of his pants. "Jason, we have to just calm down and wait for the doctor to update us." He glanced at Melissa's tearful face and opened his arms to give her a hug. "Devon's a tough kid; she'll be fine."

Brett nodded and slapped his brother almost playfully on the back. "Kevin is right. You know Devon; she's an ass-kicker." Just as Brett finished his sentence, his eyes caught the movement of his parents as they returned to the room. "Anything new?"

Ashford McKenzie led his wife, Caren, toward their sons as if she were fragile and about to break. Ashford, or Ash as he was called by nearly everyone, was a strikingly handsome man. He was well over six feet tall and had thick, broad shoulders and blonde hair that was cropped short above his neck and ears. Although his hair was mostly blonde, there were tracings of gray scattered here and there. His handsome face was dusted with brownish-red freckles that were darker on his forehead than on his cheeks or neck.

Like his oldest son, he was dressed in a dark suit and tie. He had removed the tie and wadded it in his front pocket. He led his wife toward the closest seat near his family and held her hand as she sat down.

As a young woman, Caren McKenzie, had no doubt looked a lot like Devon. It was not hard to imagine her in her twenties with the same dark hair and chiseled frame as Devon. If they were to stand side by side, Devon was probably just a bit taller, although her mother would most likely not admit it.

Caren McKenzie was also a tad bit heavier, her curves less defined. In any event, she was still a beautiful woman. She scanned the room quickly, mostly to ascertain who was there and only partly to discover who wasn't.

Kaitlin's surveillance of the McKenzie family was interrupted by the arrival of her own brother, Jarrod, his arms balancing several cups of coffee and sandwiches as he twisted his body around the human obstacles gathered in the room stopped almost ceremoniously beside his sister.

As a physician, Kaitlin more than understood the anatomy and physiology of the human body. She was an expert on the mystery of human genetics and the roles they play. For example, it never ceased to amaze her how she and Chris seemed to have been dipped in the same gene pool. They both had their mother's dark hair and golden complexion. Her brothers, Jarrod and Nick, however, had lighter hair that was almost brown in color, and fair skin that seldom enjoyed a tan.

Both her brothers were dressed as if they'd come straight from work. She could tell by the light blue tie Jarrod was wearing, that his wife, Cindy, had most likely assisted him that morning when he was preparing for work.

Even more telling was the wrinkled, spotted tie that Nick was wearing. Since his divorce recently, he frequently showed up without a tie or wearing one in desperate need of dry cleaning.

Kaitlin accepted the cup of coffee but refused the sandwich. Her stomach was so knotted, she doubted she could eat a bite. She pulled playfully at Nick's tie. "You should just trash this. That stain is never going to come out anyway."

He pulled the tie from around his neck and tossed it toward the trash can. "You sure Mom and Dad don't want one of us to pick them up at the hotel?"

Kaitlin nodded to him over the rim of her coffee cup as she took a sip. "Dad said they'd get a rental."

Almost on cue, the door to the family sanctuary opened, and her parents blended into the crowd. William and Laura Gates wandered through the room practically unnoticed. It wasn't until they were almost to the corner where their children were waiting, that they came face to face with Ash and Caren McKenzie.

William Gates was also a tall man, whose bodybuilder physique seemed to have been poured into a gray suit and jacket; his black overcoat made him look even more gigantic. His fair hair and skin seemed almost a direct contrast to the dark suit and coat he was wearing. His wife Laura was tall, especially for a woman. Her dark hair and features gave her an almost exotic appearance. She was dressed casually in a pair of jeans and a blue turtleneck sweater.

By the time the elder Gates had made it to the center of the room, Ash McKenzie had extended his hand to greet them. Kaitlin recalled how cordial and caring the McKenzie's had been two days prior, when everyone's relief was all but tattooed on their faces.

Funny how, after two days, with so many pieces still unplaced, everyone's patience was wearing thin. She swallowed and took another sip of coffee, disappointed at how quickly it had cooled. Kaitlin looked desperately around the room and thought to herself how Chris needed to wake up and tell everyone where he and Devon had been, who'd been holding them, and what had happened to cause the trace evidence they'd collected from Devon.

****

Kaitlin straightened up in the chair, letting her feet almost hit the floor. She watched his sleeping form, looking up and down for any signs that he had stirred, moved, to any degree, regardless of how minute. Several hours ago, her spirit had been lifted by a series of small seizure-like movements of his right leg.

It had taken her only a few minutes to realize they were simply reflexes and nothing more. She thought back to the utility worker who'd been interviewed that morning by the local news. He'd looked anxiously into the camera and relayed how he'd only seen one body at first, that of the male cop. It wasn't until he got out of the truck and approached him, that he realized there was another figure almost buried under the first. His words stuck deep in her mind. "It was like he was trying to protect her," the worker had said to the reporter.

She looked intently out the window; somewhat dismayed that the sun was setting on yet another day. Chris's doctor had warned them that the longer he was unconscious, the less likely he'd awaken, and the greater the probability that Chris had sustained some degree of brain damage.

No one had been able to determine how long either of them had been in the water, or how long they'd been on the riverbank. Kaitlin Gates bit nervously on her bottom lip and prayed for him to wake up. They all needed to get on with their lives. Now that he was home, that was just what she intended to do.

****

Gates cleared his throat before his mind really registered the surroundings around him. Without moving even the tiniest of muscles, he opened his eyes and took a long, silent look at the room around him. His brain filled in the pieces of the picture his mind couldn't make out. Hospital room, he thought to himself. Devon was shot and we're in a hospital. No wait, the logical side of his mind argued, there are no hospitals in Hamilton County, Nebraska.

Then he remembered, the woman sitting beside his bed earlier, Abby, no he almost cried, it was Kaitlin, his sister. They were back. Back, his mind argued, to a time where they weren't lovers, they weren't married. Back, he whined deep in his throat, to when she hated him, loathed him.

However, his heart cried in a softer, gentler tone, in this time, she wasn't hurt. She was whole again, flawless, and strong. As he weighed the pros and cons of their return, he wasn't prepared for the ache he was feeling. Not so much a physical ache, as an all-encompassing ache that started at his toes and hurt all the way to his head. It was almost as if the pain was overwhelming, he cried out with so much remorse, it brought Kaitlin to her feet in a single action.

"Devon!" he cried out, his arms flailing about, as if he intended to remove the IV lines and extricate himself from the hospital bed. With a single pull, he pulled the line, needle and all from his arm, leaving a small red, trail of blood that dripped onto the white sheet of the bed.

By the time, he'd made his way out of the bed and to his feet, both his brothers had appeared at her side to assist her. But when Kaitlin planted herself in front of the door, arms extended to block his exit, she knew she wouldn't need their assistance.

She knew her little brother would never hurt her; not once had he ever raised his hand to her in anger. Instead, he slumped to the floor, broken and beaten, his cries echoing down the hallway and into the room where the McKenzie's were praying for an awakening of their own.

Chapter Nine

Jarrod Gates paced back and forth in Chris's hospital room. Both he and Nick had managed to get their little brother to his feet and back into the bed, but it hadn't been easy. At first, Chris had fought them, but after hearing Kaitlin's soothing, comforting words, he settled calmly against the mattress and relaxed.

Jarrod rose from the chair and rummaged through the plastic grocery bag Kaitlin had left on the table. He knew his sister well enough to know there was some chocolate in the bag somewhere; he just needed to find it.

He only casually looked at the opened bag of Calvin Klein underwear and unopened pair of black lounge pants. Kaitlin had purchased two packages of men's medium boxer briefs for Chris, one package of black, and another package of blue. Additionally, knowing how much Chris hated hospital gowns, she'd opted for lounge pants, a blue and white striped pair, and a black and gray pair. He smiled to himself, knowing that his sister would most likely shop just as perfectly for Nick, Seth, or him.

Jarrod didn't notice that Chris was awake, until he heard him ask in a dry, strained voice, "Is she awake yet?"

Jarrod tried not to show his excitement as he made his way to Chris's bed and sat on the edge of the mattress. "Thank God, Chris. We've been so worried."

Chris repeated anxiously, "Devon awake yet?"

Jarrod shook his head, no. "What happened? Where have you two been?"

Chris motioned for the water pitcher on the nightstand next to the bed. "We were ambushed just after the last check with Squires and Michaels."

After taking a few sips of the water, enjoying the coolness of it as it made its way down his throat, he went on. "Esteban's crew took him and flipped the van off the embankment with us still in it."

By now, Nick had entered the room, closing the door behind him after Jarrod motioned for him to do so. Like Jarrod, Nick could not contain his excitement and pleasure at seeing his brother awake and oriented. "I'll call Mom and Katy."

He turned his attention to the phone by the bed and dialed a series of numbers scrawled on a scrap of paper. He hesitated for several minutes than announced into the receiver, "He's awake." After hanging up the phone, he took a seat on the bed next to Chris. "Go on, tell us what happened."

"We came to in the van later. It was dark and wet. Eventually, we were able to get out and make our way through the woods for several days. Finally, we encountered a farmer and his family."

Jarrod walked closer to Chris's bed. "They held you captive?"

"No," Chris said emphatically. "They helped us. They sheltered us and fed us. For a while, we were part of their family."

Nick patted his brother's leg. "Who hurt you?" He paused and then added, "Who hurt her?"

Chris pretended he didn't understand the question and motioned for more water.

Jarrod handed him the cup again, steadying it against Chris's lips as he drank in deep, hearty gulps.

"Chris?" Nick prodded.

Chris shook his head. "I don't know what you mean. Agent McKenzie wasn't hurt, at least, not that I know of."

Nick lay his hand on Chris's shoulder. "You've got a healed gunshot wound." He looked to Jarrod for support. "And Agent McKenzie's got a fresh gunshot wound to her left side. Her other wounds are of a more personal nature."

Quickly, Chris yanked the hospital blanket away from his shoulder and ran his hand across the ragged scar. He couldn't help but smile, unable to contain his pleasure. "It was real," he mumbled under his breath.

"What was real?" Jarrod asked, genuinely confused.

Chris fumbled with the sheets and stood to his feet, swaying until he found his balance, holding on to his bed for support. He cleared the immediate area of the bed and motioned for his brothers to help him out the door. "I have to see her."

****

The guard standing in front of Devon McKenzie's room, looked awkwardly at the trio of Gates brothers making their way toward him. The middle one was being held by the other two; he was barefoot and bare-chested with each arm around the shoulder of a brother as they headed to Agent McKenzie's room.

Initially, the guard placed his hand on the handle of his sidearm, but when the door to Devon's hospital room opened and Caren McKenzie poked her head out to see what was causing the commotion, she announced to the guard, "It's okay, let them in."

When the Gates brothers made their way into her room, they were surprised to see that only Mrs. McKenzie was there with Devon. From the looks of it, she'd been lying on a small cot placed very close to her daughter's hospital bed.

She motioned for Jarrod and Nick to ease Chris onto the cot. "Detective Gates, I am so happy to see that you're up and about." Before he could answer, she'd draped one of the thin hospital blankets she was using over his naked shoulders and chest.

"Has she been awake at all?" he asked, through heavy breaths; the trip down the hall had required more exertion than he'd thought it would.

"No," she said, with a weary sigh, "not at all. But at least her vital signs are good. She has a little cerebral swelling, but the doctor doesn't seem too concerned."

Gates swallowed loudly and wiped a thick layer of sweat from his forehead. "Gunshot wound?"

Caren McKenzie nodded. "Just grazed her right above her waist on the left side."

She handed Chris a glass of water and sat very close beside him, so that their knees were nearly touching. "Please tell me where my daughter has been all this time."

She smiled at him, and he couldn't help thinking of Edith Ennis when she spoke of Mary. "She's been with me, ma'am."

"Were you held against your will?" she asked, wiping her tears before they could fall down her cheek.

By now Chris's gaze was on Devon, her delicate features marred by several bruises. He knew she was breathing, because he could see the gentle rise and fall of her chest. But he couldn't help but infer that the way she was lying, with her arms planted like planks at each side and no expression on her face, her skin so white it looked translucent, she looked almost like a corpse.

Chris leaned in close to her. "Devon, can you hear me?"

He traced the outline of her cheek, just above her jaw. "Devon, please wake up. I need to talk to you. I need you here with me," he paused then added, "Please Devon, wake up." When he finished his plea, he let his tears fall so freely, that he didn't realize he was crying until he saw them dropping onto her throat.

No one noticed the door opening as Kevin and Brett McKenzie entered the room. Kevin's arms were laden with cans of soda and bags of food that smelled greasy and fried. He froze in his tracks when he saw Gates so near to his sister. But he took in the fact that his mother was nearby and was at ease with whatever the Gates brothers were doing there. He stopped, but didn't say anything.

Brett, however, was a different story. His arms and chest bumped into Kevin's back when he stopped short, and when he peered around to see what had made his brother stop so suddenly, he was so shocked that he dropped everything he was holding.

He pushed past his brother and strode toward Chris. "What's he doing in here?" he screamed, making a wild open-armed grab at Chris.

Instinctively, both Kevin and the Gates brothers caught him by the arm, effectively impeding him from closing in on Chris.

"Brett, calm down," Jarrod said. "He just wanted to see her, that's all."

Brett pushed so angrily at Jarrod's chest, that he propelled him backward into Nick's arms. Nick caught his brother and lurched him to his feet. Then he pushed Brett, and seconds later, Kevin and Jarrod were alternating between controlling their younger brothers and pushing at each other.

Almost desperately, Caren McKenzie stepped between Jarrod Gates and Kevin McKenzie, trying to diffuse the situation. The rumble in the room became so loud, that the guard on the other side of the door called for backup and entered the room.

Before he could regain order, everyone turned to look at Devon when she called out in a frail, thin voice. "Stop it! What's going on?" She looked around in confusion.

Fists halted in midair as everyone turned to Devon, who had sat up in the bed and was looking in bewilderment at the scene before her. Her brothers, mother, and Detective Gates were entwined in some sort of battle. In addition, there were several other men gathered around that she couldn't identify.

Mrs. McKenzie hurried to her daughter's side. Grabbing a wet towel and a cup of water, she wiped her daughter's face and held the cup for her to take a drink. Devon looked at Chris, who was still sitting almost in the bed with her. "Detective Gates? What happened? Why are we here?"

He reached down to trace her cheek just above her ear. She jerked away from his touch as if she'd been burned.

"Devon?" he whispered. "What's wrong?"

She pulled the blanket tighter against her chest. "I'd really appreciate it if you didn't use my first name, Detective Gates." Her attention turned to her mother. "How'd I get here?" Then she fixed her gaze on the bandages wrapped securely around her side. "Was there a shooting?"

Gates made his way back to the door with the aid of Jarrod, but before he left her room, he looked back and asked, "What's the last thing you remember?"

She sipped the glass of cool water her mother was holding out in front of her. "We were at the warehouse. Brad and I were caught in some crossfire with Esteban and his goons," she paused for a minute. "Was I shot?"

"Yes," her mother answered, before anyone else could correct her. "Yes, honey, you were."

Dr. Lawson, who had entered the room just after the brawl was resolved, approached Devon and motioned to everyone else to clear the room. "I need everyone out of the room, please."

Then he pointed to Gates. "He shouldn't be out of bed." Obediently, Jarrod and Nick wrapped Chris's arms around their shoulders and led him back to his room, protesting all the way.

****

Caren McKenzie listened intently as Dr. Lawson explained to her the condensed version of Devon's injuries. He told her that the brain was a mysterious thing, and that it had the ability to heal independently and at its own rate.

For whatever reason, Devon had regressed to a time about three and a half months ago when they'd captured Esteban in the warehouse in New York. He believed that when she was ready, her mind would effectively catch up and regain recent memories. For now, he suggested that everyone play along and not force her to recall more than her mind could handle.

"What do we tell her about the other injuries?" Caren asked.

He motioned for her to join him in the hallway, closing the door quietly behind her. "More than likely, at some point, Devon will start to recall the events she's repressing."

He rubbed his chin. "Just tell her what you think she can handle."

He squeezed her shoulder and looked down the hallway toward the rooms located at the end of the corridor. "I've got to finish rounds. I'll check back on her later."

Caren nodded and watched as he made his way down the hallway and entered one of the rooms on the left. Her hand was on the doorknob to her daughter's room, but instead of going in, she looked just to the right, two doors down to Detective Gates's room. She had to know the truth; it was the only way to prepare Devon for what was to come.

Calmly, she made her way down the hall to his room and tapped lightly on the door before entering. She waited patiently at the doorway, watching as his brothers helped him back into bed. They pulled the blankets up to his waist and refilled the water pitcher, before turning to ask what she needed.

She walked easily to the bed and pulled the heavy tan leather chair close to his side. She'd read the report from the emergency room; she already knew that the only trace evidence they'd identified belonged to Detective Gates. Now, she desperately needed to know the details of how it got there, and she wasn't leaving until he told her the truth.

"Detective," she began, "I need to know what happened to you both: where you've been, and on what terms you and my daughter had sex."

Jarrod pushed himself between Mrs. McKenzie and his brother. "Chris, don't say anything." He opened his mouth as if to add something else, but Chris interjected, "It's okay, Jarrod. I want her to know what happened. I would never hurt Devon," he paused, tears building in his eyes. "I love her."

Over the next hour, Gates related the significant events that had happened since the ambush, until he'd awakened in the hospital. Although it was hard to hear the details, Caren McKenzie sat and absorbed every bit of the story, feeling at times as if she was there watching the barn burn down, swimming in the warm waters of the river with Benjamin, tied to the cot at the jailhouse, and exchanging vows at Abby's ceremony. In her mind's eye, she saw and felt it all.

She couldn't explain how she was able to believe his story so easily. But as she sat there watching him, she realized that if nothing else, he believed what he was saying was true.

Methodically, she went over the details of his story in her mind. She'd heard her husband and sons talk about trauma and how the brain could be affected by it.

Was it possible that whatever they had endured over the last three months was so horrific, that he'd conjured up this story to protect himself emotionally?

Perhaps their captors had forced them to have sex together, and he was protecting them both from that realization. In any event, now more than ever, she desperately needed Devon to awaken and tell them where they'd been, and who'd they'd been with for the last three months. Detective Gates's story made no sense at all.

Caren McKenzie patted his hand as she stood to return to her daughter's room. "Detective, I appreciate everything you've told me, and I can see the effect this ordeal has had on you," she said, almost formally. "I'd appreciate it if you'd leave Devon alone, at least for now."

He swallowed. "Mrs. McKenzie, I ..."

She cut him off. "If what you say is true, then at some point, she'll remember it all and come find you. If she doesn't, would that really be so bad? I mean, after all, she's been through, wouldn't it be better if she could just forget?"

Gates didn't answer her. Truth be told, she was right. Maybe it would be better for Devon if she didn't remember what had happened in Hamilton.

She turned back from the door. "Don't you want her to be like she was before; strong, carefree, whole?"

He thought back to what he'd told her that night back in Hamilton, promised he'd never hurt her. And if that meant he had to walk away, he would. Maybe what her mother was saying was right; maybe not remembering any of the pain of being in Hamilton wasn't a bad thing.

He nodded. "Of course, ... I want what is best for her."

She opened the door and stepped into the hallway. "Then don't make her relive it all over again, until she's ready to do so on her own terms."

****

Gates tapped tenderly against the door to Devon's hospital room, and bent his head closer to the door, listening for consent to enter. The new jeans and shirt he was wearing was rough against his body and irritated his skin. During their time in Hamilton, he'd only had the single pair of jeans, and lord knows they'd been patched and sewn to such degree, they wore more like pajamas than dress clothes.

Kaitlin's had helped with shaving, the skin of his face and neck was pink and baby soft, sensitive to the conditioned air. She had even brought a hair trimmer to get rid of the longer pieces of hair around his neck and over his ears. Mrs. Ennis had trimmed it twice while he was in Hamilton, but she'd used a small pair of sewing shears and he'd known as he walked from the main house back to the guest house, that it wasn't a very good haircut, but he was grateful that she had tried.

Gates waited till he heard Devon answer through the thick, metal door. "Come in."

"It's me," he said, as he stepped across the threshold, stopping before he got fully into the room.

"What do you want?" she asked, sitting up in the bed, pillows lined two deep in front of the headboard. Several blankets were pooled around her knees, she pulled them up, covering herself more completely and stuffing the ends of the blanket under her arms.

"I'm getting discharged in a bit. I just wanted to see if you needed –" he began.

"There's nothing you can do for me, Detective," she interrupted, her words angry and accusing.

"Devon." He took several steps further into the room.

"I don't want you in here," she said, reaching for the nurse call button and pushing it several times. "Just leave me alone," she paused. "I don't remember all the details, but I know what you did."

"What I did?" he repeated, letting the door close behind him, but not coming any closer to her. "I didn't hurt you, Devon."

"I'm remembering bits and pieces, it's dark and it smells moldy, old. There was a fire, you raped me."

"No," he shook his head. "I didn't."

"Did you have sex with me?" she asked, letting the blanket pool back around her waist and leaning closer to where he was standing.

"Yes," he answered, feeling a bit intimidated.

"I would never have had consensual sex with you, Detective." She hit the call button again. "Get out, before I call security and have you removed."

"Devon, I would never hurt you. I told you in Hamilton, I'd walk away first."

He turned to the doorway just as it swung open, and Devon's nurse rushed inside.

"I won't bother you again, Agent McKenzie, but if you need anything, you call me and I'll be there."

"Get out," she said again.

"Detective Gates," the nurse motioned toward the door. "I think it's better if you leave," she paused. "Do you need some help getting back to your room?"

"No," he stepped into the hallway.

"I'll be there in a minute," the nurse advised, with a wheelchair to discharge you."

"I don't need a wheelchair," he said, a short distance down the hallway.

"It's hospital policy, Detective," she called back.

"I don't care," his words were faraway.

Chapter Ten

Gates made his way unsteadily up the stairs, and down the hallway to the familiar whitewashed door at the end. He waited patiently for Kaitlin to get the key into the lock, noticing how dark the hallway was even though there was a small window at the end. He glanced up curiously and nodded to himself; yep, just as he'd thought, an overhead light had gone out.

Kaitlin waited for him to get completely into his apartment, before she followed him in, setting bags and travel cases on the floor as she made her way into the living area.

She and Jarrod had come by once or twice to check on things after Chris's disappearance. She remembered how they had collected dirty clothes from just about every corner of the room and tossed them into the laundry. The last thing she wanted was for him to come home to a houseful of dirty, smelly laundry.

She made her way into the bedroom, flipping the light on, and opening the shades. The pair of windows flooded the room with sunlight almost instantaneously. She unlatched the lock and opened the windows, pushing them out as far as she could to allow some air into the room.

She smiled at the coolness of the air as it pushed past her and disseminated almost like a fresh scent throughout his bedroom. She made a point of pulling down the bedspread and fluffing the pillows, before she returned to the living area to find him sitting upright on the sofa almost statuesque. She sat down next to him. "You hungry?"

He shook his head, no, but he said nothing. In fact, he'd said very little all the way home from the hospital. She wanted to ask him about the ring he was wearing on his left-hand ring finger.

If she didn't know better, she'd think it was a wedding ring. It wasn't lost on her that he'd been toying with it ever since leaving the hospital. His interest in it was most evident during the ride home. He'd hardly said a word, since being discharged.

His nurse had mentioned in a round-about-way how he was upset over a disagreement with Agent McKenzie a few rooms down. When asked about it, he'd answered that he didn't want to talk about it. And he hadn't, he'd barely said two words the entire drive home.

Kaitlin couldn't decide if his confusion was a result of guilt over leaving Agent McKenzie as a resident of Memorial Hospital, or if there was something deeper going on, something he wasn't comfortable sharing.

Gates bent at the waist just enough to kick off his running shoes, letting them fall on one another at his feet. He leaned back against the sofa.

Kaitlin made a point of grabbing a small, white paper bag from his pack and holding it out toward him. "Your medicines are in here. If you have any pain, take a pain pill."

He replied without raising his head from the sofa. "Yes, Doctor."

He smacked his head as if he'd just remembered something previously forgotten. "Tell me the Mets didn't win the pennant and I missed it ..."

"Chris?" she asked him, her voice almost childlike. "What happened that you haven't told anyone about? And no, the Mets weren't in the World Series. It was the Dodgers and A's."

She had his attention now. "If I told you," he said reluctantly, "you'd think I was crazy."

She moved closer to him, rubbing his knee. "You're my brother. I love you. You can tell me anything."

"Kaitlin, do you believe in time travel?" he asked it so naturally, that it was almost as if he'd asked her if she believed in Santa Claus or the tooth fairy.

She jumped to her feet and made her way into the kitchen. It was a typical bachelor's kitchen with practically every device for warming or microwaving. Every appliance was stainless steel and black. The room itself looked mechanical, almost sterile. She held up two thick, white mugs. "You want some coffee?"

He smiled. "Only if there's a little Kahlua in it."

She flipped the coffee maker on and shook her head. "Liquor and pain meds are never a good combination."

As soon as the coffee was done, she poured a cup for each of them and made her way back to the sofa. She took his left hand and held it up. "Tell me about this ring."

Gates sipped at the coffee, enjoying the burn it made as the hot liquid traveled down his throat. "It's a wedding ring, Katy." His eyes met hers. "We were married while we were away."

"Married?" Kaitlin repeated. "How does this fit into your time travel scenario?"

He pulled his hand out of hers and awkwardly stood to his feet. "After the wreck, when we woke up, and after the Ennis' took us in, we discovered we were in Hamilton County, Nebraska, in the year 1869, just after the Civil War ended."

She sat quietly on the couch, listening to his every word as he related to her the significant events of the last three and a half months. He didn't confess everything they'd endured but told her just enough for her to understand not only his reactions, but perhaps Devon's as well.

At first, Kaitlin didn't say anything, and she didn't move a muscle. She merely sat still, arms folded across her chest, feet crossed at the ankles, her back just barely touching the back of the couch. Finally, she exhaled a breath and licked her bottom lip. "Chris, I don't know what to say. I know that you believe these things happened. But you had a head injury, and Devon is still recovering from a concussion. It wasn't real; none of it was. Wherever you were, it wasn't 1869."

"Kaitlin, I know you're trying to protect me. But I don't need your protection." He closed his eyes and exhaled. "Every time I close my eyes, I remember how she felt in my arms, how complete I felt."

She stood and pointed toward his bedroom. "You should get some rest. I'm going to stay tonight. Nick has tomorrow and Friday night."

Instead of getting to his feet, he reclined on the sofa. "I'm fine here. You take the bed."

She pushed at his feet. "Don't be ridiculous; you're the one recovering. Get in the bed."

Gates pulled the spread from the back of the sofa and shook his head, lying on his back against the sofa's cushions. "I sleep here on the couch more times than not."

He smiled at her as if he had a secret and wasn't sharing. "I typically only use the bed if I have company."

She rolled her eyes, sighed, and made her way to the bedroom, collecting the small bag from the floor along the way. "Speaking of," she called out hesitantly, standing in the hallway, "I'm not cramping your style, am I? If there's someone you want to call to come and stay with you, I'm fine with that."

He shook his head; there was only one person he wanted to spend the night with, and she was holed up in a hospital seventeen miles away, without any recollection that he even existed.

****

"Mom?" Kevin asked, almost in a whisper, but his gaze never left the sleeping form of his sister curled up on one side of her bed. She looked like she was seven years old again, resting on a mat at naptime. "Why won't you tell us what Gates told you about their disappearance?"

Caren McKenzie pulled the bedroom door closed, but left it ajar, so that she would be able to hear if Devon called out from the room. She led her son into the living room, careful not to disrupt any of Devon's things.

It had been many months since they'd all gathered at Devon's for dinner. Devon had spent the better part of two days preparing the meal, and everything was home-cooked and served on the remaining pieces of her great grandmother's china.

Over the years, Devon had been on the receiving end of multiple hand-me-downs, but mostly china and other assorted trinkets. In addition, she'd decorated her apartment in various holiday decorations.

Caren smiled at the recollection; she missed seeing her daughter fulfilled and complete. With Christmas just a few weeks away, she'd make a point to get some holiday flowers and decorations, and help Devon bring in the holidays.

"Kevin," she answered, "I can't tell you what Gates said. You know how incredibly private your sister is. She'd never forgiven me for sharing, nor would she forgive you for insisting."

"What did he do to her?" Kevin insisted. "I need to know."

She looked awkwardly at the door. "He says they were married and that they made love."

"Is that what he's calling it?" he asked, his fists clenching.

She smiled at him, as if he'd skinned his knee and she was spraying antiseptic on his wound. "I don't think he would ever willingly hurt her."

Kevin slid his suit jacket off, revealing his heavy service weapon hanging from his belt. "Devon would never sleep with him willingly. She doesn't even like him. I remember her talking about him those few times after they dated."

"I don't think that was the truth, honey. I think she told us that so we wouldn't see how much she liked him."

"Liked him?" Kevin tossed his arms up in the air. "You know his reputation, right?"

"Yes, your father told me about him," she said, very matter-of-factly. "And he also told me that there was nothing to suggest that the women he was with weren't consenting. You boys are going to have to realize that Devon is a vibrant young woman with the same healthy appetite for sex as your wives. She's not a child anymore; you need to stop treating her like one."

"Dad, had him checked out?" Kevin asked, making himself at home by sitting on the couch.

She handed him a beer. "Yes, when they first went missing." She sat down next to him. "Your father was assigned with Captain Adam

Goff several years ago at the forty-second precinct. When they were first reported missing, he called Adam to find out about the type of man Detective Gates was."

Kevin took a long sip from his beer. "And?"

"Adam reported that Gates was one of the best officers he's ever commanded."

"What about all the womanizing?' Kevin pointed out, making sure to keep his voice in a hushed tone.

"Apparently, anyone he's with is a willing partner." She popped open a can of Diet Coke and sipped at it almost delicately. "There's not one complaint of a sexual nature in his docket."

Kevin shook his head, as if he didn't quite believe his mother. "He just doesn't seem to be her type, that's all."

"What type is that, honey?" Caren McKenzie smiled; she was unaware that her daughter had a type.

"He's nothing like Paul."

"I think that's what attracted Devon to him. They are like oil and water. When did she date Christopher?"

"It was after Paul died."

Before she could respond, she heard Devon call out from the bedroom. "Mom?"

Without hesitating, she set her drink down and entered the room, coming out a few minutes later with Devon holding tightly to her arm. She led her slowly to the couch and helped her sit next to Kevin. "Feeling any better?" she asked, as she backed away and took a seat in the chair across from them.

"Yeah," she answered, pushing herself back against the sofa. "I am."

"Do you want something to eat, hon?" Caren asked, looking behind her to the kitchen where everything was in its place, just as she'd left it three months ago.

"No," Devon answered, sliding her feet up underneath her. "But I could use some coffee."

Kevin jumped to his feet. "I got it." He went to the kitchen where they could hear him opening and closing cabinets until he found the coffee, sugar, creamer, and a special cup and saucer. Within a few minutes, he returned carrying the delicate, white cup filled almost to the top with caramel-colored coffee.

He bent to place the cup within easy reach and kissed Devon at the top of her head. "I'd love to stay and hang out with you ladies, but I got to get home. Andrea's been working double shifts, and with the baby and all, she's …" He paused and looked at his mother, searching for the correct word.

Caren smiled and finished his sentence for him. "She's tired."

He checked his watch again and grabbed his jacket from the coat stand in the corner by the front door. "I'll check back with you guys later."

He followed his mother to the door and kissed her on the cheek. He looked at Devon, who was still seated on the couch and sipping her coffee. "If she needs anything before I get back, just call me."

Caren nodded and placed her hand against the back of his arm, as she led him out the door. She couldn't help but be proud of the adults her children had become. She knew her boys were protective of Devon, partly because she was the youngest, and partly because she was the only girl. But she was also cognizant of the fact that her children were intimately involved in each other's lives. Her house was the site of frequent impromptu cookouts and events organized by one of the children.

She knew her sons were concerned for Devon because they were her brothers, but she also knew that, as law enforcement officers, they were fearful for her life and safety from this point on. Each of them was harboring his own concerns about her welfare.

Neither Kevin nor Brett had asked about the trace evidence, although she knew they were both aware of the results. Neither of them had questioned it. But she knew her sons well enough to know that at some point, they would want to know what had happened during the three months that Devon had been lost to them.

Her thoughts turned to Jason, Devon's twin brother; they were so alike, yet so different.

Jason had approached her almost immediately, and questioned Devon's relationship with the detective. At that time, she hadn't spoken to Detective Gates and had none of the details, so in true motherly fashion, she'd evaded the question and reminded him that Devon was a grown woman.

Caren McKenzie made her way back to the couch and took a seat to the right of Devon. "What do you want to do today?"

Devon answered, "Just enjoy the day," she said, reclining back into the cushions and switching the television on so that the room was enveloped in the afternoon news. After several minutes, she asked almost casually, "Has Detective Gates called or anything?"

Her mother shook her head. "No, any reason why he should?"

"No," she answered. "He just seemed so determined at the hospital. I don't know him very well, but I do know enough about him to know that he's usually more resilient." She sipped the coffee. "I just wish I could remember what happened to us and where we were held, or something. I have flashes, but they don't mean anything, not really."

"What kind of flashes?"

"A fire, a white horse with some kind of scar," Devon didn't tell her about the dark place or man in her dreams who hurt her. "I wish I could remember."

Mrs. McKenzie patted her hand. "You will, Devon, when you're ready."

****

The air inside Gates apartment was thick and warm, too warm, he thought. Even if it weren't the middle of winter, he wasn't sure the heater in the apartment needed to be running. It was just wasted money, he'd made a promise to spend as little time as was possible in it.

Christmas had come and gone, it had felt like any other day. Despite pleas from his family to decorate a tree, come to Christmas dinner, stop by and pick up his presents, he'd done none of those things. There was no point. It didn't mean what it used to; nothing really did.

If he turned his head and squinted his eyes, the empty lot behind his apartment building reminded him of the blonde field in Hamilton; the one Mr. Ennis had planned to build the house for him and Devon. What had become of Gabriel, Edith, and Benjamin Ennis? Had they held their breath and waited for him and Devon to return? Had they mourned them when neither returned? Gates knew just as surely as he took his next breath, they would have. The loneliness they felt every time they looked at the empty guest house would have surely swallowed them whole. Had Gabriel and Benjamin gone looking for them, hoping to bring them home?

These were the questions that haunted him. He missed them just as surely as he'd missed his family while he and Devon were in Hamilton.

He didn't realize how long he'd been sitting near the window at the back of his apartment; the one that faced the empty lot until the streetlights flashed on and illuminated the alley just below his fire escape. Gates ran his hand over his chin, scratching through the beard and mustache he'd grown since they'd returned home.

Sometimes, when he looked in the mirror, he wasn't sure who the man looking back was. He was a stranger, someone who hadn't fallen in love and married Devon McKenzie. Sometimes that thought comforted him, other times, it scared him so badly, he couldn't move.

He dialed a familiar number on the phone sitting on the table near his chair, and adjusted the turtleneck of his sweater more comfortably around his neck, while he waited for the attendant to answer.

"It's Gates," he said, after the greetings were exchanged.

"Good evening, Mr. Gates," the voice on the phone replied. "We've got a special event for you tonight, sir."

"I don't think so," Gates answered. "You know what I want, she needs to be about five-seven with long, dark hair."

He paused as his sister, Kaitlin slid through the apartment door with a take-out bag in her hand. "Normal breast proportions, no schoolgirl, latex, or maids, just jeans and a shirt."

Kaitlin waited at the front door, until he hung up the phone. She watched as he sucked the last drop of liquor from the glass in his hand and made his way to the bar to make another drink. She held up the take-out bag. "Brought you some dinner. It's Chinese."

She watched as he downed the drink and made another. "Nick says you went back to work this week?"

Gates sipped from the glass and took the bag from her. "Yes, part-time, not sure how much help I was. I think Mike was beginning to enjoy his new partner."

He opened the cartons to see what type of Chinese food was in each container. "You going to join me?"

She stood up and collected her purse. "No, Tim's coming over tonight. I think he's feeling a bit neglected with everything that's been going on." It was obvious to her that he hadn't listened to what she'd said.

"You okay? You seem so distant, tonight," she asked. "I can cancel my plans for tonight."

"No, don't," he answered, comprehending what she'd said. "I'm expecting company."

"I'm happy to hear you're getting out." She tried to contain her surprise and extreme happiness. "Is this someone you know from work?"

"No, I don't know her at all. Couldn't even tell you her name."

"Your company is a hooker?" she said, trying not to sound as disappointed as she felt.

"The service prefers that you call her a companion, but yes, I'm planning on having sex with her."

Kaitlin walked toward the door, biting her lip and hoping it's contagious to her tongue.

"That's not going to solve anything."

"It's been over a month already. She's not remembered anything. Her biggest fear was once we got back, everything would return to the way it was. Looks like she wasn't far off."

Kaitlin opened the door to an attractive woman waiting on the other side. The visitor's physical appearance was similar to McKenzie. In fact, they could be twins. Kaitlin couldn't help but notice she was even dressed like McKenzie in jeans and a conservative sweater.

Kaitlin stepped back and motioned the woman inside. "I'll talk to you soon, Chris."

"Thanks, sis," Gates called back to her, as she disappeared out the door.

Chapter Eleven

The woman entered the room, dropped her purse, and assessed the immediate room. She eyed Gates hungrily and made her way closer to him as if she were a lion and him, an injured deer. She unbuttoned his shirt and opened it across his shoulders.

"Too bad, you only booked for a half-hour." She licked her lips, her fingers grazing across the skin of his chest as if his skin were burning her fingers.

Gates took her hand and rebuttoned his shirt, before spinning her around so that her back was against his chest. Gently, he eased her over the couch. "Don't talk, take off your clothes."

Boldly, she dropped her clothes to the floor, stepping out of the clothes with her back still to him. Gates unzipped his pants and lowered them off his hips, just enough to free his penis. He tore open a condom and slid it on his erect member without saying a word.

Gates initiated sex with her, screaming Devon's name as he climaxed. He didn't waste any time, pulling out and zipping up.

She turned to face him. "Want anything else? You've still got time left."

He shook his head and bent down to collect her clothes before handing them to her. "Bathroom is over there if you want to wash up and get dressed."

She ran her hand down his chest again. "We could shower together?"

"No thanks. I'm late for an appointment." He pointed to several twenty-dollar bills folded together. "Your money's over there."

She nodded and took her clothes from his hand, turning to go into the bathroom.

"Are you available tomorrow around the same time?" Gates asked, before she closed the bathroom door.

The woman nodded that she was and disappeared into the bathroom to redress. Gates waited until she came out and left the apartment, before donning his jacket and exiting behind her.

****

Frankie's bar and grill was loud, probably the loudest lounge on the block, the waiting line stretched out of the door and into the nearby alleyway. From the street, it didn't look it, but once you got inside, the bar took up nearly half of the building. Tables and booths were strategically placed so that every seat had a good view of one of a dozen or so television screens that lined all the walls. Basketball, hockey, skiing, each monitor gave play by play action of the day's games.

It was dark, only a few lights or lamps placed on the tables and walls to provide ample light to peruse the menu and navigate back and forth from the bathroom, while at the same time, provide a black screen of privacy for its many patrons.

Toward the back of the building, the lighting was a little better, as it housed a plethora of booths and tables with white linen tablecloths and an assortment of sofas and chairs positioned into social sectionals.

Devon entered the bar and removed her jacket before throwing it over her arm. She walked closer to the bar, looking for a familiar face. It only took a minute to find him, his large bulking figure, back to the door, expensive suit jacket hung over the back of the chair.

"Hey," she dropped into the chair beside him. "Sorry, I'm late. Traffic was really bad."

Richard Landers ran his hand through his blonde hair and kissed her cheek as she pulled her chair closer to the bar. "No problem." He pointed to his partially filled glass. "I started already."

He swallowed the remnants of peanuts he was chewing. "You look great!" he paused. "I tried to visit you in the hospital, but couldn't get past your brothers."

"Sorry, bout that. I never really mentioned that I was seeing anyone before we went missing…"

"What are you drinking?" He handed her a small menu of the alcoholic drink selections.

"Just iced tea, I've just been cleared to drive again. I don't want to mess it up. It's felt like I'm in middle school again, being driven around by my parents and brothers."

****

The man inside the sedan had a perfect view of Devon and her date. The man lit a second cigarette and rolled down the window, just enough to blow the smoke out of the car and into the night air.

It was hard to see her with someone else, dating again, so soon. He hoped she'd have an early night, he didn't want to follow her around all night waiting for an opportunity to prove his love for her, again.

His beard was itchy and he ran his hand up and down the hard bone of his chin. When was she going to accept that she belonged to him? Hadn't he proven his love for her repeatedly, why couldn't or wouldn't she see what was right in front of her face?

He licked his lips, remembering how she felt in his arms and how perfectly her body fit against his. He inhaled remembering the way her hair and skin smelled like rain, he felt himself growing hard at the thought and adjusted himself through his trousers.

They would be together again, soon. He felt it in his heart. Fate would bring her to him, as before. And this time, he was never letting her go.

****

The man waited and watched Devon and Richard as they finished dinner and decided on a dessert they could share.

Chocolate, the man smiled. He knew she'd pick something chocolate, maybe a dollop of whip cream on top. She was nothing, if not predictable.

It hadn't been much of a challenge to stay out of sight, hide in the shadows where she couldn't see him. At one point, he'd been close enough to smell her cologne.

It had taken every ounce of his self-control to stay hidden, just beyond the boundary of her personal space. So close, he could almost touch her. But not yet, he soothed his racing heart, not yet.

He watched as Devon excused herself and disappeared into the ladies' room, laughing to her date as she passed behind him and touched his shoulder. Was she even aware she was flirting with him?

He smiled, hearing the date's phone ring and took advantage of the time the young man had his back to Devon's drink. It took only a second to walk past and drop the tasteless, odorless powder into her iced tea. He was long gone when Devon returned from the ladies' room and reclaimed her seat at the bar.

If it hadn't been so obvious, he'd have applauded when she finished her drink and pushed the glass away for the bartender to remove.

Minutes later, he was back in his car, watching her from the front seat of his vehicle again. Soon, he promised himself, very soon and she'd be his once again.

****

"You sure you're okay to drive?" Richard asked her, rubbing her bare arm to ward off the cold while he slid her arm into her jacket.

"Yes," Devon nodded, "the tea didn't have any alcohol in it," she said, yawning as she finished the sentence and covering her mouth as if in surprise. "I'm sorry, I'm just really tired."

"I don't know," he pulled her closer to him by her elbow. "Seems like it's more than just being sleepy?"

"I'm fine," she reiterated, handing the valet the key to her car.

"Okay," he nodded. Stuffing his hands into his coat pockets and moving closer to her to wait for her vehicle.

"I was hoping we could go out again, maybe this weekend?" he asked, his eyes red and watery as a result of the cold air that blew in the space between them.

"I'd like that." She looked away from his stare.

He leaned into her to kiss her goodnight, holding her in place at each elbow. For a second, Devon had a recollection of Detective Gates. They were dancing, in what seemed to be an old wooden barn with lighted candles and lanterns scattered all about. He wasn't dressed formally, but he wasn't wearing jeans either, and she was dressed in a tight-fitting, long, yellow dress. Detective Gates was whispering into her ear, she laughed at whatever he'd said before dropping a light kiss against her cheek.

Devon shook the images from her mind, surprised that she'd even daydream such a thing. She didn't care much for Detective Gates, he was the last man she'd even be dancing with. Richard paced a few steps on the sidewalk, before coming to a stop near her.

It was obvious Richard intended to kiss her on the lips. She wasn't sure why she turned her head to evade the kiss, but she did. He seemed almost as surprised as she did when his kiss landed on her cheek, instead.

"I'm sorry," she looked down to the ground.

"It's fine," he licked his lips to ward off the sting of the wind. "I'm not trying to rush you," he paused. "We'd been talking about moving our relationship to the next level before you disappeared." He cleared his throat and looked away from her to where the valets were running back and forth, collecting car keys and parking cars. "I wasn't sure what you were expecting; what you wanted."

"I know," she pointed to a car as it came to an abrupt stop in front. "This is me." She stopped moving, before climbing behind the steering wheel. "I don't mean to be evasive. I'm just not sure how I feel right now about being intimate, with anyone." She smiled. "We'll talk about it on Saturday, okay?"

"Of course," he smiled. "Goodnight," Richard said again. "I'll see you on Saturday."

She nodded, pushed an errant strand of hair out of her eyes, and slid into the car, waving to him as he stepped off the sidewalk and crossed the parking lot to his own car.

****

The drive home from the restaurant to Devon's apartment wasn't that far but tonight, it felt as if she'd already driven a hundred miles and yet, she wasn't home yet.

Coffee, she thought to herself. She should have had a cup of strong coffee before she'd left the restaurant, maybe two cups. Focusing on the road was getting harder and harder, all she wanted to do was sleep.

She rolled down the driver's window, allowing the cool outside air to circulate through the cabin of the car. For a minute, she thought it had worked, the cold night air stung her face and neck turning her senses on to such degree she felt as if she could smell the fragrance of the evergreen trees in the field. She inhaled deeply, her thoughts steadying as if they were standing at attention and awaiting an order, a new thought.

Another image came to mind, it was dark and smelled of decaying wood and spoiled hay, a barn, perhaps? There were animals, too, horses maybe and something else, but she wasn't sure what it was, but she could feel it peering at her through the slits in the stall.

She fought the man off or tried to, but he was bigger, stronger and when they crashed through the thin wall of one wooden stall into another and she fell on her back, she knew she was losing the battle. He came down hard on top of her, holding her arms above her head and kneeing himself between her flailing legs.

Even in the darkness, she knew it was him. She'd known it all along, Detective Gates was nothing if not persistent. He tugged and pulled at her clothes, finally freeing himself from his own just enough to root against her. The pain was excruciating as he pounded into her, it felt as if she was being torn in half from her groin to the top of her head.

Like smoke rising against the blackness of the night sky, the image in her mind was gone. Her eyes fell on the road again just in time to acknowledge the headlights of an oncoming car as she drew closer and closer to it.

Devon felt her car swerve out of her lane and across the road into the other lane, before coming to rest against the trunk of a tree. It seemed as if it took forever for the airbag to explode and swallow her whole before the darkness fell all around.

****

Detective Gates was bored, he grabbed up a partially empty Styrofoam cup of stale coffee, sniffed at it as if he wasn't sure what the contents were. He dropped it back on the desk's surface not caring about the coffee splashes that covered the paper items on his desk.

He picked up one of the folders, a case number written in thick black letters across the top while on the front, it read ESTEBAN, G. There was no need to review, he thought as his eyes focused on the gold band on his left hand. He had read it a dozen times, probably more. Truth was, catching Esteban was no longer the top priority on his to-do list, praying for Devon to recover her memory was.

Gates twisted the ring around his finger several times and thought about their moments together that had led to Devon putting it on his finger. He turned it several more times hoping that like Dorothy, he might click his heels and have her back in his life.

"I need your help," a familiar man's voice caused him to look up, as Kevin McKenzie stood in front of his desk and dropped a zip drive in the middle of the pile of file folders.

Gates didn't make a move to investigate the zip drive. Instead, he pushed to his feet. "What do you want, McKenzie?"

"It's Devon?"

"Is she okay?"

"She's fine. She hit a guardrail last night coming home from a date. First, we thought she'd had too much to drink, but her blood alcohol was zero."

Gates cringed when Kevin said the word 'date'. He'd known at some point, she'd resume her normal duties, pick up with her life where she had left it months earlier. It was only natural.

Kevin went on. "Blood was positive for GHB."

"Her date slipped her a mickey?" Gates said, his hands perched on his waist as if he didn't trust himself not to hit something.

"That's what I thought too, until I received the surveillance video from the bar." Kevin slid the zip drive into Gates computer and stepped closer to Gates to watch the video.

Gates watched as the blank screen lit up with the recording from Devon's date last night. She looked happy, he ached at the thought. "Must have just been sitting waiting for her date to look away." The word tasted badly in his mouth and Gates looked to Kevin to read his reaction and hoped Kevin wasn't aware how much the conversation was bothering him.

"That's what I thought too, "Kevin tapped at the monitor where the picture was still playing. "And whoever it was, knew where the cameras were. We don't have any identifying pictures in or out, either. Don't even know if it's a man or a woman."

"What do you want from me?" Gates exhaled, hoping Kevin would take his leave soon. His head was killing him, he needed to lie down. The doctor had said he'd be predisposed to panic attacks and episodes of unknown anxiety.

"Is there any chance this could be related to the time you were missing?" Kevin asked, without taking any breaths between the words. It was like he opened his mouth and the words had simply poured out.

"Too short to be me, if that's what you're asking?" Gates flipped the computer off, since both Devon and her date were out of the video frame.

"I didn't think it was you. What about the person or persons that held you both captive?" he paused before adding. "That's what you said happened, right?"

"Everyone who was there then, is dead now. I don't think it has anything to do with Hamilton. Maybe Esteban is making a play to take her again?" Gates ran his hand under his chin, tangling his fingers in the thin hair of his beard.

"I'm going to assign a security detail to her, until I know what's going on, who is trying to hurt her again."

"Is this guy someone she's serious about?" Gates asked, the question quickly as if he were afraid he might change his mind.

"Didn't even know she was seeing anyone. The guy showed up at the hospital, but we didn't let him through," Kevin answered, not looking Gates in the eye.

Gates could tell Kevin didn't want to answer the question. He wasn't sure why he had.

Kevin paused before making eye contact again. "How are you doing?"

"Working, staying busy," Gates answered, as if he was checking items off a list. "Trying to move on, but it's hard." Gates waved his hand through the empty space between them.

Kevin caught the reflection of light off Gates wedding band and indicated to the ring. "Still wearing that ring, huh?" he paused. "Might be easier to move on if you weren't wearing that."

"For now, yes." Gates shrugged. "You want some help with her security? I don't mind sitting…"

"I don't think that would be a good idea, "Kevin interrupted, "but I appreciate the offer." He scooped up the zip drive from Gates computer. "You take care, Detective."

****

Brett McKenzie paced himself at the intersection, running in place at the crosswalk and glancing back at his sister with a half-smile. "Come on, Devon, pick up the pace. It's been three weeks; you've got to build your time back up."

She joined him on the sidewalk and bent her head toward her feet, inhaling air in large gulps in and out of her mouth. She leaned against the street post and hit the pedestrian crosswalk button to initiate the light. "Give me a second. I didn't know you meant we were going to do the entire three miles today."

He stopped running in place and pushed her chin up so that her mouth was closed. "Breathe through your nose, not your mouth."

"Shut up, Brett," she warned, pulling herself upright and placing her hands on her hips. She pulled a water bottle from her jacket pocket and squeezed it with such force, that the water spilled into her mouth and trickled down the jacket she was wearing. After replacing the bottle in her pocket, she said, "I'm done," and then she crossed the street and walked in the direction of her apartment.

"Come on, Devon, we'll go slower; I promise," he said, running up behind her and swatting at her backside.

"Knock it off," she warned him again, punching his chest once he was close enough.

He feigned a response as if he was hurt, but then fell into a walking pace next to her. "Just kidding, Dev. You did fine. This time next week, you'll be up to three miles easily."

"I could barely do three miles before I was hurt, Brett. I'm not a runner," she reminded him.

If he heard her, he pretended that he didn't and continued to urge her onward back to the apartment. They made their way quickly into the building and down the hallway to the last door on the left. Devon pushed her key into the lock and opened the door, just as her mom was hanging up the telephone in the kitchen. Caren McKenzie motioned toward the table where she had set the table for three.

"Breakfast will be on the table in five, kids. Get washed up and grab a seat," she directed them.

Devon made her way behind her to the sink and flipped the water to warm. "Who's that on the phone, Mom?"

Caren pretended not to have heard the question. "Who wants juice with their coffee?"

Devon was determined to get an answer. "Mom, who called?"

Caren wiped her hands with a nearby towel and leaned against the counter. "That was Detective Gates, Devon."

Devon froze at the sink and spun around to face her mother. "Why is he calling?"

Brett made his way to his sister and stood close by, as if to reaffirm that he had her back. "He's got some nerve, calling her."

Caren forked the last few muffins from the oven and grabbed the butter tray, as she made her way to the oak kitchen table. She set the plate of muffins and butter almost in the center next to the strawberries and grapes. "Truth is … he's called every day since you were released from the hospital, to inquire how you're doing."

"Every day?" Devon repeated. "Why didn't you say something before now?"

"I didn't see the point of upsetting you. He's just concerned, and I knew you wouldn't speak to him," Caren answered.

"Please, Mom. I can't believe you're falling for this ploy," Devon admonished her. "He's just checking to see if his story is still intact."

"Don't be ridiculous, Devon," she warned. "I don't think it's like that at all."

"Did you ever consider that he's just trying to cover his ass?" Caren answered. "I don't understand what you mean, dear."

Devon made her way back into the kitchen, opening cabinet after cabinet as if she were looking for something. "Maybe," she replied, in between the opening and closing the cabinet doors. She thought of the flashback she'd had in the restaurant. "Maybe he's wondering how much I'm remembering."

Caren met her daughter at the middle pantry and opened the door to it. She grabbed a bottle of acetaminophen and pushed it into Devon's hand. "I don't think so, honey. All he asks is how you're doing and if you need anything."

Devon downed two of the yellow tablets with a full glass of water. "Like I said, Mom, he's covering his tracks or trying to."

"Devon," her mother's tone grew harsh and impatient. "Say, what's on your mind, or let's talk about something else. I'm not getting it."

Devon glanced anxiously behind her at Brett, who had made his way into the kitchen when he heard his mother and sister's voices growing louder and angrier.

"It's no secret that I don't like Detective Gates very much," Devon began, accepting the towel Brett was handing to her to wipe the perspiration off her brow. "There's no way I would have had sex with him willingly," she paused for a minute then added, "I know about the trace evidence, and I'm telling you, it wasn't consensual."

Brett's expression had transitioned from mildly curious to over-the-top angry by the time she finished her sentence. "I'm going to beat the truth out of him," he said.

Caren McKenzie fought back a smile and directed her statement to her son. "Brett, you're not helping." Next, she fixed her gaze on her daughter. "Devon, you have no recollection of those three months. A lot of things can change in three months."

Devon tossed the towel into the sink. "I know I would never have consented to have sex with him." She made her way back to the table but pushed the plate away from the area immediately in front of her. "I'm sorry, Mom, but I'm not hungry."

Her mother slid down into the chair next to her. "Devon, I can't imagine how you must feel, so I won't try and comfort you by saying I know how you feel because I don't. But my mother's intuition is intact, and it's telling me that Detective Gates seems to be sincere and genuinely concerned about you."

She poured Devon a cup of coffee and went on. "I've spoken to Laura Gates several times over the last few weeks, and they're very concerned about Christopher. He's only cleared for light duty. He spends the rest of his time holed up in his apartment."

Devon nodded. "I told you, he's worrying about charges being filed."

"His mother described him as depressed," Caren added. "They're very worried about him."

Brett motioned to his mother. "I've got to go." He kissed her on the cheek and rubbed Devon's shoulder. "I'll see you tomorrow, and we're going to finish those three miles."

Chapter Twelve

Caren waited until Brett took his leave, before she directed her attention back to Devon. "I don't want to fight with you, honey. We're all worried; everyone is here for you, baby."

She hugged Devon, and in a tone that Devon knew signaled the discussion was over, she added, "We have to be patient; once you are able to recall what happened, we'll deal with it. But until you do, I must respond to the Gates family in a manner that is appropriate. If Christopher has hurt you in any way, we'll hold him accountable. You have to trust us, Devon."

Devon nodded and sipped the last of her coffee. As she set the cup down, she noticed a small nick in the handle. There was something oddly familiar about the cup and the nick. She had a flashback of Gates dressed in old-fashioned clothing, leaning against an old whitewashed cabinet that was surrounded by other antique furniture. He was laughing, and his smile was wide and inviting as he leaned in close to her.

The memory was so real, that she could recall his scent, how solid his arm felt against hers. She shook her head as if she could shake the recollection from her head. She cleared her throat and set the cup down loudly on the end table next to the couch. Her mother noticed the change in her demeanor and asked, "Everything okay, honey?"

Devon smiled and lifted her head, but she did not look into her mother's eyes. "Yeah, I'm fine," she said. She wiped her hands along the sides of her hips as if she were drying them on her jeans. She pushed herself anxiously to her feet. "I'm so ready to go back to work."

"Devon," her mother said, "it's going to be several weeks before you're cleared physically and psychologically. Detective Gates was only cleared for light-duty, part-time."

Before she could answer, a tap at the door caused them to spin around nervously. Mrs. McKenzie held up her hand. "Relax, Devon, your protective detail is still outside."

Devon patted the handgun sticking out from the waistband of her jeans. "Not a problem, Mom."

Caren McKenzie was only partially surprised to see Agent Brad Michaels leaning comfortably against the wall; his body was turned away from the door to engage the police officer who was stationed close by. He held out his hand as Mrs. McKenzie leaned into the hallway. "Hi, I'm Agent Michaels, Devon's partner. Is she able to receive visitors?"

Mrs. McKenzie turned toward the living room. "Devon? Your partner is here to see you."

Devon closed the distance in about three large steps and slid in front of her mother; she was obviously happy to see him. "Brad, come in."

Agent Michaels followed behind her and took a seat on the sofa, glancing around the room. It had been a while since he'd been to her apartment.

Over the last two years, he'd been up on several occasions, usually to carpool wherever they were going. It was his routine to pick her up for work and raid the refrigerator simultaneously.

Caren McKenzie could tell that Michaels was comfortable in her daughter's house. It was troubling to her, but she wasn't sure why.

Initially, Mrs. McKenzie had attempted to make herself scarce as Michaels visited. The last thing her daughter needed was her mother hovering over her. After all, Devon was a trained police officer; she didn't need a chaperone.

Caren collected the load of laundry from the dryer and spread out the warm items of clothing so that they would not wrinkle. She could hear their voices from the living room, low but not whispering. She wasn't trying to eavesdrop, but her mother's instinct was sounding alarms on several levels. She folded the last of the towels and gathered the stack in her arms.

As she passed through the living room, she could plainly see Devon still on the couch where she'd been all along. She knew she'd heard Michaels refer to Gates, and whatever he'd said to Devon had upset her. "Devon, honey, you are supposed to be resting, not working," she said, when she stopped near the entrance to the living room.

Her next comment was directed to Detective Michaels. "And I hope you'll forgive me, Agent, but she's not supposed to get upset, and whatever you're talking about is upsetting her."

"It's okay, Mom," Devon replied, shaking her head. "Brad's just updating me on the Esteban case."

Mrs. McKenzie walked toward the door and opened it wide as if she were airing out the apartment. "Agent Michaels, do you mind?"

Brad looked awkwardly around the room. "Sure, no problem. I'll call you later, Devon." He grabbed his overcoat and walked out the door, as Caren stood holding it open for him. She closed it quietly and turned to find Devon standing almost directly in front of her.

She knew from Devon's demeanor that she was angry. Devon seldom exhibited her emotions, and her mother knew that this time would be no exception. Ever since Devon was a little girl, she'd kept her emotions intact. In fact, Caren could count on one hand the number of times she'd seen Devon cry as an adult.

"Mom, you're coddling," Devon warned. "He's my partner and …"

Caren cut her off. "No, Devon, he was your partner. He has a new partner now. Once you've been cleared for active duty, you'll get a new partner, too."

Devon shrugged her shoulders and retreated to the living room, opting not to argue with her mother. She knew from times past it was pointless. Instead, she dropped back down onto the sofa. "I'm bored. I can't do this for two weeks."

Caren collected the empty coffee cups and carried them into the kitchen, noticing the one Devon had been drinking from—the one with the nick in its handle. "I can't believe you haven't broken this already." She smiled to her daughter and added, "As rough as you are, it probably would have been safer with one of the boys, Jason, maybe."

Devon laughed. "Probably right, but I don't use it very often. It's special. In fact, I seldom actually use any of the dishes Grandmother left to me. I'm always afraid the dishwasher will ruin them or whatnot."

Caren rinsed and dried the cup, being careful to replace it in the china cabinet Devon owned. No need to tempt fate, she thought. As she latched the glass door, she said hesitantly, "I heard you and Brad mentioning Detective Gates. Is there some new development in your case?"

Devon shook her head. "No, not really. Brad just keeps pushing for me to remember what happened, where we were, and anything I can recall about our captors."

Caren nodded, but said nothing. It was as if she was waiting for Devon to continue. Finally, after several minutes of silence, she asked her daughter, "Is there something I should be aware of regarding you and Agent Michaels?"

Devon's posture changed instantly. Her back went straight. "What are you asking, Mom?"

"I'm just saying that I know how it is for police officers, Devon. I've been married to one for over thirty years. When partners are of the opposite sex, the lines sometimes get blurred."

Devon stood to her feet. "He's married, Mom. You honestly think I'm the type of woman who'd knowingly become involved with a married man?"

Devon's mother caught her by the arm as she walked away. "That's not what I said, Devon."

"Are you asking me if I slept with him?" she replied angrily, her face and neck flushing dark red.

"No, honey. You're a grown woman. Who you sleep with is between you and the young man at this point," Caren McKenzie said, as she folded a thin blanket and laid it over the back of the sofa. She made a point of turning her back to Devon and pretending to look out the window.

"Did the lines ever get blurred for Dad?" Devon asked, but her voice was calmer this time, more rational.

Caren McKenzie smiled and straightened her body, so that all of her five feet eight inches were standing proudly. "Let's just say your father is a wonderful husband and he's been a great father." She paused then added thoughtfully, "But he's still a man."

She changed the subject. "I get the impression that Agent Michaels is not fond of Detective Gates."

Devon smiled to herself, thinking how best to answer her mother's question. "No, I don't think they are big fans of each other. I doubt that Detective Gates is any fonder of Brad than Brad is of him."

"I didn't know they knew each other that well," Caren said, baiting Devon and pretending to fiddle with odd items in the kitchen drawer.

"Mom, you would make a terrible investigator. What are you trying to say?"

"Nothing, just curious as to why Agent Michaels has so little regard for Detective Gates if they barely know one another, that's all," she spoke as if she were reading from a script.

"Detective Gates and I dated a few times several years ago. It wasn't the worst date I've ever had. It wasn't the best, either." Before her mother could say anything, Devon added, "And no, I didn't sleep with him. Detective Gates has quite the reputation with women and an even longer list of broken hearts. One of those walking wounded is Brad's wife, Julie."

"I wasn't going to ask if you've slept with him, honey. I bet having Detectives Gates and Michaels working together is awkward?"

"To say the least." Devon semi-laughed. "Luckily the Marshall's service and NYPD don't cohabitate much so they don't cross paths, often. But when they do, it's like fireworks."

Mrs. McKenzie smiled. "She pointed outside the window where the day was shaping into a beautiful winter afternoon. "Why don't you get a shower and we'll go out and get some lunch."

Devon smiled and made her way to her feet. "That sounds like a good idea. Maybe we can see if Andrea and Melissa want to join us." She stopped before entering the bedroom. "Any word from Emily? How's she doing after the divorce?"

Caren's smiling expression turned sad as she thought of her daughter-in-law. No, ex-daughter-in-law, she corrected herself. "Brett doesn't talk much about it or her. But I know it's hard on them both."

As Devon entered her bedroom, she said, "Maybe we should see if she wants to join us. It would be nice to see everyone."

****

The sedan parked and waited just outside her building like always. The driver with the beard was careful not to sit idle in one spot for very long, with the security officers on foot and on patrol, he couldn't be too careful.

He checked his watch, wondering how much longer before she'd make an exit. Even though she wasn't working, she was seldom in the apartment for very long. And she didn't have much company. So far, it had only been the mother and then, the brothers.

He had barely finished the thought when he saw her and her brother jogging down the steps. They ran side by side, down the sidewalk, to the intersection before crossing the crosswalk, and disappearing behind the businesses on the southeast corner. He'd have had to be blind not to have noticed her bodyguard walking quickly behind them trying to keep her insight.

McKenzie and her brother hadn't been away from her home for long, the man caught sight of them about a quarter-mile from her apartment. They took turns drinking from a spent water bottle and made their way back up the steps and disappeared into the building.

The brother appeared not long after, taking the steps two at a time until he reached the sidewalk. The way the brother turned and approached the parked sedan, the man thought maybe he'd been made and his hand dropped to the ignition in case he needed to make a fast getaway.

But the brother wasn't a cop, he was a fireman. He didn't pay any attention to the bearded man in the sedan. Instead, he slid into his car and backed out of the parking lot, giving the sedan no thought at all.

Her partner today had been an exception and the man had been surprised to see Agent Michaels strolling comfortably down the sidewalk outside of her apartment.

The man blew a stream of smoke out the window, taking a moment to bite at the tender skin of his tongue and bottom lip. The only man he despised more than Agent Michaels was Detective Gates.

The man had half expected Detective Gates to be hiding in the shadows as well, keeping an eye on her, and waiting for his chance to redeem himself and win her over once again.

He took another drag on the cigarette before pushing it through the open window, smiling as he observed Agent Michaels descending the steps and down the sidewalk away from Devon's apartment.

The man squirmed nervously in the seat; he'd need to use the bathroom soon. The mother and brother had arrived within an hour of each other, the brother had left before Michaels paid his visit, surely the mother would be leaving soon. No doubt, Devon would take her exit not long after.

Within the hour, she and the mother appeared on the front steps, dressed for lunch a little fancier than usual, meeting someone for lunch no doubt. The man started his car and watched as Mrs. McKenzie waited for Devon to get into the passenger side and buckle up.

He waited for their car to pull into the traffic and pulled quickly out behind them, nearly colliding with another vehicle. The bearded man flipped the other driver a bird and followed Mrs. McKenzie's vehicle. He wasn't sure where they were going for lunch, but he hoped the bathroom was vacant and the takeout options appealing. He hated stakeouts, almost as much as he was beginning to hate burgers and fries.

****

There was only a single lamp burning inside Devon's darkened apartment. When he'd first arrived, she'd flipped the television off and turned the stereo on so that the room was enveloped in soft, easy listening music.

She poured them both drinks, white wine for Richard, red for her and set out a few finger foods to nibble on. However, the only thing he was nibbling on currently was her right ear.

Tenderly his lips found hers, then made their way down her neck. He kissed the sensitive skin of her collarbone and careful not to leave a mark on her fair, white skin while his hands pushed under her shirt cupping the warm flesh of her breasts through her bra.

"Let's go to the bedroom?" he whispered into her neck, reaching for the top button of her shirt.

"In a minute." She returned his kisses, her hands around his neck, pulling him closer against her.

Richard unbuttoned her shirt, unclasped her bra and caressed her breasts as his lips kissed his way down her throat and to her breast. They slid down on the sofa as he clasped her fingers into his and pulled her arms over her head.

****

Like a flash of lightening, Devon was back in the dark place, her arms tied over her head, her shirt torn open, and what appeared to be a corset laying loose around her waist. The man kissed and suckled at her breast, before forcing himself into her. The pain was crippling and Devon's body jerked in response to the flashback.

****

Devon blinked and the recollection was gone, like a whisper, maybe a song. The room was hot, too hot and the air around had an unpleasant scent. It's a sweaty, musty smell and she had to force the bile in her stomach to stay down.

All she could think about was throwing up, but she managed to keep their dinner and the liquor down. She pushed at Richard's chest, forcing his mouth away. "Richard, stop," her words were hoarse.

"It's okay," he purred, his lips searching frantically for her breasts. "I brought protection."

She made the request again, several times, each time more forcibly than the previous one. "Richard, please, just stop."

He pulled away and sat up, allowing her enough room to sit at his side. Devon pulled her shirt together at the front, letting her bra hang open under her arms.

"What's wrong?" he asked, through lidded eyes. "We talked about this before you went missing. I thought you wanted our relationship to move forward?"

He took her silence as a sign of consent and pulled her closer, resuming to kiss her neck and slide into her again. "Let's go to your bedroom."

"I can't, I'm sorry." She saw the image again in her mind, and realized for the first time, that she wasn't sure her attacker was Detective Gates.

"I'm really sorry. I'm not feeling well." She ran from the room, into the bathroom.

Richard followed her to the bathroom and waited on the other side of the closed door. He heard her vomiting and wrenching from behind the door. "I'm sorry you aren't feeling well. I'll just see myself out."

Devon continued to vomit behind the closed door, as Richard exited her apartment and closed the door behind him.

****

Gates knew he should have seen her to the door, but he didn't. Instead, he'd kept his place on the sofa, zipped his jeans up, and finished the drink she'd poured him before they'd had sex.

It had been challenging finding someone who looked as much like Devon as she did. Of course, she was a hooker, a call girl, she could make herself look like whomever the client wanted. And for the last three weeks, every night he'd wanted her to look like Devon.

At first, his companion had tried to interact with him, make small talk while they had sex. He'd asked her politely to keep quiet. She couldn't speak because if she did, she destroyed the illusion. When she talked, it was obvious she wasn't Devon McKenzie, and Gates wasn't able to maintain his erection.

Now some three weeks later, his companion barely uttered a word. After entering his apartment, she stripped out of her clothes and waited for Gates to approach her from behind, doggy style was the only way he could perform. He couldn't look her in the eyes, that would also destroy the illusion.

Gates poured another drink, listening to her movements on the other side of his apartment door as she reapplied her lipstick and counted her money, dropping the rolled-up bundle of bills in the tiny blue purse she carried with her.

Chapter Thirteen

Devon hadn't gotten much sleep last night, none. It wasn't that she'd had nightmares, she hadn't. What had kept her awake all night had been thinking about the dammed flashbacks or whatever they were.

Were these memories, finally bullying themselves into her conscious memory or were they fabrications of things that she'd imagined. Since they'd returned, she considered many times how the truth might affect her and her family. How her life might be changed once the truth was evident and out in the open.

What if Detective Gates had been telling the truth, what if their feelings for one another, had over the course of those three months changed?

What then had happened in the dark places, who was the man she remembered, and what had he done? What was she supposed to tell Richard? She didn't wait for an answer. Instead, she rolled out of the bed and stepped into the shower.

The large master bathroom and shower had been a major selling point when she'd leased the apartment. The heat from the warm water had already caused the mirrors in the bathroom to fog over, before she'd even lathered her body. But Devon didn't care; she loved the way the warm water felt as it cascaded off her body.

****

Caren McKenzie entered Devon's apartment and dropped the key on the kitchen counter before pausing to take notice of the empty wine bottle, wine glasses, and dishware in the sink. She smiled, Devon had company last night she thought to herself, remembering the young man who'd showed up at the hospital. Caren couldn't help but smile, remembering how he wasn't able to penetrate through her sons, Devon's brothers.

She turned toward the bedroom and heard the water running in the shower of Devon's bathroom. "Devon," she called, as she entered the bedroom. "You alone in there, honey?"

"Yes, Mom," Devon answered, sounding more like fourteen than twenty-something. "I'm alone in the shower."

"Have you had breakfast yet?"

"No, not yet. I just got up."

"Maybe we can meet the girls for breakfast?"

"Sounds good," Devon called, from under the water of the shower. "Let me just finish up."

"There's no rush, honey. Take your time."

The water was warm against her skin and if she'd had more time, she'd have liked to take a bath. In her line of work, she seldom had time to take bubble baths, but she enjoyed them when she did have the time.

Thank God for indoor plumbing. Here there was no need to carry in bucket after bucket of water to heat in the fireplace and pour into the tub. It was as easy as turning a knob and the hot water flowed easily. That was one of the things she had missed most when she was living with the Ennis'.

She finished the thought before she realized she'd thought it. When the realization hit her, everything came flooding back as if she were facing an avalanche head-on. She heard herself scream and felt the hardness of the tile, before she realized she'd fallen to the floor and was crying out.

She rolled into a ball so tight and tiny, that the water from the shower seemed to cascade like a raging river over her shoulders and head, as the events replayed in her mind from beginning to end. It was as if she was watching a movie on fast forward. All she could do was wrap her arms tighter around her shoulders and scream. No words would come to her.

****

Caren McKenzie had just hung up the phone after speaking to both of her daughters-in-law. Luckily, they were both available to meet for breakfast. She had just started dialing the number she'd written down for Emily when she heard Devon's agonizing scream.

Caren was halfway to the bedroom, when the front door was kicked open and the security detail entered the apartment and headed toward Devon's screams.

"Wait here, Mrs. McKenzie!" the officer instructed, before approaching the bathroom with his gun drawn. Once inside the bathroom, he deduced that Devon was alone in the bathroom without an immediate threat to her.

He returned to the bedroom where Caren was waiting, pacing anxiously in place near the bathroom door with the telephone in hand. "She's alone, crying on the shower floor."

Caren pushed past him into the bathroom. "Can you call someone to fix the front door?"

The officer nodded and returned through the bedroom, to wait in the kitchen.

Without hesitation, Caren dropped the phone and made her way into the master bathroom. The bathroom was filled with so much steam it looked more like a sauna than a bathroom.

Her daughter had stopped screaming, and Caren could barely make out a low hum over the roar of the water from the shower. She almost didn't see Devon as she lay still and curled into a tiny ball on the shower floor.

Nervously, she stepped into the shower and bent down to her. "Devon? What is it? What's wrong?" she asked, although she thought she already knew the answer.

Devon was still on the shower floor, crying and screaming. "Oh God, Mom it was horrible!"

Devon pushed her mother away and screamed out above the water cascading from the shower, "Where's Chris?"

Mrs. McKenzie tried to pull her daughter out of the corner. "Devon, it's okay. You're safe. You're home."

Devon yanked her arm free and made herself even smaller in the corner of the shower as she rocked back and forth. Caren knew she was saying something, but she couldn't understand any of it.

She backed out of the stall and ran toward the kitchen. She was just about to dial 911 when she realized that her daughter's career in law enforcement would be over, not to mention, her reputation. Instead, she dialed the only number she thought could do her daughter any good.

****

The phone only rang a few times before Laura Gates snapped it up to her ear. She was considering muting the phones in all the rooms except for the kitchen. Every time Christopher relaxed or finally fell asleep, the ringing of the phone woke him. Thank goodness, she'd finally gotten him to go for a jog. He'd been cooped up in his apartment for the better part of three days.

It had taken all their attention to get him to eat and bathe. He wasn't interested in doing anything, except moping about the apartment and sitting on the sofa.

The first few days, Jarrod and Nick had slept over with the intent of getting him focused on regaining his life. But Christopher had made it plain that he didn't want a life if Devon wasn't a part of it.

Yesterday, Jarrod and Nick had packed their bags and returned to their own homes just as Mrs. Gates had packed up Chris and taken him back to the family home in New Jersey, hoping to change his perspective with a change in surroundings.

In addition, Seth, her youngest son, had finally been granted emergency leave from the military. It had taken him the better part of the last three days to be evacuated from Iran. Seth had a wonderful sense of humor; he and Christopher always seemed to find some sort of amusing trouble. Given Chris's mindset lately, she decided it would be a welcoming change.

"Hello?" she called into the kitchen phone, as she lifted the lid from a huge metal pot that was simmering on the stove. The boys had asked for pot roast for dinner, and she was excited about making it. Truth was that she seldom cooked anymore. It was a lot of trouble to cook for just the two of them. She and Ash often went out for dinner at local places just down the street. It was so close that they could walk, arm in arm, as if they were twenty years old again.

The voice on the other end was obviously upset; her words came out in intermittent exclamations of talking and sobbing. It wasn't until the caller had been on the phone for a few minutes that she realized it was Caren McKenzie. "Caren," she soothed, looking out the window to see if she could see Chris or Seth running along the path to the house. "What's wrong?"

She paused as she listened, her ear glued to the receiver. "Do you think she's remembering?" She peered out the window again. "I'll have to find him, but we'll get to you as soon as we can." She listened, and then added, "He went running with his brother. He can't be that far away. I'll get the car and find them. We'll be there as soon as I can find him."

Laura Gates slammed the phone into the receiver on the wall and grabbed her purse, before rushing out the door; she returned only seconds later to turn off the stove and grab jackets for Seth and Chris.

****

Caren McKenzie had checked on her daughter twice since she'd made the frantic call to the Gates residence. After several tries at the phone number that Gates had given her the day he was discharged from the hospital, she'd called her old friend Adam Goff only to discover that Detective Gates spent a lot of time at his parents in New Jersey. Captain Goff had been more than happy to give her the number to the Gates's summer home just off the Jersey coast.

She couldn't relate how thankful she'd been when she heard Laura Gates answer the phone and promise to bring her son as soon as she could find him. The last time she'd checked on her, Devon was still curled into a ball, rocking in the corner of the shower with the water plunging down around her.

The water had turned cold by now, but Devon didn't seem to notice. It fell like rain against her back and neck before swirling into the drain. Her flesh was covered with goosebumps.

Devon continued to hum rhythmically to herself. Caren tried to coax her daughter out of the shower and into a warm blanket, but each time, Devon either didn't hear her calls or didn't acknowledge her. Frustrated, Caren closed the shower door and waited.

****

Gates knocked on the door loudly in three successive beats, and then waited only a second before raising his fist and pounding at the door. Just as he raised his fist again, the door flung open and he was face to face with Caren McKenzie.

She stepped away to allow him and his family into the apartment. The young man with him was the only brother she hadn't met. He looked more like the older brother, Jarrod, though he was thinner than Jarrod, and about the same height as Chris, but his hair was darker than Chris's. Like Chris, he had the same intense blue eyes and charismatic smile. They were both dressed in running gear—dark sweatpants and gray sweatshirts. Chris's shirt had NYPD printed across the front in big, black letters, while Seth's shirt had USMC printed in smaller letters across the left breast pocket. Apparently, when Mrs. Gates had retrieved jackets, she only grabbed long overcoats for her and Seth; the latter looked out of place with his dark coat atop his running gear. Gates had pulled a light gray jacket on.

He pushed past her and looked awkwardly around the room. "Where is she?"

"She was in the shower when I think it happened," Mrs. McKenzie answered, raising her hand to indicate the direction of the master bedroom. The fact that he'd started walking in the correct direction before she finished, wasn't lost on her, but she thought that she'd save those questions for later.

Gates could hear the water still running in the shower. The condensation had all but dissolved, and he could see his reflection clearly in the mirror. "Devon?" he called out, his voice just a bit stronger than he would normally use.

"Gates?" she answered. "Chris, is that you?"

He opened the shower door and took in the scene before him. She was squatting against the wall, clutching her legs, rocking back and forth, and trembling. He looked behind him and flipped the water off before stepping closer to her.

"Devon," he soothed, kneeling to her so that the knees of his running pants were saturated with water from the shower floor. "I got you, it's okay." He took her wrists and pulled her up toward him, wrapping his jacket over her shoulders and pinching it together in the front. He held her tightly against his chest, leading her in small steps out of the bathroom.

As they passed into the bedroom, he whispered to her mother, "Can I get a blanket? She's shivering. I think she's in shock."

Caren returned just as he was guiding Devon toward the queen-size bed that was positioned just in front of a large window. Mrs. McKenzie yanked the comforter away and pulled the blanket down, so that he could get her into the bed. Once she was leaning against the headboard, Gates pulled the blanket over her and retrieved his jacket. With some coaxing, he convinced her to recline against the bed pillows. As an afterthought he took the blanket from Mrs. McKenzie and spread it over her.

After she was settled, he tried to pry her arms from his neck, but she held on tight to him and whispered, "Stay with me. I don't want to be alone."

Gates motioned to her mother. "Your mom's here. you're not alone."

She laid her head snuggly against his chest and held on to him even tighter. "Chris, please just stay."

He nodded to her and settled against the pillows with her cocooned tightly in his arms. He kissed her head and breathed in her scent. God, he thought to himself, there would be much to be thankful for this year. And in a few week's when everyone gathered at his parents' house for dinner, he'd make sure he was the one reciting the grace.

He could tell by the sound of her breathing that she was asleep, but was too enticed by the feel of her in his arms again to consider pulling away. He wanted to savor every minute for as long as he could.

Gates was so overwhelmed with Devon being in his arms, he'd forgotten they weren't alone and that Mrs. McKenzie was in the room. He looked up to her as if to say, *She pulled me into the bed with her. It's not my fault.*

Instead, her smile put him at ease. She handed him a satin gown and a clean pair of underwear, like the black ones Devon had worn during their stay with the Ennis,' but these were light blue.

She whispered to him, "Can we get these on her without waking her?"

He shook his head. "We can try, but I'm almost certain she'll wake up."

"Never mind, then," she said. "I just want her to be warm enough. It's cool in this room."

He smiled at her words. They reminded him of something Mrs. Ennis had said once. Whether it happened yesterday or a hundred years ago, the time they'd shared with the Ennis' would always weigh heavy on his heart. It was like finding out as an adult that your best childhood friend had passed away suddenly and unexpectedly.

The moments of missing them intersected with the acceptance that things could never be, again. His smile faded; his eyes softened. "The family that took us in, put us in a guesthouse in the yard behind the main house. It had a small fireplace in the middle of the room, and we fell asleep just about every night to a fire burning in the hearth. It was warm and toasty and smelled like cedar. It was an amazing experience to fall asleep to the crackling of the fire in the fireplace."

Caren took a seat on the edge of the bed, noticing how Chris moved his feet to accommodate her. "Sounds nice," she said. "I'm glad you were there for her." She patted his knee. "I'm happy that she has you."

He didn't miss she'd used the word has and not had. He exhaled and made a motion toward the bed. "What do you want me to do about this?"

She swallowed and closed her eyes. "I trust you'll exercise good judgment. I feel as if I can trust you to continue to take care of her."

Caren took the gown from his hand. "I'm going to see if your mother would mind dropping me home. I'll be back in the morning."

She looked lovingly at her daughter before she exited the room. Gates could hear them discussing the details just on the other side of the door. Minutes later, he heard the front door close and the lock click into place.

Within minutes, he succumbed to the darkness of sleep. The place next to her was warm and soft, and it enveloped him like a glove. It was the first good night's sleep that he'd had in over a month.

****

Gates heard the rain as it tapped against the glass of the window and slid down the pane, collecting in the windowsill and falling hard and heavy to the ground before his mind registered that it was morning or where he was and who he was with.

At first, he dismissed the feeling of her warm and soft against him as just another dream. He'd awaken any minute to find the place beside him cold and empty. At times, it was more than he could bear, waking up alone and without her.

Her hair had fallen into her eyes and between their faces, almost tickling his nose. He inhaled deeply against her, enjoying the fragrance of honeysuckle and something that he couldn't quite place. Gates pulled her as close against him as he dared without waking her, mostly to reassure himself that she was beside him and not a figment of his imagination.

Gates ran his right hand down the full length of her, coming to rest at the small of her back just above her buttocks. He'd forgotten that she'd been put to bed naked until his fingers encountered the warm spot just at the center of her back. Most of the night, she'd tangled herself up in the linen sheet, so it was now like a cocoon. He knew she was awake; he could tell by the intermittent cadence of her breathing.

"How'd you get here?" she asked, just above a whisper.

He answered softly, "Your mom called my mom; she brought me over yesterday."

Devon smiled and burrowed closer against him. "This is the best playdate she's ever made for me."

Without saying anything else, she snaked her small hand from under the sheet and caressed his chest softly just above his abdomen. He pushed against her back, so that she was slightly on top of him. She kissed at his neck, mostly to assure herself that she was awake.

He returned her kisses, hard and hungry, lips devouring lips. He pulled her hair up and away from her face, kissing her tenderly on either side of her neck, just below her ears.

She pulled at his sweatpants without breaking contact with his lips, surprised that once she managed to push them down to his knees, he still was not erect. In fact, he seemed almost bored, as if he were going through the motions on her behalf.

She cupped him in her hands, taking time to run her hands up and down his shaft the way she knew he liked her too. Minutes later, she felt him responding, growing hard and heavy in her hand. He moved uncomfortably under her hands. "Devon," he said almost painfully, "we should wait a while; it's too soon."

He attempted to sit up. "You want to take a shower?"

"No." She seemed angry. Devon stalled and sat next to him, pulling the blankets frantically around her waist and clutching the top of the blanket against her breasts. "What's wrong?"

He squeezed her shoulder. "I don't know exactly; it just doesn't feel right."

It was almost as if he'd hit her, the feeling she had as he said the words, "Just go. I knew it would be this way."

He shook his head and tried to hold her in place next to him. "You don't understand, Devon."

"Let go now, Detective Gates," she demanded.

He jumped to his knees in a single bounce and leaned in so close, that she could feel the moisture of his lips as he said through clenched teeth. "Devon, I want nothing more than to push you onto your back and bury myself so deep inside you that I can't function."

He didn't realize she'd hit him, until he heard her hand against his face. It was loud and sharp and seemed to resonate throughout the room. He calmed down and leaned back against the pillow to afford her the luxury of her own space. "I meant everything I've said to you over the last five months, Devon."

Gates paused. "I love you, and yes, I want to spend the rest of my life here in this bed making love to you over and over again."

"Then what is it?" she asked him, through tears that were cascading down her cheeks. "Why are you pushing me away?"

He reached over and pulled her to him again so that she was in his arms. "This time yesterday, you didn't remember anything about our life together." He kissed her head just at her hairline and kept her close enough that his lips were still touching her forehead. "I told you in Hamilton, I have to have all of you. I can't just have pieces. I need you here." He kissed her forehead again and added, "And here," kissing her just above her breast where he knew her heart was pounding. "And here," he said, as he pushed her against the cushions of the bed and pulled her knees gently apart, easing his erection hungrily between her legs. He pushed himself up as high on his arms as he could and plunged into her.

Devon lunged back and forth under him; it was as if they were imprinting one on the other. She felt him growing harder and bigger around her; it was evident by the way he increased the pace with his hips, that he was close to his climax. She grabbed him around the neck and pulled him closer against her, pushing his face to her breasts.

Obediently, he took as much as he could of her left breast into his mouth, pulling it by the nipple with his teeth and tongue until his mouth was full and the nipple almost square. He teased the right nipple into a tight, hardpoint with his left hand and then forced it into his mouth, licking and nipping it in and out of his mouth.

Gates was thankful everyone had left them alone; with as much noise as they were making, there would've been no doubt as to what was going on. Devon was intermittently moaning and apparently praying as he heard "God" come from her lips several times.

Frantically, he withdrew himself and pushed her back against the bed; her back arched over several pillows they'd been sleeping on the night before. He'd managed to hold on to her breasts, one in each palm, as he kissed a path between them and down to her stomach. He alternated between licking and kissing a trail of hot kisses across her abdomen and between her legs. His tongue danced in the dark curls, toying with her, pulling and biting at the skin of her mons. Gates pushed her legs apart as wide as he could without hurting her and pulled her toward him for optimal access.

He pushed her folds apart with his right thumb and ran the other fingers of his left hand over her clitoris so intensely, that she lifted herself off the mattress in response to his touch. He lowered his mouth to her center as if she were his prey. He alternated licking and plucking at her clitoris, until she cried out and came. As soon as he felt the spasm around his tongue cease, he pushed himself up so that they were face to face again, and his lips owned hers.

She felt him enter her in a single stroke. He pumped and thrust so wildly, his moans were little more than a cry deep in his throat. He exploded into her, screaming her name.

His motion slowed, and his movement stilled, but he waited, still buried inside of her.

Devon ran her hands through his wet, sticky hair, pushing it out of his eyes and around his ears. She could feel his penis still inside of her deflating. She laughed into his shoulder until he gave her a confused look. She smiled and whispered. "It tickles."

He kissed her again on the lips, pulling and tugging at her lips with his own. He pushed his tongue into hers and pulled it, suckling it until she couldn't breathe.

She pushed at his chest. "I have to pee ... Thank God for indoor plumbing."

He slid off her, but kept his place at her side, his right hand still kneading her breast and picking at her nipple with his finger. "You've been thanking God a lot today."

Devon kissed his fingertips and sat up. "I've a lot to be thankful for." She pulled a robe off the chair and slid it on. "I'm hungry."

Gates made his way out of the bed and to his feet, meeting her about halfway before she made her way into the bathroom and pulled at the belt of the robe. "Me, too."

She punched at him playfully. "Seriously, order pizza and I'll run the shower for us. Use the number on the frig. I have an account." She smiled out to him through the open door. "They know the way by heart."

He made his way into the kitchen, still naked, and opened the refrigerator. "They know the way?"

She yelled from the bathroom, over the shower, "Yeah, the owner went to school with Kevin. They're still good friends. He has a key and delivers here all the time."

He nodded and picked up the phone from the kitchen wall and dialed a number from a magnetic sticker on her refrigerator.

She could hear him on the phone, explaining to the person on the phone that the pizza was to be delivered inside the apartment where the money would be left on the table in the living room.

He flipped the stereo on and adjusted the volume so the shower (and any other noises coming from the area) would be drowned out by the music.

She smiled and stepped into the warm water and waited for him.

He didn't disappoint her; several minutes later, he opened the shower door and stepped inside to join her. The water was warm, but nowhere near as warm as the feeling of his arms around her with her back pressed tight against his chest.

It was amazing how perfect their lovemaking had become. More importantly, each time she swore it was the best, and she could never feel any more complete than she did when held in his embrace. Yet, each time was better than before.

She let her head fall back against the wall of the shower as she reveled in the sensations he was provoking. "Oh God," she heard herself saying, each time he brought her closer to the edge; she'd fall over it and tumble until she was just a small speck. Then there was the light again, the light of his face, his voice, his touch. He'd become her life, and for this moment in time, that seemed to be just fine.

Chapter Fourteen

Gates felt as if he'd run a marathon, and from the way he was breathing, he sounded like he had as well. He leaned up against the wall of the shower to catch his breath and collected a few towels. He wrapped one around his waist and handed another one to her as she stepped from the shower, soaking wet and shivering. "Pizza should be here by now," he announced.

He tucked the edge of the towel around his waist and went into the living room. Sure enough, the pizza was sitting on the table next to two bottles of beer and two cans of Diet Coke. He tossed a few slices on a white paper plate and set it next to one of the cans of soda.

He slid down to the floor and stretched his legs out, crossing his feet at the ankles as he leaned his back against the front of the sofa only partially listening to the deep, husky vocals of Michael Bolton crooning "That's what love is all about" on the radio. He had already eaten two slices when she emerged from the bathroom wrapped tightly in a towel. He patted the place next to him and handed her a slice of pizza.

She eyed him hungrily, appreciative of his lean outline only partially veiled by the thin, damp towel. "I like your dinner attire tonight," she murmured, moving closer to him so that their hips were nearly touching. He continued chewing on his pizza as if he weren't paying her any attention. He stuffed another bite into his mouth. "And I'm very enamored with yours as well." He rubbed her shoulder gently with his hand and bent his head to kiss her in almost the same spot.

"I have an idea to make it even better." She reached across their laps and pulled at his towel until it gave way. He raised his buttocks up enough, so that she could pull it out from under him and toss it behind the sofa. Gates did not seem fazed, and he continued eating as if patiently awaiting some event. After swallowing the last bite that he'd forced into his mouth, he reached toward her and announced, "You're a bit overdressed, don't you think?"

She swayed her torso just enough to avert his hand and shook her head. "No, I'm already cold."

He tugged playfully at the towel. "Ooh, even better."

She swatted at his hand and moved away just enough to evade his reach. "Seriously, I'm perfectly fine as is."

He scooted closer to fill the gap. "This hardly seems fair."

Devon blew on the slice a few times before folding it in half and eating it. She wiped her hands on a folded napkin that he'd placed close by, and then she smiled as she turned toward him with a devilish look in her eye.

Before he could ask, he felt her hand, still warm from the pizza, wrapping around his shaft, teasing him until he was hard and rigid. She pushed closer against him to get better access and stroked him hard, taking time to collect all of him in her hand as she moved in and out from between his legs. She could feel him fighting the urge to push against her hand, and to urge her closer against him.

She kissed his neck, biting at the delicate skin at his throat. "What were you saying was unfair?"

He paused for a minute, trying to focus his thoughts enough to answer her question. "Never mind," he managed to whisper, his reply almost lost in the haunting melody of Nancy Wilson as she poured out her heart's desire in the song "These Dreams."

Devon leaned back against the small table, pushing it until it gave way and provided her access to move closer to him. Lifting one leg over him, she came to rest in his lap, his erection pressing intensely against the opening between her legs.

Gates ran his hands along the length of her legs and around her back to her buttocks, as he bent at the neck to kiss her just above where the towel was still protecting her breasts. Between kisses, he said, "Not that I'm complaining, but we just did this like twenty minutes ago in the shower."

She met his kisses. "I like being close to you like this."

He pushed his hand between their bodies to adjust himself into her. She intercepted his hand with hers and tugged at her towel, until it dropped like a curtain to the floor near to them. "Not so fast; I was thinking we could just do this for a while."

Before he could ask, she pushed his hand up to her breast, pushing him backward to recline against the sofa. She had her lips on his chest, kissing the area from shoulder to shoulder. As she straightened up, she felt him pulling her breast into his mouth, nipple first, gently sucking and tugging until it was hard and taunt in his mouth.

Gates had arched his groin so high toward her, that his buttocks were off the floor and steadily rising. He made his way to his knees with her still in his lap and pushed the pizza box and all to the floor to make room on the table. As soon as her back touched the hard surface of the table, he was furiously pumping toward his release. Minutes later, he collapsed his weight atop her, calling her name as he emptied himself again into her. He pulled away, taking her with him to the floor against the sofa, rubbing her back and neck softly. "All good?"

She smiled. "What is it with you and hard surfaces?" He gave her a curious look, but said nothing.

"Tree trunks, barn walls, hay bales, and now tabletops, what do you have against beds?"

Smiling, he reached for the box and handed her a slice of pizza. "I can't seem to control myself when I'm with you."

Devon nodded and took the pizza from his hand, biting deep, thick bites of it, but never breaking eye contact with him. After a few bites, she popped the top of the soda and sipped. She looked at the beer bottle he was drinking from and asked, "Can I have a sip?"

He handed it to her. "Just a sip. Doesn't mix well with your medications."

She took two small drinks and handed it back to him. She watched his hands travel back to the box to select another slice. "Chris, when did you get your ring back?"

He wiped his mouth. "I asked for my belongings when I woke up in the hospital. I've worn it ever since." He took another drink of his beer and smiled. "I plan to be buried wearing it."

She looked anxiously at the clock hanging on the wall. "If my brother's come over and find us here like this, that might be sooner than you think."

He finished the slice he was eating and pulled another piece from the box. "It will be a death well worth facing."

She seemed sad. "I don't know what happened to my ring. I must have lost it when we were in the water."

Gates tossed the uneaten piece of pizza back in the box; his stomach was protesting that last piece, or at least the half of it that he'd eaten. "Mine was pinned to the collar of the shirt I was wearing. Did you check the clothes you were wearing when we were brought into the emergency room? Katy says they routinely pin jewelry to the clothes when there's no family member to claim the valuables."

"Really?" she asked, jumping up to locate the plastic bag of clothes she'd brought home from the hospital. She found the bag on the washer. "The skirt and shirt I was wearing aren't in the bag."

He was quiet for a second, and then added after swallowing several gulps from the bottle, "They kept yours as evidence, Devon."

"Yeah, I'd forgotten that they keep the clothes if it appears …" She realized that she didn't need to continue and motioned toward his beer again.

Reluctantly, he handed it to her, and she added, "Who knows about the trace evidence they gathered?"

Gates shook his head. "Just those with a need to know."

"So … the officers assigned to our case? And who else, my family?"

"More specifically, your mom," he answered. "The fact that I'm still breathing tells me your brothers aren't aware," he added, trying to lighten the moment.

"Don't get too comfortable. They're aware." By now, Devon had emptied all the contents of the bag onto the floor and was inspecting them item by item. Inside one of the socks was a small yellow envelope whose end was sealed with an adhesive.

Gently, she tore open the envelope and poured its contents into her hand. To her delight, a smaller, more delicate ring identical to the one Gates was wearing tumbled into her palm. Enthusiastically, she slid the ring on her left-hand ring finger.

She looked tentatively at Gates, holding her hand up for him to examine. "What do we do with these now?"

He looked her in the eyes and smiled. "Invite everyone over for a reception."

****

Mrs. McKenzie slid the key in the lock and quietly turned the knob, pushing the door open just enough to accommodate her slender form. She carried several plastic bags of groceries draped over her wrists. Before the door could close, Brett and Jason pushed through as well, taking note that their mother was motioning for them to be quiet. She pointed toward the bedroom door as if to announce that Devon must be sleeping, again. She hadn't answered the phone all day; no doubt that after Christopher left this morning, she had a lot to absorb.

She placed the bags on the counter and walked around the counter into the living room toward the bedroom. She stopped in her tracks at the scene laid out before her. Christopher and Devon were sound asleep on the couch. He was dressed in a pair of blue jeans, but he hadn't buttoned them. It looked as if he had simply stepped into them and sat down on the sofa. Devon was wearing his shirt. It was blue with tiny stripes, and it hung almost to her knees. She had only buttoned those buttons in the middle. She was lying in his lap, her head almost at his abdomen. Both were barefoot, and his feet were propped under hers against the coffee table. They looked so peaceful, as though they'd come to the end of a play date and simply taken a nap.

Brett made his way to his mother's side to see what had taken her attention and stopped in a similar fashion. He didn't say a word, but he didn't have to; his body language said it all. His forward motion was stopped by the hand of his younger brother at his shoulder. Jason shook his head and motioned that they should leave before anyone woke up. Brett was shaking his head and gesturing toward his sister. Finally, Mrs. McKenzie stepped forward and shook her daughter's shoulder gently.

Devon stirred and sat up as she stretched to the extent that Gates pushed his body upward and took her with him. If Devon was embarrassed, she didn't let it show. She smiled to her family and pushed her way to her feet, pulling at the shirt to ensure that she was covered. "Brett, Jason, do you know Chris?" she asked, as she scooted to her bedroom and grabbed her robe.

She handed Gates the shirt she'd just taken off and made her way into the kitchen to see what groceries they'd brought. Chris put the shirt on and inhaled her scent. He made his way around the couch to where the brothers were still standing, silently taking in the events of the last few minutes. Gates held out his hand to the older brother. "Nice to see you again, Brett."

Reluctantly, Brett took his hand. "Detective Gates, it's been what, about a year since the Wilkins case?"

Gates nodded. "About that, I guess." He turned to the other brother, Devon's twin, and held out his hand. "I don't think we've met."

Jason shook his hand and turned to see where Devon had gone. She was still in the kitchen rummaging through the bags, pulling one item out and then another. She finally settled on a plastic bag of yellow apples. She pulled two apples out of the bag and walked back around the sofa to where Gates was. Devon tossed him one playfully; she seemed to be enjoying how uncomfortable he was and how thick the tension was in the room.

It was odd how similar, yet different, Devon and Jason looked. They shared the same dark hair and eyes and had similar facial features, though Jason was significantly taller than Devon. Gates sometimes forgot how small Devon was, but standing next to her twin, it was obvious.

Gates buttoned the shirt and tucked it into his jeans as he gave Devon an awkward look. She just bit into the apple and fell back against the sofa. Mrs. McKenzie made her way to Devon and sat down next to her. "Devon," she said, uncertain of how to discuss the recent developments between Christopher and Devon, "obviously there's been some changes between the two of you."

Devon smiled and held up her hand to show her the ring on her left hand. "I remembered everything, Mom." She held out her hand to Gates and motioned for him to join her on the sofa.

Before he could sit down next to her, his phone rang. He checked the caller identification and stepped into the hallway so he could return the call in private.

Gates rubbed his hands on his jeans and motioned to the door. "I'm going to step out for a bit."

She shook her head. "You don't have to leave. You're my husband."

"I do, I'm sorry. Got a dead body. Squires is meeting me there. It's not too far from my place, so I can grab a change of clothes."

She opened her mouth to protest, but he added, "It will just be for an hour or so. I'll be back soon."

He kissed her on the forehead and added, "Unless of course, you want to move into my place." His expression grew more serious. "You need to talk privately with your family. I'm sure they have questions."

He hesitated on his way to the door. "I need to call a taxi. I'll just wait outside."

Caren McKenzie shook her head. "Brett can drop you wherever you need to go."

At first, it seemed that Brett was going to protest, but after seeing the look on his mother's face, he nodded. "Sure, no problem." Caren handed him the keys, and he opened the door for Gates and followed him out.

The door had barely closed behind Gates and Brett when Caren asked, "Devon, what's going on?"

Devon tossed the apple core in the trash and answered from the kitchen. "We're married, Mom." She folded her arms across her chest in defiance. It reminded Caren of when Devon was six years old and sitting at the dinner table, refusing to eat her broccoli.

Without saying anything else, Caren made her way to the kitchen, grasped Devon's arm gently, and led her into the living room. She indicated for Devon to take a seat. "Devon, I realize you're a grown woman. But you've been through such an ordeal, honey. I just want to make sure this is right for you."

"I love him, Mom, more than I ever thought I could love anyone in my life. He completes me, he makes me whole," Devon replied, pushing back against the couch.

"Okay, I get that, but you hardly know this young man, Devon. Don't you think you're taking this kind of fast? What would be the harm in slowing things down a bit and getting to know each other?" Mrs. McKenzie argued.

"I'm an adult, Mother, and he's my husband; we know each other very well."

Jason, who had been standing idly by, took the opportunity to come into the living room and take a seat between them. "Mom, Devon, let's calm down."

He looked almost sympathetically to his mother. "Mom, I know you and Dad are concerned about Dev. These last few months have been hard on us all, not knowing what was happening to her or if she was alive or dead."

He looked at Devon as he finished the sentence. "You have no idea what it was like for the people who love you. And Devon, no one is arguing that you are an adult; we know you're capable of making your own decisions regarding your life. We must figure this out, though, and find something that we all agree on. Devon, we love you. We want what is best for you; do you doubt that?"

She shook her head. "No, of course, I don't doubt that. I can't imagine how hard it was for you all during the time I was missing." She turned to face her mother again. "But, Mom, you have to understand that I love him."

Her mother's expression softened and transitioned to a smile. "I do, Devon. I understand, and I know how difficult it is for you to share this part of yourself with us." She pulled her daughter into an embrace. "I just want you to be happy."

Devon slid her arms tentatively around her mother's neck. "I am."

****

Gates approached the yellow police tape that marked off the crime scene and flashed his badge at the young patrolman standing guard at the perimeter. He shook hands with several other officers, some patrolmen like the sentry earlier, others were detectives, sergeants, and lieutenants, all offering encouraging words about his return. Once he was close enough to see the yellow blanket-covered body in the alley, he waved to his partner, Mike Squires, and waited for Mike to make his way through the maze of officers and crime scene technicians.

"Whatcha got Mike?" Gates asked, tendering his hands in his pocket and noticing how he could make out the outline of his living room window from where he was standing. Good time to move, he thought, knowing Devon's place was in a much nicer part of town. He doubted there were ever any murders in the alleys behind her house. He corrected his thoughts, there weren't even any alleys in Devon's neighborhood.

"You should brace yourself." Mike advised, motioning for Gates to follow him for a closer inspection of the body."

Gates pulled a pair of latex gloves from his pocket and followed in Mike's footsteps, as to not contaminant the scene any more than was necessary. "Not my first rodeo, Mike."

"That's not what I mean." Mike knelt just enough to grasp the edge of the cover and pulled it away from the body enough for Gates to get a look.

"What then?" His body froze as if his eyes took in all the body from head to toe. He wanted to look away but couldn't.

"She could be McKenzie's twin," Mike paused. "There's no identification on the body. Medical Examiner's running her fingerprints."

"I know this woman." Gates forced the thick saliva down his throat and looked around to see who might be near enough to overhear. "She works for an escort service."

"How well do you know her?" Squires shifted his weight from one foot to another.

"Very well, every night these last few weeks," Gates answered abruptly. "Cause of death?"

"Gunshot to the head, execution-style," Squires answered, dropping the cover back over the body.

"Sexual assault?" Gates asked sadly, remembering her alive and healthy less than 36 hours ago.

"Initially, I thought yes, but now that I know what she did for a living, it will have to be determined at autopsy." Mike pulled out a small black notebook. "When did you see her last?"

"Night before last." Gates answered awkwardly. It felt odd to be on the other side of the interrogation. It wasn't a pleasant feeling, he hoped it was his first and last crime scene questioning.

"Not last night?" Mike waited for Gates to answer.

"No, I was with Devon all night. She started remembering what happened and was upset, her Mom called. I went to her."

"Were you supposed to meet up with her last night? He pointed to the woman's body.

"Yes, but Devon needed me." Gates answered defensively, as if he were a child and was explaining how the lamp had gotten broken.

"Did you cancel your appointment with her?" Mike hand-combed his hair from one side to the other and patted it into place to cover his bald spot.

"No, when Mrs. McKenzie called about Devon, I dropped everything. I'd already paid the service for the week so---" Gates paused. "You didn't find a small blue handbag? Every time I've seen her, she's had the purse."

"You're thinking of robbery?" Squires asked, rubbing his chin awkwardly.

"Possibly."

"Well, it's not here. Maybe it was left at wherever she was killed, obviously, this was just the dumpsite."

"Yeah," Gates added. "This isn't where she was murdered. It's too orderly, no blood at all."

"Give me the number you call so I can get started on her identity."

"I'm going to run by my place and change clothes." Gates searched through his phone's contact list and turned the phone around so Mike could write the number down. "I'll catch up with you at the station".

Mike nodded and turned his attention to the crime scene.

Chapter Fifteen

Gates walked thoughtfully up the stairs, his pace on the steps slow, methodical, almost as if he were healing a wound. His thoughts were a triad of emotions, happiness for Devon's recovery, sadness as a result of the young woman's death, and guilt that he may have inadvertently played some role in her demise.

He made his way down the hallway to his apartment, tossing his keys from one hand to the other as he tallied how much time he'd give the McKenzie's to discuss Devon's awakening and by default, her recollections of the time they'd been in Hamilton.

Damn, he thought once he'd pushed the key in the lock, it was stuck again, He couldn't get the key to turn the lock and open the door. He tapped the bottom of the door with his foot and jiggled the key inside the lock.

Just as the key slid deeper into the lock and the key turned, the door to the apartment at the end of the hallway cracked open, just enough for whoever was inside to see who was at Gates's door.

"I was hoping you'd get home soon," the old lady said, as she slid through the slit in the door and approached him.

She walked slowly, her pink, fuzzy house shoes, slid against the wood floor and made a scratching noise as she moved closer. Her dress was at least a size too big and as a result, the material of the dress swayed flaglike, as she moved her arms from side to side on her journey from her apartment to his.

"Is something wrong, Ms. Fran?" He exhaled a breath, anxious to get his belongings and return to Devon. Every minute he was away from her was agonizing. He hoped whatever his neighbor needed wasn't going to take up much time.

"No, I found this in the hallway, outside your door." She pulled a small blue handbag from a wrinkled grocery bag. "Your friend must have dropped it on her way out yesterday? "

"What friend?" Gates took the handbag from her, knowing it should have been treated as evidence using the grocery bag as a glove, so that he didn't touch the handbag.

"That pretty girl that comes by almost every night."

"She was here last night?" Gates asked, already knowing the answer.

"Yes," the old lady nodded. "She went inside around the same time as most nights." She looked away from him and her face flushed blood red. "I didn't see or hear her come out, but I did find her purse in the hallway last night when I went across the hall to check on Lenora."

"Thank you, Ms. Fran." He took her by the elbow and walked her back to her apartment door. "Let's get you back inside?"

He stood in the hallway and watched until she was safely inside, and he heard the door latch before returning to his own apartment. Whereas, his triad of emotion had been sort of evenly split before he'd spoken to Ms. Fran, at the present time, he was drowning in guilt. There was no avoiding it, he was responsible just as surely as if he'd pulled the trigger himself.

****

The police station was bustling with activity, detectives sitting in the bullpen and collars in the "box."

The smell of take-out food and coffee was strong in the squad room as was the odor of cheap cologne permeating from a group of hookers who were being processed by several of the detectives.

Mike collected several empty coffee cups from Gates desk and tossed them in the trash between their desks. "You think Esteban snatched her at your place?"

"Yes, I do. I wasn't there maybe she went in to make sure I wasn't in the bedroom. Maybe he took her at the front door?"

"He realizes it's not Devon, kills her, dumps the body. The ME has concluded she was sexually assaulted before she was killed."

Gates pushed himself closer against the desk and dialed the phone before the chair's wheels had come to a stop.

"Who are you calling?" Mike asked, from the desk across from Gates.

"I'm adding an officer to Devon's detail. And I'm hoping she's still ok with me moving in. Tonight!"

"Her brother already has an officer on her, day and night," Mike reminded him, as he tapped on the computer keyboard and verified it on the screen.

"Well," Gates advised. "Now she's going to have two officers."

****

Gates shifted his weight from one foot to the other and took the opportunity to scan the office again. It was larger than it looked from the hallway and furnished more expensively than was evident through the smoked glass of the office door. He felt her hand on his right thigh; it was to still his fidgeting more than anything else. Devon leaned in closer to him, so that their hands were almost touching on the arms of the leather chairs they were sitting in. The desk across from them was empty, except for several manila folders stacked neatly in rows of three.

She ran her hand over his clean-shaven cheek, the skin still pink from where shaved his beard. "I like this much better."

He nodded and moved uncomfortably in the leather chair, noticing how it whined and moaned under his weight. He thought of the Ennis' metal bedsprings and the noise it made every time they put weight on it. The memory was bittersweet.

"You having second thoughts?" she asked, looking behind them as if she were expecting someone else to join them.

She was dressed more casually than he would have expected. Her jeans were worn, comfortable and she'd pulled a pale blue V neck sweater over a white knit shirt. She'd worn her boots today; the black ones that made her look a bit taller and with her hair pinned up in the back with a large clip, she looked a tad older, as well. Once they'd entered the office, she tossed her black leather jacket on a coat stand just by the door. If he'd hadn't known better, he'd thought she was on a stakeout instead of waiting in the office of the justice of the peace.

"No," he whispered, as if he were in the principal's office. "Just anxious to get on with this." He ran his hand over his jaws, his palm slightly irritating the sensitive skin of his cheeks and chin. "What's taking so long, anyway? All we need to do is sign some papers, right? No blood test or peeing in the cup, right?"

Devon stilled his knee with her hand and kissed his lips, before she sat back into her chair. "There's no peeing in a cup or taking of blood. We're at the justice of the peace's office, not the doctor's."

He pulled at her elbows. "You sure you don't want a real wedding with music and cake?" His eyes traveled up and down her face but locked on her lips as he finished the question.

"I had a real wedding, a country fall wedding. It was beautiful," she answered, watching his eyes closely.

He smiled and kissed her neck, pulling his kisses up to her lips. "Of course, two weddings equates to two wedding nights, right?"

Before she could answer, the office door flung open and an older man with long, thick graying hair hurried inside. He tossed a bundle of folders on the desk and slid his arms out of the long robe he was wearing.

"Detective Gates, Agent McKenzie, sorry to keep you waiting; my case ran later than we scheduled. I'm Jim Marshall, circuit court judge." He glanced at his watch before throwing himself in the chair behind the desk.

The Judge selected the top folder from those stacked on his desk and flipped through several pages. "I think I have all the information I need to marry you officially." He looked at Devon. "Your father was very helpful in getting everything together for today. He's facilitated everything very nicely."

Devon smiled and looked at Chris. "That's my dad."

"Let's get on with it, shall we?" Marshall said, almost playfully.

Within a few minutes, Devon and Chris were reciting vows and exchanging marital kisses once again.

****

"Everything looks wonderful, Laura," Caren McKenzie noted, as she looked around the banquet hall they'd reserved earlier that week.

The room itself was large, but it had been cordoned off to allow for dancing and several long tables of food. Just to the right of the dance floor, were several dozen small tables with lace cloths and a small vase of yellow fall flowers. Banners with good wishes on them such as Good Luck and Congratulations draped from the ceiling. There were yellow and blue balloons and other decorations placed around the room. Toward the front of the room, stood a smaller table with a pale blue tablecloth that contained a white wedding cake, fours layers tall, with blue and yellow flowers adorning each layer and figures of the bride and groom at the top of the final layer.

"Thanks and thank your husband for pulling some strings at city hall. I know how much this means to the kids." She paused and pulled her into a private corner of the reception area. "Can I show you something?

Laura led Caren by the arm to an area in the hallway where the lighting was slightly better. "I Know Chris shared all the details of what happened while they were missing. There's only a handful of people who know about Devon's rape and ultimately their marriage."

"I appreciate his honesty and how respectful he is of Devon's privacy. She wouldn't want her brothers or fellow officers to know what happened in that cell," Caren answered, as she checked behind them to ensure their conversation was still private.

"I have this friend who works closely with various record keeping state agencies," Laura explained. "He sorts through large amounts of data daily. On a whim, I asked him to search for any marriage documents for Chris Gates and Devon McKenzie."

"You can't possibly be subscribing to their time travel story. Obviously, they were drugged or something," Caren paused to catch her breath. "What did your friend find?"

"Nothing for Gates and McKenzie—" Laura began.

"I'm not surprised." Caren smiled with a tinge of arrogance.

"But there was a notation in the Hamilton county clerk's register for Chris and Devon Gates to validate a marriage ceremony that took place in 1869." Laura unfolded a copy of an old worn document and handed it to Caren and watched as Caren's smile faded.

"You're saying, you believe their story about traveling back in time?"

"Let's just say I'm disbelieving it less." Laura nudged Caren's arm, retrieved the document, and tucked it back into her bag.

"Thank you again, Caren and Ashton, too," Laura answered, letting her hand rest on Caren's arm. "I know this will be a night the kids will remember for the rest of their life."

Before she could answer, Ashton McKenzie almost danced up to them. "It was no trouble, I assure you." He looked lovingly into his wife's eyes and added, "I love my daughter very much. I just want her to be happy."

The attention of both couples was drawn to the front door, as several of the siblings and their spouses entered the hall. They watched from the background as the tables around the dance floor quickly filled up with family and friends. The party had been going for about an hour, when the front door opened again to allow Gates and McKenzie to enter.

Gates was still dressed as he'd been in the Judge's chambers: dark dress pants, a blue long-sleeved shirt, and a dark tie without a jacket. Devon, however, had changed into a casual royal blue dress. Its sleeves hung tight just below her elbow, and the form-fitting skirt fell just about the knee. It buttoned in the back and had a scoop neck that showed the top swell of her breasts. It was the perfect dress both in form and color, because it emphasized her slender waist and well-toned arms and legs, yet it left most of her breasts and hips to the imagination.

Devon's hair was hanging loose around her shoulders, and it was slightly more curly than usual. Her makeup was conservative, but more obvious than normal.

Gates guided her through the crowd, his hand at the small of her back, until they came to a table near the front covered in blue and yellow decorations. He indicated for her to take a seat by pulling the chair out for her. Her buttocks had just barely touched the seat of the chair, when she jumped to her feet in response to the song that started. The room was suddenly enveloped in a low rush of cheers as 'Locomotion' began to whine from the band.

The chairs were emptied as everyone made their way to the dance floor and began moving in rhythm to the beat. Devon pulled Gates by the arm and led him near the center of the room. Within minutes, they were almost obstructed from view by couples dancing all about them.

The next song that bellowed from the band was a classic; the salty, sultry vocals of Lou Gramm from Foreigner belting out "Waiting for a Girl Like You" made all the couples wrap their arms around each other and sway with the music.

"They look like they were made for each other," Detective Squires mentioned casually to his captain.

Captain Goff nodded and handed his wife a drink. "Yes, he certainly looks happy. Although, I must admit that things will most likely be a bit boring with him no longer chasing every skirt in or near the precinct."

Squires nodded and kept his gaze in their direction. "He's a lucky man."

The band switched gears and played a slow haunting melody about Main Street. The lights flickered in different colors, transitioning from dim to bright, so that the dancers' shadows were silhouetted against the wall. Squires wasn't sure when Agent Brad Michaels made his way to his side. It seemed as if he appeared from nowhere.

Squires offered his hand as soon as he recognized Michaels. Truth be told, they hadn't spoken since they'd lost the transport detail. He and Michaels had spent days searching the area for any signs of Gates and Devon. They combed acre after acre, mile after mile only to find no sign of them or the vehicle. It was almost as if they'd just vanished into thin air.

"Squires," Michaels acknowledged, "nice to see you again." He motioned toward Devon and Gates swaying tenderly in each other's arms to the romantic ballad by Bob Seger. "Can you believe this?"

Detective Squires glanced toward the dance floor and shrugged his shoulders. "Guess we should have seen it coming." He slid his arm around his wife as she made her way next to him and handed him a bottle of beer. Michaels took another sip of liquor from his glass and shook his head, almost whispering as he watched them dancing, "He is so out of her league. I can't believe he's the one she gave it up for."

Squires gave him a curious look. "You're drunk, Agent Michaels; watch your mouth." He looked around. "Where's your wife?"

Michaels answered after swallowing another drink. "She left a few months before we lost the detail. The divorce was final last week." He finished the drink and set the glass on the nearest table. "Anyone need a refill?" he asked, turning away from Squires and making his way toward the bar.

Squires pulled out of his wife's embrace and caught Michaels by the upper arm, steering him to a chair. "I think you've had enough, friend. Let me give you a ride home, huh?"

Michaels opened his mouth for a rebuttal but decided against it and nodded. "I'd appreciate that."

Agent Michaels was escorted out of the reception, with Squires holding up one side and Captain Goff holding up the other.

As they neared the exit, Devon saw them from the dance floor. She tried to step out of Gates's embrace, but he held on and indicated the door. "Mike and Captain Goff seem to have everything under control. If you run over there and make a big deal, you'll just embarrass him."

She hesitated, but then she let Gates pull her closer to him, and she fell back into pace with the music. Song after song, dance after dance, they remained on the dance floor engaging with various other dancers, but never drifting very far from each other.

About halfway through the evening, Gates removed his jacket and tie, tossing both over the chair at the table designated as theirs. It may have been nearly winter outside, but the banquet hall itself was warm, the air so hot, it was thick and almost damp. He motioned toward the hallway, where an exit sign posted at the end indicated a door might be found. "Want to step outside and get some air?"

Devon nodded and took his arm, following closely behind him, not stopping to look back. Once they got to the door, he opened it and pulled her through to the outside, stopping only long enough to prop the door open about eight inches with a small, slender, metal rod.

He fidgeted nervously in his pants pocket as if he'd lost something. His facial expression grew calmer when he realized that whatever he'd been fishing for was now residing within his palm. "Devon," he began, somewhat nervously, "I can't find the words to tell you what you mean to me."

"Chris?" she interrupted. "What's this about?"

"I didn't realize until I found you back in Hamilton, how lonely I was," he answered. "I mean, I was with people all the time, but at the same time, I was alone."

He glanced quickly to the open door acknowledging the soft, yet rhythmic beat of George McGray's "Rock Your baby" as it echoed loudly from the dance hall and vibrated against the walls of the alley.

He opened his hand to her to reveal a large diamond engagement ring. "I know we did this backward, but I don't want you to feel as if you've missed out on anything." He pushed it gently on her hand. "Thank you for marrying me, again."

Devon smiled and practically fell into his embrace, pulling at his lips with her own and pushing so tightly into him, that he could feel her heart beating all the way down to his feet. Devon undid the top three buttons of his dress shirt and kissed his chest almost directly atop his left nipple and rubbed her hands up and down the length of his ribs and abdomen.

Gates had admired the fullness of her body all night through the confines of her dress. He ran his hand up and down her back and around to the curve of her ass, taking a moment to clutch both her cheeks and push her against him as hard as he could.

As much as he liked the dress, he knew there was no way he would be able to get his hands up any part of it; it was just too tight on her. Gates pushed the skirt as high up her thighs as he was comfortable with, sensitive to the fact that they were in the back of an alley and anyone could pass by, it would be hard not to notice her skirt up around her waist.

Instead, he pulled her as flush against him as he could and, with one hand, managed to slide her underwear down her legs and off, holding them, triumphantly, out for her to see. If he noticed they were smaller than those she normally wore, he didn't acknowledge it. Instead, he folded them into a tiny wad and slid them in his pants pocket.

He felt her unzip his pants and reach her hand inside, until she met the warm soft skin of his penis, already erect and pushing its way through his zipper. Gates pushed her up against the wall and slid almost snakelike up the length of body her on his knees, until his mouth stopped between her legs, his tongue dipping in and out of her folds hungrily, while his finger

manipulated the moistness he encountered around her opening.

His lips latched on again, struggling to stay attached amidst the grinding of her hips against his mouth. He'd just pushed his tongue as hard as he could against her core, when he felt her spasm against it, pulsating against his tongue until it tickled.

If she'd been looking down at him, she'd probably have threatened him again. His smug look of satisfaction was evident; he couldn't recall her ever coming so quickly before.

Urgently, he practically clawed his way back up her body to collect her lips within his own. His hands pawed at her breasts, until they fell out and over the bodice of her dress, stretching the material across her rib cage. He felt her hands, warm and soft, pulling his penis toward her opening, coaxing it into her entrance.

Gates had just pushed himself flush into her when they heard a familiar voice at the other side of the doorway. "Devon? You out here?"

Instantly, they separated and pulled desperately at their clothes, putting them back in order. Devon pulled her dress down over her hips and yanked the bodice up over her breasts, pausing just long enough to run her hand through her hair, before coming face to face with her brother, Jason, and his wife, Melissa.

Her brother stuck his face through the door opening, first allowing his eyes to adjust to the darkness. "Dev?"

"We're over here," she answered, hoping he didn't notice how peculiar her voice sounded.

Jason appeared through the door holding tightly to Melissa's hand. "Everything alright?" If either of them noticed how oddly Gates stood, making sure to keep Devon between himself and their visitors, they said nothing.

Devon nodded and leaned her head back against Gates's chest. "Just needed a little air. I think we've had a bit too much to drink."

Jason edged closer to her, trying to ascertain that everything was as she was saying. "Well, you've both earned a little overindulgence, right?" He pulled Melissa closer against him. "I mean, you only get married once, right?"

Devon and Gates glanced at each other smiling and nodding, but not moving. Melissa pulled at Jason's arm. "Jay, I think they want to be alone. Let's go back inside."

"Don't be ridiculous," Devon corrected, and pulled at Gates's arm, "We're just getting a little air. We were just heading back inside, right, honey?"

Desperately, he pulled her back in front of him, most specifically his groin area and obvious, still-lingering erection. "Before you go, sweetie, I need your help with ... ah ... " Gates hesitated, struggling to come up with something that sounded believable. "My contact lens."

Melissa smiled. "Chris, I didn't know you wore contact lenses."

"Yes," he replied, shaking his head up and down as if the action might make it sound more plausible.

Jason smiled and nodded to his sister. "Okay, we'll see you back inside then?"

Devon nodded and kept her place, until her brother and Melissa were deposited back on the other side of the door. Once she was sure they were gone, she pulled away from Gates, turning quickly around to face him, she asked, "Why didn't you just let me go with them?"

Gates shook his head. "I really wasn't interested in showing your brother and his wife the "tent" I'm sporting in the groin area." He patted his jacket pocket. "And I've still got your underwear in my pocket."

Devon couldn't help but laugh. "I forgot how hard it can be for men to disguise these things sometimes." She motioned toward his pocket, indicating with her open hand for him to hand the underwear back to her.

"Ha, Ha," he mocked. "Very funny." Gates made as if to hand them to her, then jerked them out of her reach. "We could work out a trade?"

She pointed to the dumpster just behind them. "Just go over there and take care of that, quickly."

He shook his head and tossed her the small bundle from his pocket. "It'll be quicker if you help out."

"Chris, you really want me to do this here, now?" she asked, stepping quickly back into the small, blue knit underwear.

He shook his head that he didn't and walked uncomfortably behind the dumpster. "I thought once a guy got married, he didn't have to resort to this anymore?"

She smiled and went quickly back inside, hoping to avoid Jason and Melissa for now.

Chapter Sixteen

Devon spotted them standing over by the bar, leaning close into each other; Melissa's back to her as she whispered tenderly into Jason's ear. He was listening intently to his wife, his gaze intermittently going back and forth from Melissa to the other occupants of the ballroom. Jason nodded, his fingers moving up and down Melissa's arm, as if he were examining a treasure map and was measuring the distance with his fingertips.

Devon smiled to herself, feeling his contentment in her very soul. After all, they were twins; it was true what was said about twins. They could at times read each other's thoughts and feel each others emotions as if they were their own. It was a feeling that gave her much comfort.

****

Jarrod Gates sipped patiently from the glass in his hand, letting the liquid swirl around in his mouth as if he needed to savor every drop. He didn't notice his brother close against his arm until Nick pushed another drink, identical to the one he was drinking, into his peripheral vision.

Nick took a large drink from his beer bottle and indicated to the dance floor where Chris and Devon were swaying back and forth to the music, their lower bodies pressed close to one another, and his hands caressing small circles into her lower back. Nick took another sip. "Looks like little brother made out like a bandit?"

Jarrod nodded, looking anxiously behind where they were standing to pinpoint the location of his wife. "She's a beautiful woman," referring to Devon.

Nick nodded. "Yes, and I am definitely sure she's not armed tonight."

After finishing the last of the drink and dropping the glass on the nearest table, Jarrod glanced back in the direction of Devon, and asked, "How do you know that?"

Nick smiled and answered, finishing the last of the beer as he did so, "There's no possible place to conceal it in that dress."

Even if she hadn't heard the last of the conversation, Kaitlin Gates would have known what her brothers were conversing about. The expressions of guilt as she stepped almost between them relayed everything she needed to know. "What are you guys studying so hard? I mean, besides your sister in law, of course."

Jarrod wrapped his arm around his sister. "We're just admiring how lovely she is. There's no sin in that, is there?"

Kaitlin nodded and pushed herself closer between her brothers. "No, I guess not." She paused a minute and then added, "Isn't there something in the Bible about coveting thy brother's wife?"

Jarrod grabbed a glass of white wine from the server as he passed by and handed it to his sister. "Yeah, right next to the passage that reads look, but don't touch." He snaked his arm around his sister's shoulder and pulled her close against him. "Seriously, they both look happy, healthy, and healing, I hope."

Kaitlin took a sip of wine, looking over the top of the glass to her brother and Devon. "I think they're both doing better. Chris hasn't said much about it since the day I brought him home from the hospital."

Nick finished off his beer and motioned to the server that he'd like another. "Well, if tonight is any indication, I'd say she's better."

Kaitlin nudged her brother. "You're incorrigible. And you know that time and patience is really the only cure for what she's been through. He loves her, and he's going to support her in any way that she needs."

Jarrod looked curiously at her, taking in her words as he digested what she'd said. "Patience has never been Chris's greatest virtue."

Kaitlin patted his arm. "You don't give him enough credit, Jarrod. He loves her, and I don't think our little brother has ever been in love before, until Devon."

Before she could say anything else, a man about her age with blonde hair and intense blue eyes, approached her and handed her a drink.

Jarrod offered his hand to the newcomer. "Hi, Tim, good to see you again."

The man nodded and motioned for Kaitlin to join him on the dance floor. She punched her brother playfully on the arm and followed her friend to the dance floor, where they positioned themselves not too far from where Devon and Chris were still dancing near the corner, almost in the back of the room.

As the reception wound to an end, and the guests began to depart, Devon found herself and Kevin rocking gently to an older song they'd enjoyed as children. At some point, Brett made his way to the floor and pushed himself between them, so that a brother was at each arm.

The trio smiled and continued swaying together in perfect cadence to the song. However, it wasn't complete until Jason embraced his sister from behind and joined in on the dance. The four of them connected through her, each moving in perfect time with the song and each other. Caren McKenzie watched her children with tears in her eyes. "Quick, Ash, take their picture before they realize we are watching."

Obediently, Ashton McKenzie snapped the photo of his children, a moment frozen in time, and hoped they could always be this close. His mind flashed to an hour or so earlier when he nearly bumped into his new son-in-law coming out of the men's room. Christopher had smiled nervously and stepped to the side to allow Ashton access to the men's room. Instead of stepping past him, and proceeding into the men's room though, he placed his hand firmly on Gates's shoulder and motioned toward a private area to their left. "A minute, Christopher, please?"

Gates nodded and followed him to the corner of the room. The area was dimly lit and smelled like stale laundry that had stayed in the washer until almost dry, then tossed into the dryer to finish. "What can I do for you, sir?"

"Take care of my daughter, son. That's all I want from you."

Gates's initiated a smile but didn't complete it. He couldn't decide if a warning was forthcoming or something else was on his mind. "I love your daughter. I'd give my last breath to protect her, sir."

Ashton smiled nervously opening his hand out between them. "So, how is she? Truthfully, I mean."

He shifted his weight anxiously from one leg to the other. Gates considered how to answer, wanting to be truthful, yet maintaining the discretion he knew Devon would demand of him. "Good days and not so good days, sir," he answered, almost as if he were having second thoughts.

Ashton leaned in closer to Gates. "What do you mean, 'not so good days'?"

Gates thrust his hands into his pockets and pushed his weight to the tips of his toes as though balancing on a beam. "The first few weeks after she was hurt, she spent a lot of time sleeping and resting, with very little interaction." He looked awkwardly around behind him, as if he were expecting company. "It took her a long time to talk about what happened."

Gates's expression grew softer. "But once she did, she started healing and things got better. We fell into a very fulfilling life together."

By now, Kevin had joined his father and was standing supportively nearby listening as if invited into the conversation, although he was aware that he hadn't been. The two men exchanged a smile as if one could comfort the other and listened as Gates went on.

"After she was hurt," he began, "there were nights she'd wake up screaming as if she were reliving it all again. Other nights, she'd sleep without incident."

When Ashton seemed to be processing the information positively, Gates continued, "There are times she just wants me to hold her until she falls back asleep." Looking back to where she was standing with Kaitlin, talking as if they were old friends, he added, "Other times I have to get out of the bed and sleep in a chair, because she can't stand having me so near, but yet, needs me to be close by."

Ashton bit down on his lip until it was almost blue. "I'm sorry, I didn't mean to upset you. I'm just concerned, and Devon tells us so little about what's going on."

Gates shook his head, indicating that it was okay; their concern was understandable, as he added, "She has flashbacks while wide awake in the middle of the day, and panic attacks so severe, she is nearly crippled." His expression softened. "Then there are times when we are making love that she's so at ease, I can't believe everything she's been through.

"She's hardly slept much the last three nights, because her nightmares are so vivid." He paused for a second, trying to read his father-in-law's expression, to see if he was sorry he'd asked the question. "So, all in all, sir," he summarized, "she has good days and then days that I wish were better."

Ashton smiled and nodded to Kevin as if to acknowledge that the conversation was finished. He held out his hand to Chris. "Thank you for telling me the truth. I appreciate your honesty."

Ashton paused, "Have you considered taking her back to Nebraska?"

"Why?" Gates fought to keep quiet, but the words tumbled out. "I wouldn't think she'd ever want to see that place again."

"You said there were good times, too, Yes?' Ashton asked, looking into the crowd for Devon. "Maybe going back might trigger something the two of you forgot?"

"Like what, Sir?"

"To be honest, son, I'm having a hard time believing this time travel story."

Gates opened his mouth to speak, but Ashton held out his hands to quiet him. "I'm not saying anyone is lying, son. I know you believe what you're saying is true." He put his hand on Gates's shoulder. "It's just hard for the rest of us to understand."

"It happened just as we said." Gates paused before adding, "Sir,"

"Then maybe she might start to recover, start sleeping better if she could see there's no one left to hurt her."

"Maybe," Gates nodded. "I'll think about it, Sir and talk to Devon."

As he was turning to leave, Gates caught his arm. "Mr. McKenzie, sir, Devon mentioned to me that she was almost married once, but she wouldn't tell me what happened. How did he die?"

Ashton shifted his weight, weighing the pros and cons in his mind of what, if anything, the man had the right to know. He shifted his head as if hearing someone approach from behind. He looked almost relieved to find no one there. "Devon was engaged to be married a few years ago. He was killed in an accident the night before the wedding."

Gates's stomach churned. "Was he a police officer?"

"No, Paul was an artist. He died in an automobile accident."

He watched as Devon made her way toward the center of the dance floor with Kevin wrapped around her arm. "My daughter is an incredibly strong young woman. I know that, but she can only take so much, Christopher, and I think she's just about reached her threshold. I don't know all the details about what happened while you were missing, but I know enough to know that she has to be the strongest woman I've ever known." He looked at Gates. "Do whatever you need to do to keep her safe. My sons and I will support you in any way that you need. You understand?"

Gates nodded and watched the other brothers as they wrapped their arms around her in a sort of group slow dance. "Yes, Sir, I understand. You have my promise."

****

Gates poured himself into the bed, pausing only to step out of the dress pants and underwear and to toss the shirt and tie toward the big easy chair in her bedroom. He was still trying to orientate himself to her place. It had taken him several minutes this morning, before he recollected where he was. After he fell into the bed, he pulled the flowered comforter up to just over his waist and laid back against the thick white pillow.

He didn't realize that he had dozed off, until he felt the bed move under the weight of her pushing close beside him. As soon as he raised his head to validate that it was she, he was awake, some parts of him more than others. In fact, sleep was now the last thing on his mind.

Devon was wearing a thin, silky light-colored gown that hung almost to her ankles. It was tighter around the waist and had a V-neck at the bodice. But the V was deep and contained some type of support inside that made her breasts look incredibly snug. It was a perfect fit in every way.

Almost as soon as she made herself comfortable at his side, his hand was already snaking around her waist and pulling her as close to his chest as he could. He turned to his side so that he could pull her flush against him, his hand moving in small circles up and down her stomach, his teeth biting at her naked shoulder. He moved his arm around, so that his free hand was inching from her waist toward her full, plump breasts. He grazed his fingertips over the thin material at her nipples, until he could feel them hard under the material.

Gates thrust his hips against her, so that she could feel how hard he was, how much he needed her, how much he wanted her all the time. He pulled the material of the long skirt to her thighs, so that he was able to slide his right hand gently between her legs. She moved her legs to accommodate his fingers, which pushed up hungrily into her.

After he plunged several fingers deep inside, he could feel her moving her lower body against his hand, grinding herself against him. He could tell by the way her pace increased, that she was working toward her own satisfaction and he placed his hand on her breasts, to assist her in her quest.

Gates felt, rather than saw, her adjust herself fractionally almost to the point of pulling her breast from his touch. Insistently, he palmed her again, a bit more passionately than before, and so much so that she cried out. At first, he thought that she had found her release, but he realized something was making her uncomfortable.

Gates's hand retreated from her breast and made its way near to her waist. He didn't remove his hand from between her legs, but stalled his thrusts. "What's wrong?"

She smiled and took his hand at her waist and placed it back to her breast. "Just a little sore, that's all."

He palmed her breast again, but gentler, more cautiously, as if she were fragile and might break. Gates slid out from under her and pushed her back against the mattress, pulling at the bodice, so that her breasts were freed. He cupped, kissed, and licked at her nipples until she was squirming frantically under him, her hands leading his to and away from her sensitive nipple area. He'd have had to be blind not to have noticed her discomfort. "Devon," he asked, between mouthfuls of breast and nipple, "What is it?"

She pushed his head away. "I'm going to get my period soon, that's all. Don't worry."

He pulled her with him and sat up on his heels, so that she was sitting in his lap with her back flush against the chest. He kissed at her shoulders again, and pulled the gown up to about her waist, lifting her up just enough to adjust his penis, and then slid her back down into his lap.

At first, she seemed a little panicked, as if he had something else in mind, but when he eased himself into her and then pulled her almost backward atop of him, the sensation was new, but not unpleasant. He pushed himself and her upward, and then let them both fall back down. "Relax, Devon, I'm not going anywhere I haven't been before." He smiled. "Just taking the scenic route." He pumped higher, almost feeling the vibrations into her stomach where his hand was placed. "Is this okay?"

She moaned, nodded, and arched her back harder against his chest and let her head fall back against his shoulder. As soon as she had picked up the same rhythm as him, he let his hand fall back down between her legs to her folds, separating them until he found her nerve center.

He stroked her with his fingers, slow at first, but he picked up his pace until he could feel the tension building from her toes to her head.

Gates continued pumping from behind and stroking at the front until he was sure that he was going to burst. He increased the pressure and the pace of his fingers, and then added a second finger, almost as a caveat.

It was the second time in a week that he was glad their room was somewhat isolated. Gates pushed himself, so that he was nearly on his toes, and his kisses at her neck were nearly drawing blood. His fingers were desperately working her clitoris from the front, and his penis was buried so deep inside of her from behind, that he wasn't sure either of them would be able to walk in the morning.

He knew by the force of her thrusts, that she was close to her climax; he could tell that she just needed a bit more to be past the point of no return. He lifted her off his penis just enough to free his testicles, and then let her fall forcibly back onto the shaft. As soon as his penis hit her vaginal roof, she cried out and found her release. He emptied himself into her seconds later, until there was nothing left. He pulled her back against him, both panting and fighting for breath until they drifted off to sleep, exhausted and complete.

****

The flight to Nebraska was only a few hours long, and they'd managed to find a row of empty seats near the back of the airplane. The plane had maybe a hundred fifty seats, and at least half of them were empty.

Gates collected two blankets and pillows on his way to their seats. He took the window seat and slid the armrest up before she sat down in the center seat next to him. She pulled the armrest to her left up and tossed the blanket and pillows into the aisle seat. Although she was sure that no one would sit next to her on a mostly empty plane, it didn't hurt to have it appear occupied.

Devon leaned into Gates's embrace, her head pillowed atop his chest. She was asleep before the plane even took off. The last few nights had been challenging for them both. Devon had been plagued by nightmares almost continually for the better part of the last week. Gates hadn't heard her right away the first night, usually, he could sense her distress before she'd awakened.

Instead, he jolted himself to his feet just as she had propelled herself into a sitting position with arms outstretched in a defensive manner. He stayed awake most of the night, his arms wrapped protectively around her, coaxing her back to sleep. It had taken them both several hours to fall asleep.

Her flashbacks had begun earlier that day, waking nightmares prompted by the smallest thing, a wind chime, the strong fragrance of cedar, or something as insignificant as the aroma of warm bread baking in the oven at the café on the corner. By the end of the fourth day, they were both beyond tired. It was all he could do at night to lie down and pretend sleep was forthcoming.

They hadn't made love since the night after the wedding reception. Her emotions were strongly tied to her dreams, and he hadn't dared touch her in an intimate way.

Truth be told, he was just as exhausted as she was, maybe more so given how his every waking thought centered around her and her safety, her comfort, and her needs.

He glanced quickly at her in the seat next to him and felt guilty for his admission. These last few weeks without her in his life had been torture, worse than torture. He'd forgo ever sleeping again if it meant they were together and could be forever.

Gates slid his hand into hers and moved in his seat, so that she'd have better access to his shoulder to use as a pillow. He kissed her forehead as she leaned into him, her head planted gently on his shoulder, and hoped she found an hour or two of sleep during the flight.

Gates was surprised when his new father-in-law suggested he and Devon return to Nebraska, back to the town of Hamilton where Mr.

McKenzie believed he and Devon had been held against their will. It was easier for everyone to accept they'd been drugged and their story a fabricated result of the hallucination.

Upon his son's return, William Gates had deployed dozens of agents and officers to Nebraska to apprehend the persons responsible for his son's kidnapping and the man who'd shot him. One by one, the agents returned home without anyone in custody and nothing to explain where Gates and McKenzie had been held or why.

It had become less troublesome for Gates to accept everyone else's version of the events, as opposed to a debate over what had really happened to them. Once McKenzie had awakened, she faced the same skepticism and worried expressions as she recounted the events repeatedly.

It was easier for her family to accept she was recovering from the effects of being drugged and assaulted, instead of being transported back in time and attacked.

One thing they did all agree with though, is that it may be beneficial to take Devon back to Nebraska, only if to help her abate the nightmares. Gates did agree with Ashton that it might be worthwhile to return to Hamilton and determine what, if any, pieces might be linked together almost as if it were part of an unfinished puzzle. Maybe if she saw with her own eyes that it was gone, the town, the people, all of it, maybe she could put it in the past and rebuild her life, their life.

Gates looked over at her, hoping she knew how worried he was about her safety, mentally and physically. He glanced around the plane's occupants carefully, his eyes lit on two men dressed in black suits a few rows ahead of them. No doubt, the FBI detail that had been assigned to Devon.

Initially, Gates really didn't think a security detail was necessary, the creep in the bar could have been just that. But after the death of the call girl, Gates had to admit something was amiss. Someone had their sights on her, there was no denying it anymore. The only question remaining was who stalking her.

Devon was certain Gregor Esteban was responsible. After all, she'd tracked him all over the county and to other countries. Gates wasn't so sure, there was nothing to incriminate Esteban except Devon's accusation.

At the warehouse, Devon had reminded him, he shot his own associate for unbuttoning her blouse. Gates hadn't flinched remembering the moment like it was yesterday. Esteban had a score to settle, Devon had said, and the packages she received every now and then was merely a way of getting under her skin.

What packages? Gates had asked, genuinely curious and slightly jealous.

Initially, she thought the lacy lingerie was a gag gift from someone, maybe a sister-in-law determined to make Devon's wedding, a celebration never to forget. But the next gift had a less than humorous theme and much more violent undertones, that unnerved her more than she would have liked to have admitted.

Yesterday's package contained a tube of lubricant, a sexually explicit videotape whose female lead looked surprising like Devon, and furry handcuffs. "At first I thought the package was from you, until I put the tape in the player and saw what he was doing to her," she paused. "I knew you would never send me something like that, even as a joke, not after everything we've been through."

After the videotape came, Gates had collected the gifts, wrapping and all for Mike to pick up and drop off at the police lab for fingerprinting. Gates didn't feign surprise when Mike reported back the only fingerprints on the tape had been Devon's and her sister-in-law's.

Melissa had jerked the tape out of the player, before anyone else at the get-together and dropped it in the trash. "I can't believe he'd get this for you, even as a gag gift," Melissa had argued.

"He didn't," Devon had explained, her eyes on the floor, hands in her lap.

The packing had dozens of prints, mostly mail carriers, while the lingerie and lubricant had been wiped clean, the only prints pulled off them was Devon's.

"I know it's him," Devon was certain. "He's trying to get under my skin, throw me off my game," she paused. "But it's not going to work, I caught him once, I can do it again."

Gates wrapped his arms around her and held her as tight as he could, without hurting her thinking to himself. I think that's his intent.

Chapter Seventeen

A few minutes after the plane had taken off, Devon leaned into his embrace. Gates wrapped his arm around her shoulder and pulled her as close as he could, pulling the blanket up and over them at the same time. "Your dad told me about Paul," he said, barely above a whisper. She swallowed loudly; she knew at some point he'd ask. It was evident.

She settled her head against his chest with her gaze locked straight ahead. "Paul was a long time ago, and when he died, I put all those feelings away. It just hurt too much to think about him."

He stroked her hair and kissed her head as he tucked her under his chin. "It's okay." Gates held her tight against his chest, until he was sure that she had drifted off to sleep.

He looked out the window at the clouds, white and thick, with sunlight streaming through at such odd angles, it looked more like floodlights than sunlight. He pulled the blanket over them as far as he could, without exposing her feet, which were tucked into the empty aisle seat.

Gates wasn't sure what woke him up, the turbulence that tossed him from one side of his seat to the other side, or the barely audible plea he heard coming from her lips.

He wiped awkwardly at his eyes, not realizing he had drifted off to sleep, until he heard Devon's second plea, only louder and more agonizing than the first "Please," she begged, "stop!"

Gates leaned in closer, nudging her shoulder gently, yet urgently. "Devon?"

He soothed her as his eyes looked around at the other passengers anxiously.

She pushed at his arm and screamed louder, more frantically. "Get off of me!"

Devon lunged forward, almost knocking heads with him, her breathing coming in great gasps, as if she couldn't get enough air into her lungs through her nose.

She had awakened, her head bowed against his chest in embarrassment. "I'm sorry," she whispered.

He kissed her forehead and pulled her as close against him as the confined space of the row of seats would allow him. Gates wasn't surprised to see the flight attendant making her way curiously toward them. By the time she'd reached them, Gates had slid his detective shield from his jacket pocket and held it out for her to see.

The flight attendant walked by, smiling and noticing their seatbelts weren't secured. "Is she okay?" she asked, more as a formality than out of concern.

Gates nodded. "She's fine. Just exhausted." He presented his badge again, in case she hadn't seen it as she'd made her way toward them. "My wife is a US Marshal recovering from an injury."

She handed him several packets of salted peanuts and held up the coffee thermos to ask if he'd like some. He didn't and motioned for her to lean closer. "How long is the flight?"

She answered quickly. "About an hour and a half." She pointed to Devon. "Newlyweds?"

He smiled, squeezing Devon even tighter against him. "Very newly." He looked past the attendant to the two men three rows up who were on their feet and making their way into the aisle toward Devon. He smiled to himself; Devon's FBI detail stood out like a whore at church.

He pointed to the officers and said to the flight attendant, "I'd like to buy those two gentlemen a round of drinks." He handed her a twenty-dollar bill and waved off his change.

As she stepped away to serve the drinks to the FBI agents, Gates asked, "Once we land and I rent a car, how far is it to Hamilton County?'

"Hamilton County?" she questioned. "You mean, Aurora?"

"Aurora? As in the Northern Lights?"

She smiled and handed him several more packets of snacks, indicating they were for Devon when she awoke. "Yeah, I grew up about thirty miles from Aurora. No one calls it Hamilton anymore, haven't for a long time." She checked her watch then answered his initial question. "Aurora's about forty miles driving, so probably less than an hour."

She was about halfway up the aisle when he asked her, "Have you seen the lights?"

The attendant nodded as if he'd made a joke or something. "Everyone who's from around there has seen the lights."

****

The flight attendant had been correct; it was almost exactly forty miles from the airport to where the sign on the interstate read Aurora — Next Exit. Accordingly, Gates veered the gray rental car to the right and took the exit. The scenery from the airport had been mostly rural landscape, barren and chilled from the cool weather.

The huge, black tree trunk stood out in great contrast to the relatively white ground and snow-covered rooftops. Several inches of snow had already fallen and clung to the ground, which, although usual for Nebraska, was less infrequent than it had been in previous years.

Off in the distance, they had noticed several farmhouses festively anticipating the holiday season with Easter decorations on full display.

Devon ran her hand over the windshield on her side of the car, making figures in the condensation. She smiled as if she were remembering something that she hadn't thought about in many years. "It's hard to believe it's nearly Easter," she said, running her hand over the condensation again. "My brothers and I used to love being outside this time of the year, the last few days of snow fights and sledding before spring arrived."

Playing outside took up most of our days, she thought to herself, followed by warm hot chocolate and marshmallows by the fireplace.

Gates smiled and nodded. "Yeah, I remember." When he stopped the car at a stop sign, he looked to his left, and his eyes opened wide in astonishment. He could hardly get the words out, but managed to finally announce. "Devon, look; it's the big tree!"

Devon turned her attention to where he was pointing. "What tree?"

"The one we saw before we found the Ennis ranch." He paused for a second. "Remember the big snake? Heimdail called the tree Idresil. It's where Hayden and the Ferris brothers intercepted us?"

"It can't possibly be the same one. Surely someone must have cut it down by now." She shook her head doubtfully, as he pulled to the side of the road to get a better look. Right there in the middle of a relatively barren field, was the enormous tree they'd come across during their trek away from the crashed van.

Devon squinted her eyes and looked across the field. She could barely make out the skeletonized frame of an old bridge. She smiled and pointed toward the horizon. "The bridge is that way, too."

"What should we do?" His questions was genuine.

Devon pointed toward the road. "Just ahead is town; we need a hotel room for the night." She fiddled with her hands in her lap.

He noticed her discomfort and placed his hand on hers. "Honey, there's no need to be nervous." He waved his hands around, as if he was hosting a game show and all the potential prizes were on the stage with him. "Look around you. Anyone from that time is dead and gone."

"Yet, here we are," she whispered.

"Together," he added. "Here we are together."

She smiled warmly at him and nodded in agreement.

****

Laura Gates circled the row of cleverly parked cars one more time in search of a parking spot that didn't include a twelve-mile walk to the restaurant where she was meeting Caren McKenzie.

She didn't know Caren very well. Although, it seemed as if recently, they were becoming better friends. They had talked almost every other day on the phone since Devon and Christopher were discharged from the hospital. In addition, they had connected almost daily, even twice daily, while planning the wedding reception.

She checked her watch again and made one more sweep of the lot in the hopes of finding a spot closer to the restaurant. Just as she made her way to the end of the last row, a white Mercedes was inching out from the spot. Laura waited for the Mercedes to get clear, and then pulled her black BMW into the spot. Once the engine was off, she collected her purse and umbrella and slid out of the car, hoping that Caren wasn't in a hurry.

The gods must have been on Laura's side; just as she closed the door of the restaurant behind her, the winter sky opened and the rain cascaded down like a waterfall.

She nodded to the man at the counter, who acknowledged her and returned his attention to the unhappy customer on the phone. Laura mouthed the words meeting someone to him as she glided past him and into the dining room.

The room was only about half-filled with customers gathered at their tables and engaged in conversations over food and drinks. The lighting in the main room was dim, and even the flames from the small lamps in the middle of each table did little to light it. It took her several minutes to locate Caren at a small table near the back.

Caren stood when she saw Laura approaching and leaned toward her to plant an informal kiss on her cheek. Laura unbuttoned her coat and handed it to the attendant standing nearby.

"Sorry, I'm late. I must have driven around four times before I found a parking spot."

Caren pointed to the large window and indicated the rain. "Looks like you made it just in time." She collected her cloth napkin as she sat down. Once she was seated, she took the wine bottle from the center of the table and motioned for Laura to hand her the wineglass closest to her plate. "I hope you don't mind. I ordered some wine; I recalled from the reception that you like white."

Laura smiled and accepted the glass. "Thank you. And yes, I do like white." She sipped at the edge of the glass and adjusted the utensils around her plate. "So, what did you want to talk to me about?"

Caren cleared her throat and leaned in closer to Laura. "I don't know what to make of all of this."

"All of what?" Laura questioned, choosing a small piece of bread from the basket in the middle of the table.

"The kids were missing for so long, and then they reappeared as if out of nowhere with this story about traveling back to the eighteen hundred's," Caren said in a single breath.

She took another drink of wine and went on. "You're the only other person who understands how I feel about having them back." There were tears in her eyes when she looked up. "She's my baby."

Laura nodded and smiled. "Yes, I know how you feel, and I feel the same way. I can't imagine my life without my son."

Before Caren could continue, the waiter approached to take their order for lunch. He waited patiently as the women mulled over the menu, finally settling on chicken and salad. As soon as he was out of earshot, she continued. "I spoke to Christopher in the hospital, and he shared with me where they'd been and some of what they'd been through. I didn't believe what he said was possible, but I also got the sense that he believed it to be true."

"Chris would have no reason to lie to you or to make up this story," Laura challenged.

"I know," Caren answered, as if trying to explain. "Then, when Devon was better, she corroborated his story, which was just too unbelievable to be true." She finished her glass and poured another, but only about half full. "What did he tell you?"

Laura hesitated, thinking at first that it might be a trap to uncover more about the events than she knew. However, Laura Gates knew her son well enough to know that he would have told Caren McKenzie everything she needed to know to care for her daughter.

"I know that they believe they were transported back to the late eighteen hundred's and were taken in by a family who cared for them.

Lisa Colodny

During their time, Devon attracted the attention of a corrupt officer who raped her. The same officer shot my son. If not for this family that cared for them, I believe both would have died."

She paused as she allowed the waiter to place salads in front of them. "After a time of recuperation, they exchanged marital vows." She sliced thin, long pieces of lettuce into strips and forked them into her mouth. "There was some kind of chase and they ended up going over a hill and into a river."

Caren smiled, realizing the versions of the events were similar. "Remember my colleague at the Department of Records?"

"The one who uncovered the marriage notation you showed me at the reception?"

Caren nodded. "I asked him to look deeper for anything that might help us explain what really happened to them."

Laura's posture changed; Caren had her attention. "Did you find anything?" She asked, setting her fork down and her napkin on the table.

Unfolding a set of papers, Caren pushed them toward the center of the table. Laura collected the papers and pushed them toward the lamp to determine what the documents were. She looked in frustration at the papers. "I can hardly even see the paper, let alone read it. What does it say?"

Caren swallowed a bite of grilled chicken and answered. "This is another version of the legal document that authorizes the marriage of Devon and Chris Gates in Hamilton County, Nebraska." She separated the documents into two piles and smacked the second pile as if she were angry.

Laura smiled. "The time travel evidence." She sipped at the wine again. "Is there any chance your friend is playing a joke on you?"

Caren pulled the papers closer to the lamplight. "No, he wouldn't do that."

"What are those?" Laura asked, eyeing the few documents still under Caren's hand.

"These are news bulletins dated a few weeks apart."

"You mean, like wanted posters?"

Caren nodded and held them up to Laura. "Look at the dates."

"December 1869," Laura read the first one and filed it under the top one before reading the date on the second bulletin. "May 1870."

"And look at the drawings." She held up the bulletins so Laura could get a better look. "It looks just like them, even down to the tiny scar over Devon's eyebrow."

"Someone continued looking for them for the next six months," Laura answered, her words drifting off as if she had something else to discuss.

"It doesn't seem as if kidnappers would distribute posters looking for them and offering a reward for information regarding their whereabouts."

"No, it doesn't" Laura finished the last of her wine and refilled it. She picked up the bulletin again. "And this drawing is done with such detail, such tenderness, it's almost as if whoever drew the pictures was emotionally invested in them."

"Devon mentioned the young man who lived at the ranch house was always drawing the stars." Caren suggested, "Maybe he drew these?"

"Maybe," Laura nodded, her mind recollecting the story Chris had told her about the drawings by the man who had hurt Devon. She doubted Caren knew about those and there was no need to tell her anything more.

"What does all this mean?" Caren asked, her eyes tearing and watery.

"I'm not sure, but it certainly gives more credibility to their story." Laura sipped the wine again. "Don't you think?"

"Absolutely."

****

Lisa Colodny

By the time Gates and Devon were within the Aurora city limits, it was well past lunchtime. He pulled the rental car into a metered parking spot and fed the meter several dollars' worth of quarters.

Snow had just started falling again; he buttoned his coat as far against his throat as he could and made his way around to the passenger side to open her door. As usual, she was already out of the car before he could help her out. His hand touched hers as she closed the passenger door.

"Sorry," she said, but she did not really mean it.

He slid his hand to the small of her back and led her toward the hotel. "Would it kill you to stay in the car until I can get the door?"

"No, but I feel silly just sitting there. I'm perfectly capable of pulling the handle. The door actually opens by itself." Her attention was on the rows of majestic art deco buildings that lined the main street. The buildings were old, but immaculately restored and painted in pastel shades of blue, yellow, off white, and gray.

Each building was augmented by coordinated colors for shutters or gutters. The three-story hotel was the largest of the buildings; it was painted a pale yellow with red shutters and had window boxes. The double doors were painted red as well. Its thick, brick chimney hovered several feet above the roof, smoke flowed thick and black into the sky, trailing like a pathway to heaven.

She stopped just at the stairs and looked up to the hotel. "It's in the same location, but it looks really different." She leaned back to get a better look. "It's beautiful."

He took her elbow and pulled her toward the hotel, making sure he got to the door first and opened it. She went in quickly, mostly because she couldn't take the cold anymore, but partly out of curiosity.

Once they were inside, he went to the counter to check them in while she investigated the lobby. She'd gotten about halfway down the hallway when she saw an old portrait of Thomas Hayden Sr. on the wall. Below it was a memorial plaque mentioning him as a great humanitarian and resident of Hamilton County. According to the plaque, he died in 1874, five years after they left.

She jumped as he came up behind her jingling the car key, stopping when he saw the portrait. "Mr. Hayden?" he said, looking at her almost mournfully. "I asked at the desk. There's a library at the end of town named for him."

He led her toward the elevator. "Let's unpack and then see what we can find out."

Chapter Eighteen

The café was busy, but not so busy that they had to wait for a table. The young blonde woman led them to a small table and handed them a menu as they took their seats. Devon stacked several stapled pieces of paper on the table and took a seat. Before the waitress could retreat, Devon held up her hand to get her attention. "Can you just bring us two burgers and two drinks, please?"

The waitress nodded and disappeared through the dining area and into the kitchen. Almost as soon as she left, they began going through the newspapers they had collected at the library. Paragraph by paragraph they filled in the timeline starting with when they'd left Hamilton.

It reminded Gates of being back in school, college, with endless hours of research and studying. Sometimes he'd studied independently, others he's crammed with a pretty female coed or even a group. It was odd how the hours he and Devon spent reviewing one hundred plus years of newspapers, felt nothing like that.

Gates folded the document in quarters, as if it were a newspaper and laid it on the table next to his plate. "There's something in this one about Benjamin and Hannah's wedding."

Devon placed her hand on top of a stack near her side of the table. "We've read about Gabriel and Edith's death, Thomas Sr's death, the birth of Abby and James' children, Abby and James' death."

Gates held up another newspaper microfiche but didn't hand it to her. "There's brief mention in this one of Hayden Jr.'s escape from the authorities. It also speculates that he may have something to do with the disappearance of a deputy and his wife."

Devon folded her chin into her hands and leaned with her elbows against the tabletop. "Edith and Gabriel must have been devastated. Not knowing what had happened or if we'd come back." She wiped the tears from her cheek, "And Benjamin, he must have been so sad, helping his Mom put our stuff away." Devon thought of all the trunks in Mrs. Ennis' room with Mary's belongings tucked safely inside. Had Mrs. Ennis started such a trunk for her and Gates' things?

"Makes me sad to think about that especially after they lost Mary." She added.

"You ready to head out, see what's left before it gets too dark."

She nodded and watched as he collected all the documents from the table.

He collected their coats and helped her with hers, making note that she'd waited for him to help instead of just putting it on.

They walked up and down Main Street several times arm in arm, reminiscing and looking for something that resembled the town they remembered. As they finished the second lap, they came to what was left of the jailhouse. It had been preserved as part of the National Historic Preservation Act and was currently a tourist attraction.

He swallowed and held on tighter to her hand. "Looks like just the jail, hotel, and livery stable survived the past hundred twenty years pretty well."

"I don't want to go in there," she whispered.

He pulled her tighter against him. "We aren't." He kissed her cheek, "No one's going to hurt you here, Devon." He looked behind them to ensure the security detail was close by. "I promise."

"Are the FBI agents going to follow us around for an extended period of time?" She asked, her words muffled against his chest.

"How long have you known?" he asked, looking down at her.

"A day or two after I hit the guardrail." She paused. "I was angry at you, you know."

"I didn't assign that one," he relaxed his arms around her.

"I know," she answered. "Kevin did." She paused. "What about the second one?"

"That one is all me." He admitted.

"Why?" She pulled out of his embrace awaiting his response.

"There was a murder in the alley close to my house." He paused, wetting his lips and searching for the right words. "The woman who was murdered was a call girl. She'd made herself look exactly like you."

"Like me?" She took a step away from him. "Why would she do that?"

"Because I paid her to," his words were soft, apologetic.

"You paid a hooker to look like me so you could have sex with her?"

It sounded bad when she'd said the words aloud, while at the time it was happening it didn't seem like a big deal at all.

"Yes," he dropped his head. "I'm sorry."

"How long?" she asked

"Only a few weeks before you got your memory back." He pulled her into his arms. "Devon, I was so scared when you woke up and wanted nothing to do with me. You didn't remember anything about our life together except that you hated me."

He took her by the arms so that she had to look him in the eye. "I couldn't take it anymore, being without you." He paused. "I wasn't going to live without you, I'd already decided that."

"So, you decided you'd go out with a big bang, literally?"

"I'm sorry, Devon, that's all I can say. It was wrong of me to use you like that. Every day, I prayed that today would be the day you remembered, but as time went by, I was less and less certain," he paused. "Being with her was the only time I felt close to you."

"What happened to her?"

"I think she was snatched outside of my apartment after someone thought she was you. And when they realized she wasn't, they killed her."

"Was she raped?"

He nodded. "We believe so, yes."

"Oh my God," Devon's hand went to her mouth. "I'm sorry. I didn't know." She thought back to the videotape and sexy lingerie. "You think Esteban killed her?"

"I think it's a definite possibility."

"What do we do now?" She asked pulling her coat tighter around her body.

He checked his watch and took note of the sun as it made its descent from the sky. "Let's drive over to the Ennis place and see what's left."

****

It took a while for Gates to navigate the road that lead to where he thought the Ennis's ranch had been. The roads had changed many times since the 1800s. It wasn't as easy as it was when they were riding horseback on the dirt roads.

After about forty-five minutes, they began to see familiar landscapes in the distance. They parked and walked solemnly through the field until they came upon the old barn. Its frame was beaten and battered, a mere black skeleton against the white sky and clouds.

He took her hand as they went inside. It was new and old all at the same time. Its tall, dark rafters ascended like a steeple into the darkness. If she squinted her eyes, Devon could just make out a metal hook with remnants of a worn rope just partially visible.

The stalls that had once been separated into sterile and non-sterile were all but intermingled. The back ones had been removed to allow more room for tractors and other machinery. The area with cabinets and shelves where she and Mr. Ennis had doctored the animals were also gone. In its place were rows and rows of bins filled with seeds, bolts, and blades.

Gates smiled to her as if an idea had come to him and pulled her away from the stalls.

"What are you doing?" Devon asked, following him back to the barn's entrance.

"I want to see if the treasure box is still here."

Quickly, he led her to the back of the barn to where a desecrated bin was placed. He pushed it aside and pulled the bottom piece of the wood away removing a worn wooden box.

The box itself has rotted to such extent, the dried-up pieces crumbled in Gates's hand and slipped through his hand onto the dirt floor of the barn.

He motioned for Devon to open her hands and transferred the decaying box and contents to her. "What's in there?" He asked once she closed her hands over the contents.

"Pressed flowers, rocks, an old piece of train track." She answered as if she were cataloging the contents for a crime scene. She paused, her mouth dry and her eyes watery.

"Your watch and my lipstick are in here."

Gates ran his fingertips over the rusted face of the watch. "Benny must have put them in there after we left?"

"I'm taking it with us." She pushed what was left of the box and its contents into the deep pockets of her winter coat.

They walked quietly hand in hand toward the main house, which was in fairly good shape considering it was over a hundred years old and uninhabited. The door was open and hanging at an uneven angle to the frame. The pane of glass in the front window was broken. The steps leading to the porch were no longer there, and access to one side of the porch was easier since the porch itself had sagged unevenly over the years.

Devon put her foot forward to step onto the porch, but Gates took her shoulder and held her in place. "I don't think it's safe, Devon."

He stepped back and looked up to the second floor. It was easy to see how the second floor had sunk over the years. No doubt the foundation had shifted. "Whole house might come down on us."

"I really wanted to go inside." She said.

"Me too," he led her around to the back close to the hand pump and peered through the door into the kitchen. What little they could see looked as they recalled except for the modern appliances." He pointed toward the kitchen sink. "Indoor plumbing."

She spun around to investigate the space between the houses, a worn path that led to an empty place where the outhouse had previously stood. "Yes, the outhouse is gone."

He walked away from the main house to the little house he and Devon had shared, a home of their own, Mrs. Ennis had called it. The guest house was still standing, but barely; its walls were pushing against themselves like playing cards, each holding the other in place.

Like the main house, the porch and floors sat on the ground unevenly, a sure sign the foundation was compromised. "I guess we can't go in here either?"

Gates shook his head. "I don't think so, honey."

Between the two buildings was the old hand pump. At some point, someone had built a stone wall around it. Other than that, it looked just the same. They walked past the house toward the river until they came to the old tree that had sheltered Edith every morning as she paid respects to Mary, her daughter's, grave.

The area was severely overgrown with hibernating bushes and thick, black trees that stood as if at attention. Since it was winter, acquiring passage was easier than it would have been in the summer when everything would have been green and alive.

After a few minutes of kicking at dead vegetation with their boots, they came to Mary's tombstone. It was just as Devon recollected, only older with the addition of Gabriel and Edith's stones. Looking at the dates, they could ascertain that Gabriel had died the next fall in 1870, and Edith much later in 1879.

Devon smiled as she ran her hand over their names, wiping at the tears that were falling from her eyes. She tapped at the name on Edith's stone: Edith Ennis-Hayden. This should have been a surprise, but after reading the papers during lunch, they already knew that after Gabriel's death, Edith and Thomas Sr. were married. Gates had mentioned that he didn't find that unusual knowing that it had been Thomas Sr.'s nature to take care of people, especially the Ennis'.

She looked curiously around, kicking at the tall dead weeds as if she'd lost something.

"What's wrong?"

"I wonder where Benjamin and Hannah are buried?"

"We can ask in town," Gates offered, pointing her back to the rental car.

By the time they had made their way back to the car, it was close to dinnertime. Since they had eaten a late lunch, neither really felt like eating. As he was backing the car out onto the road, Gates suggested, "Let's see what is left of the Hayden House."

She smiled and nodded, anxious to see how well it had survived the years. It was odd how quickly they made the trip to the Hayden place. Gabriel had been right; it really was just over the ridge. The sun was just setting as they made their way onto the property. It shone like a halo against the metal roof and radiated down the sides of the house so that its white-painted sides looked blood red.

The house had been maintained well, very well; it looked better than it had when they'd enjoyed breakfast there. It had been renovated with electricity, and its landscape was manicured perfectly. When they got out of the car, a park ranger came over to them and explained that the park closed early in the winter.

She was an older woman, shorter than most, with lighter hair that was more gray than blonde. She had a round face with light eyes and a pale complexion. She wasn't an overly large person, but because she was shorter, her weight was distributed in such a way that made her look fatter than she probably was. The tan pants had a black stripe down the sides of each leg. Her belt was secured tightly, so tightly that her stomach muffin-topped over her waistband. Her black coat was short and heavy, and made her look more like a police officer than a park ranger.

Noticing the disappointment on their faces when she told them the park was closing soon, she slid her clipboard under her arm and whispered to them, "If you're already in the house, I have to wait for you to finish the tour." She smiled as she finished her sentence.

Taking the hint, they ran toward the front steps while she made her way around to the back of the house to finish her rounds. Gates couldn't help but hold his breath, as he entered the room.

He'd only been in the house that once for breakfast, but it was even more extravagant than he remembered. Heavy chandeliers hung from every ceiling of every room, and thick dark mahogany stairs and rails led to the second floor. The same dark wood-lined the walls of the library and complimented the wooden desks and tables on the first floor. The room looked like something out of Gone with the Wind, only the curtains weren't green. They were a deep, rich red, and they hung from the ceiling to the floor, pooling almost puddle-like against the floor.

The kitchen looked exactly as it did when they had breakfast in it that morning other than a few upgrades and renovations. In fact, most of the house seemed physically like how they remembered it. After a few minutes of exploring the first few rooms, they were heading into the living room when the front door opened and the park ranger stuck her head inside. "You kids about done?"

Devon nodded and went over to the front door. "This has been kept incredibly well. It's beautiful; almost exactly as it was."

The ranger looked curiously at Devon as if to question what she'd said when Gates interjected. "She means what she imagines it probably looked like in the eighteen hundreds." He pulled Devon close against him and leaned in to read the attendant's name badge.

"Agnes," he read her badge and flashed her a handsome smile. "My wife's a bit of a history buff."

She smiled. "Really?" She stepped more fully into the house. "Well, this place is full of history."

Gates unzipped his jacket. "What can you tell us about the house?"

She set the clipboard on a nearby table. "Samuel Hayden built this house in the mid-1700s. He and his wife Rebecca had two sons. The oldest son, Lionel, died in his teens from smallpox, and Rebecca soon after. Samuel died in 1835, leaving everything to his son, Thomas, whose wife Sara died very young, several years after giving birth to a son, Thomas Junior."

She cleared her throat as if she were reciting something she'd memorized. "Thomas Senior was a beloved man to Hamilton County. His monetary support provided for everything that the county needed, from schoolbooks to mattresses for the jail. He was a great humanitarian." She cleared her throat and took a deep breath. "Thomas Jr., however, was a completely different story."

Gates jumped in. "Thank you, Agnes, but we don't want to hold you too late." He took Devon's arm and steered her toward the door.

Agnes shook her head. "Ain't no trouble; most folks either know the stories or don't care to know them."

"We're familiar with the gist of the story, and we need to head back to the hotel." Gates explained hoping to protect Devon from hundred-year-old gossip.

Devon jumped in. "It's okay; I want to hear the rest of the story."

Agnes smiled, pumping her chest out as if she were standing at attention. "Thomas briefly served as the town's deputy, but there were scandals almost from the beginning."

"Scandals?" Devon asked a bit uncomfortably, and she moved closer to Gates.

"Yes," the ranger said. "Junior drank too much and had a reputation with the women." She paused for a minute. "There are at least two references in court records where he forced himself upon a woman, and several cases where women came forward claiming that he had fathered their children."

"When did he die?" Devon almost whispered.

"Not sure," Agnes answered. "He was arrested in the autumn of 1869, but never appeared to face the charges. There's no mention of him after that. It is assumed he died elsewhere and was buried as an unknown."

She smiled and opened the front door for them. "Thomas Senior remarried in 1871. He married the widow of his best friend. He died in 1874 and left everything to his second wife Edith and stepson Benjamin. Thomas Senior put in his will that upon his death, he was to be buried with his first wife, Sarah, and Edith would be buried with her first husband, Gabriel."

"What about Benjamin and Hannah?" Devon asked, her voice soft.

Agnes smiled, thinking to herself that this young woman really was a history buff. "Benjamin and Hannah lived in the house after his mother's death. They had four children, all sons. Benjamin built the first college here in Hamilton, and he was the source of hundreds of scholarships for women. He also built a conservatory up north in Denver. He was fascinated by all his life with astronomy. He added the observation deck to the roof of the house after the birth of his first son." She glanced anxiously at her watch. "Sorry, folks, but I've got to close up now. I'm on again tomorrow if you want to come back."

Gates smiled and thanked her. "We're on a plane tomorrow morning to New York, but thank you for your patience." He held his hand out to Devon and waited for her near the front door.

Devon took her time, taking in the richness of the stairsteps, the charm of the piano and furniture. She was most taken by the old pictures that lined the wall along the stairs to the second floor. She took her time, studying one and then the other. Some people she recognized, others she didn't. There were singles of Hayden Jr and Sr. Others were group pictures of the Callahans, Haydens, and Ennis.'

"Honey?" Gates asked looking apologetically to Agnes. "She needs to close up."

"Let her look," Agnes commanded, moving the clipboard between her waist and arm.

"There are some really wonderful pictures, here." Devon touched the wooden frame of a family photo of the Ennis.' "I wish I had some copies of some of these."

Agnes handed her a pin and a piece of paper. "Write down which ones you want and leave me your address. I'll see that you get a copy."

"Thank you," Gates handed her his card with name and address on the back.

"I've seen this one before," Devon pointed to one of Benjamin and Gabriel. "It must have been when we were here that morning."

Agnes looked at Gates, her face flushed with concern. "What does she mean when you were here before?"

"We visited the park briefly, a few years ago," Gates explained, walking the short distance to the steps where Devon was still studying the photos.

He climbed the steps to join her. "Honey," he whispered. "This picture was taken after we left." He took her arm. "There's no way you could have seen it before."

Gates led her down the stairs and handed the piece of paper back to Agnes. "I'd be happy to pay you for the pictures." He reached for his wallet. "I can leave you whatever you think it will cost."

"No," Agnes shook her head. "We have a copier in the back, won't cost but the time to take it off the wall and out of the frame. No problem at all."

"I know I've seen that picture before Gates." Devon folded her arms over her chest defiantly.

"It's time-stamped after we left, honey," he whispered, taking Devon's hand and leading her out of the house and down the snow-covered steps to their car.

"I know," she shook her head, "But I know I've seen it before."

"Maybe it was in one of the old newspapers?"

"Maybe," she smiled, and followed him down the steps and into the rental car.

Chapter Nineteen

Gates poured her another glass of wine and looked around for Devon's FBI detail. He'd seen them several times in the rearview mirror after they'd left the Hayden house, but hadn't seen them since. Where were they now; had the bosses given her rookies?

He chewed thoughtfully on his steak and tapped his Glock holstered under his arm, before pushing her wineglass close to her plate.

She sipped from the water glass, looking at him over the rim. "Detective Gates, you wouldn't be trying to get me drunk, would you?"

He smiled and toasted his wineglass to her. "Is that an option?" He scanned her face for any sign of discomfort. It had to be hard for her to hear what had become of everyone. It was, he thought, as if time had stopped for them when they hit the water of that icy river. "You sorry we came?"

She smiled. "No. As happy as I am that Benjamin had a good life, it still makes me sad to think of Edith and Mr. Ennis, and Mr. Hayden." She sipped her wine as if she were the baby bear tasting hot porridge. "Let's finish dinner and take the rest of the wine upstairs to the room." She thought for a minute then added, "We'll make a nice toast to them, and then I'll make love to you, slow and sweet."

He spat out a thin stream of wine and reached quickly for his wallet, alerting the waitress he was ready for the check. He didn't see the bulky figure approach them, until the giant man was already at their table.

The next thing he knew, the man was being forced to the ground by Devon's FBI detail, and he had thrown himself across the table to cover her. Her chair fell backward with the weight of them both in the chair. Gates had his gun drawn, as did the other FBI agents, but Devon didn't have a chance to break her fall, and the concrete floor collided with the back of her head, and everything went black.

****

"Devon?" she heard his voice, faint and far away. "Devon?" he called her again, louder and more impatient. Her first thought was that she was cold, maybe even wet. Her second thought was that the floor was soft. As the blackness gave way to the fog, she realized that she was in the bed of the hotel room.

The front of her shirt was wet, and from the smell of it, it was soaked with wine. It felt like someone was using the back of her head as a door. She tried to sit up, but stopped when the wave of nausea hit her. "What happened?" she asked, pulling herself up to lean on her side.

She could hear voices coming from the other side of the door; it was Gates and someone she didn't recognize. "Chris?" she called out into the other room. She heard the talking cease, and then the sound of footsteps making their way toward her. He cracked the door open and peeked in. "You're safe; just a misunderstanding."

She pulled herself into a sitting position. "Who hit me?"

He bit his lip. "I did. When I leaped across the table, I took you to the floor, and you hit your head."

"Who's with you out there?" she asked, pulling at the blankets to get to her feet.

"His name is Dale Hyman. He works for the US Border Patrol, stationed just north of Denver, Colorado." Gates walked into the room. "If you feel up to it, come on out and listen to his story. It's amazing."

Gates waited for Devon to get to her feet before following her into the living area of the hotel room. He took a seat on the couch next to her. "Mr. Hyman, my wife, Devon."

Dale Hyman was huge, a mountain wearing a shirt, like Lou Ferrigno, but taller and without the green complexion. He had dark hair styled in a buzz cut. In addition to the blue denim shirt, he wore navy blue pants that had a tan stripe down each leg.

He stood up as soon as he saw Devon approaching them. The smile that crossed his face gave Devon the feeling that he was an old friend that she hadn't seen in a long time.

"Mrs. Gates," he said, smiling in a way that made him seem enamored with her. "I have waited for many years to meet you."

She took a seat and smiled. I must have really hit my head hard, she mused, because I have no recollection of this man. "Have we met before, Mr. Hyman?" she asked.

"No," he replied. "But my father's told me to expect you."

"Fathers?" she asked, not understanding.

He nodded. "Yes, my fathers in the lights."

Devon looked curiously at Gates. "I don't understand."

Gates shifted closer to her. "Mr. Hyman's descendants are Native Americans. Heimdail was his grandfather's grandfather."

"Heimdail is your ancestor?" she asked.

"Yes," he said. "Two nights ago, I went to Idresil while the lights were high and bright in the sky, and I saw my father in them. He told me that you were coming and that I should come and warn you."

"Warn us?" she asked, her hand instinctively going to her back where she would normally have secured her gun.

"Yes, the lights that took you back will burn bright again soon. You should take heed."

Gates leaned in closer. "We don't understand," he said, as he set down three cups of coffee that he had poured for each of them.

Hyman took a seat closer to her and rubbed soot onto her head. "It is a burnt offering from Idresil, the tree of life."

Devon was reluctant at first to allow the man to bestow the charm on her head, but after seeing that Gates was not concerned at all, she sat still while he applied the confirmation for her.

He then turned to Gates and motioned for him to bend down so that Hyman could bestow the same symbolic gesture on his head. "Many religions believe that souls travel together. From the beginning, they transition from life to life in proximity, never venturing very far from each other."

He looked around the room as if he were expecting someone or something to pounce on them at any minute. "The one that hurt you will come for you again."

Gates was on his feet before Hyman had even finished his sentence, his hand on his sidearm. Devon held him at bay with a simple touch of her hand at his forearm. "Chris, it's okay."

She gestured to Hyman. "What do you mean, he's coming for me?" she asked, her composure failing quickly. "The taste he had, has ignited his thirst; he will come again for more," he said, looking directly at Devon.

Gates moved closer to her. "How did Hayden get here into our time?"

Hyman rose to his feet as if he were in a trance, bending at the waist to collect a multicolored pelt that he placed on the couch. "Hrungnir could have crossed over with you. His soul may have been born again in this time. How he got here is of little importance. He is here for her."

"Hrungnir?" Gates questioned. "Is that the name he is using now?" He opened the door and motioned the FBI detail standing guard outside to come into the room.

Hyman opened several glass bottles of different colors and sizes, sniffing before selecting several and setting them aside. "He has had many names during many periods of history, but his name matters not; he is here." He looked at Devon. "You need to be cleansed."

Devon took a step closer to Gates and her protective detail. "Pardon?"

"He has your scent." He began pouring small amounts from the bottles he'd set aside into an empty vial. "The lights will be at their brightest in three nights, and the channel will be at its strongest."

He handed Gates the corked vial. "She should not be near here."

Once Gates took the bottle from his hand, Hyman collected his things and returned all, but one to the pelt. He kept it palmed and out of view of the others. When Gates turned to escort the FBI detail back to the hallway, Hyman poured the contents into Devon's cup and made his way out of the door behind them. Once they were in the hallway, he handed her another bottle and said, "You must heed my warning. Use this anywhere he may have touched you."

Devon closed her eyes and shook her head. "How do you know what happened?"

Hyman whispered as he walked away, "I saw it in the lights."

Devon waited until everyone had left the room before she sank into the couch. "I can't believe this is happening again." She held up the bottle to Gates. "Am I supposed to rub this all over my body?" Frustrated, she sipped her now lukewarm coffee, finishing in several swallows.

Gates took the bottle from her and opened the cork, sniffing it cautiously. He noted the strong smell of flowers and licorice. He smiled. "Might burn your more sensitive areas, but I doubt it will cause any permanent damage."

She set the vial on the coffee table and made her way to the large sliding glass door in the room that led out to the balcony. Peering outside, she scanned the rural countryside, enjoying the way the light of the moon cast shadows across the snow. "I want to go home tonight," she stated, unemotionally.

He walked up behind her and wrapped his arms around her shoulders. "We're already booked on the first flight in the morning. There are two armed agents outside, and one sleeping in the bed with you. You couldn't be safer."

She closed her eyes and leaned back against his chest. "I can't go through that again. I'd as soon be dead."

He didn't let her go as he kissed her ear innocently. "Then I'd be dead, too." He turned her to face him, holding tightly to her forearms and pulling her near. "We will get through this together."

****

The first time he heard her cry out he thought she was having a bad dream. After all, even without the news, she'd gotten that day, her mind was still coping with what her body had endured. It should be no surprise she'd continue to have bad dreams in Aurora.

He turned his body to hers, his hands reaching out to still her. As soon as his hand touched her arm, he realized she was soaking wet and had managed to pull everything off except her underwear.

He flipped on the lamp on the nightstand and jumped to his feet. When he took a good look at her, he knew she was feverish. She looked as though she'd stepped out of the shower and fallen into bed. Her face is so saturated with sweat that it dripped from her chin like rain. The sheets under her were soaked, and her body had left a wet impression on the sheets underneath her.

"Devon," he called, lifting her head just enough to ensure that she was conscious, "can you hear me?"

"What's wrong?" she mumbled.

He shook his head and picked up the receiver to call 911, when a light tap at the door interrupted him. Gates dropped the phone and went to the door, opening it just enough to see who was there.

He opened it to the older officer of the FBI detail. "Mr. Hyman is back; he says he's needed in there." When he finished talking, he jerked his head toward the end of the hallway where the other agent was holding Dale Hyman with his hands cuffed behind his back.

Gates opened the door just enough to peer into the hallway. "What do you want, Hyman?"

Dale Hyman calmly asked, "Has her fever broken yet?"

Gates opened the door wider and motioned for the other agent to bring him into the hotel room. He turned back toward the bedroom and closed the door so that the men wouldn't immediately see Devon tossing and turning.

As the trio entered the room, he motioned to the younger FBI agent. "Stay there in the hallway, gun ready." He looked at the older agent. "Stay here in the living room with your weapon in your hand, safety off. If anything happens in there that doesn't seem right, come in there and shoot him." He leaned into the agent's personal space. "You understand?"

He pulled Hyman by the arm toward the bedroom. "I swear, as God is my witness, if you hurt her, I will kill you myself. I don't care who you are."

Dale Hyman made his way into the room and dropped to his knees near the bed. If he was unnerved by Gates or his weapon, he didn't show it. As soon as his knees hit the ground, he began chanting.

Devon twisted and turned, tugging and pulling at the sheets, moaning and crying. "Chris," she pleaded. "It's so hot in here. I need some water."

Gates moved to pour her some from the pitcher near the table, but Hyman intercepted him by grabbing his wrist. "No, the fever is good. It will protect her; she is being cleansed." He sprinkled more ash around her as if chalking the outline of a body at a crime scene.

Hyman pushed Devon's hair away from her eyes. Gates nudged Hyman's shoulder with the gun. "Hands off, Hyman." Gates looked at the unopened vial that Devon had placed on the bureau and asked, "So what's in that one, then?"

He thought he saw Hyman smile. "Just some fragrances, flowers, and candy, nothing that does anything except smell good." Hyman put his hand on her forehead. "Her fever is breaking. She'll start to settle down now."

Hyman gathered his belongings once again and headed for the bedroom door. He stopped short and said, "I've done all that the fathers asked me to do for her. The rest is up to you now."

He entered the living room and passed the FBI agent. The older agent stuck his head into the bedroom. "Everything okay in here, Gates? He free to go?"

Gates nodded and turned his attention back to Devon who was attempting to pull herself up and retrieve a glass for water. He caught her hand, kissed it in midair, and filled the glass of water for her. She drank it and handed the glass back to him for a refill.

"What happened?" she asked, breathlessly.

"Hyman slipped something in your drink. The bottle he left was a decoy. You've had a hell of a fever the better part of the night. I think we should consider that you've been cleansed."

She wrapped the sheet tighter around her chest, looking awkwardly around the room. "What happened to my clothes?"

He pointed to the pile on the floor near the bed. "You had a fever and ripped them off in your sleep." He offered his hand. "Let's get you in the shower. I'll call for some clean linen while you're in the shower.

She nodded and made her way toward the shower, still wrapped in the sheet she pulled off the bed. "Did you check on the detail?" she asked, before entering the bathroom.

He nodded, pulled the wet fitted sheet off the bed, and called the number for the front desk. By the time Devon emerged from the shower, the bed had clean linen on it, and Gates was waiting for her in it.

She flipped the light off as she passed by the nightstand and slid into bed next to him. For comfort, she'd dressed in a knit shirt and underwear. She settled under the sheet to reclaim whatever was left of the night's sleep.

****

Devon opened the door to the hallway and handed two steaming cups of coffee to the agents who were still standing guard at the door. "Everything okay?" she asked, already knowing that it was, but feeling the need to make some type of attempt at conversation.

Gates came from the bedroom just as she was closing the door. "Devon, standard protocol is that you don't touch the door. Did you hit your head harder than I thought?"

"No, I just thought they might like some coffee." She motioned for him to shove the suitcase toward her so that she could carry it herself. "What time is our flight?"

He looked at his watch. "We've plenty of time. I just ..."

The annoying call of his beeper interrupted the rest of his thought. He checked the number on the tiny screen and reached for the telephone. He dialed the numbers from memory because he knew them by heart.

"Mike," he said into the phone, "I got the 911 beep. What's up?" Devon watched him closely, as he paced as far as the cord would allow.

"When?" His gaze traveled to her, and she knew the call had something to do with her. "As soon as the plane lands."

He placed the receiver into the cradle and took an extraordinary amount of time to look up at her.

"What's happened?" she asked.

"DEA bust earlier this morning at a big beach house off the Jersey coast," he reported it, as if he were a newscaster and was reading it from the teleprompter. "Miguel Raynaud was apprehended by the DEA and FBI in a joint bust. They're holding him in interrogation until we can get there."

She grabbed her jacket and threw it around her shoulders, pulling at the handle of the carry-on as she made her way to the door. "But we're still on medical leave?"

He nodded, opening the door for her. "We're in the observation room. We get to listen in, try and get a bead on Esteban, Hayden, Hrungnir, whatever the hell name he's using."

"Raynaud isn't going to give up Esteban. Esteban is Raynaud's right hand."

"He will if we make him an offer he can't refuse."

Let's do this," she said.

Chapter Twenty

Miguel Raynaud was still a handsome man. At sixty, his salt and pepper hair was wavy; he was well-groomed. He had aged with great distinction. His gray suit was expensive. His blue shirt was Italian, as were his shoes. Around his neck and one wrist, he wore thick gold chains, and on his other was a heavy gold Rolex.

He rubbed his chin calmly as he looked around the interrogation room. The room was bigger than most; it figured that the DEA would rank the grand suite. There were two chairs in the room, and he sat in one of them. The other was on the other side of the table. Almost directly across from him was a huge mirror, no doubt a two-way device, he thought.

Raynaud pretended to have something in his right eye and rubbed it as he watched the mirror for any movement or shadows behind the glass.

He cleared his throat. "How is Agent McKenzie? I hear she's recovering nicely, recently married, yes?"

Agent Brad Michaels answered from where he was leaning against the wall, just to the left of the door. "Raynaud, we got your crew, we got your drugs, and by this time tomorrow, we'll have your houses and your cars."

Raynaud gave a perfect smile. "Very sure of yourself, aren't you Agent Michaels? Who's behind the window?"

Michaels smiled and dropped into the chair across the table, sliding it as close to the table as he could. "My boss. He doesn't like you very much, and he wants to make sure that I do everything by the book so that you go away for a very long time."

Raynaud almost seemed nervous. "What do you want?"

"Esteban," Michaels answered confidently, picking an imaginary piece of lint from Raynaud's left shoulder.

"What's in it for me?" Raynaud asked, in a singsong voice, looking toward the mirror again.

"You give me Esteban, and the DEA will see that you serve your time in a cozy, very private federal prison." Michaels flipped through the papers of the file in front of him.

"Why is the DEA willing to make me a deal?" Raynaud asked, genuinely curious.

"We protect our own, Raynaud. We want to make an example of Gregor Esteban," Michaels answered. "You mess with a fellow officer; you mess with us all!"

Raynaud pushed his back against the chair to make his chest seem broader than it was. "You sure you're not just angry that Gregor tapped your partner?"

Michaels's jaw clenched, but he kept his composure. "She's not mine to tap."

Raynaud looked at the mirror again. "So, it doesn't bother you then, the thought of him and her together for what, three months?"

Michaels stood up, looked toward the mirror, and spoke loudly into it as if he were speaking into a microphone. "I don't think he wants a deal."

He leaned in close to Raynaud. "Agent McKenzie has no recollection of those events. I doubt that Esteban spent any time with her." Michaels grabbed the stack of file folders near the edge of the table and turned toward the door to exit the interrogation room.

His hands were on the doorknob when Raynaud called out, "Okay, okay, I don't know where he is right now." Michaels shook his head and opened the door to exit as Raynaud finished. "But I know where he'll be at three p.m. today."

"Where?" Michael's asked, turning back to the table and taking his seat.

"Warehouse over on Bayshore. He's transporting a load from Miami. I'll write the address down for you," Raynaud spoke, as if he were ordering his dinner to go.

****

It was shortly after 6:00 p.m. by the time the DEA transported Gregor Esteban to the federal building. He looked as if he'd resisted arrest; his face was beaten and battered, and the blood that must've run down his face in the scuffle had dried brown on the pink shirt he was wearing. He was sitting in the same chair that Raynaud had occupied earlier, only during his interrogation, Esteban was shackled to the table.

Esteban sat arrogantly at the table stealing glances at the two-way mirror directly across from him. She was on the other side; he could feel her eyes on him through the glass. He licked his lips in the direction of the mirror and smiled, hoping that she would get his message.

Agent Michaels looked tired as he perched himself across from Esteban, his hand toying with his very evident five o'clock shadow. Detective Squires, on the other hand, was calm and cool, leaning against the wall next to the mirror.

"Okay, Esteban," Squires said. "Tell me again: What happened after your men rammed the van and pushed it to the side of the road?"

"I told you a dozen times already," he said loudly. "I didn't touch a hair, anywhere on her, I swear."

"That's not true; you did touch her. You had her by the hair at the warehouse the night of the bust. I saw you," Squires yelled, moving closer to him. "In fact, you threatened to do her right then and there in front of us if we didn't give up our weapons." Squires leaned in so close that he covered Esteban in spit as he spoke. "Fact is, she busted your balls right there in front of us all, didn't she, Brad?"

Michaels slammed his hand down on the table and yelled, "She sure did. That's my partner!"

Esteban ran his hand through his hair; it had grown out over the last few months and most of his face was covered with a thick, graying beard. "That's not what I mean; I mean after that, I never touched her. I never got close enough to."

Squires dropped a thick, black book on top of the table so hard it resonated into the observation room and made Devon and Gates jump. "What's this, Gregor?" He flipped the book open to a random page where several pictures of Devon had been placed inside, and covered with a protective seal, a manila envelope fell out from the back of the book.

Esteban's demeanor changed when Squires opened the book and flipped page after page, and he yelled. "Where'd you get that? It doesn't belong to you; it's mine!"

Squires gave the mirror an awkward look before turning the next several pages. "You're a sick son of a bitch, Esteban. You like watching her?"

Esteban gritted his teeth and looked at the window. "Yes, I do."

Michaels glanced at the mirror and then flipped to another page. He smacked the page and said, "Even when she's having sex with her husband?"

Esteban ignored the question. He looked intently at the mirror as if he could see through it. "Devon and I have a connection. I've followed her for years, waiting for just the right time. That night, after the wreck, we couldn't get her out of the van. The door was pinned."

"You expect me to believe," Michaels yelled at him, "that the woman you've lusted for all these years was lying hurt and defenseless in the middle of nowhere, and you didn't seize the opportunity to take her?"

"My men were nervous," he said. "Those dammed lights had freaked them all out. The other officer, the man, was conscious of the passenger's side. I could see him trying to reach around to get to his weapon. We didn't know how far behind the second federal car was. When we saw the lights, I thought it was the other officers."

He looked at the glass again. "She broke my nose, and yes, I was gonna pay her back, but I couldn't get her out of the damn van." He swallowed. "So, we rammed the van over the edge and watched it until it disappeared into the darkness below. Then we got the hell out of there."

Esteban paused as if he was trying to remember something pertinent. "A few days later, I saw the story on the news about them still missing, and we went back to finish what we'd started. My boys and I walked the area several miles in each direction. There was no sign of them or that van."

Michaels looked at Squires and collected the envelop, tearing the seal open and pouring a handful of pictures out on the table. Michael flipped through them quickly, his attention settling on black and white photos of Devon inside the restaurant with Richard. Several pictures weren't of Devon, but the woman looked eerily like Devon.

Squires picked up the ones of the woman who wasn't Devon. "I know this woman."

"You do?" Esteban looked away, his eyes on the floor.

"Yes, her body was found in an alley near Detective Gates place," Squires informed him and handed Michaels the photo of Devon and Richard at the bar.

Michaels pulled a photo from his desk, a copy of a picture he'd received from Kevin McKenzie. "Is this you?" He tapped the photo of the man dropping something in Devon's drink."

"No, of course not," Esteban said.

"I think that it is," Michaels said. "I think you've been following her and I think you're the one who spiked her drink."

"You have proof of that?" Esteban asked, watching the mirror again.

"Did the Medical examiner run that DNA, yet from the hooker's body?" Michaels asked, changing the subject.

"Don't try and bluff me, Agent," Esteban said arrogantly. "You didn't get any DNA off that girl's body."

"He's not bluffing, Esteban." Squires dropped another folder under Estaban's face. "I know you used a condom, but the DNA we pulled from the body was from her fingernails." Squires opened the folder to an eight by eleven photo of Esteban.

"We matched the DNA under her nails to you," Michaels smiled. "You are under arrest for her murder."

Squires bent closer to Esteban's face, his breath blowing hot across Esteban's mouth. "You stalked Devon, thought you grabbed her at

Gates apartment, and killed this woman when you found out you got the wrong woman."

Squires words were loud and angry, as he finished his summary.

"I'd like to speak to my lawyer now, please," Esteban said as if his words were part of a song.

Squires shook his head and smiled toward the glass, then reached over and grabbed Esteban around the throat, almost lifting him from the chair. "I want the truth, you sick bastard. Just tell us the truth. Where did you hold them? Who else was with you? Who'd you share her with?"

Squires heard the door to the observation room slam and then the sound of footsteps stomping down the hall. Esteban seemed to take great offense at Squires' question. "Share her? I would never share her with anyone," his voice rose with anger. "She belongs to me!" he yelled to the mirror. "You hear me, Devon? You belong to me! You will never be free of me!" He screamed and threw himself, still attached to the table, toward the mirror as Squires, Michaels, and two other agents wrestled him to the floor and drug him from the room.

****

By the time Gates and the protective detail caught up to Devon, she was already out of the building and was headed to the car. He grabbed her by the arm. "Devon," he pleaded. "Wait."

"Did you know they had pictures?" she questioned.

"No, not until we were going into the observation room. Mike mentioned to me that it was going to get messy." He waved the FBI detail away, mouthing to them that they should return to her apartment and wait. The older one nodded and went into the alley to retrieve the car.

"It's just like before with Hayden and his sketches," she exclaimed, crying into his chest. "And now, everyone I work with has seen them."

Gates caressed her head. "This case has been on a need-to-know basis.

Only those assigned to the case know any of the details."

She wiped at her eyes. "Brad and Squires?" she whispered.

He opened the car door and motioned for her to step inside. "Yeah, I don't like it, Devon, but they're working on the case. They must evaluate all the evidence. The pictures are evidence."

She pulled her coat tighter around her chest as if she was cold. "I'll have to transfer to another unit."

Gates made his way around to the driver's side and climbed in beside her. "We can talk about this later, let's just get home and celebrate that this nightmare is over." He smiled. "Esteban, Hayden, Hrungnir—whatever his name is—is in custody. He can't hurt you anymore. You're safe."

As the car pulled away, she looked up to the sky, only half-believing that what he said was true. The sky was picturesque: thick heavy clouds filled most of the canvas. A small light of pale blue was visible through the smoke-like clouds. Interestingly, a series of small, darker clouds marched in alignment across the sky in perfect sequence. It looked like the perimeter to heaven.

She smiled, thinking to herself that her grandfather would have been able to evaluate the sky and the cloud cover and predict within an inch how much snow they would get before daybreak. He was an amazing man; he'd always had a way of making her problems seem smaller.

If ever she could have used a discussion with her "fathers" in the clouds, it was now. She looked over at Gates, but he didn't glance at her because he was concentrating on the surrounding traffic. Devon reached over and took his hand in hers, acknowledging to herself that she was lucky to have him. He'd been her rock since the minute the van had gone over the cliff. Gates had her six. She smiled at him, realizing, as he smiled back, that he knew exactly what she was thinking. It gave her great comfort.

By the time they arrived at the apartment, both FBI agents were already at their posts. The younger one was at his usual spot near the end of the hallway, while the older one was in his position directly in front of the door. Although she liked them both, Devon was especially fond of the way the older agent announced their visitors. He'd been holding their visitors, mostly family members, at the top of the stairs with the younger agent, until he was able to determine whether Devon and Gates wanted company.

The younger agent would announce into his earpiece that one of the brothers, parents, or sisters was there, and then would allow them to proceed to the older agent. Once they approached the older agent, he'd simply nod and tap their front door.

The older agent had ceased formally announcing their family members several days ago. And although Devon was thankful for their thoughtful consideration, she missed having a few minutes' notice that they had visitors. She smiled, remembering the day before they'd left for Aurora; Gates's father, not one from the clouds, had stopped by unannounced and nearly caught them in the shower.

Devon spoke to the older agent. "Agent Harris, we're hoping for a quiet night tonight." He nodded to her and adjusted his earpiece more comfortably. Gates opened the door for her and motioned her inside. "We'll bring some coffee out to you later," he said, as he shut the door for the evening.

****

Darkness fell quickly that night as the chill of winter settled comfortably around them. The snow fell in thick, damp piles that stuck together unevenly on the terrain. From the balcony outside the apartment, Gates watched it fall, looking into the streetlight to determine how much was falling and how fast. At certain intervals, it looked like a wave of snow bent at an angle against the wind.

"Come inside," Devon said to him. "It's too cold to be out there."

"Just a minute; I like to watch it fall against the light, especially when it falls this fast." He watched a little longer. Truth be told, the cold air helped him think. He couldn't get Esteban's words out of his head. It had been the ranting and raving of a madman obsessed with her in a way that bothered him tremendously.

There was one comforting factor that came out of the interrogation today. With Esteban in custody, she was safe. He'd never send anyone else after her. And if, as Dale Hyman had explained, souls traveled together, reborn through time, Hayden and Esteban were potential, one in the same.

Although Gates didn't understand it, couldn't objectively prove it, he knew somehow the channel was opened and Hayden had escaped from the lights and his evilness reborn in Gregor Esteban.

Gates took a last look at the falling snow and went back into the apartment to find her. He could hear the water of the shower over the hum of the heater; it had kicked on in response to the sliding glass door being open so long. He kicked off his shoes and walked toward the shower to join her, undressing as he did so. He'd just stepped out of his jeans and put his hand on the outside door when he heard her crying.

He hesitated, waiting at the door as he ran all the potential outcomes through his mind. He could rush into the bathroom and comfort her or wait, until she came out all warm and toasty from the shower and offer her a nightcap to ward off the cold.

Instead, he stepped back into his jeans and grabbed his shirt. He was in the living room when he heard the water turn off.

When she emerged from the shower with her hair wet, and a warm robe tied around her flannel pajamas, he was just placing thick slices of chicken atop luscious beds of green lettuce and red tomatoes.

Gates motioned for her to take a seat, and then he poured two glasses of white wine. They ate quietly, smiling awkwardly in the long intervals of silence. When she finished eating, he collected the plates and placed them in the dishwasher before turning off the light and falling into the seat next to her. "Devon," he said, pouring her another glass of wine, "I heard you crying in the shower." He stroked her hair behind her ears. "What's this about? Esteban is in custody. It's over."

"I hope so," she answered. "I feel as if my professional life is all but over. I feel so open and exposed knowing that creep has been following me around and documenting my most private moments." She rubbed his chin with her forefinger and added, "Intruding on my most intimate moments with you."

"I love you," Devon whispered, planting several small kisses on his lips before pulling him closer to her and kissing him deeper, harder, and more intense. She locked her arms around his neck and pulled him back so that he was almost reclining on top of her. Devon pulled his shirt out from his jeans, unbuttoned it, and pushed it off his shoulders before she reached for the zipper of his jeans. She pushed them down as far as she could and felt him reach behind to the waistband and get them the rest of the way off.

Gates pulled at his underwear and pushed them to the floor. The fact that her hands seemed to be everywhere at once did not escape him. He could feel her hands rubbing up and down his chest, scratching the sensitive skin around his nipples. Then he was aware of her hand pulling at his shaft, her hands moving up and down, until he was rigid and grinding rhythmically into her grasp.

He untied the belt to her robe and separated it until his hands touched the button of the pajama top. He opened it and slid his hands around the warm skin of her waist; it was as if his body melded with hers. He pushed the bottom of her pajamas down to her ankles, and then off her feet, dropping them to the floor.

His mouth clutched onto her breast, first one, and then the other. He tugged at her nipples so that her body moved in motion with his mouth. He pushed her as close against him as he could with a hand on either side of her buttocks, as he guided his erection into the warmth between her legs. There was very little foreplay this time; as soon as he was fully engulfed within her, he moved in and out, deep and slow. He knew she liked it that way. Gates pushed himself high onto his arms and moved his groin rhythmically up and down; he felt her opening herself wider and wider to accommodate his hips between her legs.

Gates felt himself growing harder, bigger as he pushed himself in and out of her. The pressure was building so that he was almost hurting as he slapped his body against hers. He could feel her squirming under him as his warm hands pushed up and down against her opening. Gates made several desperate groans to prolong his release. He dropped his hands between her legs, his fingers frantically searching for her moist folds.

His middle finger had just contacted with her center, when he cried out and emptied himself into her. Quickly, he returned both hands to her waist so that he could pump against her until he stilled and settled gently on top of her. His breath came in great gasps at her neck.

"I'm sorry," he said between deep, shuddering breaths. He reached for her breasts again, palming one and then the other, his fingertips teasing her nipples until they were hard against his skin. He kissed her abdomen, carefully planting his kisses horizontally from hipbone to hipbone, as he slid his hands to rest between her legs and pushed tenderly at her thighs until there was enough room to accommodate the width of him between her legs.

He trailed his kisses into the dark curls, licking at her folds until he heard her moaning and felt her undulating against his mouth. He pushed against her with such pressure that he was sure she could feel the small, prickly bumps on his tongue.

He knew she was close, he could tell by the sounds that she was making and the pace that she was setting. He slid his hands under her buttocks and pushed her against him as hard as he dared. She came almost instantly, calling out his name as she finished.

She grabbed a handful of hair at the back of his head to pull him away, but he held on as if she was the water of life, and he wanted every drop. She pushed at him again and was able to unlatch his mouth from her body.

"Let's go to bed," he suggested. "Give me a few minutes, and I'll be ready again." He smiled, pulling at her arm to get her to her feet.

She put her pajamas on and stood to meet him. "Although I appreciate the thought, I'm really tired." She rubbed her hands up and down his biceps. "How about we just lie naked, wrapped around each other until we fall asleep. I'll take you up on the double feature some other night soon."

He pulled her into an embrace and kissed her on the forehead. "Deal."

Chapter Twenty-One

Devon awoke as the sunlight cascaded through the window and reflected off the mirror in their bedroom. Gates was still asleep with half of his body on her side of the bed and a half on his. The fire that he had built before they'd retired to bed had burned out, except for a few glowing embers. She turned to look at him sleeping; he was relaxed and unbothered by his vulnerability. He was innocent, childlike, with his feet hanging off one side. The long length of his back faced her.

As soon as her feet hit the floor, he raised into a sitting position. "Can you come back to bed?" he asked, holding on to her hand. She pulled free and slid the robe back on, getting it nearly tied before he caught her from behind and pulled at it again.

They struggled and giggled as they pulled at each other until she managed to place herself in front and push through the bedroom door and into the living room. She heard the noise from the kitchen and saw the movement almost at the same time.

Her first thought was that Hayden or Esteban had escaped and had come for her. But the rational side of her recognized his familiar form and cried out half in surprise and half in embarrassment.

"Dad?" she almost screamed, tying the belt on her robe and pushing a naked Gates back into the bedroom to dress.

"Hi, honey," he said, waving to her. "Didn't mean to scare you. I was hoping it would be a surprise." He held up a spatula and announced, "Surprise." He stirred the eggs that he was scrambling. "I thought Christopher would have left for work already. He returns to full duty today, right?"

She nodded, tucking her hair behind her ears. "Yes, he'll be in the office today."

Ashton McKenzie stopped as if he'd just remembered something. "Honey, I'm sorry. I didn't mean to interrupt anything." He paused and smiled, looking at his watch. "I could come back in what, eight minutes?"

"Dad!" she almost screamed, looking behind her to ensure that Gates was still out of earshot.

He laughed and came from behind the counter and embraced her. "I'm sorry, pumpkin. Look at how red your face is."

She pulled away. "Dad, what are you doing here?"

"I came to have breakfast with my girl." He smiled and kissed her on the forehead. He stepped away just as Gates came from the bedroom, pulling on a sweatshirt that matched the running pants he was wearing. "Christopher," her dad said, offering his hand. "Didn't mean to intrude, son."

Gates smiled. "No intrusion, sir. You're welcome here anytime." He grabbed a cup of coffee from the kitchen counter. He took two sips and handed the cup to Devon. "Here, hon, I'm going running." He looked at them. "You guys want to join me?"

"Not me," Devon said. "Jason and Melissa are coming over later today. We're going running to map out a new route."

Gates smiled, happy to see her making progress in getting on with her life and putting things back in order.

By the time Gates left for his run, Ashton had filled two plates with eggs, bacon, fruit, and toast. They sat at the table and enjoyed their breakfast together as father and daughter. Devon missed having private time with him. He was an incredibly busy man who had many responsibilities to both his family and his post.

Over the years, since she'd joined the US Marshals, their private breakfast mornings had been rare. Their last one had been the weekend before she was assigned to Miami. "Dad," she asked, pushing her plate away and leaning up on her elbows, "is something wrong?"

"No, I'm just worried about you, Devon. When you were missing, our family wasn't whole." He kissed her hand and held it up to his cheek. "You're home, and you're safe. I want to keep you that way."

"Dad," she said again, "I'm fine. We're getting through."

"Devon, I want you to leave the Marshal's service," he said.

"I'm on medical leave, Dad," she reminded him. "I'll be cleared in two weeks, and then I'm going back to work."

"I've already spoken to the bureau chief, Devon. Your assignment to the Marshal's service has been terminated. Once you've been cleared for active duty, you're to report to the DEA. I want you reassigned to something safer for a while."

"Dad, I'm a grown woman. You can't just ground me from retaking my post," she argued.

He stood up and held out his arms to her. "I'm sorry. I want you to be safe. It's already been done, Devon. There's nothing to argue about."

It was obvious that she was angry. "When Kevin was shot two years ago, you didn't have him reassigned."

"Kevin is my son, and a man. You're my daughter, my baby," his voice grew sterner, yet softer as tears welled in his eyes. "I read the file, Devon. I know what happened, what they did to you."

It was almost as if he'd struck her; she stepped back with her arms folded protectively over her chest.

He was crying openly now, wiping awkwardly at his tears as they rolled down his cheeks. Then, as if he flipped a switch and composed himself, he said, "You're safe now." He cleared his throat and swallowed, making a final wipe of his eyes. "I know you're angry, Devon. I only hope you'll be able to understand in time."

"I have to take a shower. I have some things to do before Jason and Melissa arrive." She walked slowly to the bedroom. "Lock the door when you leave."

He nodded to her then gathered the remnants of their breakfast and put everything back in order. He heard the shower come alive, just as he closed the door behind him.

****

Gates leaned back in the chair and propped his feet on the worn and beaten desk. He'd only been back in the squad room for a few hours, and there were stacks and stacks of file folders waiting for him. He looked around the room; everything was familiar, but at the same time, it seemed different.

Everything was different now: the air he breathed, the food he ate, the people he encountered throughout his day. It was all less important than she was, her needs, her happiness, and her safety.

The ringing of the phone made him jump; he grabbed the receiver before it finished its third ring. "Gates," he barked into the phone. He listened patiently as the caller spoke for several minutes. He nodded. "Keep me in the loop."

Squires leaned into Gates's space. "What's up?"

Gates moved uncomfortably in his chair. "They're still interrogating Esteban. But they won't let me participate." He smiled, but there was no laughter in his eyes. "I'm banned."

Squires lips twitched as if he had to spit but didn't, his eyes darted back and forth as he asked. "You really think Gregor Esteban is some evil incarnate of that deputy from the other time?"

Gates nodded. "I do." He tapped his fingers impatiently on the desktop. "I can't really explain how we got back there, but we were there just the same."

"Isn't it more plausible that you were drugged and the entire events fabricated in your minds," Squires asked, as he leaned across the desk to minimize the space between them.

"You mean some kind of Folie A Deux?" Gates stared angrily at him.

Squires nodded.

"Might be more plausible, but that's not what happened."

They stared each other down, the silence between them so deafening, all the other noises in the squad room were muted.

Squires looked away first, he cleared his throat picked up the folder on the top of the stack and handed it to Gates. "Are you planning on working any at all today?"

"I don't want to get too far away from the apartment; it's the first day Devon has been without me. I want to be close by," he stated, looking at his watch.

Squires pointed toward the back of the squad room where two interrogation rooms were visible. One was empty other than the table and two chairs placed in the center of the room. The other housed a young woman about twenty-five years old with blonde hair.

She was pretty in a plain sort of way, and of average height and weight. Her hair was long, just below her shoulders, but cut irregularly, most likely the result of it being trimmed unprofessionally. She was wearing blue faded jeans and a black, wrinkled T-shirt. Her tennis shoes were expensive, but worn and old. They were laced, but untied so that it made her feet look wider than they really were.

Her left eye was sporting a dark bruise just above her cheekbone, and although there was no bleeding, it looked as if she'd had a nosebleed, as there were small dark drops of dried blood under her left nostril. Squires handed him the file. "You want to see if you can get this one to talk?" He took a large drink of his warm coffee and added, "I tried, but she keeps saying she fell."

Gates looked at her as if he were bored. "Maybe she did."

"Come on, partner, I know it's the husband or boyfriend. She could be a poster girl for domestic violence." He pushed the file toward Gates. "Go on, flash that smile. Make her talk."

Gates reluctantly stood to his feet and headed toward the room. Squires watched through the window as Gates took the seat across from her. He couldn't tell what they were talking about without activating the speaker. Several times during the engagement, he was able to see that she was relaxing and talking more freely to his partner.

****

Squires leaned against the wall closest to the interrogation room. He watched Gates smiling at her, leaning in and away from her, her lips moving in response to his questions. Squires didn't notice that he had a visitor until he heard the voice. "Detective Squires?"

Squires turned toward the voice and attempted to hide his disappointment when he encountered Agent Brad Michaels. Squires flipped back around, as if he hadn't noticed him. "What do you want, Michaels?"

Michaels pointed toward the room where Gates was sitting. "You know who that is?"

Squires shook his head, but offered no other conversation. He didn't like Brad Michaels, and there was no point in pretending that he did. Agent Michaels leaned against the desk opposite where Squires was standing. "Her name is Vanessa Raynaud. She's Miguel Raynaud's daughter-in-law."

Squires nodded. "So that's why you're here. She's married to the drug lord's son?"

"Yes, her husband is Elliot Raynaud. He's known to have a bit of a temper," Michaels answered.

He looked pensively around the room and jerked his head toward Gates. "When did he get back?"

Squires nodded. "Today is his first day back."

"Thought he'd still be on his honeymoon with my former partner," Michaels replied. "How is Devon holding up?"

The older man exhaled a deep breath. "I haven't seen her, but he seems to be doing okay if that's any reflection of her current state."

Michaels wiped anxiously at his chin. "Detective, off the record, we weren't that far behind them the night they went missing, maybe fifteen minutes, twenty miles," he paused, as if he was unsure if he wanted to say more. "I don't remember seeing any lights; do you?"

Squires shook his head that he didn't and continued looking through the window.

"So, what do you think really happened to them?" Michaels almost whispered.

"I think it's just as they described. They couldn't get in touch with us or call for backup. They did what they needed to do to survive," Squires replied coldly, as if he were trying to maintain his composure. "What other reason could there be?"

"To cover up that they were holed up somewhere together playin' house," Michaels answered.

Squires smile was disinguinine as he pushed warningly at Michaels's chest. "That really bothers you, doesn't it?" He leaned in closer so that no one else could hear. "As close as the two of you were for all those years, you didn't get anywhere with her. She didn't even like him, and he ends up married to her in what, six months."

Squires could see that he'd hit a nerve. "I mean, it must really make you feel bad thinking about him and her together every night."

Michaels reached out to grab Squires by the shirt, but the older man had anticipated the reaction and caught his arm just around the wrist. They both jumped when an authoritative voice called out, "Detective Squires, is there a problem?"

They turned to see Captain Goff looking curiously in their direction; he had observed the entire event. Squires pushed Michaels's arms away and said, "No, sir, not at all."

Goff nodded and looked at Michaels. "Good, glad to hear that. Agent Michaels, collect your witness and get the hell out of my squad room." He turned and stormed back into his office, slamming the door as if to announce to the squad room that he was angry.

Michaels nodded and walked into the interrogation room, emerging with Vanessa Raynaud in tow. He gave an arrogant smile to Squires as he exited the squad room. Gates came out a few minutes later and handed the file back to Squires. "What was all that about?"

Squires said, "I don't think he likes you very much."

Gates looked at his watch again; maybe he'd drop by the apartment and have lunch with Devon today. "What did you say, Mike?"

Squires heaved himself into his big chair at his desk. "I said he don't care much for you; although he does have an unholy interest in your wife."

Gates nodded. "Yeah, I know. Devon doesn't get it, but I do. I got it loud and clear the night after we busted Esteban. I told her his interest was more than she thought." He dialed his home phone and waited for her to pick up. "Hey, it's me. Have any plans for lunch today?"

He paused, listening to her reply. "Okay, no problem. I'll see you at home for dinner, then."

Squires held up his hands. "Honeymoon's over already?"

Gates tossed a rubber ball in his direction. "Her brother and his wife just got to the apartment. They're going running. It will be good for her to get out."

"FBI detail still attached to her?" Squires asked.

"Like glue," Gates answered. "Now that Esteban's in custody. I'm sure they will be reassigned soon."

"Probably been good to know they are there, backing you up?"

"Yeah, but it's been a bit awkward at times, especially when we want to be alone."

"Which is like all the time, you being newlyweds and all," Squires chimed in.

Gates shook his head, laughing. "Although Agent Harris is letting up a bit. He's stopped announcing the family," Gates paused. "Of course, on second thought, we could've used a heads-up this morning. Her old man showed up for breakfast unexpected."

Squires smiled, eager to hear more, but Gates had finished talking. "Guess, my detail days are over, huh?" Squires said, with a rueful look on his face.

Gates laughed. "Since my lunch plans have changed, looks like you're stuck with me. Let's grab a bite before we have to meet that guy from the gang division."

****

The knock at the door caused Devon to jump, knocking one of the three bottles of water over that she had poured. She'd become accustomed to Harris's radio announcement that her mother or Gates's mom was on the way up. Between Kaitlin and their brothers' visits, it had been like Grand Central Station at their place over the last few weeks. And since Harris had learned everyone's names and recognized their faces, his messages had been very brief and to the point. "Kevin is on the stairs," or "Nick is at the door."

Since she hadn't gotten a radio message, the knock must be Jason and Melissa. She made her way to the door, eager to spend some time with her twin and his wife. With all the excitement, she couldn't recall the last time she'd spent any time with just the two of them. She couldn't count running into Melissa the night of the transport. It had been late, and she had barely enough time to say hello, much less actually converse with Melissa or her brother.

The door handle turned and Jason entered before Devon had gotten to the door. Her arms went around her brother's neck instantly. "Jason, Melissa," she welcomed, "come on in. I can't tell you how good it is to see you."

Jason held on to his sister for what seemed like a long time, and then held her at arm's length. He took all of her in, happy to be able to hold her again, healthy and safe. "Dev," he said, smiling at her, "you look great, and happy."

Melissa bounced joyfully between them. "Jay, don't hover. Let her have some air."

He ran his hand over her head. They might have been twins and shared similar facial characteristics, but Jason had always been bigger and taller than his twin was.

Clutched in his embrace, she came just above his chest. Jason may have been the youngest of the brothers, but he was just as tall as Brett was. Devon recalled how angry Kevin was when both his younger brothers grew taller. As a girl, the only girl, she really didn't care that her brothers were taller. But today, as he held her, she was keenly aware of the difference in their size. It was the first time that she recalled being so aware.

Melissa almost fell into Devon's embrace, finding comfort in being so close to her. They'd known each other since middle school, moving in the same circles and sharing common acquaintances. Devon was close to her other sisters-in-law, but she and Melissa had been friends before Jason came along. At first, it had been a little odd, having her brother dating a friend. But once Devon saw how happy Melissa made him, she knew she could adjust. Melissa and Jason were true soul mates, and Devon had once been envious of their relationship, hoping to one day find her life partner.

Devon pointed to the vegetables and thawed chicken on the counter. "I thought we could have a late lunch after we run. Chris won't be home until later, and I like eating dinner with him. We always seem to eat dinner late."

Jason smiled and arched his eyebrows suggestively. "Is that so?" He paused then added, "So, married life is good, then?"

The red flush that came over her face was not lost on Jason or Melissa. "Jason," Melissa warned, "don't embarrass her. That's private."

He punched playfully at his sister's arm. "Don't be ridiculous, honey. We're twins; we know things without being told." He looked into Devon's eyes. "Don't we?"

Devon nodded and smiled, rubbing her hands against her leg, as she thought of how Jason knew exactly where her wound was after she'd been shot. Oh God, she thought to herself, hoping their connection would afford her and Chris a little privacy.

She grabbed her jacket from the couch. "Are we ready? I filled three water bottles for us."

"Before we go," Jason said, "we have some news."

Devon poised herself; she had learned that in her family, news wasn't always good. "What's wrong?" she heard herself ask, before she was mentally ready to hear the answer.

Jason pulled Melissa closer to him. "We're pregnant."

Devon couldn't believe her ears! They had waited so long for a baby. Treatment after treatment at the fertility clinics, and finally they were to be parents. She could tell by the smile on Jason's face that he had never been happier. Melissa, too, looked as if she was going to burst at any minute. Devon couldn't recall a time when she'd seen them more pleased with themselves.

"When?" Devon asked, barely able to contain her excitement. "Do mom and dad know?"

Jason answered. "We're about three months along. I stopped by to tell them this morning. Apparently, Dad was here bright and early, I take it."

She smiled. "Oh yes, very early. He made me breakfast, and then he told me that he's suspending me from active duty with the Marshal's service."

"What?" Jason asked, unsure of what he'd heard her say.

Devon jumped to her feet. "Let's go running. We can talk about this later."

Jason stood up to join her, motioning Melissa to the door. "Okay, but I've got to hear the rest of this when we get back." He threw his jacket on and headed for the door.

"You guys," Melissa interrupted, "I think I'm just going to hang around here if that's okay." She unzipped her jacket and removed it, tossing it against the back of the sofa.

Jason was by her side in an instant, rubbing her back and shoulders. "Honey, is something wrong?"

Melissa shook her head. "No, I'm just tired, and to be honest, my breasts are so sore. I don't think I'll be able to run very far, with or without a sports bra."

Devon unzipped her jacket. "We don't have to run today. Let's just do something else."

"No, really," she said, as she urged them both toward the door. "You need some time together. I'm fine. I'll start on lunch, and when you get back, we can eat, and maybe walk down to that café later for a celebratory drink, non-alcoholic for me, of course."

Before he could protest, Melissa held up two fingers in the air and waved them. "I mean we don't want the twin thing to get out of whack, do we?" She smiled to them, hoping to make them feel comfortable with her staying behind.

Devon took Jason's arm and led him to the door. "Okay, you're sure?"

Melissa nodded and turned her back to them to prepare the items Devon had laid out for lunch.

Devon followed her brother out of the door, stopping to advise Agent Harris. "My brother and I are going for a run; we won't be gone long. Melissa's inside making lunch."

Harris nodded and spoke into the radio indicating that the other agent was to follow Devon while he would remain on point at the apartment. There was a crackle over the radio. "Roger that."

Chapter Twenty-Two

Devon hated to admit it, but her legs were killing her. In truth, it wasn't just her legs; her thighs and her ass hurt, too. Every part of her body was aching. She looked quickly at her brother; he was hardly even sweating. She supposed that a firefighter's muscle groups were used differently from a police officer's.

He handed her his bottle of water, still about half full, when he noticed that hers was empty. "Here, drink. You need to stay hydrated." She drank about half of the contents then handed it back to him. They were walking back to the apartment, using the last half mile to cool down and stretch.

They made the last turn and headed up the street. "Devon," he asked in an even, yet concerned tone. "How are you? I mean, with everything that's happened."

She paced herself a step ahead. "I'm fine."

He grabbed her arm, effectively stopping her next to him. "Devon, it's me. I just hope, I mean that you're healing. I'm not talking about knowing the details." His eyes softened. "Just knowing that you're happy and fulfilled."

She bit her lip, considering what she could say to give him peace of mind. "Jason, I am very happy. I have a husband who is a passionate and considerate person in and out of bed. I'm healing; we are both healing."

She poked at his ribs and looked back to see how far behind them the agent was. She didn't see him, but that didn't bother her. She seldom saw them, even though she knew they were there. "If I wasn't so tired, I'd challenge you to race up the stairs."

He swatted playfully at her behind as she pushed past him and ran up the stairs. "If I wasn't so tired, I'd accept."

Devon slid the key in the lock and pushed the door open without considering that Agent Harris wasn't at the door. She smiled down the hallway to her brother and pushed into the apartment to inform Melissa that they were back and hungry. She didn't get any of the words out because her attention was drawn to what was left of her apartment.

Almost every item in the living room and kitchen was destroyed; it looked as if a truck had driven through. The lamps were broken, and the tables were upturned and smashed. However, most disturbing was the blood; it was everywhere. Devon's hand went instinctively to her sidearm, removing and aiming in almost the same motion. "Melissa!" she screamed. "Harris!"

She heard steps behind her and turned to face Jason. After that, the world faded to black, starting at her peripheral vision, until she was encased in total darkness.

****

Gates looked impatiently at his watch again. He ran his hand through his hair, pausing to inspect his wedding ring. He felt like a silly girl, always looking at it, but he couldn't help it; every time he acknowledged it, he felt as though he was acknowledging her again and announcing to anyone who would listen that they had found each other. It was also a testament to the fact that he was never letting her go.

The detectives with the gang division talked incessantly. They had hardly stopped talking for the better part of two hours. Gates and Squires sat at either end of the table, looking at the folders the detectives slid to them.

Gates checked his watch again: 6:45 p.m. Devon would be expecting him soon.

He leaned over and whispered to Squires, "Excuse me; I'm going to step out and make a call."

Squires nodded and waved him off, whispering, "No sense in them both being in the doghouse tonight."

Gates paced the hallway, disconnecting the call and redialing before he reached the end of the hallway. Both times, her cell phone went automatically to her voicemail.

By the time Gates started his second lap down the hallway, he had dialed the house phone and waited, hoping she'd pick it up, breathing loudly into the phone and explain how'd she been outside or in the shower and didn't hear the phone ringing.

Gates returned to the table, not surprised to see the detectives were still rambling on about the various gang tattoos and initiation tactics. He sat down moments later, with a worried expression on his face and took his seat next to Squires.

After several more minutes, he interrupted the other detective, who was delineating the different tattoos specific for gang identification. "Agents, excuse me, but I need a moment with my partner, please." Squires rose and followed Gates over to a private corner. "Mike, something's wrong. Devon's not answering the phone, and her detail isn't returning my pages."

Squires dismissed his concerns. "She probably sent the detail home already. With Esteban in custody, she knows she doesn't need them. She's probably in the tub or something, getting all prettied up for you tonight."

"I don't think so," Gates said. "She would've taken the phone with her." He looked to where the other agents were waiting. "Mike, finish this up. I'm going home to check on Devon."

****

Gates heard the sirens even though his vehicle was still several blocks away. He flipped the button on the console and accelerated his vehicle, just as the lights and siren on his own unmarked police vehicle exploded into life.

He parked the car erratically in the street almost parallel to one of the two ambulances that were waiting in front of their apartment building. Gates pulled his badge from his jacket and wore it so that he would be allowed entrance.

"Devon?" he cried out, his pace increasing so that he was nearly running up the stairs and down the hallway. An officer that he recognized from another precinct accosted him just outside the door to the apartment. However, it was pointless; Gates could see the blood smeared on the walls and saturating the wood floor. The trail of blood leading into the bedroom was so red that he could barely breathe as he considered the horrific possibilities.

He pushed at the officer, screaming and pulling away from him and another who had come to assist. "This is my house! Devon?"

Gates fought his way to the bedroom, dragging the officers with him. His right hand touched the doorframe of the bedroom, but then he pulled away realizing that it was sticky with blood. "Devon?" he screamed again. "Just let me see her, please!"

He was startled to come face to face with his captain. Goff reached out and forcefully pulled Gates away from the other officers and led him from the bedroom. "She's not here, Chris."

His head was spinning, and the room was so hot that he couldn't breathe. He reached out to steady himself on the nearby wall. "What?"

Goff took him by the arm and guided him into the bedroom where the badly beaten and bloodied dead body of Agent Harris was staged across their bed. The scene was still being processed: Technicians were measuring and photographing the body and recording where items were dropped and fingerprints were lifted. It was evident that he'd put up a fight; he had multiple defensive wounds on his hands and arms. Gates took note that his gun was still holstered.

Gates looked around the room, partially to ascertain who else was affected and partially to hide his relief at discovering that the body inside wasn't Devon's. "Where's the other agent?" he asked.

Captain Goff gave a defeated sigh. "We pulled Agent Daniels from the river in the park. He was shot at point-blank range. His gun was still in his holster; he had no defensive wounds."

Gates rubbed his chin. "Safe to say that he knew his attacker." A few minutes later, he had a thought. "Is Esteban still in custody?"

The captain nodded. "Yes, I verified that myself."

Gates turned toward the door. "I've got to call her parents."

Goff took his arm. "Listen, your brother-in-law was airlifted to the hospital. He was stabbed several times. I think the perp left him for dead."

Gates had forgotten that Jason and Melissa were coming over for lunch. He made for the apartment door. "What about his wife, any sign of her?"

The captain shook his head.

Gates made his way down the hallway. "So, he has them both."

****

Gates parked his jeep at the hospital in the area designated for police officers and recognized his partner's vehicle two parking spots over. Thank God, he thought, Mike already would have collected as much information as he could. His mind was racing; with Esteban in custody, he had no idea where to begin the search for her.

He pushed through the double doors as if he were searching for someone. He anxiously approached the nurse's station, pulling his badge from his pocket. "Excuse me," he said, motioning toward the corridor. "I'm looking for Dr. Gates."

The nurse was about forty years old with short blonde hair cut into a wedge just about to the nape of her neck. She was wearing white pants and a white scrub top with pockets on each side, both of which were so full that they drooped heavily toward her hips. She tapped the keys on the keyboard and read the screen quickly. "She's with a patient right now."

Gates indicated his badge and looked frantically around the patient care area. "It's kind of an emergency."

The nurse almost laughed and waved her hand out in front of her. "This is an emergency room, everything's an emergency."

Gates had to restrain himself from reaching across the counter and slapping her. He supposed that he could claim temporary insanity brought on by his missing wife as his defense. Instead, he leaned in close and warned her. "Listen, Nurse Ratchet, unless whoever Dr.

Gates is working on is in dire trouble, you better page her and get her here now, or you will be."

Before she could answer him, Kaitlin Gates emerged from the patient room just across from the Nursing Unit. "Chris!" she yelled, meeting him at the station and pulling him over to the side for privacy.

"How's Jason?" Gates questioned, pausing for a second then adding, "I need to talk to him."

Kaitlin led him toward the large family room in the back. It was a rather large room with tables and plush, comfortable blue chairs. There was a worn yellow sofa pushed to the back wall with a coffee table in front of it. Toward the right was a small kitchen area with a sink, microwave, and small refrigerator.

Someone on the hospital staff had already started a fresh pot of coffee; the aroma was strong and welcoming as they stepped into the room. "I reserved the room for the McKenzies'. I expect them any minute."

"How is he?" Gates asked, fearing the answer she might give.

"Not good," she answered. "I was able to get him stabilized and transported upstairs for surgery. He lost a lot of blood. I think the blood bank is going to ask the family to donate some blood in reserve for him and possibly Devon."

Gates couldn't hide his expression as soon as Kaitlin said Devon's name. "Just give me the facts, Kaitlin."

She nodded. "He was stabbed four times, all in the abdomen and chest area." She paused then went on. "I can't believe he didn't bleed out; there's so much blood loss."

"Is he gonna make it?" Gates asked, trying to get to the bottom line.

Kaitlin shook her head. "I honestly don't know. He's in great shape and he's strong. At this point, it's in God's hands."

Almost at that time, the door opened as Ashton and Caren McKenzie bolted into the room. "Chris, what the hell happened?" Ash asked, advancing to where Gates and Kaitlin were standing.

Chris motioned to his sister. "You remember my sister, Dr. Kaitlin Gates? She cared for Jason here in the Emergency Department."

Gates quickly stepped away and let Kaitlin answer their questions about Jason's condition as best as she could. Once Kaitlin had answered their questions, Caren walked over to where Chris was standing. "What about Devon and Melissa?"

"All I know is that the two agents assigned to Devon are dead. The apartment is trashed; there was a hell of a fight in there. Devon and Melissa are missing, but presumed to be alive." He turned back to the door where Laura and William Gates were just entering, followed by Kevin McKenzie and his wife.

As the group made its way to Kaitlin for an update, Jarrod and Nick came bursting through the door, and like the other men, all had their police badges prominently displayed on their jacket pockets. Gates waited as Kaitlin updated everyone on Jason's condition. The silence in the room was deafening as the realization of what she was saying set in.

Everyday phrases took on a completely different meaning as the McKenzie family had to accept the fact that one or both twins might be lost forever.

The last brother to arrive at the hospital was Brett. It was obvious he'd come straight from work. He was wearing a dark suit jacket with the holster hanging just under his arm. His eyes were red and wild, almost frantic. "How did this happen?" he yelled, as he closed the door behind him. His eyes searched through the crowd until his gaze lit on Gates. He almost ran to him, his finger pointed and his face enraged. "Where were you?" he screamed. "Why weren't you with her?"

Gates didn't say anything. He couldn't find his voice; instead, his eyes met the floor. Finally, he sighed, almost relieved. Someone had said what everyone else was thinking. It was out, and he didn't have to dance around it anymore. He had failed her again. It was just like being back in that cell and listening to her muffled cries and restrained pleas for help. He had tried to block out their moans of satisfaction and her pitiful attempts at resisting.

Nick Gates wasn't the most patient brother, but he was probably the most loyal, the brother most likely to take a beating for one of the others, especially Seth, the baby.

He knew how much Chris loved this woman, and her family was part of that package. He wanted nothing more than for this to work out, but this was his brother, his little brother. "Hold on, McKenzie, I know you're upset and all, but this isn't his fault."

"Whose fault is it then?" Brett screamed, almost crying.

Kevin stepped in between them, putting a hand against each of their chests. "The fault is with whoever took them." He smiled. "We have to work together, you guys." He looked at Chris. "When you married her, our families became one. We have to see this through for each other, and for Devon and for Melissa."

Ashton McKenzie stepped into the circle and motioned for William Gates to join him. "Kevin is right, boys. We're in this together. From this point on, you are all brothers." He put his arm around William's shoulder and patted him affectionately.

William leaned in and looked almost directly at Gates. "I suggest we figure out who's got them and go get them." His meaning was not lost on his son, and he nodded his head to affirm that the message was received loud and clear.

Jarrod looked around, noticing that the number of people in the room far outweighed the available seating. He left to locate someone who could commandeer more chairs for the room. Within a few minutes, the staff had put together an area that looked more like a command center than a consultation area.

Gates sat at the table near the back of the room, his attention only partially on the caller on the other end of the phone. Even without a spoken word, it was obvious he was upset by the telephone call, his posture was stiff, frozen almost.

Devon was his world, his air, his very life's blood. He remembered the life he had before she was in it, it wasn't a life he wanted anymore.

He perked up when he saw Mike Squires come into the room, and jumped to his feet, getting to him in about four large steps. "Mike," he said, desperation evident in his voice. "What can you tell me?"

Squires rubbed his face. "Captain has been very specific that you are not to be involved in this investigation."

"Mike, cut the crap. What angle are they working?" he asked.

Squires flipped through his notepad. "Most of the blood is either Harris's or Jason McKenzie's. From the blood splatter, Harris was killed in the living room, right at or near the sofa area, and his body was dragged into the bedroom for staging. Your brother-in-law was stabbed just inside the living room. It looks as if he'd just stepped into the apartment when he was struck. I'm sure your sister already told you that there were four stab wounds."

Gates motioned for him to go on, and Squires continued reluctantly. "There is a small amount of blood just outside the kitchen that is Devon's."

Squires flipped the page. "No one in your apartment complex saw anything unusual." Squires shook his head. "We're still gathering data, but there are very few leads to follow up on."

He motioned for Gates to get closer. "Brad Michaels has not reported for his shift and has not returned any of the bureau's calls. There's a BOLO out for him."

Gates flinched. "What does Michaels have to do with this?"

"Not sure if the two events are related at all. It's no secret to anyone but Devon, that Michaels has a thing for her. The fact we can't locate him is concerning."

Squires noted. He looked awkwardly toward the door. "I've got to go before the captain finds me here."

Gates shook his hand and slapped his arm as he left, then retreated to his seat to rehash everything that Squires had shared with him.

Chapter Twenty-Three

An unfamiliar sound penetrated the darkness; it was mechanical and heavy with an intermittent clash that echoed all around her. The cushion beneath her head and body smelled musty and old as if it had been stored away for a long time, and then suddenly brought out for airing.

Her eyelids were heavy, and she struggled to lift them, if only just for a second or two. She didn't know where she was, but she knew that she wasn't supposed to be there. She managed to open her eyes for a second or two, before she gave way to the darkness again and drifted back to sleep.

The figure concealed in the back stepped out from the darkness and approached her cautiously, almost as if he were afraid of her. After edging closer, he ran a gloved hand across her left cheek and along her neck, and then took his time with her left breast, pushing and pulling it under the material of the knit running shirt she was wearing.

She stirred, protesting in her sleep and adjusting herself away from the intrusion. Quickly, the gloved hand pulled away and the figure disappeared into the darkness again.

****

The surgeon Kaitlin escorted from the second-floor surgical bay into the family consultation room was younger than anyone was expecting. Ash and Caren McKenzie broke into tears of joy to discover that Jason was out of surgery.

Although his condition was still listed as critical, he was expected to recover. But to everyone's dismay, he hadn't regained consciousness yet and probably wouldn't until tomorrow, at the very least.

Kaitlin convinced the surgeon to let his parents visit him in the PACU, and then she left with them to show them the way. Almost as soon as they returned, Ash approached Gates. "Are we just supposed to wait until we find their bodies?" The question prompted discussions all over the room that broke out like wildfire.

Gates ran a shaking hand through his hair and motioned for everyone to settle down. "There's something that we aren't seeing." He looked around the room and almost laughed. "I mean, we have a roomful of detectives here. We've missed something."

He looked at Ashton and Caren. "Before we went missing, was Devon ever harassed or followed, anything like that?"

Devon's family shook their heads.

"What about her fiancée? Any chance his death could be related?"

Once again, the brothers and her parents shook their heads.

"What about this guy she was seeing?" He motioned to Kevin. "The one from the bar video, the night before her accident with the guard rail."

"Richard?" Caren McKenzie asked. "I don't think she was serious about him."

Gates went on. "Any chance he might feel differently?"

"I don't think so," Caren added. "I think their relationship was more casual. I don't think it progressed to anything other than dinner every now and again."

Gates went on. "So other than what happened to us as well as this event, there's been nothing out of the ordinary."

Ash McKenzie swallowed as if he was trying to find the right words. "Any chance that this can be related to the man who hurt her while the two of you were missing?"

Gates recalled Dale Hyman's warnings about the one who was coming for her. Whoever took her, came for her, and killed or intended to kill anyone who got in the way of him doing so.

Most likely, Melissa was dead already; her body just hadn't been found yet. His rational mind screamed out. Esteban was still incarcerated, so if it wasn't Esteban, then who?

Hayden, he thought to himself, Hayden had managed to come through the portal with them and was here in his own physical body, not hiding in Esteban's.

It was the only thing that made any sense. Gates looked around the room so quickly it was almost as if it were spinning. "I think that we've been going about this all wrong."

He looked at her parents and considered asking them to step outside for a minute, but he decided to continue. "The man that hurt her before, he let other men hurt her as well." He wiped at his forehead, suddenly aware of how warm it was in the room. "I mean, once he finished with her, he let two other men have a turn."

The room was silent except for the sounds of gentle weeping from Caren and Laura. Gates gave Mrs. McKenzie an apologetic look. "When we interrogated Esteban, he made it a point that he wasn't sharing her with anyone. In fact, he boasted that he'd given all his men a directive that she wasn't to be touched. She belonged to him."

He shook his head. "I don't think Esteban is responsible. It is someone else who is attracted to her, someone who wants her, but can't have her." He didn't say the name, but his mind finished his thought: Brad Michaels.

Caren McKenzie inquired almost casually, "Does this have anything to do with her former partner?"

Gates looked at her but didn't respond right away. "I don't know him that well, but he didn't report for his shift and is not responding to his Captain's calls."

"You think he's somehow involved with this?" Ash asked, moving closer.

"It's possible," Gates answered.

"Where do we start looking for them?" Kevin pulled his phone from his pocket and barked into the receiver. "I want everything on Agent Brad Michaels, any building, storage unit, anything in his or his ex-wife's name, ASAP."

Kevin put his phone away as Brett approached. "Where would he take her?"

Gates jumped to his feet. "My God, three nights!"

Jarrod was at his side within minutes and placed his hands on his shoulders as if to calm him down. "Three nights?"

Gates strode to the door. "This all started in Aurora, and I think that is where it is supposed to end tomorrow night. If we don't find her before the lights are the strongest, we might not find her at all."

William Gates called out to Chris, "Where are you going?"

"To the airport; I've got to get to Aurora before tomorrow night," Gates answered.

Kevin raced across the room and said, "Hang on, Chris. You can't go alone. You'll need backup."

Gates nodded, thinking to himself that they were right. "Okay, I'm getting my gear. Whoever's going with me, be at the airport in two hours." He turned to his father, "Dad, I'll need help getting the FBI jet."

"Head to the airport," William said. "I'll have it cleared by the time you're ready to leave."

Gates kissed his mother and sister's cheek and left the room, before running down the hallway and exiting the hospital.

****

Devon's head was pounding; it was a dull, hard pain that started at the top of her head and ended just about where her neck and shoulders came together. She opened her eyes; still feeling sluggish, but she was able to get them open more easily than before.

She exhaled a deep, breathy moan, mostly in response to the aches and pains of her lower legs. She didn't know how long she'd been there, but she was sure by the way her legs were cramping that it had been a while.

She was still in the dark, musty place, but there was some lighting in the room. There were at least four lights, one in each corner of the room. The room was larger than she thought; the lights cast an eerie shadow that bathed most of the room in darkness.

Devon knew she wasn't alone; she could hear him breathing. Esteban, she thought; he must be lurking somewhere in the shadows. The best chance she had of escaping was to lure him into a false sense of compliance, then attack him when he was vulnerable and not expecting it.

She tried to move her arms, but couldn't and turned her head to determine what was binding her. She was surprised that there was no binding; her arms and legs were free. Devon realized she had been drugged. She shook her head, trying to clear some of the cobwebs that had taken up residence there. How long have I been here, anyway, she thought. Chris would be frantic, not to mention her parents and brothers.

Brothers? It came back to her in a flash, the sight of Jason falling to the floor in agony, blood welling from his gut and pooling on the floor like rain. Her last thought was the sound that their bodies made as they hit the floor almost simultaneously. She hadn't even seen who had hurt him and hit her.

As she lay there bound, she tried to turn her head to see if there were any other prisoners. Where was Melissa? Had Esteban already killed her? No, she thought, he would need something to control her with, and what better leverage than her family?

She felt the sting of the needle in her bicep without seeing anyone nearby, but as the clouds formed in her head and the room began to spin, she realized that he had been in the shadows just to her right. "What do you want?" she mumbled, as the darkness engulfed her again.

The voice replied from his hiding place, "You."

****

Gates parked his car at the small lot beside the hangar. The man that walked out knew him, and Gates waved familiarly and extended his hand as they approached each other. "Eric, thanks, man. I appreciate your help."

Eric nodded and pulled a gray baseball cap off his head and wiped the sweat that had saturated his forehead. It may have been cold outside, but inside the hangar, the air was thick and sweaty. He was about the same age as Gates, and tall and thin with blonde hair. He wore a worn pair of gray overalls smeared with oil and dirt, especially, on the chest and arms.

"I worked with Devon on a case a few years ago. I hope she's okay," he said.

Gates nodded and walked inside the hangar. Just as he and Eric walked through the big open door, several cars pulled up as Jarrod and Nick Gates spilled out of one vehicle while Kevin and Brett McKenzie stepped from the other. Each of them was carrying a backpack, and three were carrying packages that looked suspiciously like rifles wrapped in leather cases.

Eric gave them a curious look, concerned with all the firepower. "Everyone here is a cop?"

Everyone nodded, and they all walked into the hangar. As they entered the building, Eric looked around in confusion. "Which of you is the pilot?"

Gates stopped and looked at him with concern. "What do you mean?"

"You know the guy behind the wheel? Pulls the flaps up and down?"

"I thought you were flying us?" Gates dropped his bag.

"Na, I haven't flown in a few years, I had eye surgery and something didn't heal right." He smacked the belly of the plane. "Now, I just fix them."

A car's squealing breaks coming from the direction of the hangar's opening drew everyone's attention. Gates didn't try to hide his surprise. "Dad? Mr. McKenzie?"

Gates offered his hand to each one. "We weren't expecting you?"

"I want to make sure you have whatever you need to bring her home, son," William said.

He disappeared behind the plain, duffel bag in hand.

"Mr. McKenzie?" Gates asked. "Are you coming along or just here to see us off?"

"I'm the pilot, son," Ash explained, as he stepped up the step and into the cockpit. "I need to start on the safety check."

"Let's load up," Gates advised, motioning everyone to stow their bags and climb aboard.

****

It was almost midnight by the time the FBI jet took off with Gates and everyone else aboard. Gates rubbed his eyes, noticing how tired his brothers and Devon's brothers looked. He knew the smart thing to do would be to lay down in one of the empty couches along the back part of the plane and try and get some rest. He let his head drop on top of the headrest instead and closed his eyes.

"Chris?" His father was kneeling in the aisle. "What is the plan when we land?"

"I don't know, Dad," Gates blew a sigh. "There's no protocol for something like this, but my instincts tell me it's about Hayden. And when we find her, he won't be far behind."

"You have to tell them, you know?" William looked behind their seat to where the others were either resting or talking. "Everything about what happened, not just bits and pieces."

"They won't believe me," Gates words were exact, confident.

"You have to give them a chance. You're asking them to risk their lives," he paused. "You owe them the truth."

Gates stood up from his seat and addressed the group. "I know some of you don't believe that Devon and I were sucked into a time warp that dropped us in the middle of 1869. But it happened. The night we wrecked, the aurora borealis was whacked, it lit up the night sky for miles. We saw those lights both nights we slept in the woods and again the day we were pulled back to our own time."

"What does this have to do with Melissa and Devon's abduction?" Kevin asked.

"The Indians who inhabited the area believed the lights were markers to points in time where the channel connects all generations is open. There's an old tree, about thirty miles from the Ennis ranch, they called it Idresil, which means tree of life," Gates explained.

"You think he came through this portal somehow and is taking her back with him to his time?" Jarrod's question was on everyone's mind.

"I think whoever has Devon is following this legend. The lights burn their brightest tonight at midnight. This is our best shot at getting them back." Gates shook his head.

"So that's where we're headed? To this big tree?" Nick asked.

"It's one of a handful of places; Hayden feels in control. My instincts tell me this has something to do with him." Gates pointed to the map spread on the table. "He'll be holding her somewhere he feels in control until he takes her to Idresil. What's left of the Ennis barn and house, or the jail are all possibilities for places where he was in control. However, the Hayden house is where he felt the safest."

"So, we're going to those places before we end up at Idresil?" Nick asked.

"Yes, if we haven't found them at any of the other places, we all head to Idresil." Gates took his seat and finished the last bit of water from the plastic bottle he'd snagged at the hangar.

"When we get where we're going, you have to be prepared for all outcomes, Christopher." William stepped over Gates and took the empty seat beside him.

"I'm bringing her home, Dad."

"I hope so, son." He looked across the plane to where his own sons were retaking their seats on the small couch while Devon's brothers took their several rows ahead.

"Once we start the search and rescue, I think it would be best to separate the siblings into pairs for the search."

"Why?" Gates yawned, looking to where his father's attention was focused, watching Devon's brothers as they whispered, their heads close to one another.

"If this turns out badly, I'm not sure how those boys are going to react. We are all still officers of the court." He swallowed, 'I expect everyone to remember that."

His warning wasn't lost on Gates, "I made Devon a promise once that I wouldn't take the law into my own hands," he paused. "I kept that promise, although it wasn't an easy pledge to keep. There were times, that all I could think about was killing him."

"Yet, you didn't"

"Because I promised her I wouldn't" he exhaled, and let his head fall back against the seat and closed his eyes. "Course, killing him won't be the first promise to her that I've broken."

"How's that?"

"I promised her, he'd never hurt her again." He didn't open his eyes as he spoke. "

"Let's just hope that we find them and everyone comes home safe," William said, leaning into the cushion of the empty seat and closing his eyes to rest for a moment.

****

When the plane's tires hit the landing strip, the plane and its occupants were thrust forward, everyone including Gates were startled awake. Gates looked at his watch: 2:00 a.m., they had less than twenty-four hours to find them. He waited for everyone to grab their packs and disembark from the plane before grabbing his own and following them clutching his rifle in his hand as he climbed down the stairs.

"Chris?" Brett asked, wiping diligently at his tired, red eyes.

"Yeah," Gates answered, noticing that he'd called him Chris instead of Gates.

"I need some coffee or something, and we need to catch a few minutes of sleep. We can't help them if we end up shooting each other," he paused. "How far from here?"

Gates answered walking faster out of the hangar and into the darkness of the night. "About sixty miles, so about forty-five minutes; maybe less."

"Where are you going to get a rental car at this time of the morning?" Jarrod asked, stepping into pace with Gates and Brett.

Lisa Colodny

"Yeah, be a shame to come all this way and then have to wait until eight o'clock to get a rental car," Nick added, walking a few steps behind.

Gates pointed to an old blue van waiting near the chain-link fence that bordered the perimeter of the private airport. Dale Hyman was sitting in the driver's seat with the engine idling; his breath settled like clouds against the windshield.

Hyman stepped out of the old van as soon as he saw them emerge from the hangar. He looked over his shoulder into the darkness, but indicated the town located near the airport. "We have about a forty-five-minute ride."

He pointed up to the sky where the pulsating red and yellow lights were still visible. "You should hurry," he advised. "You have less than twenty-four hours to find her."

"I know," Gates tossed their bags into the van and climbed into the front seat, letting Brett pile in beside him while everyone else climbed in the back.

Hyman drove the van onto the street toward Aurora and said to Brett, "You are of her lineage?"

Brett looked curiously at Gates, but Gates simply said, "Yes, he is one of her brothers." He pointed with his thumb to the seat behind them. "Her father and other brother are in the back."

Hyman nodded and edged his head under the roof of the truck cab to peer into the lights. "The one who is like her will recover physically, but his wound is deep."

Gates yawned and were surprised to feel Hyman place a thermos into his hand; it held very strong coffee. Gates poured some into the thermos cup and handed it to Brett. He drank from the thermos and passed the thermos to the back seat. "How do I find her, Hyman?" Gates shook his head. "I misread your warning. Who has her?"

Hyman said, "You already know the answer to that, son. He has her, as before."

Brett interjected, "You mean, that son of a bitch who raped her, and let those others rape her?"

Gates couldn't bring himself to answer, and he hoped Hyman wouldn't, either, Devon didn't like that word. She seldom used it. "Hyman," he pleaded, "just tell me where she is. I'll go get her."

"It is not in the lights, son. I don't know. But if she is to survive, we must get to her soon," Hyman warned.

Chapter Twenty-Four

It was just after 3:00 a.m. when the blue van rolled into Aurora. Hyman drove toward Main Street; the hotel would have to serve as their command center. They couldn't very well go to the police with a crazy time travel story. Once they were able to get a lead on her, they'd involve the authorities; but for now, they were on their own.

Brett had to bang at the window for well over ten minutes before the innkeeper came to the counter. It was obvious that he had been sleeping.

The innkeeper was younger than he looked. His complexion was pale, most likely because he was inside most of the day and night. For this reason, he was overweight: A round protruding belly poked through and under his stained white undershirt. His dark, curly hair was longer in the back and sides than the front or the top. It was mostly black with just a few strands of gray scattered here and there. He sluggishly checked them in and handed them a handful of keys.

"Four rooms," the innkeeper clarified, "they are all together. Two are connecting," he yawned, "Anything else?"

He peered through the glass window to where everyone else was waiting. The innkeeper was curious as to what could possibly bring so many out so late. "What's going on?"

Brett answered with the only lie he thought would be believable. He smiled a sincere smile. "It's a bachelor party for our friend here." He smacked Gates on the back.

"A hunting bachelor party?" The innkeeper yawned again. "Never heard of that before."

"It's a city thing," Brett smiled. "And we will probably need more towels."

"Of course." The innkeeper waved as he turned toward the door behind the counter.

Before the innkeeper left, Gates asked. "There's an older woman who works at the Hayden House. I believe her name is Agnes. Do you know her?"

The innkeeper wiped at his eyes and nodded. "Yeah, I know her, you guys know what time it is, couldn't signing up for the Hayden tour wait until daybreak? "

"I just want to ask her some questions about the Hayden house."

"Yeah, Agnes Robards, she knows everything about that house and that family," he said.

Gates perked up. "You wouldn't happen to know where she lives, would you?"

The innkeeper nodded and pointed down the street where streetlights illuminated a pathway about ten feet ahead to the next lamplight. "She rents a room over the café at the end of the street."

He put his elbow on the counter and practically poured his chin into his extended hand. "Anything else?" he asked, yawning as he finished the question.

Gates looked out the window to where he'd indicated. "How do I get to her place?"

The innkeeper answered without looking up or opening his eyes. "Go down the street and enter at the door between the bank and the café. Take those stairs and look for her apartment on the left. I think its apartment C; look for the one that has a door knocker with a cat design," he yawned again. "Old woman's crazy about cats."

Gates smiled and tossed a twenty-dollar bill near his elbow. "Thank you for your help, and sorry we woke you."

He pulled Brett out to the street. "Listen, I'm going to go wake up Ms. Robards and see if she can tell me anything else about the Haydens that I don't know already."

He handed the keys to Brett and added, "Can you help everyone get settled in? I won't be gone long."

Brett nodded and grabbed as many bags as he could carry from the van and made his way up the stairs, motioning for the others to follow him in search of rooms D through G.

****

The door between the café and the bank was just where the innkeeper said it would be. It was an older door and was stuck so tight that Gates had to tug at it several times before it wailed like a siren and gave way to reveal a darkened staircase leading to a second level with better lighting.

The stairs creaked and crackled as Gates climbed them. He checked the landing before heading in the direction indicated by the innkeeper. Sure enough, there on the door of the third apartment on the left was a metal door-knocker shaped like a cat.

Gates tapped at the door several times, before he saw a sliver of light glowing under the door. Several minutes later, she opened the door, but only as much as was allowed by the safety chain.

Agnes, like the innkeeper, had no doubt been sleeping. Her gray, curly hair was pointing out in numerous directions. She had hurried into a bathrobe before opening the door. Now that the door was open, she was struggling to push her arms through the holes, but it remained open, the belt hanging untied at each side. She squinted her eyes and pushed her head close to the opening. "What do you need?" she asked.

Gates flashed his badge close to her face. "Do you remember me, Agnes?"

She looked at him intently, assessing whether he seemed dangerous or not. "You do look familiar," she said.

"I came by the Hayden House a few days ago and found myself so fascinated by your stories that I may have kept you a little bit past your quitting time." He smiled, hoping to shake her memory.

She smiled at him through the chain. "I remember you. You were with that pretty girl. Newlyweds, if I recollect." Before Gates could reply, she pushed the door shut. He heard the chain lock slide out and the knob turns again before the door swung open. "What can I do for you this time of the morning?"

She left the door open, but turned and walked to a big, gray, leather chair. He followed behind her and took a seat on the sofa. "I need your help."

It was obvious by her reaction that she had no idea what he was referring to. "Son …" she started, but he broke in.

"My wife has been taken by someone, and I believe he has a relationship to the Haydens," he said it so quickly, that he had to give her a minute to process everything. Once he was sure she'd caught up, he went on. "I need to know if there's any sort of hiding place in that house where someone could hold a person against her will."

She pushed herself to her feet, letting the belt of the robe almost drag the floor as she made her way into the kitchen, flipping lights on as she went. "You know most of the house is just for show, son. There's hardly any space suitable to actually live in."

Agnes moved from cabinet to cabinet, pulling the doors open and looking inside. Finally, she held up a bottle of acetaminophen as if she'd found the golden egg. After setting two cups on the counter, she filled a coffee pot full of water and set it to heat on the stove. "Many of the hallways are just dead ends to accommodate the public area. And most of the bedrooms have been converted into offices or storage rooms." She thought for a minute and added, "Most of what you can see is the touring area, which you and your wife toured."

"What about the barn or any exterior buildings? Nothing comes to mind that might be useful?" he asked as she handed him a cup of coffee.

"Not inside the house," she answered.

He made as if to stand on his feet, and disappointment was on his face like a raw sore. "But under the house," she announced, "there's a lot of possibilities there."

"Under the house?" Gates asked.

She returned to the living room and took her seat. "Thomas Hayden Senior was a wealthy man, Detective Gates. But his father, Samuel Hayden, was even richer. He had one of the largest plantations in the area, and he managed it with dozens and dozens of slaves."

"Slaves?" Gates asked. "I didn't know that. I thought Nebraska supported the Union during the Civil War."

"Most did," she answered, "but it wasn't exclusive, and there were a lot of Confederate supporters. Samuel Hayden III had more than fifty slaves, and he took good care of most of them. He had a special affection for his female slaves, as did his father and grandfather before him."

Gates shook his head and thought to himself, how he wasn't surprised.

"The slave quarters are actually under the house, almost like a basement that runs the full length of the house. Over the generations, many of the slaves and Union sympathizers dug a series of tunnels extending out from the slave quarters that ran for many miles in all directions."

"An underground railroad of sorts?" Gates asked.

Agnes smiled. "I don't know much about the tunnels, just that they're there. There're no access points from the house anymore, I know that. They've all been closed up and sealed, permanent walls placed and so on."

"Come on, Agnes, there has to be someone who can help us. My wife's life might depend on it."

She stood up and smiled. "Bryan Keyes, he's a photographer in town, but he's also a knowledgeable historian. He lives about an hour north of here."

"An hour?" Gates frowned. "I don't have two hours to get there and then get back. I have to search for some other places, too. My gut tells me there's a relation to that house, but my gut's been wrong before."

She called from the dressing room, "Why don't you go ahead and start your search of the other areas, and I'll bring Bryan to the Hayden House."

"Agnes," he called out, "I could kiss you." He grabbed his jacket and made his way out the door and into the street.

****

"Devon?" Devon heard a frantic voice calling her name; she felt her shoulder shake so that her head rocked back and forth as if she was drunk. "Oh, God, Devon, please wake up."

"Melissa?" Devon mumbled through a throat so dry, that she couldn't even swallow. She managed to lift her head to assess that it was indeed her sister-in-law. Melissa's hair was tangled and matted with mud, and dried blood clung to her forehead. She had a bruise almost bulls-eyed on her left cheek. Devon could only see her from the waist up, but her shirt was bloodied and torn, and hanging off her shoulders.

Devon licked her lips, desperate for water to quench her parched throat, as she attempted to push herself into a sitting position. But the ropes attached at her wrists held tight and she couldn't get free. "Please," she pleaded, trying to get Melissa to focus. "Untie my hands."

Melissa shook her head and continued to babble, crying intermittently between sentences. "He'll be back any minute," she managed to blurt out, looking behind her frantically.

Devon knew that Melissa was in shock. "Melissa, please just reach up and untie me." Devon pulled on the ropes binding her hands, hoping she could loosen them. "Melissa, honey, please, please, untie my hands."

Melissa reached toward Devon's hands as if she were going to untie her, and then she stopped and jumped to her feet. She turned around to face the darkness behind them and screamed in a hushed tone. "Oh, God, he's back."

Before Devon could say anything else to her, Melissa ran off into the darkness, away from the direction she'd indicated. Devon pulled frantically at the ropes, but they were so tight, that her skin under the rope began to bleed.

Minutes later, Devon heard Melissa screaming again, and a struggle not too far away.

Devon kicked at the structure she was bound to, trying to create some slack in the ropes. "Esteban, you bastard! Let her go," Devon screamed, pulling at the ropes, but her struggle was to no avail. She could hear Melissa begging and pleading with him, followed by a hoarse, masculine voice warning her to cooperate.

After several minutes, the noises stilled and the darkness became silent again. Devon heard steps approaching her and braced herself for what she knew was coming.

His image in front of the light made it hard for her to distinguish all his features, but she recognized his walk and his clothes. She knew it was him, and the fear was so overwhelming that it reached down and swallowed her whole. Thomas Hayden Jr made his way purposefully toward her with a knowing smile.

He stopped before he reached her and paused as if he were waiting for an invitation. She could hear his breathing, deep, heavy, and erratic. She couldn't tell if it was the result of his altercation with Melissa or in response to seeing her again, helpless and at his mercy.

"Where's my friend?" she asked, pulling at the rope, praying that it would just magically break away or dissolve into thin air, so that she could get to her feet and repay Thomas Hayden Jr. for all the horrible things he did to her and the people she loved.

He stepped close enough to reach out and touch her, but not close enough so that she could see his face against the reflection of the lights. He ran a gloved hand from her ankle just to the inside of her knee, and only pulled his hand away when she kicked him. "She's a little tied up right now, but she'll be out soon to assist me with a little something," he teased.

"Let her go, Hayden, I'll do whatever you want," Devon offered.

He stepped forward, but stayed far to her left, still in the shadows. She saw the syringe in his hand, but could do little, if anything, to defend against it. She felt the needle prick into her shoulder, and then the world around her went black once again.

****

The sun was just beginning to rise when Gates parked the rental car near what was left of the rotted and worn fence that once marked the boundary of the Ennis ranch. In almost synchronized fashion, all the doors of the rental vehicle were thrown open and the occupants stepped out.

Ashton McKenzie stepped from the front passenger seat and looked around curiously. He waited for Jarrod and Kevin to exit the rear passenger side before shutting the door. They walked around to the front of the car to where Gates was gazing at the landscape with an almost nostalgic look on his face. Nick opened the trunk and pulled out one of the rifles. He handed it to his father, William Gates, as he slid out of the middle seat and joined the others at the front of the vehicle.

Ashton pointed to the barn, and then asked Chris, "Why are we ruling out these places? If you think he's in the tunnels with them, why are we wasting time with other places?"

Chris pulled his gun and walked toward the barn. "It's just a hunch. If Hayden is trying to relive the past, he'll bring her to one of the places where he felt he was in control before."

"You mean reliving the rush?" Jarrod asked.

"Yes, that means we check the barn and main house here and the jail cell in town. If that's not his motivation, a comfortable place where he's the most at ease, then he'll be at the Hayden House.

The ground was frozen so solid that the crunching of the snow as they walked into the barn was rhythmic. The rise and fall of their steps sounded like a platoon marching toward the battle. It didn't take long after inspecting the barn to classify it as a waste of time.

Within minutes, they reached the same conclusion about the skeletal remnants of the main house. Disheartened, they secured their weapons in the trunk and crammed themselves back into the van.

Chris pulled the car into gear and hit the gas, and they rode along in silence so loud that it was deafening. Everyone was vividly aware that the clock was ticking, and they were no closer to finding Devon and Melissa than they'd been yesterday when they left New York.

"Chris," Ashton asked, his voice solemn and hoarse, "I know why we're going to the jailhouse, but why did we come here?"

Gates did not answer immediately. "A few nights after we got here, a man with a sack on his head approached Devon from behind and tried to attack her. That's where the cut on her head came from. He slammed her headfirst into the counter too. She needed stitches to close the wound."

Kevin added, "The house is something similar?"

This is going to be tough, Chris thought. Very tough. "Yes." Right before we were returned, Hayden came to the ranch for some payback. He took everyone hostage and tried to force Devon to have sex with him," he paused to catch his breath. "She didn't actually have sex with him, but he humiliated her with everyone watching."

"If you don't kill that bastard. I'm going to," Kevin argued, through gritted teeth.

****

By the time they had returned to town, the old jailhouse tour was open for admission. Luckily, there was no great desire or need for most of the townspeople to tour the old jail. Chris hesitated before going inside; he'd only been in the holding area a handful of times. And he hadn't been inside the first cell since the night of the rape. Even during his few days as deputy, he'd managed to steer clear of that cell.

William Gates approached his son and placed his hand on his shoulder for support. "Why don't you wait out here? We've got this one."

Gates shook his head. "No, Dad, I'm fine." He took a deep breath and paid for seven adult admissions. After everything that had happened, he would remember his return to the jail for the rest of his life. It was like knowing where you were when John Lennon was gunned down and killed, or when Ronald Reagan was shot. It was like a photograph of a moment in time burned into his mind's eye.

It was surprising to realize that it hadn't changed much since 1869. His and Devon's scars were but a few months old, but in the passage of time, several lifetimes had passed. The lighting, although electric now, was still dim and sparsely integrated throughout the rooms, so that some cells were still darker than others.

It was evident that at some time the floors had been replaced. Although the floors were presently tile, the room still smelled damp and musty.

The cells were still in the same proximity as they had been that night. The cots were still placed just as they had been as well. It truly was a picture frozen in time.

In the office, Callahan's desk was not only still there, but it was in the same place in the room. Everything in the sheriff's office was the same.

Gates went outside to get some air before meeting up with the others. "Let's get back to the hotel and see if Brett has everything ready for the tunnels."

Brett had been the logical choice to act as the tactical leader for the search. The years he'd spent in search and rescue, had given him exceptional experience in searching for and retrieving victims alive, dead, and everything in between.

****

When Ashton opened the door to room D, he was only partially surprised to see multiple backpacks lining the wall. Each pack had a specific color rectangle on it, designating the color flashers and reflective paint that each contained.

Brett stood up and checked his watch as the group entered the room. "I was thinking I'd be searching for you all."

"Sorry," Chris said, motioning toward the rooms. "Let's eat something and head to the Hayden House." He retrieved his pack and grabbed a clean shirt and underwear from the compartment as he walked toward the bathroom.

He'd almost gotten to the bathroom when he noticed Ashton McKenzie sprawled across the bed on his back, facing the ceiling. It was his first consideration to pretend he didn't see him, but the expression on his face was so forlorn, Gates couldn't help, but pause and inquire if he needed anything.

Ashton didn't sit up or move his forearm away from his forehead. He looked almost as if he was lying on the beach and using his arm to block the sun from his eyes. "Chris, do you think they're still alive?"

Chris pulled his T-shirt over his head with one hand. "I don't believe Hayden wants Devon dead. He could've killed her at least twice already." He walked into the bathroom, unzipped his jeans, and stepped out of them.

"What about Melissa?" Ashton asked, although he feared he already knew the answer.

Gates stepped back into the room. "He needs Melissa, so I don't believe he will kill her."

Ashton sat up. "What does he need Melissa for?"

"To control Devon," he answered. "He'll use her as leverage against Devon."

Chapter Twenty-Five

Devon awoke with a start, jumping forward as far as the ropes on her wrists would allow her to. Her first realization was that she was cold and shivering. She blinked several times, each time hoping her visual field would be better. Whatever sedative he was using on her was strong; each time she came to, it was harder and harder to focus, more difficult to coordinate her movements, and more challenging to believe that rescue was imminent.

The cool air on her belly and chest alerted her that he'd removed her shirt and running pants. Since her hands were still tied, she could only assume he'd cut the shirt off, because nothing else was amiss.

He'd also rearranged the torches so that the light was directed to where she lay bound.

She heard him approaching before she saw him step into the pool of light. "Hayden, where's Melissa?" she asked, her voice barely audible.

He took a glass of water from the table next to her and motioned for her to raise her head to drink. She considered refusing his offer, just on principle. But she was so thirsty she licked her chapped, dry lips and lifted her head to the glass he offered. The water tasted cold and bitter, and she realized too late that it was spiked with something. Once she'd satisfied the dryness in her throat, she pulled her mouth away from the glass and let her head fall back against the cushion.

The room had already started spinning again, just not as violently as when he'd injected her. She'd been cold earlier, but now her skin was warm and moist, and she was sweating. She felt his hands pushing against her ankles, forcing her legs apart, and sliding himself between them at her knees. He raised his hands over his head, grabbing her breasts through her bra until they spilled out over the top of it.

She opened her mouth to protest, but she knew that he would ignore her pleas. She squirmed as if she could pull away enough to get out of his reach, but he grabbed her breasts and pulled so hard that she cried out. Devon jerked her knee upward and caught him in the groin.

He curled up defensively and cupped himself. When he could speak, he croaked,

"Do that again, and I'll bring her back to watch."

He traced the elastic of her underwear with two fingers of each hand, pulling them all the way down and kicking them to the floor with his boot. He stroked the insides of her thigh, his lips following the trail left by his fingers. He kissed her knee and pulled at the dark hairs between her legs.

A loud whine escaped from her throat, and she bit down on her lip, hoping the pain would distract her from crying out.

Devon raised her head unsteadily to look down at Hayden; she noticed that his hair was longer and was almost touching the soft skin of her stomach. He was kissing just above her hairline now, his tongue intermittently dipping in and out of the curly hair.

Propped up between her legs almost on his elbows, he pulled his gloves off and separated her labial folds with his pointer finger, dropping his mouth down on her almost at the same time. She lurched her hips upward, lifting herself off the hard edge of where she lay, hoping she could get him to unlatch from her center. "Hayden, please, please; not again."

He was biting and licking at her, pushing several of his fingers in and out of her, and pumping as if they were a thick penis. He pulled himself away from her just long enough to address her. "Don't pretend you don't like this. I've watched you with him. I know you do."

She responded through gritted teeth. "He's my husband."

If he heard her, he gave no indication. Instead, he slid his other hand under her hips to her buttocks, pushing her groin as hard against his mouth as he could.

Devon closed her eyes and willed her body not to respond to his mouth and fingers, but her body had a mind of its own and was responding to the mechanical stimulation. She felt the pressure building at her core and extended all the way through her groin. Finally, she gave in, and turned her face into her forearm and cried out, as she felt herself spasm against his tongue.

As soon as he felt her release, he pulled his fingers out and his mouth away, and began kissing and licking a trail to her right breast. Devon couldn't see his face, but she was sure his expression was one of smug satisfaction. She could feel him hard and erect against her thigh, pressing forcefully and impatiently from one side to the other.

She squirmed again to push her legs together, but he'd already anticipated her move and responded accordingly. He was positioned so that her legs were almost spread into a V.

"Why do you still fight me?" he asked, surprisingly sincere. "You know we are meant to be together. You belong to me. You always have."

His touch was unusually gentle, almost loving, and Devon jerked away in repulsion. "I thought you'd learned your lesson after the artist. It's unfortunate for Detective Gates that you didn't. When he comes to save you, I'll make sure he's enlightened as well."

She was surprised to feel how gently his fingers snapped the band of her bra apart and pulled it down to her wrists. He cut it at the shoulder straps and pulled it away, letting it fall to the floor.

Her mind was so fuzzy; she couldn't make out everything Hayden had said. Did he just mention Paul? What was he planning for Chris? "What does any of this have to do with Paul?" she asked, finally settling on which question to ask first. Her growing anger was evident in her voice.

He raised his head so that they were almost face-to-face, and she could smell his breath, warm and foul against her cheek. "You remember Paul; he was the one always trying to separate you from your clothes," he remarked.

"Did you have something to do with his accident?" she spat out at him, tugging her arms at the ropes with the hope that, by some chance, she would have use of them.

"You should have seen his face that night," he said, taunting her. "He was so eager and excited about spending the evening with you."

Smiling, he made a gesture with his fingers to his lips as if he was telling a secret that he wasn't supposed to share. "He might have gotten a message to meet you at the studio for an unprecedented evening of romance. The message may have led him to believe that you'd had a change of heart about waiting until your wedding night."

Devon shook her head, obviously distraught; tears were falling rapidly down her cheek. "He was such a gentle man. He never laid a finger on me. What did you do?"

Hayden smiled. "I waited until he parked the car and opened the door to get out, and then I came out from the studio with some wine and a piece of paper he thought was from you. I hit him over the head while he was reading the letter, still sitting behind the wheel."

Hayden traced his finger down her right cheek to her neck and then to her breast. "He never had a chance to get out of the car. I pushed him over and drove the car west, to the harbor, put him back in the driver's seat, and popped his head against the steering wheel as hard as I could before I watched the car roll into the bay."

Devon was crying more freely; she couldn't get Paul's smiling face out of her mind.

He kissed her right breast again then moved to the left, biting at the nipple and sucking as much of it as he could into his mouth. "I've been patient with you these last few years, Devon. Haven't I tolerated him just to be near you? I've waited so long for you," he said, between mouthfuls.

She knew his demeanor was changing as he finished his last sentence. He was growing angrier by the minute. "And you betray me again with the detective, a man who you don't really even like. You're no better than all those other women he sleeps with. You're a whore. You'll spread your legs for any man with a penis, any man but me, that is."

As if to illustrate his point, he pushed her thighs so far apart, it was painful. She cried out in response and tried to adjust the angle to provide some comfort.

He'd mentioned Chris again, she realized. Whatever his plans were, both she and Chris were a part of it. It was as if he knew what she was thinking. "When he comes for you, I'll kill him this time. We're going away, just you and me."

Devon could feel him fumbling with his pants and zipper, struggling to free himself from his trousers. She knew by the way he was thrusting against her that he was finally successful. "A trip?" she questioned between breaths, trying to distract herself from the discomfort.

He ran his hand against her opening, using his thumb to prepare her once again. He pushed his thumb several inches into her then pulled out and pushed himself into her in a single motion. "We're going back to Hamilton," he whispered against her neck.

Devon screamed out unable to maintain her silence anymore; it was different this time, and it hurt like hell. She screamed again, arching her body as if she could separate his body from hers, but she was not successful. He rammed even harder into her, causing her to scream out with each thrust he made.

"Tonight, when the lights are the brightest," he threatened, between clenched teeth in time with his forward thrusts, "we will wait at Idresil for the lights to take us home."

There was something different this time, she thought. Rigid was one thing, but the feeling wasn't like anything she'd felt before. And although her experience might be classified as limited, she knew something just didn't feel right. It felt more like an inanimate object then warm, flesh and skin.

She raised her head to him again to determine what he was doing to cause her so much discomfort and pain. Maybe it was the timing or maybe the way the light bounced off the torch at just the right second. Her breath caught in her throat, a breath that she couldn't release as she came face to face with Melissa.

She was dressed in tan trousers and an old blue shirt; the light from the torch was reflecting off the infinity necklace hanging loosely around her neck. Her hair was cut just below her ears, just as Hayden had worn his the last time she'd seen him in 1869.

Maybe it was because of the dim light, but Devon could see that Melissa could have been Hayden's identical twin.

****

It was late in the afternoon when the van rolled to a stop near the Hayden House, followed minutes later by Dale Hyman's old blue pickup truck. Chris slammed the van door shut and motioned for the others to join him. Everyone was dressed in dark SWAT attire complete with boots and vests. He pointed to Brett. "I can't believe you were able to requisition all this on such short notice."

Brett smiled and threw his rifle over his shoulder. "I spent six years as part of the FBI's Elite Squad before I joined the police force. I had everything flown in by chopper from Denver." Brett indicated his pack and motioned the others to gather around him to go over the finer points of search and rescue underground.

"First, everyone's equipment has a different reflective color. Mine is blue, so my lights, tags, paint, everything is blue. As we search the tunnels, it's important to know where we are and where we have been; as you enter the tunnel, mark your reflective paint at the top middle of the area you are entering, and place your tags along the right side of the path to mark your trail."

He looked around to ensure that everyone was paying attention, and then he went on. "This is important so that you can find your way out, or we can get to you if you need help. Everyone has white paint, and this is to indicate that a tunnel is a dead end and you have come out and gone to the next one. So, if you see a tunnel with blue paint sprayed at the top and then white next to it, it means that I searched it, it was a dead-end, and so I exited and moved on."

Chris pulled his pack over his shoulder and adjusted his earpiece more securely into his ear canal. "Is everyone's equipment working and ammunition checked?"

William Gates nodded and pointed to the house where an older woman was approaching them.

"Agnes," Chris exclaimed, running to meet her, "I was getting worried you couldn't find Mr. Keyes."

She nodded to everyone, as she made her way down the incline to where the group was waiting. After almost stumbling into them as if they were bowling pins, she managed to grab onto Jarrod and bring herself to a stop. Agnes was breathing heavily, her warm breath expelling into the cool air and rising like steam.

She handed Gates a rolled-up blueprint that looked old. "He couldn't come back with me to help, but he gave me this drawing notated with where he thought the easiest access into the tunnel would be."

She motioned for them to follow her as she moved past the house and to the barn. Once she was inside, she checked the blueprint and went into the third stall on the left. All the way to the back of the stall, where the wall met the floor, was a small trap door with an old, rusted handle. She pointed to the handle. "There it is."

Gates thanked her and said, "You should leave for the day. Call your boss and tell him you're sick and you're going to close the site down for the rest of the day."

She agreed, exited the barn, and walked toward the Hayden House.

Chris pulled the trapdoor open and flashed his light into the small opening. "Hope no one's claustrophobic." He pushed his feet through first, holding himself as if he were doing a chin-up until he had no choice, but to let go and drop the rest of the way. It was only about three feet until the bottom of his boots collided with the wet, hard ground. He jumped to his feet almost instantly, shining his flashlight in all four corners before calling up to the others. "Toss me my pack, then drop down one at a time. "

One by one, each of them forced themselves through the small opening into the tunnel until only William Gates was the only one still on the surface. "Brett," he called into the hole below, "are we using a line to get out, or is there an easier way?"

"Chris's expert says this is the best way in or out, so let's just hope everyone is able to walk on his own. Dad, tie your rope to the rafter above you and drop the rest of the rope into the hole."

Ashton tied a secure knot at the top of the rafter and let the rope fall into the opening. He tugged on it a few times to ensure it would hold, and then he climbed on the rope and made his way down into the darkness.

His first thought, once his feet were planted firmly on the ground, was that it was cold and dark. The second thought was that there was an old odor, not necessarily a musty odor, but an unusual scent. The location they'd dropped down into was facing a darkened area where the path ventured into three different tunnels. Ashton motioned to Brett. "I believe this tactical command is yours, son."

Brett nodded and looked around the area, nothing seemed unusual or out of place. He acknowledged Nick. "Dad and Nick take the first tunnel. Good luck." Seconds later, he threw his pack on. "Jarrod and I will take this one." He pointed to the third one. "Chris, you and Kevin take the last one, there." Brett looked at William Gates. "I need you to stay here and secure our exit and monitor these tunnels."

Gates pointed upward to the opening. "Hyman is waiting in his truck. If we aren't out by midnight, he'll alert the authorities. He can also call for medical assistance, should we need it," he paused. "If anything happens or if we haven't found them by 11:30, Dad you and Hyman need to head for Idresil. It's our last chance to find them."

Brett paused a second, then nodded. "Everyone ready?" No one said anything; they all just nodded and looked at the tunnel they'd been assigned to. "Let's roll, then. Good luck," he said, motioning Jarrod toward the second tunnel.

****

Devon had finally given up on struggling against the ropes and focused on a plan for talking Melissa into releasing her. Why would she do this? Devon couldn't think of anything that made any sense. She had known Melissa almost all her life. She cataloged the years and events she and Melissa had shared, even before Melissa had married Jason. There had to be something she could use to trigger a connection and elicit some kind of empathy.

Her mind drifted back to what Melissa had said earlier about Paul. Devon pressed the rewind button of her mind, trying to ascertain if she had ever shared anything intimate with Melissa about Paul. Sure, she did, she told herself. She and Melissa had been close, and when she and Paul first started dating, he was always trying to sketch her. It had become a joke between them. Later, after they were engaged, she had posed for him, but never naked.

At the time, she didn't want it to be an issue between Paul and her brothers. It would have been easy for Melissa to trick Paul into a meeting, and he never would have suspected there might be a danger. Why would he? Melissa was family, her family.

Whatever Melissa had drugged her with was finally wearing off. She'd left about thirty minutes ago without sedating Devon again, which could only mean that the second phase of the plan had been initiated.

Devon was confused by Melissa's actions as she was leaving; she'd pushed herself to her feet and thrown a blanket over Devon to ward off the chill in the room, almost as if Melissa had been concerned for Devon's comfort.

Devon heard her coming before she saw the shadow nearing her, and she braced herself for another round of physical abuse. From the shape of the shadow, Devon could tell that Melissa was still dressed as Hayden, but she had donned a worn looking, long, brown leather coat and a western hat that looked oddly like the one Hayden had worn in Hamilton.

She could also tell that she was carrying something in her hands, but she couldn't identify what it was. As Melissa stepped out of the shadows and made her way closer, Devon could tell that some of the items were food, and the other was an odd-looking metal stick.

"Melissa," Devon whispered, pulling at the ropes, "please let me go. I promise I'll see that you get some help."

Hayden slid down to sit next to her left hip. "Don't call me that! She's not here anymore," she said in a deep, masculine voice. "I don't think she knows about me."

It's Hayden, Devon thought with alarm. He unwrapped a sandwich from a clear plastic bag and pulled off a small piece, which he pushed toward Devon's mouth.

Devon turned her face away, refusing to eat. "Come on, Devon, I know you're hungry." He sounded almost concerned for her welfare.

He turned Devon's head forcefully back toward him. "Open your mouth and eat this. You won't get anything else for a while." As if to make his point, he plugged her nose until the lack of air forced her to open her mouth. Once she did so, he forced the bite into her mouth and held her mouth closed until he felt her chewing.

She hated to admit it, but peanut butter and bread had never tasted so good. It had already been thirty-six hours since she'd eaten anything, and her stomach growled and churned in anticipation of more. Hayden continued to tear off pieces and push them into her mouth until the sandwich was gone. He unscrewed the cap from a bottle of water and gave her several large drinks before he recapped it and dropped it to the floor.

"She's a strong woman, you know." He referred to Melissa, as if they were talking about a common ally, a family member, or a friend. "We've battled many times over the years; she's usually able to keep me at bay, but not anymore. I am in control now." Devon knew by the pace of his breathing that he was admiring her shoulder and the curve of breast tissue that wasn't concealed under the blanket.

"You like having control, don't you, Hayden? Is that what happened with Mary?" her question came out, as if she were sitting with him in an interrogation room.

"Mary was going to leave me and take our baby away," he answered, not looking up to meet her eyes. "I tried reasoning with her that day after school. I knew she'd be at the river like always. I waited there just to talk to her, but she wouldn't listen to reason. She'd made up her mind about going away to some school back east."

He finally looked up to face her. "I couldn't let her go. If she couldn't be with me, then she couldn't be with anyone." He looked away and caressed her shoulder with the back of his hand gently, intimately, as if they were lovers.

Patiently, he tugged the blanket away just enough to expose her breast. Once uncovered, it responded in record time, rising against the cold air of her prison. "You're a beautiful woman, Devon. I can't think about anything except how good you feel in my hands and mouth."

She moved as far away from his touch as she could, but the ropes wouldn't let her go very far. "Melissa, please help me," she pleaded. "I know you're in there somewhere; just let me go."

"I told you not to call me that!" He pinched her nipple between his two fingers then palmed the entire mound roughly. "I can't let you go," he whispered more calmly, bending to kiss her neck. "I just can't. I have no choice," he hesitated for a minute, as if reconsidering, and then went on. "My father never understood that, but my grandfather did." He lifted his mouth from her neck, but his hand continued to toy with her breast. "He had hundreds of slaves when my father was a boy; many of them were women."

He reached across her and lifted the corner of the blanket from the breast that was still covered, and then he grasped it roughly and gave it the same attention as the other one. "My grandfather enjoyed beautiful women all of his life, but my father never understood his needs or mine."

Hayden let her go and stood up to retrieve the metal rod that he'd brought with him. "My grandfather and I had many things in common." He held the item up to her. "You know what this is?"

She exhaled a breath that she didn't mean to hold and shook her head no. She tugged at the ropes one more time, wishing against all hope that they would somehow come loose.

He walked to the back of the room and removed one of the torches, and then he bent down to ignite what looked like a small campfire at the end of where she was bound. He returned the torch to its holder, so that it lit the corridor ahead of them. He dropped one end of the metal rod into the fire. "I was so intrigued with that necklace you were wearing the first night we made love."

"We didn't make love," she corrected him.

He ignored her. "I've studied what it means, and it's perfectly symbolic of our time together." He leaned in closer to her. "No matter where you are, in any time, you belong to me. I plan to see that you don't forget that." He grabbed her chin and kissed her hard on the lips, pushing his tongue so deep inside of the mouth that she choked.

He pinched her chin so tight in his hand that it was painful, and through gritted teeth, he warned, "Don't contradict me again. I'll teach you the same lesson I taught your partner."

"What partner?" Devon asked, tears gathering in her eyes.

"The one who's always putting his hands on you," he answered confidently.

Hayden jerked himself away and entered the darkness, adding, "He won't be bothering you anymore."

Devon buried her face against her forearm and cried silently for Brad Michaels.

Chapter Twenty-Six

The first tunnel was dark with rock-like walls whose segments seemed to be alive as if blood pulsated under the surface. At certain points, the floor was uneven and dropped off a foot deep and then inclined again to become almost level. Luckily, after about a half-mile, it did level off, but it split into two with neither entrance looking any more promising than the other.

Nick paused to catch his breath, surprised at how easily Mr. McKenzie was keeping pace with him. Nick pulled his water bottle from his pack and took several sips, and then handed the bottle to the older man. "You pick one and I'll take the other."

Ash McKenzie returned the bottle and nodded toward the tunnel closest to him. "I'll take this one." He yanked out his can of yellow reflective paint and sprayed a circle on the tunnel, and then he disappeared into the tunnel with his flashlight lighting the way. Nick sprayed his color on the other tunnel and went in it.

****

Jarrod and Brett took the second tunnel at a cautious pace because it narrowed and widened at will. There were times when they turned their bodies sideways to get through the passageway. They had traveled about a mile when Brett stopped; a bootlace had come undone, its strings hanging from the boot like legs of a spider.

Using hand motions, he indicated to Jarrod to continue onward and he would catch up with him. Jarrod had gone about twenty feet when his boot tripped a thin string of wire draped across the tunnel. He knew he'd made a mistake, but by the time he heard the mechanical click of the device, he heard the arrow release and felt the sting of something penetrating his thigh.

Brett was able to get to Jarrod before he hit the dirt floor of the tunnel. He whispered into his microphone, "Man down, tunnel two," and guided Jarrod to the ground to better assess the injury. Brett pulled the arrow from his thigh and managed to stop the blood flow with a series of bandages. He was just pulling Jarrod to his feet when Ashton McKenzie's beam of light was visible to them.

He raised a hand as if to question what had happened. Brett shined the light down to the wire and then to the device mounted on the other wall. He picked up what was left of the arrow and aimed the light on it. Ashton nodded that he understood when Brett signaled to him to help Jarrod out of the tunnel while he continued clearing tunnel two.

Ashton offered his arm to Jarrod, practically carrying him back to the rope that led up into the Hayden barn.

****

Chris and Kevin had few surprises in tunnel three other than the bending and winding of the pathway. It was probably wider than the other passages, and at times it seemed more like a roadway than a tunnel under the ground.

All along the way, there were ledges that ran parallel to the walls decorated with drawing and sketches. There was no doubt that once the passage had been utilized frequently, and Chris's heart beat frantically at the thought that their luck might be turning.

Both quickened their pace, hoping to finally get to the end and find Devon and Melissa safe and sound. Chris held up his hand indicating they should pause as he listened to Brett's message in his earpiece.

Jarrod was hurt; Ashton had accompanied him to the waiting ambulance at the house. William was waiting with Hyman at the entrance where the rope was hanging, preparing to leave for Idresil. That meant both Nick and Brett were still in the tunnels on their own without any support.

He motioned to Kevin to continue and adjusted his earpiece, listening for more updates. They continued the hike, almost running at times to get to the end of the tunnel.

In discussion with Bryan Keyes, they'd agreed that if Hayden and the girls were underground, they wouldn't be that far away from the house. Keyes doubted that Hayden would use any of the entrances farther away from the house.

There must have been an entrance that only the Haydens used. The entrance most likely would be inside the house and therefore only known to them. As a result, they had marked off an area with a two-mile radius as the search area. It was doubtful that Hayden would set up a sanctuary any farther than that.

Chris looked at his watch, illuminated for night vision; they were running out of time. Nick and Brett would most likely be coming to the end of the two-mile search area soon, if they hadn't already.

He looked at Kevin, his eyes almost in a panic; what had they missed? He had been so sure the Hayden house was the key to finding her and saving her. Gates flipped the safety off on his gun. He'd made the decision about an hour ago; if Devon didn't come out of the tunnel tonight, he wouldn't, either.

****

This time Devon didn't hear Hayden return until he was standing next to her. He was dressed in his full western attire this time, tan trousers, blue denim shirt, black vest, black boots, a long coat, and cowboy hat. Additionally, hanging low at his hip was his holster and gun. It was obvious to her that he was leaving to go somewhere; her biggest fear was that he planned to take her with him.

It was ironic how this time he looked less like Melissa and more like Hayden. He stopped as soon as he was at the foot of the ledge near her feet. He yanked the blanket off her and tossed it away so that it flew in the air and seem to float like a feather to the dirt floor. His hands were cold on her ankles, and she kicked out at him without really knowing what direction to kick in.

"Devon," he warned, wrestling with her legs, "I'm just going to turn you over on your stomach."

My stomach? The fear exploded inside of her as she recalled the last encounter she'd had with him on her stomach. "Hayden, you son of a bitch, get off of me!" She could feel his hands at her hips, pushing at her buttocks until her groin was pressed against the hard surface she was lying on.

"My grandfather used to mark his possessions so that there was no doubt that they belonged to him," he whispered into her ear, using his body as leverage to hold her in place. He slid his knee up and into the small of her back, forcing her still.

In her peripheral vision, she could see he had something in his left hand. Using his right forearm against her back, he held her still as he placed the hot metal apparatus into the skin of her right buttock. The smell of seared flesh filled the area and made her eyes water.

She heard screaming echoing from somewhere in the tunnel before she realized the sound was coming from her own mouth. She tasted blood in her mouth, noting that she'd bit her bottom lip, and blood was oozing from it.

She couldn't get her breath, and she struggled to refocus her vision. Her head was spinning; the room was spinning; she rested her forehead against the hard surface and succumbed to the darkness once again.

When he pulled the branding iron away, it was obvious the design was an infinity symbol. He'd branded on her ass, as if she were a cow or a horse. "Every time you run," he whispered into her ear, kissing and biting at her earlobe as he spoke, "I'm going to mark you again."

****

It wasn't clear who heard the scream first, Chris or Kevin, but it didn't matter because they both tore through the tunnel as if they were running a foot race. Chris called into his microphone that they'd heard screams in tunnel three. He was certain that Brett and Nick would leave their tunnels and join them in tunnel three, at least he hoped so.

Kevin saw the torches in the distance before Chris did, and he held up his hand to signal they should halt and proceed with caution. Both dropped their packs and drew their guns and crept toward the lights.

About fifty feet ahead, the tunnel expanded into a large room lighted by torches burning in sconces on the walls. It took several minutes for their eyes to adjust to the dim light; before they saw Devon's naked form stretched out on some sort of ledge that looked like a bed.

Chris couldn't see Hayden, but he knew from the way Devon was moaning that he couldn't be far away. For a moment Kevin dropped his weapon by his side and stepped towards her, but Chris caught him by the shoulder and shook his head negatively.

He pointed to another thin wire draped across the area where the tunnel and room met. Kevin followed the line to the device mounted on the wall and untied it from the metal box, effectively disabling the mechanism that would've shot an arrow at them.

When Kevin returned, Chris made another series of hand signals directing Kevin to wait until he had eyes on Hayden while Chris flanked the other side and waited. He finger signaled that they needed to identify Melissa's location, too.

Chris had just gotten into position when he saw the familiar form of Thomas Hayden Jr. reappear from the darkness to Devon's right. Chris couldn't determine exactly what Hayden was saying or doing, but it was obvious that Devon was not cooperating.

He looked at his watch again and quickly scanned the area. It was well after eleven already; what time had Hyman said the lights would burn their brightest?

He whispered into his microphone and hoped to catch Hyman and his father before they headed to Idresil. "Target in sight but not secure, suspect not in custody."

****

Devon could hardly find the strength to fight him anymore, and in all actuality, it had become pointless. Every muscle in her body was either bruised or bleeding; and every inch from the waist down was on fire, including the severe burn on her ass where he'd branded her.

She pushed to her knees hoping to turn over so that she was lying on her back again.

It was obvious she had more cover when she was on her stomach, but she couldn't handle him sneaking up on her anymore. Good or bad, she wanted to know when he was coming.

She felt him behind her again, pulling her hips toward him. "Mrs. Gates are you trying to tease me?" he asked climbing onto the ledge and pulling her into his lap.

Devon jerked her head backward, feeling justified when she heard the crack of his nose and felt blood dripping down her back. But her victory was short-lived; he wrapped his forearm around her throat and applied just enough pressure to still her.

"I know you don't like it from behind," he stated, moving his left hand up again to grope her left breast. "Just be still, and don't fight me, and I won't take you like that again. Just lay still and let me touch you."

She weighed the pros and cons; knowing that Melissa wasn't anatomically capable of penetration certainly gave her something to consider. But whatever she was using was just as uncomfortable as an unwelcomed penis, maybe more so.

Devon continued to struggle with him in an effort to slide herself out of his embrace. After all, Hayden was completely dressed; it didn't appear as if he truly planned on having sex with her. She got the distinct impression that they were leaving soon, but she had no idea where they were going, but felt as if they were going to Idresil.

Before she was able to contemplate it any longer, she felt him plunge another syringe into her thigh and inject the contents. Her head fell against his chest almost instantly, her eyes rolled back in her head, and her entire body went limp.

He collected her in his arms and walked them backward until his back was against the wall. "We have to leave soon for our trip," he whispered into her ear, "but we have a little time." He reached up and slit the ropes that had bound her hands to the top of the structure, but he kept them bound together in front. "I know you can hear me and feel me," he stated with a despicable chuckle. "That's why this potion is my favorite." He took both of her breasts in his hands, enjoying the fullness of them.

Devon willed her mouth to move, to shout some statement of protest, but like her arms and legs, she was unable to move it. Hayden stopped touching her just long enough to remove his gloves. He hated barriers, any barrier, between them.

He lifted her up just enough to unzip his trousers, fumbling with one hand to retrieve his member and position it so that he could place her atop it. Since she wasn't fighting him, it took very little effort to place her where she best met his need. Hayden pushed up against her as soon as he'd penetrated, his left hand still playing with the nipple of her left breast, his right slipping between her folds, plucking at her as if she were the strings of a guitar.

Devon was dead weight in his lap, but the pressure of her weight against his member still attached somewhere to Melissa's groin was extremely exciting for Hayden.

He pushed his fingers as far inside of Devon as the angle would allow and separated her folds as if he were flipping through file folders and latched onto her core. He could tell he had her close to her release.

Devon was very predictable, whether she wanted to be or not. Hayden pumped up into her as hard and fast as he could, increasing the pressure on his own pleasure center. He wanted their release to occur simultaneously, a symbolic gesture for the trip they were going to make. He felt her coming in his hand and thrust even harder to bring himself some closure and satisfaction.

Hayden knew by the way she'd stilled that he'd been successful. Her breathing was still coming in great gasps against his chest, but he could tell it was becoming more normalized, as was his own. He pushed her forward so that he could climb out from behind her, laying her back gently as he pushed his way to his feet. The lights would be at their brightest very soon. It was nearly time for them to head to Idresil to ensure they crossed together.

****

Kevin remained hidden in the shadows for as long as he could, taking care to avert his eyes from his sister and that lunatic. More than twice, he'd risen from his hiding spot to go to her and stop what was going on, but both times Chris had signaled to wait until Hayden had moved away from her and was not so close to her.

He looked awkwardly at Chris and thought the man must have nerves of steel. He couldn't imagine how difficult it must be to stand by and observe what had occurred, although each time he'd looked at Chris, Chris didn't seem to be watching. Instead, he had his head down, gun in his lap with his finger resting on the trigger.

He knew Chris was aware of the storm that had begun about forty minutes ago. Even down below in the tunnels, they could hear the crash of thunder and lightning. As soon as Devon's captor had crawled out from under her and made his way to his feet, he looked to Chris for a sign. With or without one, he was freeing his sister from the arms of this crazed mad man.

Chris nodded to him and indicated he should advance toward Devon from the side he was covering while Chris did the same from his side. Crouching as low as he could, Kevin advanced to her, seizing the opportunity before Hayden could reach her. The sound of quickly advancing steps made both look to their right as Nick and Brett advanced from their tunnels almost at the same time with weapons drawn.

"Hold it! Hands in the air!" Brett directed, his voice quivering in anger. "Back away from her."

The figure didn't move, but he didn't follow Brett's instructions, either. Instead, he hesitated as if waiting for option number three. Nick stepped out from the darkness of his tunnel.

"Do you mind if I zip up?" Hayden asked in sardonic amusement, his right hand in the air and his left hand still on Devon's knee.

"Yes, I do mind," Brett warned. "That's what I'm aiming for. Now get your hands off her, now," his voice grew louder and more insistent, as he finished his instructions.

"She's a beautiful woman, isn't she?" Hayden taunted, dismissing their warnings. "Throughout history men have written and painted about women they'd die for." He paused for a second before adding, "How many of them do you think actually meant it?"

He asked loudly, "What about you Deputy Gates? Would you die for her?"

Chris stood up and walked out of the tunnel making a point of tossing his gun away so that Hayden could clearly see that he was unarmed. "You already know the answer to that question," Chris answered. He walked close enough to see that Devon was still drugged and that Hayden had a large knife in his left hand, the hand resting on Devon's knee.

Since Chris wasn't aware of the knife from his vantage point, he was pretty sure the others couldn't see it, either.

It definitely altered their strategy because it transitioned them back to a point where they weren't assured of her safety. "Put the knife down, Hayden."

He could tell from Brett's reaction that he hadn't realized Hayden had a knife. Brett flipped his visor down over his eyes and held his position as he leveled his rifle to his face.

When the shot rang out, it echoed like a train horn throughout the tunnel, Gates was surprised to see Hayden still standing, unfazed. It wasn't until he noticed Kevin lying on the ground that he realized the shot had been another one of Hayden's booby traps. Hayden was still standing over Devon unbothered by their presence. Gates could see that Kevin was pushing himself onto his buttocks to seek cover behind a cluster of large rocks.

"Sir," Brett advised, "I'm going to ask you one more time to step away from her, or I will be forced to shoot you."

"You'd really shoot me with this long beautiful knife so close to, how do I put this delicately, her treasures?" Hayden was so amused with himself that he didn't see Chris give Brett the signal to take the shot.

This shot wasn't as loud as the first one. In fact, it was barely audible, and there was no echo. If it hadn't been for the way Hayden's head snapped backward and the spray from behind him as the bullet exited the back of his head, it would have been difficult to know that a shot had been fired at all.

Chris made his move for Devon as soon as he'd given the signal to Brett. When his body reacted to the gunshot, Hayden fell backward almost on top of Devon; he was dead the instant the bullet tore into his forehead.

Brett flipped the visor up and spoke into the microphone. "Suspect is down, officer is down, and the target has been acquired." He looked at Kevin leaning behind a large rock holding his right shoulder. When he moved toward him, Kevin gave him thumbs-up, and Brett's attention was redirected to Devon.

Gates pushed Hayden's body off Devon, taking pleasure from the sound it made as it hit the dirt floor. He yanked the blanket from the floor and wrapped it quickly over her, stopping only a minute to ensure none of the blood that covered her was hers.

She struggled to sit up, dazed from the drugs. After taking a quick glance at Hayden's body, she opened her arms to Gates and began crying uncontrollably against his chest.

"Devon, baby, where's Melissa?" Brett asked, looking around for where Hayden had trapped his sister-in-law.

Devon's crying became louder, more intense, almost hysterical. "Hayden," she managed to say through the tears.

Chris cut the ropes away from her wrists, trying to keep her covered as best as he could. He knew she was cold; her entire body was shaking vehemently. "We're going to need stretchers to get them out," he barked into his mouthpiece, hoping to set the first responders in motion.

"I don't need a stretcher," Kevin advised, walking over to Chris with Nick's support. He pulled away from his brother and approached his sister with caution. "Honey, we're gonna get you out of here. But what did he do with Melissa? Where is she?"

Devon pointed to Hayden's body and fell into Kevin's chest. "Oh God," Devon said. "Jason is going to be devastated."

Kevin looked up at Chris. "Is she dead?"

Chris shook his head and shrugged his shoulders slightly. He had no idea, and he didn't want to push Devon for an explanation. She was in no shape to talk coherently.

Needing an answer, Kevin rubbed Devon's back soothingly and said, "We want to take Melissa home, Devon. Do you know where her body is?"

"It's here," Brett announced, standing up from where he had been kneeling beside Hayden's body.

Chris looked at Brett as if he'd lost his mind. Deciding to remain calm, however, he walked closer to the body and said to Brett, "I don't understand. How can Hayden be Melissa?"

"This body is that of a woman, not a man," Brett said very clinically, as if he was trying to detach himself from the realization of what had transpired. "The body has some kind of tape around the chest to conceal her breasts." He pointed to the groin, more specifically, the penis, and said, "That's not real. It's some kind of prosthetic penile apparatus. It's Melissa dressed as a man."

"She made herself to look just like him. Why?" Gates asked.

"She doesn't just look like him. It's him," Devon cried, into Gates chest.

Kevin hesitated for a few minutes, trying to process the thoughts and emotions reeling through him. "Let's just get out of here."

Nick returned and reported, "The area is clear. There's no one else here but us."

Brett walked toward the tunnel in a daze. "I'll help with the stretchers," he said numbly. He disappeared into the darkness to make peace with the fact he'd just blown his sister-in-law's head off.

Chris helped Devon to her feet, pulling his jacket off and nestling it around her shoulders. "I want out of here," she mumbled, her words still slurred as she stumbled into Chris's arms.

"Stretcher's on the way," he reassured her, holding her close against him to keep her steady. He couldn't let her go. It was as if he feared she'd disappear again, only this time, she might be gone for good.

"Get me out of here," Devon said, trying to stand on her own and walking unsteadily toward one of the tunnels. Chris took several steps to catch up to her and walk at her side.

"I can't stay in here a minute longer, either," Kevin said, looking back toward Melissa's body. "Let's start walking and meet whoever has the stretchers."

Chris looked awkwardly at Nick, who was milling around behind the ledge where Devon had been bound. "Can you wait with the body?"

Nick nodded and unbuttoned his protective vest before letting it fall to the damp ground. He set his gun tentatively against the wall, but close enough so that he could get to it if he needed it. "Of course, just don't forget me down here," he said. He leaned closer to Chris and whispered, "I don't have a camera, so I can't document the scene."

"Good," Gates said, walking away. "I don't want there to be any pictures."

Chris pulled Devon into his arms and led her out of the room and down the tunnel, with Kevin following protectively behind them.

About half the way back, the group encountered two young men carrying stretchers. He tried twice to get Devon to get on the stretcher, but both times she refused. Instead, she held on to his arm and pushed on toward the end that she could only hope would come soon.

Chapter Twenty-Seven

The hotel was buzzing. Police officers from Aurora, New York, and New Jersey, as well as agents of the FBI and DEA, were roaming about. Some were there in an official capacity, some because they were connected to the families, others because they were curious.

It had taken a while to get everyone safely from the tunnel and aboveground. Devon and Kevin couldn't hoist themselves up by the rope, so it was tied under their arms, and they were lifted to the ground where they were carried to the waiting ambulances.

The FBI had commandeered the entire floor of the hotel they'd previously leased mostly to accommodate the numerous forensic specialists and investigators, but partly to make it convenient for the Gates and McKenzie families until the investigation was closed.

Ashton McKenzie hung the phone gently on the receiver and absent-mindedly perused the hotel room. It was an average looking room, a little on the small side, but not really that bad. Truth be told, they had stayed in much worse places, but he doubted he'd ever been in such a bad place, physically or mentally. He knew his family would never be the same; the physical wounds might heal, but the scars would last a lifetime.

He wiped awkwardly at his eyes, mindful that as the patriarch of the family, he needed to stay focused and strong. His family needed him to anchor them safely to shore. He had to be strong even though all he wanted to do was sit down in his big, comfortable blue chair in his study at home and cry.

Chris hadn't said much about what had happened; Brett had told him only enough for him to know that ambulances were needed. It was his oldest son, Kevin, who had filled in the details in vivid color, so much that he knew he'd have nightmares for many months to come.

Would any of his children ever be the same? He couldn't imagine Devon's pain after having been tortured and abused by someone she loved like a sister. He couldn't imagine Jason's anguish knowing that his wife was the source of that pain, and that he knew so little about her even though he had shared his life with her.

And Brett, his hurt must surely be the greatest of all, knowing he'd killed someone he loved like a sister and weighing how his decision would affect his brother's life forever.

He wiped his face again and pushed himself wearily to his feet. He needed to talk to Christopher and share with him and the authorities some of the pieces that his wife Caren had been able to put together.

****

No one said much when Chris opened the door to their motel room and led Devon slowly into the room. Kevin and Jarrod had already been released from the hospital and had returned to the hotel. Kevin was resting in the room just off the main room while Jarrod was sitting comfortably on the sofa, his leg poised on the ottoman elevated at a forty-five-degree angle.

Brett disappeared almost as soon as everyone started arriving at the hotel. That left only Nick, William Gates, and Ashton McKenzie sitting impatiently in the main room of the suite when Chris and Devon came in. She was wearing hospital scrubs and surgical booties over her bare feet and holding tightly to Chris.

Ashton stood to his feet, but the others remained sitting, looking awkwardly around the room, hoping she wouldn't notice them. Ashton went toward them, his arms outstretched to her. Devon held up her hand as if to hold him back. "Dad, I've got blood and stuff all over me, but especially in my hair." She smiled at him. "I'm fine. I just want to take a shower. The hospital let me rinse off, but I really need a shower, okay?"

He let his hands fall to his sides, deflated as if the wind had gone out of his sails, but he just nodded and said, "Of course, baby."

Chris opened the door to the room he'd slept in the previous night, or at least for the forty minutes that he'd attempted to sleep. She stopped at the bathroom door. "Do you think Melissa was anywhere in there or was it all Hayden?"

He tried to avoid the question and divert her attention by steering her toward the shower. "Devon, let's just get you in the shower." Gates led her closer to the shower and attempted to help her off with the shirt.

She pulled away and sat on the edge of the tub. "Jason, does he know?"

"I believe so, yes. Your Father contacted your Mother while we were at the hospital. My Mom is with him at the hospital until one of your brothers can get back. Your Mom is catching a flight out tomorrow morning," Gates advised.

"He must be devastated," Devon cried.

Gates recalled Hyman's premonition how the one who was like Devon would recover, but be deeply scarred. "Yes, he probably is, he loved her."

Devon fell into his arms and walked further into the bathroom. As they walked past the large bureau next to the bathroom, Devon caught her reflection in the mirror. Her hair was tangled and matted with a combination of blood, sweat, and something else. Her hand went to her head, and she cried out in such distress that Chris thought his heart was going to break. "Oh God, Chris! What is in my hair?"

It was hard to watch, hard to intervene, hard to really know what to do as Devon decompressed right there before his eyes. He knew it was blood and brain matter stuck in her hair, and Devon realized it, too. She began slapping and pulling at her head and hair, her arms flailing about.

"Let's get your hair washed."

She moved farther from him and pulled at the bloody pieces, sobbing, her cries coming in big hiccups.

Chris tried to pull the scrub top over her head, but he couldn't keep her arms still long enough. He didn't think it was a good idea to push the scrub bottoms off without her consent. He looked around the room for another option, and finding none, decided on the most obvious solution.

Gates kicked off his boots and guided her into the bathroom, turned the water on as hard as it would go, and got into the shower with her fully clothed. He adjusted the water to hit her almost fully on the face, noticing that once the water was running, she began to cry unabated as if she needed the sound of the water hitting the floor to drown out her cries.

Once she was calmer, he was able to shampoo her hair, trying not to notice the pale reddish color of the water as it drained and swirled dance like down the drain.

He had been able to get the wet scrub top and pants off her as well as peel his own shirt and pants off. He'd left his underwear on in the shower, for now, more as a precaution than anything else. After the water flowing off the long strands of her hair ran clear, he released her and leaned back against the shower wall exhaling a breath of warm air into the steam that enveloped them both,

"Would you mind if I had a minute or two alone?" she asked.

As she lathered the soap against her palm, he whispered, "I'll be outside the shower door. Take your time."

He stepped out of the stall leaving a path of water on the bathroom rug. After yanking a towel from the rack and drying himself quickly, he stepped into a clean pair of jeans and put on a long-sleeved knit shirt.

Chris stood outside the shower stall the better part of an hour waiting for her to finish. He'd tried to leave twice: once to give her some privacy and the second time because he needed to take a piss. Both times, she'd called him back before his distorted image on the other side of the shower door had gotten very far.

He heard the tap at their hotel room door over the sound of the shower, and he stuck his head out far enough to call out, "Door's open." He knew it had to be one of the family; the FBI and DEA would not let anyone else even get off the elevator, let alone into the hallway.

Chris couldn't say he was surprised to see her father practically dragging himself into the room. He realized that as hard as it had been on him and the brothers to bear witness to the trauma, it most likely paled in comparison to the pain of participating in it as a parent.

He knew Ashton wanted nothing more than to take his daughter's pain away, and he probably felt like he had failed as a father because he couldn't.

Chris motioned for Ashton to come into the hotel room and close the door, and he indicated that Devon was in the shower. He stepped outside of the bathroom, but left the door open just enough so that he could hear the shower running.

"I don't want to over-step any boundaries, Chris. I realize you're her husband, but I'm her father, and I want to know what happened. I want to know that she's okay."

Gates shrugged his shoulders, moving to take a seat on one of the two beds. "I'll answer any question you have as honestly as I can."

Ashton looked toward the bathroom door trying to gauge how much time he had to ask his questions before she turned it off and joined them in the room. "First of all, how badly is she hurt? I'm having a hard time understanding how Melissa was able to pull this off. Devon's a trained agent with an extensive defensive skill set."

"She was heavily sedated throughout most of the ordeal," Chris replied. He hesitated briefly then added a further explanation quickly as if he feared he'd lose his nerve. "Devon was restrained almost immediately after being captured. And at some point, some type of muscle relaxant was used on her so that she was awake and aware, but unable to respond."

He ran his hand through his hair so that the front stood up almost on its own until he brushed it back into place with the other hand. "I don't know at what point she realized it was Melissa."

Ashton's face was pale as if he'd come into the sunlight after being in a cold, dark place for an inordinate amount of time. "How badly is she hurt?" He paused for a second and then added, "Did Devon realize it was Melissa before or after the assault?"

"Physically, I don't think she has any permanent injuries. Devon's injuries are the same as if she'd been hurt by a man. She has multiple bruises and abrasions on both breasts and on the insides of her thighs. Devon was forcibly penetrated vaginally with some sort of prosthetic penis; she's really swollen and sore, but the hospital reports there's no bleeding or tearing.

Her entire body is bruised and marred, and there's a two-inch by two-inch infinity symbol branded into her right buttock."

Gates was amazed at how objectively and unemotionally he answered the question. It was as if he were bringing a fellow officer up to date on an open case.

He motioned toward the minibar in the hotel room and got up to pour them both drinks. "The emergency room processed a rape kit on her even though we told them they didn't have to. They documented the absence of semen, which, according to their logic, meant the rapist wore a condom."

Gates handed Ashton his drink and went on. "I didn't tell them any different. They also tried to admit Devon for overnight observation, but she refused."

Chris fell into a chair in the sitting room. "As far as when she realized who Hayden really was, I don't know and she didn't say." He paused and swallowed another drink, as if it gave him courage. "She definitely knew when Brett took the shot."

Gates rubbed his hands up and down his thighs as if he were cold. "Mr. McKenzie, when Devon's ready, she'll tell me everything. She did last time. But it took her a while, and it was hard for her. I know she'll tell me when she's ready."

Ashton set his drink down on the table and went to stand behind Chris. He put his hand on his shoulder and said, "Son, it's okay." He patted him as if he was Chris's coach and Chris had just missed the winning field goal. "There's no way you could have seen this coming. None of us could have known that Melissa was ill."

"They had been friends for a long time, hadn't they?" Gates asked, thinking he'd heard that from someone else.

Ashton nodded. "Yes, Devon introduced Melissa to Jason," he paused. "I'm still trying to understand how all of this happened."

"Don't understand it all myself. Hyman told me that souls travel through time together, different on the outside, but the same inside. Hayden believed his and Devon's souls were together in other lifetimes. Somehow, he was able to merge into Melissa's body, take her soul to finish what he started in Hamilton," Gates explained.

"This sounds like a science fiction movie. How's that even possible?" Ash asked, combing his hair from his eyes.

William Gates appeared at the bedroom door and entered, closing it behind him as Gates stepped behind partition to change out of his wet underwear.

"I may be able to offer some insight. I went to visit my grandfather at the nursing home last week to share the good news about Devon being home. He's ninety-five, has bouts of dementia but he has some clear moments. Kept calling me Ray, explained how his father wanted him to name me after a lawman in our family tree," William explained.

Gates stepped from the partition, holding a dry shirt in his hand. He leaned against the bathroom door to check on the sounds of the shower before returning to the conversation.

"When Mr. Hyman and I were at Idresil watching for Hayden and the girls, I started thinking about what he said about the generations," he paused. "I just got off the phone with one of my analyst's in Boston. She was able to trace our family back several generations. Abby Callahan Middleton was my great-great-grandmother," William went on.

"I'm not surprised. I felt a connection with them from the beginning, especially Abby," Gates admitted.

"On a hunch, I took the liberty, had the same analyst run yours, Ash. Benjamin Ennis was your great, great, grandfather." William smiled.

"There was something between them and Devon from the minute they met, especially Benjamin. He was so protective of her from day one," Gates whispered.

"How does this affect Hayden's family? Where's the link with him?" Ash asked.

"Melissa's great-great grandmother was Marissa Montero," William said.

"She was the daughter of one of the servants that worked for Mr. Hayden. She was sent away soon after we arrived. We never met her, but I heard the rumors, she was pregnant with Hayden, Jr's child," Gates said, looking back at the slightly open bathroom door.

The door opened and Devon stuck her head through the door. "Can I get a robe?"

Gates handed her one of the complimentary robes from the closet. She reappeared at the door dressed in the robe and took a seat next to her father on the bed.

"Idresil, the lights? Time just snapped us all back to Hamilton? Why?" She asked.

"It's no secret, the probability of us or our souls getting together before Hamilton was pretty low." Gates took her hand and kissed it. "We weren't the presidents of each other's fan club."

"Fate's way of correcting itself?" Devon smiled a tired smile.

"Maybe." Gates handed her a bottle of water. "You hungry?"

"No, but I need some clothes. I don't have anything to even change into," she answered, pulling the robe tighter around her body.

Ash stood and disappeared out of the bedroom, returning moments later with a forty-niner's shirt and a pair of boxer shorts. "I didn't pack much." He handed the clothes to her. "Not a perfect fit, but all the boys' will be too big for you."

"Would you mind? I'd like to lie down for a few minutes?" Devon asked, taking the shirt and shorts from her father.

Instantly Ash and William were on their feet and vacated the room, closing the bedroom door behind them.

"We're going to get through this, I promise." Gates pulled the blankets down for her and waited while she slid between the sheets.

He covered her up and took a seat next to her. She kissed his hand and pulled herself as close to him as was possible. "I knew you'd come for me. So, did he."

He kissed the top of her head. "Get some sleep. You're safe now."

****

Caren McKenzie had spent the better part of the last two days sitting in her son's hospital room making phone calls to fill in as many blanks as she could regarding her missing daughter-in-law. It had come as a major surprise to discover that the bi-monthly visits to the fertility physician had in fact been visits with a psychiatrist. Melissa had been diagnosed with schizophrenia in her teens and had been treated pharmacologically ever since.

It had taken a significant amount of truth-stretching and dozens of phone calls whereby the callers may have mistakenly believed that Caren McKenzie was a police officer working an active case. After all, her husband and three of her four children were in police enforcement, so she was an expert in the lingo. But it had been worth it, because Caren was able to determine that her meek, mild daughter-in-law of nearly ten years was leading a sort of double life. She'd been pregnant twice during the last ten years but had aborted the child both times for reasons that still weren't clear.

Also noteworthy was the fact that Melissa had indeed been pregnant when she went on her killing rampage. She was about three months along, and it seemed she had decided to bring this child to full term. When Jason had regained consciousness the previous night, Caren had tried to determine what if anything he could contribute to the mystery that was Melissa.

She was sure he wasn't aware of the abortions or the pretend trips to the fertility clinic. Caren knew her children well. It didn't go unnoticed by her how upset he became when asked what he recalled about the stabbing. She thought he must still be in shock, and therefore was unsure of what had transpired in Devon's apartment.

Tonight, though, after hanging up the phone with her husband and having more pieces of the puzzle, there were questions she needed answers to. For the rest of her life, she would never forget the look of desperation on her son's face to discover that his wife Melissa was dead, killed in the shootout that occurred during Devon's rescue.

He was relieved to learn that Devon was safe, released from the hospital, and recuperating with her husband at a hotel in Aurora. Jarrod Gates and Kevin had been injured, but their injuries weren't critical. Both were treated at the Emergency Department and released. Tears had fallen from his eyes when he attempted to understand that the only fatality had been Melissa.

Jason had sat up in the hospital bed independently. "Mom," he whispered, holding his hand out for her to come closer to him, patting a place on the bed next to him. He leaned over to grasp a paper cup of water near the bedside. After drinking it greedily, he asked his mother, "What aren't you telling me?"

"Honey," she said, patting his arm, "it can wait until tomorrow. You're getting stronger every day."

"I'm fine. The doctor has said so several times, Mother," his tone was serious and stubborn. He'd made up his mind already. He wanted to know the truth, no matter what it was.

"Jason," she began, pausing to find the right words. "Do you remember anything else that happened in the apartment when the girls were taken?"

He shook his head as if he had an image in his mind, but he couldn't discuss it because it was just too horrendous. "Was Melissa involved in Devon's abduction?"

She pulled back almost as if he'd hit her. "Why would you ask such a thing?"

He swallowed as if he were stalling for time. "Because I have this image in my head of Melissa stabbing me with a knife." He looked up at his mother as if he wanted or needed her to tell him how ridiculous it was. "Crazy, right?"

Caren McKenzie cried as she answered him. "No honey, it's not crazy. Melissa did stab you, and she drugged Devon. We also believe she killed the two FBI agents assigned to protect Devon from Gregor Esteban."

He opened his mouth to speak but couldn't find the words. It took him several minutes to ask, "Was Melissa working for Esteban?"

Caren pushed herself to her feet and walked to the window and peered outside. It was snowing again; every perspective was improved with the falling of crisp, white snow. It made everything new again. "No, honey," she said quietly, and then she paused. "Gregor Esteban has nothing to do with this."

Jason shook his head, slightly agitated. Maybe he was more medicated that he thought; he wasn't getting it. "Mom, please, just tell me the truth."

"Do you remember the man that raped Devon while she and Christopher were missing?" she asked the question, without any emotion in her face or voice.

"Harris, or something like that?" he answered, somewhat confidently.

"Hayden," she corrected. "Thomas Hayden Junior. When Melissa was killed, she was dressed as this man and answering to his name."

If Jason could have gotten to his feet, he would have. "That's ridiculous," he replied. "Dressing like a man wouldn't make her able to actually perform as a man."

"Jason, honey, I know this is an impossible thing for you to believe. I can hardly believe it myself. Your brothers and Christopher approached where Devon was being held early this morning. They waited in hiding for the suspect to get far enough away from Devon to guarantee her safety. The suspect finished assaulting your sister, and when he stepped away, he was shot."

She paused to collect her thoughts. "After they untied Devon and got her to safety, they realized that it was Melissa dressed as this man."

"Who shot her?" he asked, incredulous. His face flushed red and then blanched almost white.

"The boys haven't said which one fired the shot."

"How was Melissa able to assault Devon like that?" Jason asked this without looking up. It was an uncomfortable topic considering he was talking with his mother.

"She was wearing some type of prosthetic device," Caren answered, just as uncomfortably. "Jason, I spoke to Laura Gates, and she's going to come and stay with you. I want to go and care for Devon. She's in a hotel full of men. I think she needs me."

Jason nodded that she should go to Nebraska and ensure that Devon's needs were met, and then he slid back down into the bed and pulled the sheet up to his chin.

Chapter Twenty-Eight

As the morning sun broke just off the horizon, darkness steadily gave way to the light, Gates wished he felt as if the night had gone quickly. It was an odd feeling to sense that time stood still in her arms. His critique of his nights with her usually involved the time getting away from him as though it had sped forward, stealing precious moments with her from him. But last night, it had felt as if time had literally stalled and then slipped backward.

He'd been awake the better part of the night, holding her close to him. He kept one arm under her body just at her waist, and the other resting loosely across her hip.

The heat from the fireplace kissed both their bodies so that they were warm and toasty. He thought again of the guest house in Hamilton and smiled.

He felt Devon stirring, slowly, gently on his chest, gradually acclimating herself to the surroundings as if she had detected a threat. Ultimately, she gradually settled back down against the warmth of his skin.

She knew even before she opened her eyes that it was him. The feel of his chest and abdomen under her hand, the scent of him warm and musky under her nose, were familiar to her. It was comforting.

She raised her head just enough to smile at him, but her attention was drawn to something scratchy and uncomfortable at her chest. Her hand went curiously to her chest and felt the fabric of the T-shirt she was wearing. It was an old red T-shirt with gray faded lettering for the 49ers football team. She could feel the fabric of the shorts she was wearing against her legs and buttocks. It was thick and not as soft as the shirt. She pulled impatiently at the shorts, straightening the waistband comfortably around her waist.

Chris smiled. "Your dad's boxers. We got back from the hospital too late last night to go to the boutique downstairs." He cleared his throat and added, "We'll get one of the guys to run down and pick up some things for you. I don't know sizes, sorry."

He wiped away a strand of hair that had fallen into her eyes. "We'll get you some undergarments, too."

She shook her head, smiling at him. "I'm not telling my brothers or yours my bra size, Chris."

He held out his hands, palms up, slightly cupped, and joked, "'Course I could go down to the shop myself and tell them I need a bra about this big." He thought he saw her smile and was hoping for some typical banter, but it was not forthcoming.

Instead, she settled in closer to him and inhaled. "I can't explain any of this; can you?" Before he could answer, she added, "Melissa confessed that she killed my fiancée, Paul, many years ago. Something that she said made me think of Brad Michaels. Have you spoken to him? Is he okay?"

"I'm sorry, Devon," he said kissing her head. "Brad's body was discovered in his apartment the day after you disappeared. He was stabbed to death."

She didn't cry this time; she didn't think she had the strength. Instead, she closed her eyes and said a small, silent prayer. "How was she able to disguise herself as Hayden?"

Gates made gentle circles on the small of her back. "I think the clothes and hair helped some, especially in the dimness of the tunnel. Probably those things and the drugs she gave you may have helped her pull off the ruse."

Devon rubbed her right cheek against his chest, enjoying the friction it produced. "I was so scared."

"I know, me too. I love you, Devon." He pulled her close against him until he felt her drifting back to sleep. He waited until he was sure she was asleep, and then he pushed himself skillfully to his feet and slipped quietly out the door.

****

The scream broke the stillness of the room and produced a flurry of movement and weapon alignment that the small town of Aurora had never seen before and most likely would not see again. Chris jumped from the couch in the other room and was by her side within seconds while the others waited just outside the door.

"Devon," he soothed. "You're okay; you're safe. Your dad is here and your brothers; we're all here. No one's going to hurt you, I promise." It took several minutes before she settled against the mattress, clinging to his arm as if she were a child. Several attempts later, he slid back into bed next to her and wrapped her protectively in his arms.

Ashton pulled the connecting door closed and returned to his empty room. He felt sad; except for Caren, Laura Gates, and Jason, all the other families had flown to Nebraska to console their spouses. His daughters-in-law and the wives of the Gates brothers had all arrived earlier in the day after learning the news.

Hell, he thought, even the ex-wives were rallying in support. It was hard to describe the gratitude he felt the previous night after opening the external door to discover Emily McKenzie, Brett's recently divorced former wife, here with her carryon bag in her hand. Ashton could barely contain his relief as he invited her into the room and went to find Brett. Ashton was grateful Emily had come for Brett. He desperately needed someone, even if it was only temporary.

He had always had a hard time being alone after getting bad or sad news. He knew that most of the occupants of every room on this floor were probably making love or had been.

Ashton wished his wife Caren was there so that they could comfort each other. He was still very distraught over the horrendous ordeal his daughter had endured. He couldn't get Devon's face out of his mind as Chris had made his way out of the tunnel with her in his arms wrapped in his coat. He hadn't been there with the boys, but Kevin had given him the details of what was happening when they got to her. She looked like a wounded, dazed animal, eyes darting back and forth waiting for the next attack to come, making herself smaller as if hoping to occupy less space and attract less attention.

He kept asking himself how this was possible. Ash's thoughts were interrupted as Chris crept quietly into the room and sat next to him on the sofa. "Mr. Ashton, you okay?"

Ashton nodded. "Just worried about my baby." He looked curiously at Gates.

Chris explained. "Jarrod spoke to Melissa's psychiatrist this afternoon. He was saddened by her death, but not surprised. He reports that Melissa suffered from schizophrenia and has been medicated for many years. Most likely, this other personality was there all along, but she wasn't aware of it. She was the dominant personality, but when she became pregnant, she stopped taking her meds and the other personality, Hayden, took control."

"You think it's just a coincidence that Melissa married Jason, considering that he's Devon's twin?" Ashton asked.

"No," Chris answered. "I think Hayden settled for the next best thing, though he inhabited a female body this time." Chris rubbed his forehead as if he had a headache. "I mean, Jason and Devon are twins, so they have some commonalities, yes."

"You think Melissa was subconsciously drawn to Jason because of her ancestor's obsession with Devon."

Ashton stated rather than asked before he pushed himself to his feet and made his way into the small kitchenette. He pulled the refrigerator door open so quietly that Chris didn't realize what he had done until he saw the bottle of cold beer come into view.

He smiled and accepted the drink. "I think Melissa had most likely been battling a personality disorder whereby she and Hayden battled for control. I doubt she even knew she had another personality, and she probably never knew that Hayden even existed."

Chris took a long drink from the bottle and held it up against the light as if to assess how much remained in the bottle. "Wish I could get Devon to have a couple of these; it might help her sleep."

Ashton smiled and nodded, finishing what remained in his own bottle before setting it on the table. "You should try and get some rest, son. She'll need to lean on you for a bit, and you'll need your strength."

He slapped playfully at Chris's shoulder as he walked into the bedroom. Gates remained on the sofa a few minutes longer than rose to his feet and slipped quietly back through the connecting door and into bed next to her.

****

Brett McKenzie tossed the blanket to the floor, taking extra care to kick it with more force than needed. The bedroom was draped in shadows from the fire that burned low in the small fireplace just across from where the bed had been placed in the small room. It made the objects in the room seem almost animated pulsating up and down in rhythm with the wavering flames.

There was barely room for the bed; it took up most of the room. He looked anxiously to where his wife, make that his ex-wife, Emily, had drifted back to sleep after their lovemaking. Her naked back was turned toward him, the sheet and comforter resting against the top of her hip artfully. He traced the outline of her hip against the sheet and looked longingly at her back, envious of the movement it made from her breathing. Her breaths were deep and long, indicative of her peaceful slumber. He hadn't slept well in months, since Devon had gone missing. He hadn't closed his eyes since Jason was stabbed. His mind just wouldn't shut down; even now, when Devon was home and Jason was safe, he couldn't just close his eyes and rest.

Every time he closed his eyes, he replayed it in his mind, the way Melissa's head snapped back after the impact with the bullet; the expression on her face as the back of her head opened and spilled out onto Devon.

Brett rubbed his eyes as if he could erase the image from his brain. He couldn't help but think of Jason and the path he would now be forced to take. If only there'd been another choice, his mind questioned. But that was not to be; he'd taken the shot, possibly saving his sister's life, yet devastating his brother's with the same pointer finger reflex. All their lives had changed with the caress of that trigger.

It gave him some comfort to consider that had he known who Devon's abductor was, maybe he'd have done things differently. Perhaps he would've exercised more patience, negotiated more intently to find a resolution, or aimed his shot differently before pulling the trigger.

Without deliberating it any further, he swung his feet to the floor and stepped into his jeans that were lying on the floor near the foot of the bed. Emily had been relentless in her attempt to take his mind off the event and focus it more determinedly on the celebration of life.

He didn't bother to button his jeans or put on a shirt. Instead, he stepped quietly back to the door and slipped out of the room and into the small kitchen. He'd heard his father and Chris talking about an hour ago, their voices low and steady. Brett was headed to the refrigerator, but paused before he reached it and made his way to the bedroom with the door slightly ajar.

Although he felt guilty about peeking inside, he assured himself it was more a result of the need to validate that she was safe. After all, given everything she'd been through the last twenty-four hours, he doubted sex was on either of their minds. It wasn't like he'd be interrupting anything. He inched closer and pushed his head in so that his cheek just brushed the edge of the door.

Like his room, it was enveloped in a warm glow from the fire in the fireplace so that most of the room was in the shadows. She was sleeping on her left side, her back to the door and her body turned toward Chris. She was almost on top of him, her face barely resting on his naked chest. Brett wasn't sure, but he thought he recognized the worn red shirt she was wearing as one formerly belonging to their father. The boxers she was wearing were too big for her, so much so that they hung loosely around her hips rather than at her waist. He was able to make out the top portion of a gauze bandage on her right buttock. His mind reregistered the blood-curdling scream they heard while they were in the tunnel. He thought he remembered something about a burn on her hip. No doubt, the two were most likely related.

He looked around the room before pulling the door back to where he'd found it. Brett had just gotten to the kitchen and opened the refrigerator when he heard her familiar voice just on the outside of the bedroom door.

"I hope there's enough in there for two," Devon whispered, indicating the bottle of beer in his hand. Brett removed another from the top shelf and shut the door, motioning toward the sofa just on the other side of the half-wall that separated the two areas.

Devon got to the sofa first and slid gently into the thick cushions keenly aware of the burn on her buttock. She pulled Chris's long-sleeved shirt tighter around her body and accepted the bottle her brother handed to her.

He took three long successive swigs before looking at her and stating almost defensively, "I meant to check on you before now," he stuttered, stopping and starting his sentence several times before saying in one quick breathless sentence, "I thought with everything, I mean, with all that happened, it would be easier if you had some time to process what happened … what I did."

"What you did?" she repeated. "Brett, you're not responsible for Melissa's death."

He dropped his gaze away from her eyes and went on. "I don't want to talk about that. I've already acknowledged what I did. It was my call. I want to know that you're okay or will be." He took two more large swallows of beer and chewed at his lip as if he were studying a question on an examination.

"I'm sore and swollen," she said, "but I'll live. We will both recover."

Brett finished his beer and went to get another, pausing at the kitchen door before asking, "And Jason? Will he?"

Devon rose and met him in the kitchen. "With our support, yes, he'll recover in time."

If she didn't know him better, she'd have thought that he was crying, the way his eyes were watering and his voice was wavering. "When he finds out that I took the shot, our relationship will never be the same, Devon." There was no doubt that he was crying now. "He's my brother. I love him, but it will never be the same for us."

Brett wiped his face and pulled her into an embrace. "For the rest of our lives, he probably won't ever ask, but he'll always wonder if I could have made another choice." He released her arms when he saw how uncomfortable she was with him so close in her personal space. "It's all gone to hell," he said as if he were summarizing.

She handed him the bottle she'd been drinking from and motioned for him to finish it for her. "I don't believe that, Brett. It's not all gone."

She turned to go back to her room when he asked, "When did you realize it was her?" He drank the last few drops of beer from her bottle and added, "I mean, was it before he ... I mean she ..." Brett paused, not sure of the right words to choose, then he went on as if he'd found his way. "Was it before she forced you?"

"No," she answered. "I didn't realize at first. I was drugged," she paused, trying to align the events in the order that she recalled them. "The last time I saw Melissa, she was frantically trying to escape." Devon paused, not missing the fact that she needed some time to gather herself. "I thought I'd convinced her to untie me."

Devon's tears started flowing freely down her cheeks, so that she was wiping them almost as quickly as they formed. "She was so scared, crying and begging me to protect her from him."

Devon paused, reliving the moment in her mind. Once again, she was seeing Melissa's torn clothes and mangled hair as well as the blood and bruising on her face. Was there something she missed? Was there any way she could have known that the wounds were?

self-inflicted, and the demon chasing her was pursuing her from within? Devon went on, biting her lip to ward off the tears and keep them at bay. "I thought I could save her."

Brett opened his arms and allowed her to fall into his embrace. "It's not your fault, Devon. There's nothing to feel guilty about. "

"I know," she admitted, pulling away and glancing back toward the bedroom door still ajar. "I'm tired," she said wearily. "I think I'll go back to bed." She folded her hands, one into the other, and headed back to where Chris was sleeping.

Brett followed her to the door, kissing her on the forehead and smiling at her tenderly like the good big brother he was. "' Night, Devon. I think I'm going to like your husband."

She smiled and closed the door, letting it latch tight against the frame, but securing it quietly so as not to awaken Chris, who was adjusting himself around the empty place in the bed. It wasn't long before she heard his voice barely above a whisper. "Everything okay?"

Even in the dim light, she knew he was pushing the blankets away, making it easy for her to take her place in the bed. Once she had snuggled in, he pulled the blanket around her and wrapped his arm loosely over her torso. After almost rooting down close to him, she finally answered his query. "Everything's fine."

He nodded against her shoulder, kissing her gently as he settled close to her, clasping her hand within his and pulling their conjoined hands between them. Almost as an afterthought, he pulled their hands out and kissed the back of her hand before letting it fall again. Pulling himself almost horizontal alongside of her, he kissed her neck, gently and

tenderly. "You want to make love?" he asked, barely above a whisper. He couldn't imagine that she'd want to, but he remembered that after the ordeal Hayden had put her through at the Ennis' house, that's exactly what she'd wanted, what she needed.

She shook her head, stilling his kisses at her neck with her hand behind his head. "Not tonight, but soon, I promise." She took her hand from his embrace and flipped over so that her back was tight against his chest, and she spooned into him.

She felt him kiss the back of her head. "There's no rush, Devon. You've been through a lot," he soothed. He buried his face tightly into her neck, and she felt him nuzzling against her skin. At first, she thought he was kissing her; it wasn't until she felt the dampness on her shoulder that she realized he was crying softly. Before she could ask, he whispered between wet breaths, "Devon, I was so scared that I'd lost you forever this time."

She ran her hand gently through the back of his hair. "I know; it's okay," she soothed him, whispering into his ear. "I'm here." It was an odd feeling for her to be comforting him. All along, he'd been her rock and her strength when she'd had none left; he'd been her voice when the words just wouldn't or couldn't come to her. She'd never considered how it might have been for him to be left alone and fearful that all they had was lost.

She slid her hand down to his lower back and caressed the soft skin around the waistband of his underwear. He intercepted her hand without pulling his face off her shoulder. "I don't want to have sex tonight, Devon." He kissed her shoulder again. "I just want to lay here in your arms; that's all."

"The longer we wait, the harder it will be for me," she admitted.

"Making love shouldn't be hard, Devon, for either of us," he reminded her, pulling her closer against his chest as he exhaled a warm breath into her hair and drifted back to sleep.

Chapter Twenty-Nine

The fire had died down when dawn broke bright pink and yellow across the horizon. A foot or so of snow had fallen sometime in the night and covered everything in a thick, fluffy white blanket, making everything look new again. Chris gently extricated himself from around her body and grabbed his shirt from the back of the chair. He knew she'd been wearing it as a cover of sorts over Ash's 49ers t-shirt, and he could still smell her shampoo in its fabric. He buttoned the shirt so that a thin patch of dark hair was visible on his chest.

Before exiting the room, he stacked another log on the fire and set some kindling close. He looked back quickly behind him to where she was still sleeping, making sure to leave the bedroom door ajar so that he could hear her if she needed him.

Chris was only slightly surprised to find Ashton McKenzie already dressed for the morning and hovering impatiently over the coffee maker. "You know what they say about a watched pot, sir?" he asked.

Ashton smiled and motioned for him to take a seat. "You can call me Ash or Ashton, Chris. You've married my daughter; you're not taking her to prom." He placed a cup in front of Chris. "You want cream or sugar?"

Gates nodded. "No, black is fine." Noticing that they seemed to be alone, he added, "Is everyone sleeping in?"

"No, everyone's out and about already. I think they're trying to give her some space. Devon's always been so private about everything. Her brothers left early to access what's left to process of the crime scenes." He slipped a piece of toast and jam into his mouth. "Your dad went to pick up some things he thought we needed, and I think your brothers and their families are out and about."

Pausing to chew his toast and take a swig of coffee, Ashton asked, "How is she this morning? She slept better last night?"

Chris nodded. "Physically, she's really just sore and bruised. Mentally, I really don't know. Like you said, she doesn't say much about her feelings."

****

The knock at the door made them both jump, Ashton opened it to find his wife Caren standing there with tears in her eyes and holding two pieces of luggage, one for herself and one most assuredly for Devon.

Ashton didn't say much, but just opened his arms to her as she fell into his embrace. She looked tired, he thought; spending the last few days at the hospital alone with Jason and then catching the first flight out of New York this morning had been hard on her. He'd been surrounded by family throughout the event, which had helped him make it through. She'd had no one to lean on; no one to hold her or comfort her.

He took the bags from her and motioned for her to come inside. She went immediately to Chris and embraced him. "How are you holding up?"

Chris led her to the couch and eased her into a seat, holding on to her longer than he intended.

When she was settled, he said, "I'm fine."

She looked around the suite. "Where is everyone?"

Ashton handed her some coffee. "Devon's still sleeping; the boys have been out and about for a bit. We're hoping the CSI teams clear us to leave today. We're ready to get out of here."

Chris looked at Caren with an awkward expression. "Devon needs some clothes. She's kind of sensitive about the sizes. I think I can pick out jeans and a shirt, but I've no idea about the other items." Caren knew by his expression he was referring to undergarments.

She smiled; he was blushing. "It's okay; I stopped by your place and picked up some clothes for her and an extra set for you as well."

She couldn't help but notice the smile that crossed his handsome face when she referred to Devon's apartment as their place. To be perfectly honest, she doubted Devon would ever want to return there.

It would be too painful for her to surround herself with the painful memories of what happened there.

"How's Jason holding up?" Ash asked, as he pulled her to the couch and motioned for her to take a seat.

"He's just broken, honey. His wife and baby are gone. His sister hurt again. Thank God Laura was able to stay with him. I don't think I could have left him there all alone."

"Were you able to speak to Melissa's family?" he asked, as he walked to the minibar and poured his wife a drink.

"There's just her brother. He didn't even seem that surprised when I told him what happened," Caren paused. She'd been fighting psychiatric issues all her life, she just didn't share that with us. She was compliant with her meds and they were working for her.

"What changed?" he asked sitting next to her as she finished her drink.

"She stopped taking her psych meds so she and Jason could have a baby."

"Christopher," she said, her expression was softer. "I want you to know how grateful we are that Devon is home safe and that I realize you are a big part of the success. I'm not sure we'd have gotten to her in time if not for you."

Chris cringed a bit when she used the words "in time." In his own mind, he'd arrived too late. Devon was hurt again; Melissa was no more. Her perspective on success intrigued him, but he pushed it away and buried it deep within.

"I know, Mrs. McKenzie," he admitted. "I'm not the kind of man you'd have picked for your daughter. But I want you to know that I love her. I would do anything and give up everything to ensure her safety and happiness."

She patted his hand. "My daughter and I are very close, Christopher. She told me that while the two of you were gone, you chose to stay there with her and never return here. I know how much you love her; that's exactly the type of man my husband and I want for her."

Caren set the empty glass down on the coffee table. "Where is she? Can I see her?"

Ash pointed to the bedroom door. "Chris was able to get her to shower and sleep a bit."

Caren stood up and walked toward the door. "Is it okay if I just peek inside?

"Of course."

Caren stood and made her way to the bedroom door; she paused as her hand touched the cold metal of the knob. She exhaled a long cleansing breath that seemed to Chris and Ashton as if she'd been holding it forever. She placed her free hand against her chest as if she were in pain, and then she took another breath and went into the room.

Once inside, she paused just long enough to orient herself to the room. Devon was sleeping with her back to the door. In other circumstances, the picture she presented in her father's old, worn 49ers shirt and boxer shorts might have been amusing.

Caren's mind regressed to a time when Devon was about eight years old playing dress-up with her brothers. Devon seldom got to play princess or ballerina when she was younger. Instead, they pretended to be cops, pirates, and athletes.

But the situation didn't call for nostalgia or strolls down memory lane. It was all she could do not to collect her daughter in her arms and just weep for all that had been sacrificed.

As Devon lay sleeping, it occurred to Caren that she'd never seen her daughter look so small, so vulnerable, and so defenseless. Truth be told, Devon looked more fragile than she had a month ago lying in that hospital bed.

Caren had gotten almost to the bed when she heard Devon stir, shifting her weight from one side to the other. Her father's boxers were extremely loose around her hips, so much so that a fair amount of her right buttock was visible. Caren could decipher on her buttock an angry red puckered scar that looked like a sideways number eight.

She felt her anger building; what had been the purpose of branding her daughter like an animal? What was Melissa thinking? She wasn't sure what awakened Devon, but by the time Caren may it to the bedside, Devon was pulling herself into a sitting position.

It was hard to describe the emotions that flashed across her face. Caren saw everything from fear, shame, relief, and joy, almost at the same time. "Baby?" Caren whispered pulling Devon to her chest as if she were an infant.

She felt rather than heard Devon crying into her embrace, her sobs becoming harder with each breath she took until her body was jerking in rhythm to her cries.

"Mom," Devon finally said barely above a whisper. "I'm so glad you're here." She wiped at her eyes with the back of her right hand. "How's Jason?"

Caren smiled a mother's smile. "He's hurting, but he's healing." She put her hands to Devon's shoulders and looked directly into her eyes. "He just has to take it day by day. She paused then added, "We all do."

****

Dale Hyman adjusted his pipe more solidly in his mouth, kicking his heel against the thick carpet in the hotel room. He dropped the spent match into an ashtray and looked awkwardly around the room where most of the Gates and McKenzie families were sitting on the sofa, chairs, arms of chairs, and any other place that served as a stool or chair.

He smiled at Devon propped up against Gates, almost sitting in his lap. She was wearing the jeans her mother had brought her and an NYPD t-shirt that probably had belonged to one of the boys, but Devon had claimed it at some point through the years.

"You look well, pretty one. Find peace," he said to her.

"Hyman," Chris asked, "How did this happen? How was he able to merge his spirit with Melissa's?"

Hyman took a long puff from his pipe and blew a steady cascade of smoke into the air around him. "I told you once before, the souls travel together through time. You are destined to be together; you are soul mates, and you should not fight it." He looked anxiously from one to the other. "You must accept this."

Chris smiled and kissed the top of her head, noticing how she edged even closer to him. All he could think was how deeply they'd accepted it. They listened as Dale went on. "The path you were on before you went back was not going to bring you to each other. When you passed through the lights, it was perfect timing, and it took you back to the last place in time when you were together."

"But Melissa wasn't with us that night," Devon said. She paused, her hand to her mouth. "Oh God, we ran into her at that truck stop. She was there."

Chris pulled her hand into his. "It's okay," he whispered.

Dale Hyman nodded and went on. "When you were returned through the lights, your souls were united, and the past was corrected. But Hayden's desire was great, and once he united with her, he couldn't let her go. He desires her; he will always desire her. His lineage is strong, and that desire has been passed from generation to generation." He paused a moment as if in deliberation. "The girl probably did not realize she was sharing space with him until his soul took over. You should not blame her. She, like yourselves, was trapped."

"Is he dead?' Devon asked.

"As much as anyone can be, his soul will live on with the fathers in the lights. It is their hope that their strength will hold him in the lights." He looked at Devon and Chris. "It is time for me to leave."

He shook hands with everyone, taking care to hug Devon gently before exiting the door and waving goodbye.

"Christopher," Caren began, "your mother and I have been doing lots of research into our family trees since we found out about the family lineage." She looked at Devon. "I was looking at your wedding ring, and it reminded me of a ring my Aunt Isabel used to wear. When she died, she left it to her daughter, who of course was also my cousin. I stopped by her house and asked if she still had it, and she did." She pulled a small box from her pocket and held it out to Devon. "Open it up, Devon, and compare it to your ring."

Devon did and was surprised to see that except for the small diamond on the top, it was identical. Both rings had the same intricate design that wove in and out, up and down, around the band.

Chris held out his hand and plucked the ring from the box. "I've seen this before. It's just like the one Benjamin gave to me that night at the campfire, the first night I asked you to marry me for real." He paused and then added, "The one I returned to him."

She shook her head, rubbing her hands on her face as if to gain clarity. "It's Benjamin's ring?" Her hand flew to her mouth, eyes teary, it was as if he was there with her. "

"I miss him," she said, through the tears. "I miss all of them."

Gates pulled her into his arms, "I know I do, too."

The ringing of the phone interrupted her thoughts as Kevin, his arm still in the hospital-issued sling, picked it up. He handed it to Devon. "Mrs. Gates, it's the hospital," he said kiddingly.

Devon took the phone and listened intently, nodding her head intermittently as she answered yes and no to specific questions. Finally, she said, "You're sure?"

She waited a few minutes and then said, "Thank you for calling."

Devon walked quietly over to the kitchenette in the suite and poured a glass of water. She took several large gulps before setting the empty glass on the counter.

"Dear," her mother chided, "you drink like a sailor." Devon smiled, remembering the last time that something she'd done had been compared to the habits of a sailor. Grandmother Edith would not have been pleased, she told herself.

"Chris," she said, speaking barely above a whisper, "can you help me with something in the bedroom?"

He followed closely behind her, stopping only to shut the bedroom door behind him. He noticed how nervous she was as soon as he turned to face her, but he pretended not to notice. Instead, he smiled at her and leaned closer toward her so that they were almost locked in an embrace. "What's up? Who was on the phone?"

She pinched her bottom lip with her front teeth. "I know the scene's been cleared and we're all heading back to New York today or tomorrow, depending on available flights, but …"

Chris pulled her toward him so that he could lock his fingers behind her back. "I know you're apprehensive about going back to the apartment."

She interrupted him. "I'm not going back there; I can't."

He kissed her forehead and let his lips remain there instead of pulling away. "Your mom has already hired a moving company to pack up your things from your apartment, and my apartment too, actually." He kissed her again in almost the same place on her forehead. "We're going to stay at my parents' summer house in New Jersey until we can find a place of our own."

Devon slid her arms around his neck and pushed herself as tight against his chest as she could. "Would you be okay with us going away for a few days, just the two of us, to rest and unwind?" She paused then added before he could say anything, "I was thinking maybe a bed and breakfast in Montana."

"What's going on, Devon?" he asked, his concern was evident in his voice.

"I just think some time alone together might be nice," she said. "We've hardly had any time together where we could just enjoy each other without worrying about anything."

He bent his upper body, so that he could rest his chin on the top of her head. "Sounds nice. You have a specific place in mind?"

Chris felt her shake her head that she didn't. "Doesn't matter; I'd just like for us to be alone together, just a day or two before we return home and the craziness begins again."

****

Terminus

The room was bigger than she was expecting; in fact, it was huge. It very easily could have housed several more occupants comfortably. Chris had really gone all out to make their private time special. There was only one window in the room, but it was a big window. It took up almost one wall entirely, just to the right of a mammoth king-sized bed. A stone fireplace with a dark wooden mantel dominated another wall; it served as the perfect place to display a variety of antique collectibles. The comforter was pale blue, but the staff had turned it down to expose stark white sheets and pillows, so many luxurious pillows that were lined two-deep across the head of the bed.

Devon looked at her watch; it was just after two in the afternoon. In some parts of the world, lunch was just finishing. Did housekeeping really expect them to get off the airplane and jump straight into the bed?

If Gates noticed her nervousness, he gave no indication. Instead, he tossed their overnight bag to the floor and turned his attention to the fireplace. It was funny, he thought; prior to living at the Ennis' ranch, he could have counted the number of fires he'd started on one hand. Now he was an expert. It took him only a minute or two before the room was bathed in the warm breath of the burning flames.

He didn't see her open the curtains covering the window. But when he turned his attention from the fire, he couldn't help but gasp at the wondrous view of the snow-covered mountaintops. Large, thick evergreen trees stood close to the window and outlined the landscape like soldiers ready for battle. They were the only source of color in a world of winter white.

Movement to his left caused him to turn his gaze just enough to notice she was pouring amber liquid into a small clear glass. Once she finished, she capped the bottle and made her way to where he was standing.

"A toast?" she asked, handing him a glass.

He took the glass from her and asked, "You're not having any?" She smiled, but never broke eye contact with him. "You first."

His expression was serious yet jovial at the same time as he took it from her hand. He was reminded of the scene in Romeo and Juliet where the star-crossed young lovers share a poisonous drink so that they can be together in heaven for all eternity.

He wasn't sure where she was going with the toast, but he'd already decided to play along. Gates lifted the glass to his lips and emptied its contents in one long drink. He broke eye contact only long enough to turn around with the intent of refilling the glass for her. However, she placed one hand gently on his chest and took the empty glass with the other hand.

Before he could ask, she descended on his lips, delighted at their softness and warmth. She licked his lips enjoying the taste of liquor clinging to them. She smiled against his lips and added before he could ask, "Now I've had mine."

"Devon," he whispered, reluctantly pulling at her hands as she fumbled with the buttons of his shirt. "There's no rush. We don't have to do this until you're ready." He kissed her hands, clasping them together against his chest. "I want us to make love; you've nothing to prove to me. You know that."

"I'm ready," she said, her kisses making a path from his Adam's apple down to the midpoint of his chest.

Although his mind was formulating a dozen reasons why they could wait, his body had other ideas. He could feel himself responding to her as if he were sixteen years old and had just jumped into the backseat with Tiffany Jones at the drive-in during Jaws. In fact, he didn't realize she'd undone his jeans until he felt her hand warm and soft wrap around his swollen member, encouraging it to attention. He kissed at her neck, pulled her as close as he could, and stepped out of his jeans in one movement.

It was an odd feeling for him to be completely naked and wrapped around her fully clothed body. Devon walked him backward gently, their lips and bodies never breaking contact. She pushed him gently until the back of his legs contacted the edge of the bed. He fell back onto it bringing her down with him.

He toyed with the buttons of her shirt as she lay on top of him; he had to resist yanking the last two off in his eagerness to feel her skin against his. Finally, the shirt fell gracefully from her shoulders. He made quick work with the clasp of the black bra. She wasn't sure how, but she ended up on her back with him pulling at her jeans and boots. He buried his face against her breasts, lifting her at the waist so that he could pull off her black Ralph Lauren underwear. Once his hands were free, he wasted no time. His hands were everywhere almost at once it seemed.

She felt him caressing the fullness of her breasts, pinching her nipples, and pushing against her legs to move her closer into him. Devon opened her legs enough to accommodate the width of his body; her hands pushed against the back of his head as his lips paid homage to her breasts, going back and forth from one to the other until she was sure he must be dizzy. It wasn't until she felt his lips moving south that she pulled him gently by the hair back up to meet her eyes so that she could see his face.

His expression changed to one of great concern as he pulled himself upward and focused his attention on her eyes. "You okay?"

She smiled to him, a comforting smile. "I'm not going to tell you this is easy, 'because that would be a lie. It is very hard to lay here and not think about what happened and how it felt. I keep having flashbacks, no matter how hard I try not to."

Devon's honesty was sometimes a mystery to him, but there was never a time that he didn't appreciate it. It was oddly unnerving and refreshing all at the same time. He pushed himself away. "Let's stop and relax a bit; you want to take a bath?"

"Chris, I don't want to stop," she insisted, holding him in place with her hand clasped gently around his upper arm.

He shook his head and dropped it just enough to plant a tender kiss at her shoulder. "I would never want you to feel you have to do anything, Devon. I told you once before, I want it all, every time."

"Please," she was almost begging him. "I really do want to make love with you here, now, today."

He eased himself off her but remained close against her body. "What is it then?"

She stroked his chest, gently at first, then with more force as she trailed her hand over his abdomen, tickled the hair around his navel, and encountered the thickness of his shaft, coaxing it back to a rigid state. "We have to talk first," she answered.

He swallowed the knot that was forming in his throat. Currently, it seemed as if all the blood was rushing southward to fuel his erection growing harder by the second. "That's not fair, Devon," he stuttered. "Whatever you're wanting, count me in."

She smiled, secretly pleased with her ability to bring this powerful, capable man to the point where he was almost fragile and unable to put more than a few words together to form a sentence.

She released her hold on him and redirected his attention to their conversation.

Before she could say anything else, he said, "There's nothing you can say to me that will change anything between us. I love you, and I don't care what you did or said or felt. You did whatever you needed to do to survive." He pulled her back toward him so that she was on top of him again. "You're here; right now. This moment in time is all I care about."

She laid her head on his chest. "I'm pregnant."

She could feel his body tense underneath her chin and along the muscles of her arms where they rested against him. "What?" he asked, just barely above a whisper.

She repeated it, watching his eyes this time, trying to gauge his reaction. Everything he was feeling was evident in his eyes. The eyes truly were a window into the soul, and Chris's were no exception in this moment.

He paused, as if he were memorizing a long paragraph. Then, brushing back the hair that had fallen over her eyes, he asked, "How do you feel about that?"

"Chris," she stated, her voice deep and throaty as if she'd just woken up, "I'm going to have a baby, our baby."

He smiled, hearing Gabriel's voice in his head about needing a bigger house for them sometime in the spring. The old man was amazing, he told himself, one hundred twenty years later, and the old man was still there for them.

When she took his silence as a summation of his displeasure, she pulled away from him to isolate her body from his. He stilled her, taking her around the waist and pulling her close to him again. "Devon, I know this is a shock, but we've known this was a possibility since we've never used protection."

She felt his hand moving toward her abdomen, stopping just about her navel. "How many weeks are we?" he asked.

The fact that he'd used the word we instead of you did not escape her.

She placed her hand on his and said, "Just a few weeks, maybe two?"

He smiled and kissed her stomach just above where their conjoined hands were resting on it. "A baby, huh?"

She nodded, gently bumping his forehead with her own, letting it rest against his as she gazed into his eyes. "Are you upset?"

He shook his head that he wasn't. "I love you, Devon. It would have been nice to have a little more time to figure out how to be a couple, but it's not going to work out that way." He pulled his head away from hers to face her again. "Make no mistake, Devon. I'm very happy." He scooted himself a little further down against her and kissed her on the lips. "I'm happy to be your husband." He kissed her softly on the neck and shoulders. "Happy that we're pregnant."

As he caressed her breasts, one in each hand, his thumbs rotating circles against her sensitive nipples, teasing them until they were red, hard nubs against his fingers, he kissed her stomach and added, "Happy to be here making love to you." He leaned in close to her stomach and whispered as if he were talking to the baby. "Look away, little one, Daddy is about to make Mommy feel very good." He felt her laugh against his cheek, but continued his journey until he reached his destination between her legs, his fingers marking the path for his mouth and tongue.

Chris took his eyes off his fingers just long enough to look upward and assess her reaction. If she was having any issues, it was certainly not discernible. Instead, she looked like a woman in the throes of passion on the edge of a blissful fall. Devon was lying against the pillows, her head thrown far back, her eyes closed, and her hips grinding against his chin. He could tell by the intensity of her undulations and the pace she was setting that she was close to her release. Chris pushed his fingers deeper and harder against her center as if he knew she liked it. The feeling of her hand on his caught him by surprise, and at first, he thought she wanted him to stop.

As he pulled his hand away, she whispered to him in a tone that was unfamiliar yet recognizable, "Can we do sweet and slow now?"

He smiled and buried his mouth between her thighs, kissing, rubbing, and biting gently at her core until he felt her push against him with such intensity, he couldn't get his breath.

He continued holding her with his mouth until he felt her spasm subside and she calmed against the mattress, her breath coming in great gasps.

Without waiting for her to recover, he pushed his erection eagerly between her legs and guided himself gently inside of her, setting a slower pace than he normally would have. He felt her responding, pushing against him to meet his thrusts. He pushed her knees apart just fractionally to give himself better access, better leverage, to push deeper into her. He lifted her at the knees, pulled her almost into his lap, and pumped frantically against her.

He slid his hand down between their bodies to where they were connected and found her center again; he pushed and pulled at it until he could hear her moaning and groaning with pleasure beneath him. He wasn't sure who cried out first. But if it had been a race of some kind, the referee would have called it a tie. Gates held on to her until both their respiratory rates were within normal limits. Then he slid off her to reclaim the empty place alongside her.

He looked past her reclining form to the majestic landscape framed by the window. The sun was making its descent for the evening, and the Montana skyline was ablaze with color—waves and rolling waves of color. Red, yellow, blue, and white pulsating lights were just appearing for the evening. He pulled her up to a sitting position so that she could see them. "Look, Devon, it's the lights."

She smiled, surprised that unlike the previous time, she was not fearful. She was almost comforted by the pulsating sequence as it rolled from yellow, to red, to blue, and finally white, only to start again. She grabbed the blanket from the bed and went quickly to stand next to him, wrapping him with half of it. "Do you believe the things Heimdail said about our ancestors and these lights?"

He smiled. "I don't know, but I figure it can't hurt." He kissed her hand and gazed out the window at the lights, and then he called out the names of his ancestors. "Ray and Audra, James and Abby."

She took his hand and added, "Gabriel, Edith, and Benjamin." She turned her face toward him and whispered, so that he could barely make out the name. "Melissa."

He smiled and kissed her again, softly, tenderly, endlessly.

The lights continued to dance and transition from color to color, moving along an infinite wave until the colors seemed to merge into a single band before separating into individual bands of color again. He couldn't help but consider how the lights symbolized their life together.

In such a short time, they had come full circle. Like the blink of an eye, they could look ahead and see their sons and daughters, grandchildren and great-grandchildren in the lights. They could find comfort in knowing that love, like life, is endless, an infinite loop that lasts for all time, perfectly entwined with no beginning or end, just like the love they shared.

About the Author

Lisa Robin Phillips Colodny was born and grew up in the rural countryside of Kentucky. She attended the University of Kentucky and Broward College in Fort Lauderdale and graduated with a Doctorate in Pharmacy from Nova Southeastern University.

Her non-fiction publishing history includes numerous publications in the health and science industry. Other titles currently available by this author include an award-winning children's book, Ms. *Abrams' Everything Garden*, and adult fiction, *The Town Time Forgot,* and *Yellow River Pledge*.

Dr. Colodny currently works in the healthcare industry and resides in South Florida with her daughter and their Labrador retriever, Cooper.

About the Publisher

#KINGSTONPUBLISHING

Kingston Publishing offers an affordable way for you to turn your dream into a reality. We offer every service you will ever need to take an idea and publish a story. We are here to help authors make it in the industry. We've been hurt by publishers in the past and we want to provide a positive experience that will keep you coming back to us.

Whether you want a traditional publisher who offers all the amenities a publishing company should or an author who prefers to self-publish, but needs additional help - we are here for you.

Now Accepting Manuscripts!

Please send query letter and manuscript to:

submissions@kingstonpublishing.com

Visit our website at www.kingstonpublishing.com

Extras

Dr. Jordan Chamberlain is a successful, beautiful, young medical examiner with the perfect husband, the perfect life, and perfect friends. Somewhat of a whiz, kid, she's younger than most Medical Examiners and enjoys a bit of glamour whenever her forensic data is sent to trial. To an outside observer, Jordan has it all, until that is, her husband, Jason, announces without warning that he doesn't want to be married anymore and Jordan's perfect life crashes and burns around her.

Jordan buries herself even deeper in her work, temporarily embarking on a career consulting with the FBI's Violet Crimes Division under the careful eye of college friends turned colleagues, who support her during her as she tries to rebuild her life.

Her future, however, is about to be compromised once more when she becomes the target of the serial killer she's been pursuing.

Milton Keynes UK
Ingram Content Group UK Ltd.
UKHW032143170324
439604UK00012B/1797